MARTIN CRUZ SMITH

STALIN'S GHOST

PAN BOOKS

First published 2007 by Simon & Schuster, Inc., New York

First published in Great Britain 2007 by Macmillan

This edition published 2008 by Pan Books
an imprint of Pan Macmillan, a division of Macmillan Publishers Limited
Pan Macmillan, 20 New Wharf Road, London N1 9RR
Basingstoke and Oxford
Associated companies throughout the world
www.panmacmillan.com

ISBN 978-1-4472-0876-1

1 3 5 7 9 8 6 4 2

A CIP catalogue record for this book is available from the British Library.

Typeset by Intype Libra Ltd
Printed and bound by CPI Group (UK) Ltd, Croydon, CR0 4YY

Also by Martin Cruz Smith

Arkady Renko series

Gorky Park

Polar Star

Red Square

Havana Bay

Wolves Eat Dogs

Three Stations

Other titles

The Indians Won

Gypsy in Amber

Canto for a Gypsy

Nightwing

Stallion Gate

Rose

Tokyo Station

STALIN'S GHOST

Martin Cruz Smith's novels include *Gorky Park*, *Stallion Gate*, *Polar Star*, *Red Square*, *Rose*, *Havana Bay* and *Three Stations*. A recipient of the CWA Gold Dagger for fiction in the UK, he is also two-time winner of the Hammett Prize in the United States. He lives with his wife and children in northern California.

'Cruz Smith writes extraordinarily well in a genre not usually considered literature . . . [He] is not merely our best writer of suspense, but one of our best writers, period'
New York Times

'When Cruz Smith is at his best, it is impossible to tell how much is research and how much imagination . . . he moves into the realm of high adventure, alongside such writers as John Buchan, Hammond Innes, the great Lionel Davidson and Geoffrey Household'
Guardian

'Cruz Smith understands pace, plot, character, not wearing your research on your sleeve, and all the other old-fashioned virtues. In short, he can write'
Independent

'Martin Cruz Smith is one of the finest writers at work today'
Sunday Herald

'You'll be engrossed in the atmospheric setting and the complexity of Renko's pained character'
Observer

Praise for MARTIN CRUZ SMITH

'Cruz Smith is brilliant at both building atmosphere and charting detail'
Daily Mirror

'An extraordinary portrait of the New Russia . . . an exceptional novel'
Independent on Sunday

'You can almost taste and smell the terrifying landscape . . . a richness and depth that is quite exceptional'
Daily Mail

'Cruz Smith's great gift is his painstaking recording of minutiae, compiling his descriptions with the skill of a pointillist painter'
The Times

'Cruz Smith not only constructs grittily realistic plots, he also has the gift of characterisation of which most thriller writers only dream'
Mail on Sunday

'One of those writers that anyone who is serious about their craft views with respect bordering on awe'
Val McDermid

For Knox and Kitty

ACKNOWLEDGMENTS

I thank Ellen Irish Branco, Luisa Cruz Smith, Don Sanders and Annie Lamott for reading *Stalin's Ghost* over and over, and Sam Smith for sharing the research at the Moscow Metro Museum.

I also want to acknowledge Doctors Nelson Branco, Michael Weiner, Ken Sack and Wayne Gauger for answers to medical matters and George Young for firearms. In Russia, I was aided by Nina Rubashova, matchmaker; Carl Schreck, reporter; Colonel Alexander Yakovlev, detective; Lyuba Vinogradova, interpreter; Andrew Nurnberg, accomplice; and the Red Diggers of Tver.

First and last, of course, I thank Em.

STALIN'S GHOST

PROLOGUE

Winter was what Muscovites lived for. Winter knee-deep in snow that softened the city, flowed from golden dome to golden dome, resculpted statues and transformed park paths into skating trails. Snow that sometimes fell as a lacy haze, sometimes thick as down. Snow that made sedans of the rich and powerful crawl behind snowplows. Snow that folded and unfolded, teasing the eye with glimpses of an illuminated globe above the Central Telegraph Office, Apollo's chariot leaving the Bolshoi, a sturgeon sketched in neon at a food emporium. Women shopped amid the gusts, gliding in long fur coats. Children dragged sleds and snowboards, while Lenin lay in his mausoleum, deaf to correction, wrapped in snow.

And, in Arkady's experience, when the snow melted, bodies would be discovered. In Moscow that was spring.

1

It was two in the morning, an hour that was both early and late. Two a.m. was a world to itself.

Zoya Filotova wore her black hair severely trimmed as if to defiantly display the bruise below her eye. She was about forty, Arkady thought, stylishly sinewy in a red leather pantsuit and a golden cross that was purely ornamental. She sat on one side of the booth, Arkady and Victor on the other, and although Zoya had ordered a brandy she had yet to touch it. She had long red fingernails and as she turned a cigarette pack over and over Arkady was put in mind of a crab inspecting dinner. The café was a chrome affair above a car wash on the beltway. No car washes tonight, not with snow falling, and the few cars that made it to the café were SUVs with four-wheel drive. The exceptions were Arkady's Zhiguli and Victor's Lada crouching in a corner of the lot.

Victor sipped a Chivas, just maintaining. Drinks were expensive and Victor had the patience of a camel. Arkady had a modest glass of water; he was a pale man with dark hair and the stillness of a professional observer. Thirty-six hours without sleep had made him more still than usual.

Zoya said, "My heart hurts more than my face."

"A broken heart?" Victor suggested as if it were his specialty.

"My face is ruined."

"No, you're still a beautiful woman. Show my friend what else your husband did."

The drivers and bodyguards who occupied stools along the bar were contemplative, cradling their drinks, sucking their cigarettes, keeping their balance. A couple of bosses compared Florida tans and snapshots of Sleeping Beauty. Zoya brushed the crucifix out of the way so she could unzip the top of her pantsuit and show Arkady a bruise that ran like a grape stain on the smooth plane of her breast.

"Your husband did this?" Arkady asked.

She zipped up and nodded.

"You'll be safe soon," Victor reassured her. "Animals like that should not be walking the street."

"Before we married he was wonderful. I have to say even now that Alexander was a wonderful lover."

"That's natural," Victor said. "You try to remember the good times. How long have you been married?"

"Three months."

Would the snow ever end? Arkady wondered. A Pathfinder rolled up to a gas pump. The mafia was getting conservative; now that they had seized and established their separate territories they were defenders of the status quo. Their children would be bankers and *their* children would be poets, something like that. Count on it, in fifty years, a golden age of poetry.

Arkady rejoined the conversation. "Are you sure you want to do this? People change their minds."

"Not me."

"Maybe your husband will change his ways."

"Not him." She smiled with an extra twist. "He's a brute. Now I don't dare go to my own apartment, it's too dangerous."

"You've come to the right place," Victor said and solemnized the moment with a sip. Cars droned by, each at a different pitch.

Arkady said, "We'll need phone numbers, addresses, keys. His routine, habits, where he hangs out. I understand you and your husband have a business near the Arbat."

"On the Arbat. Actually, it's my business."

"What sort?"

"Matchmaking. International matchmaking."

"What is the company's name?"

"Cupid."

"Really?" That was interesting, Arkady thought. A quarrel in Cupid's bower? "How long have you had this business?"

"Ten years." Her tongue rested for a moment on her teeth as if she were going to say more and changed her mind.

"You and your husband both work there?"

"All he does is stand around and smoke cigarettes and

drink with his mates. I do the work, he takes the money and when I try to stop him, he hits me. I warned him, this was the last time."

Victor said, "So now you want him . . ."

"Dead and buried."

"Dead and buried?" Victor grinned. He liked a woman with zeal.

"And never found."

Arkady said, "What I need to know is how you knew to go to the police to have your husband killed."

"Isn't that how it's done?"

Arkady ceded her the point. "But who told you? Who gave you the phone number? It makes us nervous when an innocent citizen, such as yourself, knows how to reach us. Did you get our number from a friend or did a skywriter spell out Killers for Hire?"

Zoya shrugged. "A man left a message on my phone and said if I had a problem to call this number. I called and your friend answered."

"Did you recognize the voice on the message?"

"No. I think it was a kind soul who took pity on me."

"How did that kind soul get *your* phone number?" Victor asked.

"We advertise. We give our number."

"Did you save the message?"

"No, why would I want anything like that on my machine? Anyway, what does it matter? I can give you each two hundred dollars."

"How do we know this isn't a trap?" Arkady asked.

"This phone thing bothers me. This could be a case of entrapment."

Zoya had a throaty, smoker's laugh. "How do I know you won't simply keep the money? Or worse, tell my husband?"

Victor said, "Any enterprise demands a certain amount of trust on both sides. To begin with, the price is five thousand dollars, half before and half after."

"I can get someone on the street to do it for fifty."

"You get what you pay for," Victor said. "With us, your husband's total disappearance is guaranteed and we'll handle the investigation ourselves."

"It's up to you," Arkady emphasized. "Your decision."

"How will you do it?"

Victor said, "The less you know about that the better."

Arkady felt he had a front row seat to the snow, to the way it tumbled in foamy waves over parked cars. If Zoya Filotova could afford an SUV, she could pay five thousand dollars to eliminate her husband.

"He's very strong," she said.

"No, he'll just be heavy," Victor assured her.

Zoya counted out a stack of much-handled American bills, to which she added a photograph of a man in a bathrobe at the beach. Alexander Filotov was alarmingly large, with long, wet hair and he was showing the camera a beer can he had apparently crushed with one hand.

"How will I know he's dead?" Zoya asked.

Victor said, "We'll give you proof. We take a picture."

"I've read about this. Sometimes so-called killers use

makeup and catsup and pretend the 'victim' is dead. I want something more solid."

There was a pause.

"More solid?" asked Victor.

"Something personal," Zoya said.

Arkady and Victor looked at each other. This was not in the script.

"A wristwatch?" Arkady suggested.

"More personal."

"As in . . . ?" He didn't like where this was going.

Zoya finally picked up her brandy and sipped. "Don't kidnappers sometimes send a finger or an ear?"

There was another silence in the booth until Arkady said, "That's for kidnapping."

"That wouldn't work anyway," she agreed. "I might not recognize his ear or his finger. They all look pretty much alike. No, something more particular."

"What did you have in mind?"

She swirled her glass. "He has a pretty large nose."

Victor said, "I am not cutting off anybody's nose."

"If he's already dead? It would be like carving a chicken."

"It doesn't matter."

"Then I have another idea."

Victor put up his hand. "No."

"Wait." Zoya unfolded a piece of paper with a photograph of a drawing of a tiger fighting off a pack of wolves. The photo was murky, taken in poor light, and the drawing itself had an indistinct quality. "I thought of this."

"He has a picture?"

"He has a tattoo," Arkady said.

"That's right." Zoya Filotova was pleased. "I photographed the tattoo a few nights ago while he was in a drunken stupor. It's his own design."

A sheet covered one corner of the tattoo but what Arkady could see was impressive enough. The tiger stood majestically on its hind legs, one paw swiping the air as the wolves snarled and cringed. A pine forest and mountain stream framed the battle. On the white arm of a birch were the letters *T, V, E, R.*

Victor asked, "What does that mean?"

"He's from Tver," Zoya said.

"There are no tigers in Tver," Victor said. "No mountains either. It's a flat, hopeless dump on the Volga."

Arkady thought that was a little harsh, but people who made it to Moscow from places like Tver usually shed their hometown identity as fast as they could. They didn't have it inked on them forever.

"Okay," Victor said. "Now we can definitively ID him. How do you propose we bring the proof to you? Do you expect us to lug a body around?"

Zoya finished her brandy and said, "I need only the tattoo."

Arkady hated Victor's Lada. The windows did not completely close and the rear bumper was roped on. Snow blew in through floorboard holes and swayed the pine scent freshener that hung from the rearview mirror.

"Cold," Victor said.

"You could have let the car warm up." Arkady unbuttoned his shirt.

"It will, eventually. No, I'm talking about her. I felt my testicles turn to icicles and drop, one by one."

"She wants proof, the same as us." Arkady peeled adhesive tape from his stomach to free a microphone and miniature recorder. He pushed Rewind and Play, listened to a sample, turned off the recorder, ejected the cassette, and placed it in an envelope, on which he wrote, "Subject Z. K. Filotova, Senior Investigator A. K. Renko, Detective V. D. Orlov," date and place.

Victor asked, "What do we have?"

"Not much. You answered the phone on another officer's desk and a woman asked about doing in her husband. She assumed you were Detective Urman. You played along and set up a meeting. You could arrest her now for conspiracy but you'd have nothing on the detective and no idea who gave her his phone number. She's holding out. You could squeeze her harder if she pays for what she thinks is a finished assassination, then you'd have her for attempted murder and she might be willing to talk. Tell me about Detective Urman. It was his phone you answered?"

"Yes. Marat Urman. Thirty-five years old, single. He was in Chechnya with his buddy Isakov. Nikolai Isakov, the war hero."

"*Detective* Isakov?" Arkady said.

Victor waited a beat. "I thought you'd like that. The file's in back."

Arkady covered his confusion by fishing a ribbon-bound folder out of the dirty clothes and empty bottles on the back seat.

"Is this a car or a laundry chute?"

"You should read the newspaper articles. Urman and Isakov were with the Black Berets, and they killed a lot of Chechens. We fucked up in the first Chechen war. The second time we sent in people with, as they say, the proper skills. Read the articles."

"Would Isakov know what Urman was doing?"

"I don't know." Victor screwed up his face with thought. "The Black Berets make their own rules." He kept his eyes on Arkady while he lit a cigarette. "Have you ever met Isakov?"

"Not face to face."

"Just wondering." Victor snuffed the match between two fingers.

"Why did you pick up Urman's phone?"

"I was waiting for a snitch to call. He'd called Urman's number by mistake before; it's one digit off. These guys on the street, in the wintertime they drink antifreeze. You've got to catch them while they're able to talk. Anyway, it might be a good mistake, don't you think?"

Arkady watched a group leave the café and head for an SUV. They were heavyset, silent men until one of them built up speed and slid on the ice that covered the parking lot. He spread his arms and moved as if his shoes were skates. A second man chased him and then all the rest joined in, clowning on one leg, executing spins. The lot rang with their laughs, for their own impromptu performance, until one went down. Silent again, the others shuffled around, helped him to the car and drove off.

Victor said, "I'm no prude."

"I never took you for one."

"We're underpaid and no one knows better than me what a person has to do to live. There's a break-in and the detective steals what the robber missed. A traffic cop milks drivers for bribes. Murder, though, that's over the line." Victor paused to reflect. "Shostakovich was like us."

"In what conceivable way?"

"Shostakovich, when he was young and hard up for money, played the piano for silent movies. That's you and me. Two great mentalities wasted on shit. I've wasted my life. No wife, no kids, no money. Nothing but a liver you could wring the vodka from. It's depressing. I envy you. You have something to fight for, a family."

Arkady took a deep breath. "Of sorts."

"Do you think we should warn the husband, the guy with the tattoo?"

"Not yet. Unless he's a good actor, he'd tip her off." Arkady got out of the car and immediately began stamping his feet to stay warm. Through the open door he asked, "Have you let anyone else in on this? The station commander? Internal Affairs?"

"And paint a target on my head? Just you."

"So now we're both targets."

Victor shrugged. "Misery likes company."

Arkady's headlights concentrated on a hypnotic reel of tire tracks in the snow. He was so exhausted he was merely coasting. He didn't mind; he could have circled Moscow forever, like a cosmonaut.

He thought of the conversations men in space had with their loved ones at home and called the apartment on his cell phone.

"Zhenya? Zhenya, are you there? If you are, pick up."

Which was useless. Zhenya was twelve years old but had the skills of a veteran runaway and could be gone for days. There were no messages either, except something angry and garbled from the prosecutor.

Instead, Arkady called Eva at the clinic.

"Yes?"

"Zhenya is still not back. At least he didn't answer the phone or leave a message."

"Some people hate the phone," she said. She sounded equally exhausted, four hours left on a sixteen-hour shift. "Working in an emergency clinic has made me a firm believer that no news is good news."

"It's been four days. He left with his chess set. I thought he was going to a match. This is the longest he's been gone."

"That's right and every minute has infinite possibilities. You can't control them all, Arkasha. Zhenya likes to take chances. He likes to hang out with homeless boys at Three Stations. You are not responsible. Sometimes I think your urge to do good is a form of narcissism."

"A strange accusation coming from a doctor."

He pictured her in her lab coat sitting in the dark of a clinic office, feet resting on a coffee table, watching the snow. At the apartment she could sit for hours, a sphinx with cigarettes. Or wander out with a small tape recorder and a pocketful of cassettes and interview invisible people, as she called them, people who only came out at night. She didn't watch television.

"Zurin called," she said. "He wants you to call him. Don't do it."

"Why not?"

"Because he hates you. He would only call you if he could do you harm."

"Zurin is the prosecutor. I am his investigator. I can't totally ignore him."

"Yes, you can."

This was an argument they had had before. Arkady knew his lines by heart, and to repeat them by phone struck him as unnecessary misery. Besides, she was right. He could quit the prosecutor's office and join a private security firm. Or—he had a law degree from Moscow University, after all—become a lawyer with a leather briefcase and business card. Or wear a paper hat and serve hamburgers at McDonald's. There weren't a great many other careers open to a senior investigator, although they were all better than being a dead investigator, Arkady supposed. He didn't believe Zurin would stab him in the back, although the prosecutor might show someone else where the knife drawer was. Anyway, the conversation had not gone as planned.

Arkady heard a rustle, as if she were rising from a chair. He said, "Maybe he's stuck somewhere until the Metro starts running. I'll try the chess club and Three Stations."

"Maybe I'm stuck somewhere. Arkady, why did I come to Moscow?"

"Because I asked you to."

"Oh. I'm losing my memory. Snow has wiped out so much. It's like amnesia. Maybe Moscow will be buried completely."

"Like Atlantis?"

"Exactly like Atlantis. And people will not be able to believe that such a place ever existed."

There was a long pause. The phone crackled.

Arkady said, "Was Zhenya with homeless boys? Did he sound excited? Scared?"

"Arkady, maybe you haven't noticed. We're all scared."

"Of what?"

This might be a good time to bring up Isakov, he thought. With the distance of a telephone cord. He didn't want to sound like an accuser, he just needed to know. He didn't even need to know, as long as it was over.

There was a silence. No, not silence. She had hung up.

*

As the M-1 became Lenin Prospect it entered a realm of empty, half-lit shopping malls, auto showrooms and the sulfurous blaze of all-night casinos: Sportsman's Paradise, Golden Khan, Sinbad's. Arkady played with the name Cupid, which on the lips of Zoya had sounded more hard-core than cherubic. All the time he looked right and left, slowing to scan each shadowy figure walking by the road.

The cell phone rang, but it wasn't Eva. It was Zurin.

"Renko, where the devil have you been?"

"Out for a drive."

"What sort of idiot goes out on a night like this?"

"It appears we are both out, Leonid Petrovich."

"Didn't you get my message?"

"Say that again."

"Did you get . . . Never mind. Where are you now?"

"Going home. I'm not on duty."

Zurin said, "An investigator is always on duty. Where are you?"

"On the M-1." Actually, at this point, Arkady was well into town.

"I'm at the Chistye Prudy Metro station. Get here as fast as you can."

"Stalin again?"

"Just get here."

Even if Arkady had wanted to race to Zurin's side his way was slowed when traffic was narrowed to a single lane in front of the Supreme Court. Trucks and portable generators were drawn up in disorder on the curb and street. Four white tents glowed on the sidewalk. Round-the-clock construction was not unusual in the ambitious new Moscow; however, this project looked especially haphazard. Traffic police vigorously waved cars through, but Arkady tucked his car between trucks. A uniformed militia colonel seemed belligerently in charge. He dispatched an officer to chase Arkady, but the man proved to be a veteran sergeant named Gleb whom Arkady knew.

"What's going on?"

"We're not to tell."

"That sounds interesting," Arkady said. He liked Gleb because the sergeant could whistle like a nightingale and had the gap teeth of an honest man.

"Well, seeing as how you're an investigator . . ."

"Seeing that . . . ," Arkady agreed.

"Okay." Gleb dropped his voice. "They were doing renovations to extend the basement cafeteria. A bunch of Turkish workers were digging. They got a little surprise."

Excavation work had torn up part of the sidewalk. Arkady joined the onlookers on the precarious edge, where klieg lamps aimed an incandescent light at a power shovel in a hole two stories deep and about twenty meters square. Besides militia, the crowd on the sidewalk included firemen and police, city officials and agents of state security who looked rousted from their beds.

In the hole an organized crew of men in coveralls and hard hats worked on the ground and up on scaffolding with picks and trowels, plastic bags, surgical masks and latex gloves. One man dislodged what looked like a brown ball, which he placed in a canvas bucket that he lowered by rope to the ground. He returned to his trowel and painstakingly freed a rib cage with arms attached. As Arkady's eyes adjusted he saw that one entire face of the excavation was layered with human remains outlined by the snow, a cross section of soil with skulls for stones and femurs for sticks. Some were clothed, some weren't. The smell was of sweet compost.

The canvas bucket was passed fire brigade style across the pit and pulled by rope up to a tent where other shadowy bodies were laid out on tables. The colonel went from tent to tent and barked at the men sorting bones to work faster. In between orders, he kept an eye on Arkady.

Sergeant Gleb said, "They want all the bodies out by morning. They don't want people to see."

"How many so far?"

"It's a mass grave, who can say?"

"How old?"

"From the clothes, they say the forties or fifties. Holes in the back of the head. In the basement of the Supreme Court yet. March you right downstairs and *boom!* That's how they used to do it. That was some court."

The colonel joined them. He was in full winter regalia with a blue fur hat. Arkady wondered, not for the first time, what animal had blue fur.

The colonel said loudly, "There will be an investigation of these bodies to see whether criminal charges should be brought."

Heads turned along the line, many amused.

"Say that again," Arkady asked the colonel.

"What I said was, I can assure everyone that there will be an investigation of the dead to see whether criminal charges will be brought."

"Congratulations." Arkady put his arm around the colonel's shoulders and whispered, "That is the best joke I've heard all day."

The colonel's face turned a mottled red and he ducked out of Arkady's grip. Ah, well, another enemy made, Arkady thought.

Gleb asked, "What if the grave runs under the entire court?"

"That's always the problem, isn't it? Once you start digging, when to stop?"

2

Arkady took his time. His relationship with Zurin had deteriorated to a game like badminton, in which each player took mighty swings that feebly propelled loathing back and forth. So instead of racing to Chistye Prudy Metro station, Arkady stopped in a lane of brick buildings hung with banners that filled and emptied in the wind. Arkady couldn't see all the banners, but saw enough to learn that "Studio Apartments–Concierge Services–Cable" would soon be erected on the site. "Interested Parties Should Subscribe Now."

He kicked his way through snow down a flight of stairs and knocked on a basement door. There was no answer but the door was unlocked and he pushed his way into a black space with no more than a seam of street light along the top of the basement windows, about as hospitable as an Ice Age cave. He found a light switch and an overhead rack of fluorescent tubes flickered to life.

Grandmaster Ilya Platonov sat sprawled face down on a table, asleep between chessboards. Arkady thought the fact that Platonov had found that much room was remarkable since chess sets and game clocks covered every surface:

antique, inlaid and computerized boards, men lined up like armies summoned and forgotten. Books and magazines on chess crammed the bookcases. Photographs of the Russian greats—Alekhine, Kasparov, Karpov, Tal—hung on the walls along with signs that said, "Members Are Requested Not to Take Boards to the W.C." and "No Video Games!" The air reeked of cigarettes, genius and musty clothes.

Arkady stomped the snow from his shoes and Platonov's arm compulsively shot out and hit the game clock.

"In your sleep. That's impressive," Arkady said.

Platonov opened his eyes as he sat up. Arkady guessed his age at about eighty. He still had a commanding nose and a pugnacious gaze once he rubbed the sand from his eyes.

"In my sleep, I would still beat you." Platonov felt his pockets for a wake-up cigarette. Arkady gave him one. "If you played your best game, maybe a draw."

"I'm sorry to bother you, but I'm looking for Zhenya."

"Zhenya, that little shit. I say that most affectionately. A frustrating boy." Platonov hobbled to a desk and began searching loose papers. "I want to show you the results of the last junior tournament, in which he was a complete mediocrity. Then, the same day, he defeats the adult champion, but for money. For money your little Zhenya is a different player altogether. This is a club for people who love chess, not a casino."

"I understand." Arkady noticed a "contributions" jar half full of coins.

Platonov abandoned his search. "The main thing is, Zhenya is ruining his game. No patience. He surprises opponents now because he's just a boy and then he swoops in for the kill. When he encounters the next level of players they will wear him down."

"Have you seen Zhenya in the last twenty-four hours?"

"No. The day before, yes. I threw him out for gambling once again. He's welcome back if it's to play and learn. Have you ever played him?"

"There's no point. I'm no competition."

Platonov scratched his chin. "You're in the prosecutor's office, aren't you? Well, intelligence isn't everything."

"Thank God," Arkady said.

"Chess demands discipline and analysis to reach the top. And in chess if you aren't at the top, where are you?" Platonov spread his arms. "Teaching idiots basic openings. Left, right, left, right! That's why Zhenya is such a waste." In his passion the grandmaster backed into the wall and knocked a framed photograph to the floor. Arkady picked the photograph up. Although the glass was a whirl of shards he saw a young Platonov with a vigorous head of hair accepting a bouquet and congratulations from a round man in a bad suit. Khrushchev, the Party Secretary from years ago. Behind the two men stood children in costume as chess pieces: knights, rooks, kings and queens. Khrushchev's eyes sank into his grin. Platonov gently took the picture away. "Ancient history. Leningrad, nineteen sixty-two. I swept the field. That was when world chess was Soviet chess and this club, this undersea wreck was the center of the chess world."

"Soon to be apartments."

"Ah, you saw the banner outside? Apartments with all the modern conveniences. We will be demolished and replaced by a marble palace for thieves and whores, the social parasites we used to put in jail. Does the state care?" Platonov rehung the photo, cracks and all. "The state used to believe in culture, not real estate. The state—"

"You're still a Party member?"

"I am a Communist and proud of it. I remember when millionaires were shot on principle. Maybe a millionaire can be an honest man, maybe pigs can whistle. If not for me, they'd already have their apartment house, but I have petitioned the city, the state senate and the president himself to bring this architectural obscenity to a halt. I am costing them millions of dollars. That's why they want me out of the way."

"What do you mean?"

"Why they want to kill me." Platonov smiled. "I outfoxed them. I stayed here. I never would have made it home safely."

"Who did you outfox?"

"Them."

It struck Arkady that the conversation was taking a strange turn. He spied an electric samovar on a side table. "Would you like some tea?"

"You mean, has the old man been drinking? Does he

need to sober up? Is he crazy? No." Platonov dismissed the cup. "I'm ten moves ahead of you, ten moves."

"Like leaving the front door unlocked and falling asleep?"

Platonov forgave himself with a shrug. "You agree then that I should take precautions?"

Arkady glanced at his watch. Zurin had called him half an hour ago. "For a start, have you informed the militia that you feel your life is in danger?"

"A hundred times. They send an idiot along, he steals what he can and then goes."

"Have you been attacked? Been threatened by mail or over the phone?"

"No. That's what all the idiots ask."

Arkady took that as his cue. "I have to go."

"Wait." For his age, Platonov maneuvered around the game tables with surprising speed. "Any other suggestions?"

"My professional advice?"

"Yes."

"If millionaires want to raze this building to erect a palace for lowlifes and whores, do what they say. Take their money and move."

Platonov sucked up his chest. "As a boy, I fought on the Kalinin Front. I do not retreat."

"A wonderful sentiment for a headstone."

"Get out! Out! Out!" Platonov opened the door and pushed Arkady through. "Enough defeatism. Your whole generation. No wonder this country is in the shit can."

Arkady climbed the stairs to his car. Although he didn't think Platonov was in any real danger, he drove only a block before returning on foot. Staying away from streetlamps, he slipped from doorway to doorway until he was satisfied they were clear of anything but shadows and then lingered another minute just in case, perhaps because the wind had dropped and he liked the way the snow had gone weightless, floating like light on water.

No militia guarded the Chistye Prudy Metro station. Arkady tapped at the door and was let in by a cleaning lady who led him across a half-lit hall of somber granite and around turnstiles to a set of three ancient escalators that clacked as they descended. Maybe they weren't so old, only used; the Moscow underground was the busiest in the world and to be virtually the only one in it made him aware how large the station was and how deep the hole.

His mind returned to the excavation outside the Supreme Court. There they were, eminent judges with the modest ambition of upgrading their basement cafeteria, adding perhaps an espresso bar, and, instead, they had unearthed the horror of the past. Stick your shovel into the ground in Moscow and you took your chances.

"The people on the train must be crazy. He's been dead for fifty years. It's a disgrace," the cleaning woman said with the firmness of a palace guard. She wore an orange vest she smoothed and straightened. The outside world might be scribbled with graffiti and reek of piss, but it was generally agreed that the last bastion of decency in Moscow was the underground, discounting the gropers, drunks and thieves among your fellow passengers. "More than fifty years."

"You saw nothing tonight?"

"Well, I saw that soldier."

"Who?"

"I don't remember his name, but I saw him on television. It'll come to me."

"You saw a soldier but not Stalin."

"On television. Why can't they leave poor Stalin alone? It's a disgrace."

"Which part?"

"All of it."

"I think you're right. I think there'll be disgrace enough for everyone."

"You took your time." Zurin was waiting at the bottom, cashmere coat worn impresario-style on his shoulders and a froth of anxiety in the corners of his mouth.

"Another sighting?" Arkady asked.

"What else?"

"You could have started without me. You didn't have to wait."

"But we do. This is a situation of some delicacy." Zurin said the sighting had taken place, as before, on the last car of the last train of the night; even to the same minute—0132—testimony to Metro punctuality. This time two plainclothes officers had been stationed on the car in case. As soon as they noticed signs of a disturbance they radioed the driver not to leave the platform until all thirty-three passengers of the last car were off. The detectives had taken preliminary statements. Zurin handed Arkady a spiral notebook open to a list of names, addresses, telephone numbers.

I. Rozanov, 34, male, a plumber, "saw nothing."

A. Anilov, 18, male, soldier, "maybe saw something."

M. Bourdenova, 17, female, student, "recognized him from a history course."

R. Golushkovich, 19, male, soldier, "was asleep."

V. Golushkovich, 20, male, soldier, "was drunk."

A. Antipenko, 74, male, retired, "witnessed Comrade Stalin on the platform."

F. Mendeleyev, 83, male, retired, "witnessed Comrade Stalin wave from the platform."

M. Peshkova, 33, female, schoolteacher, "saw nothing."

P. Peneyev, 40, male, schoolteacher, "saw nothing."

V. Zelensky, 32, male, filmmaker, "witnessed Stalin in front of Soviet flag."

And so on. Of the thirty-three passengers, eight saw Stalin. Those eight had been detained and the rest released. The platform conductor, a G. Petrova, had seen nothing out of the ordinary and was also allowed to go. The notes were signed by Detectives Isakov and Urman.

"Isakov, the hero?"

"That's right," Zurin said. "He and Urman were called

to another case. We can't have good men wasting their time here."

"Of course not. Where is this other case?"

"A domestic dispute a couple of blocks away."

The platform clock read 0418, the same as Arkady's watch. Time until the next train stood at 00, because the system wouldn't start up again for another hour. Without a background rumble of trains the platform was an arcade of echoes, Zurin's voice popping up here and there.

"So, what do you want me to do?" Arkady asked.

"Nail things down."

"Nail down what? Someone on a subway puts on a Stalin mask and you pull people off their train?"

"We want to keep the lid on."

"On a hoax?"

"We don't know."

"Are you thinking of mass hallucination? That calls for exorcists or psychiatrists."

"Just ask some questions. They're old, it's past their bedtime."

"Not theirs." Arkady nodded toward a rail-thin man chatting up the schoolgirl. She plainly had trouble resisting flattery.

"Zelensky is the provocateur, I'm sure. Do you want to start with him?"

"I think I'll end with him."

First, Arkady walked to where the last car had stopped. A service gate and doorway stood at the platform's end. He hoisted himself up on the gate and saw nothing but electrical cables on the other side. The door was locked. The platform conductor might have had the key and some idea of who had been waiting for the train, but, thanks to Isakov and Urman, she was gone.

"Anything wrong?" the prosecutor asked.

"Couldn't be better. These were the only two sightings, last night and tonight? Nothing previous?"

"That's all."

Arkady questioned witnesses one by one, having each mark on a sketch of the subway car where they had been sitting. The pensioner Antipenko admitted that he had been reading a book and hadn't had time to switch to his distance glasses before the train rolled into the station. Antipenko's elderly friend Mendeleyev had slept earlier on the train, although he claimed he awoke when they pulled into the station. Neither of them felt threatened by the platform Stalin. In fact, two ancient babushkas said they recognized Stalin by his benign smile, although neither saw well enough to read the platform clock when Arkady asked them to. Another retiree wore eyeglasses so scratched, the world was a blur, and the final senior witness wasn't sure if he'd seen Stalin or Father Frost.

Arkady told him, "You've been up all night. Maybe you're tired."

"They kept us here."

"I'm sorry about that."

"I know my granddaughter is worried."

"Didn't the detectives call her and tell her you would be late?"

"I couldn't remember her number."

"Perhaps if you show me your papers?"

"I lost them."

"I'm sure there's something on you somewhere." Arkady opened the old man's overcoat and found, pinned to a jacket lapel, a tag with a name, address, and phone number. Also the soiled ribbons and hardware of a Gold Star Hero, Order of Lenin, Red Star, and Patriotic War hero, so many campaign medals that they were stitched in overlapping tiers onto the breast of his suit. This doddering ancient had once been a young soldier fighting the Wehrmacht in the rubble of Stalingrad. "Don't worry. The prosecutor will call your granddaughter and the trains will be running soon."

The student, Marfa Bourdenova, changed her mind because she wasn't clear who Stalin was. Besides, she was out past her curfew and hadn't been allowed to call home on her mobile phone. If the girl was a little plump it was also clear what a beauty she would soon be, with an oval face, a sharp nose and chin, huge eyes and light brown hair she blew away from her cheek in exasperation. "The reception here sucks."

From the next bench the filmmaker Zelensky stage-whispered, "Your reception sucks because you're in a hole, honey, you're in a fucking hole." He hunched forward in a scuffed leather jacket and told Arkady, "You can mess with their minds all you want, but I know what I saw. I saw Iosif Stalin standing at this platform tonight. Mustache, uniform, short right arm. Unmistakable."

"What color were his eyes?"

"Yellow eyes, wolf eyes."

"Vladimir Zelensky?" Arkady asked to be sure. He felt Zurin creep to the other side of the pillar.

"Call me Vlad, please." As if it were a favor.

Zelensky stood in the umbra of fame. Ten years before he had been a young director of rough-and-ready crime films, until he sniffed cocaine himself and performed the magic trick of disappearing up his nostril. His smile said the boy was back and the frizz of his hair suggested ideas on the simmer.

"So, Vlad, what did you say when you saw him?"

Zelensky laughed. "Something on the order of 'Fuck your mother!' What anyone would say."

As Arkady remembered, Zelensky got by on porn, grinding out films that required nothing more than two willing bodies and a bed. Films where everyone, including the director, used pseudonyms.

"Did Stalin say anything?"

"No."

"How long was he visible?"

"Two seconds, maybe three."

"Could it have been somebody wearing a mask?"

"No."

"You are a filmmaker?"

"An independent filmmaker."

"Could someone have rigged a film or a videotape?"

"Set it up and broken it down? Not fast enough." Zelensky winked in the girl's direction.

"He stood where?"

On the sketch Zelensky marked the platform directly opposite the last car.

"Then?"

"He walked away. Vanished."

"Walked or disappeared?"

"Disappeared."

"What did he do with the flag?"

"What flag?"

"You told the detectives that Stalin had a flag."

"I guess it disappeared too." Zelensky lifted his head. "But I saw Stalin."

"And said, 'Fuck your mother!' Why the Chistye Prudy Metro? Of all the stations for Stalin to show up at, why here?"

"It's obvious. You went to the university?"

"Yes."

"You look it. Well, I'll tell you something I bet you don't know. When the Germans bombed Moscow, when this was called Kirov Station, this was where Stalin came, deep underground. He slept on a cot on the platform and the General Staff slept in subway cars. They didn't have a fancy war room like Churchill or Roosevelt. They put plywood up for walls and every time a train came through, maps and papers would fly around, but they put together a strategy that saved Moscow. This place should be like Lourdes, with people on their knees, plaster Stalins for sale, crutches on the wall. Can't you see it?"

"I'm not an artist like you. I remember *One Plus One.* That was an interesting film."

"The serial killer. That was a long time ago."

"What films have I missed?"

"How-to films."

"Woodworking? Plumbing?"

"How to fuck."

Arkady heard Zurin groan. The schoolgirl Marfa Bourdenova blushed but didn't move away.

"Do you have a business card?"

Zelensky gave him one that read Cine Zelensky on new, crisply cut pasteboard suitable for a comeback. The address given was on fashionable Tverskaya, even if the phone prefix was for the less elegant south end of Moscow.

The clock over the tunnel read 0450. Arkady stood and thanked all the witnesses, warning them that it was snowing outside. "You're all free to leave or wait for the first train."

Zelensky didn't wait. He bounced to his feet, spread his arms like the winner of a match and shouted, "He's back! He's back!" all the way to the escalator. He clapped as he rode up, followed by the Bourdenova girl, who was already fumbling for her phone.

Zurin said, "Why didn't you warn them not to talk to people outside the station?"

"Did some riders have cell phones?"

"Some."

"Did you collect them?"

"No."

"They have had nothing else to do but spread the word."

Arkady almost felt for Zurin. Through coup and countercoup, Party rule and brief democracy, fall of the ruble and rise of millionaires, the prosecutor had always bobbed to the surface. And here he was in the subway, shooting spittle in his confusion and rage. "It's a hoax or it didn't happen. But why would anyone perpetrate such a hoax? And why would the bastards do it in my district? How am I expected to stop someone from posing as Stalin? Should we shut down the Metro while detectives search on their hands and knees for the footprints of a ghost? I'll look ridiculous. It could be Chechens."

That was desperate, Arkady thought. He looked toward the tunnel. The time was 0456. "You don't need me for this."

The prosecutor shifted close enough. "Oddly enough, I do. Zelensky acts as if this was a miracle. I tell you that miracles only happen on orders from above. Ask yourself, where are the agents of state security in all this? Where is the KGB?"

"FSB now."

"The same can of worms. Usually, they're everywhere. Suddenly, they're not. I'm not being critical, not a bit, but I know when someone pulls down my drawers and fucks me from behind."

"Wearing a mask in the subway is not a crime and without a crime there's no investigation."

"That's where you come in."

"I don't have time for this." Arkady wanted to be at Komsomol Square when the Metro began running.

"Most of our witnesses are elderly people. They have to be treated with sensitivity. Isn't that what you are, our sensitive investigator?"

"There was no crime, and they're useless as witnesses."

Antipenko and Mendeleyev sat side by side, like the stones of a slumping wall.

"Who knows? They might open up. A little sympathy goes a long way with people that age. Also, there's your name."

"My name?"

"Your father's. He knew Stalin. He was one of Stalin's favorites. Not many can say that."

And why not? Arkady thought. General Kyril Renko was a talented butcher, not a sensitive soul at all. Even given that all successful commanders were butchers—"None more passionately loved by the troops than Napoleon," as the General used to say—even given that bloody standard, Kyril Renko stood out. A car, a long Packard with soldiers on the running boards, would come for the General to take him to the Kremlin. Either to the Kremlin or the Lubyanka, it wasn't clear which until the car turned left or right at the Bolshoi, left to a cell at the Lubyanka or right to the Kremlin's Spassky Gate. Other generals fouled their pants on the way. General Renko accepted the choice of fates as a fact of life. He would remind Arkady that his own swift rise through the ranks had been made possible by the execution by Stalin of a thousand Russian officers on the eve of the war. How could Stalin not appreciate a general like that?

Arkady asked, "What about the detectives who were on the scene?"

"Urman and Isakov? You said yourself there is no question of criminality. This is a matter we may not even want on the books. What is more appropriate is a humane, informal inquiry by a veteran like you."

"You want me to find Stalin's ghost?"

"In a nutshell."

3

A heavyset man in underclothes sat at the kitchen table, his head resting on his forearm, a cleaver standing in the back of his neck. One forensic technician videotaped the scene while another peeled the dead man's hand from a water glass. Vodka was still in it, Isakov told Arkady. A tech poured half the dead man's glass into a vial to test later for rat poison, which would show premeditation. Crusted dishes, pickle bottles and glittering empties of vodka were piled in a corner to make room on the drain board for open packages of sugar and yeast, and in the sink for a pressure cooker, rubber hoses and plastic tubing. Alcohol formed at the end of a tube, hung and dripped into a jar. Otherwise, the kitchen was decorated with a mounted wolf head and bushy tail, a tapestry with a hunting motif and a photograph of the dead man and a woman as two people younger and happier. The refrigerator hummed, speckled with blood. Snow fidgeted with a loose windowpane. For the moment no one smoked, despite the flatulent stink of death. According to a cuckoo clock it was 4:55.

Arkady waited at the door with Nikolai Isakov and

Marat Urman. Arkady had imagined Isakov so many times that the real man was smaller than expected. He wasn't particularly handsome, but his blue eyes suggested coolness under fire and his forehead bore interesting scars. His leather jacket was scuffed from wear and his voice was almost whispery. Arkady's father had always said that the ability to command was innate; men would either follow you or not. Whatever the quality was, Isakov had it. His partner Urman was a Tatar built round and hard, with the broad smile of a successful pillager. A raspberry red leather jacket and a gold tooth revealed a taste for flash.

"It seems to be a case of cabin fever," Isakov said. "The wife says they hadn't left the house since it started snowing."

"Started like a honeymoon." Urman grinned.

Isakov said, "It appears that they could drink vodka faster than they could make it."

"At the end they were fighting over the last drop of alcohol in the house. Both so drunk they can barely stand. He starts hitting her . . ."

"Apparently one thing led to another."

"She slices him between the sixth and seventh vertebrae and right through the spinal cord. Instantaneous!"

The cleaver had been dusted with gray powder and the ghostly print of a palm and fingers was wrapped around the handle.

"Does he have a name?" Arkady asked.

"Kuznetsov," said Isakov. Selecting a professional tone, he commiserated with Arkady. "So you got stuck with Stalin's ghost."

"I'm afraid so."

"Chasing a phantom through the Metro? Urman and I prefer ordinary cases with real bodies."

"Well, I envy you." Which hardly told the whole story, but Arkady thought he was controlling his bitterness fairly well. He stole a glance at the clock: 4:56. His watch said 5:05. "I had a question about the phantom, as you put it. I was wondering, did either of you search the subway platform?"

"No."

"Open any maintenance gates or doors?"

"No."

"Why did you let the platform conductor leave the station?" It came out more brusquely than Arkady had intended.

"That's more than one question. Because the conductor didn't see anything." Isakov was patient. "People who weren't crazy, we let go."

"What else, besides seeing Stalin, did they say or do that was crazy?"

Urman said, "Seeing Stalin, that's crazy enough."

"Did you get the number of the car?"

"Number?"

"Every car in the Metro has a four-digit number. I'd like to see that car. Did you get the name of the driver of the train?"

Isakov was categorical. "We were ordered to ride the last car, whatever its number was, and observe. We were not told what to watch for or at which station or to get the driver's name. When we pulled into the Chistye Prudy stop we saw nothing and heard nothing unusual until people started to shout. I don't know who shouted first. As instructed, we separated the positive witnesses from the rest of the passengers and held them until we were called out on this case."

The forensic team announced that they were finished with the kitchen and moving to the bathroom, where shiny surfaces beckoned.

Arkady waited until the techs had passed before saying, "Your report was a little sketchy."

"The prosecutor didn't want an official report," Isakov said.

Urman was puzzled. "Why all the fucking questions? We're on the same side, aren't we?"

Don't complicate things, Arkady told himself. This wasn't his case. Get out of the apartment.

A whimper sounded from another room.

"Who is that?"

"It's the wife."

"She's here?"

"In the bedroom. Take a look, but watch where you step."

Arkady went down a hall littered with newspapers, pizza boxes and KFC tubs to a bedroom where the squalor was deep enough it seemed to float. A redheaded woman in a housedress was handcuffed to the bed. She rose out of an alcoholic stupor, legs and arms spread, hands in plastic bags. An array of blood spots covered the front of her dress. Arkady pushed up her sleeves. Her flesh was slack but by a comparison of forearms she was right-handed.

"How do you feel?"

"They took the dragon."

"They took what?"

"It's our dragon."

"You have a dragon?"

The mental effort was too much and she sank back into incoherence.

He returned to the kitchen.

"Someone took her dragon."

"We heard it was elephants," Urman said.

"Why is she still here?"

Isakov said, "Waiting for an ambulance. She already confessed. We hoped she could reenact the crime for the video camera."

"She should be seen by a doctor and in a cell. Save the housedress. How long have you two been detectives in Moscow?"

"A year." Urman had lost his good humor.

"You moved over to detective level direct from the Black Berets? From Hostage Rescue to Criminal Investigation?"

"Maybe they bent the rules for Captain Isakov," Urman said. "Why the fuss? We have a murder and a confession. It's two plus two, right?"

"With one swing. She must have had a steady hand," Arkady said.

"Just lucky, I guess."

"Do you mind?" Arkady stepped behind the dead man for a different perspective. One arm still stretched out for the glass. Without touching, Arkady studied the wrist for bruising from, say, being clamped down by a stronger man while a blow was struck.

Urman said, "I've heard about you, Renko. People say you like to stick your dick in. We didn't have time for people like you in the Black Berets. Second guessers. What are you looking for now?"

"Resistance."

"To what? Do you see any bruises?"

"Did you try a UV scan?"

"What is this shit?"

"Marat." Isakov shook his head. "Marat, the investigator is only asking questions born of experience. There's no reason to be taking it personally. He's not." He asked as if making sure, "You're not taking this personally are you, Renko?"

"No."

Isakov didn't smile, but he did seem amused. "Now, Renko, you'll have to excuse us if we work our own case our own way. Is there anything else you want to know?"

"Why were you so certain the glass held vodka? Did you just assume it?"

There was still some in the glass. Urman dipped his first and middle fingers and licked them. He dipped the fingers a second time and offered them to Arkady. "You can suck them if you want."

Arkady ignored Urman and asked Isakov, "So you're

satisfied what you have here is an ordinary domestic homicide due to vodka, snow and cabin fever?"

"And love," Isakov said. "The wife says she loved him. Most dangerous words in the world."

"So you think love leads to murder," Arkady said.

"Let's hope not."

Snow packed on the windshield. At five minutes before the Metro doors opened, Arkady didn't have time to stop and brush the wipers clear, but he decided that as long as he followed taillights he was on the right side of the road and headed into Three Stations, as everyone called Komsomol Square for the railroad stations gathered there. Traffic lights swung, lenses packed with red and green snow. Leningrad Station's Italian pomp, Yaroslavsky Station's golden crown, Kazan Station's oriental gate: the windshield wipers smeared them together.

Arkady left his car in a snow drift in front of Kazan Station. A few passengers had already come out to search for taxis. Most arrivals streamed next door toward the Metro: oilmen from the Urals, businessmen from Kazan, a ballet troupe returning home, day trippers with caviar to trade, families with small children and huge suitcases, commuters and budget tourists following a dim path of half-smothered streetlamps. They hurried in the steam of their breath, hats pulled low, bags and packages tightly clutched, perhaps more eager to leave than arrive someplace else. Snow had driven away the usual pimps and

Gypsies and wholesome country women who sold their poisonous homemade brew and drunks who gathered empty vodka bottles to pay for new. A hazardous undertaking. The year before, five bottle scavengers had their throats slit in and around Three Stations. For bottles. Until the Metro doors opened, people would be pressed against a dead end in the dark. There were militia officers assigned to outdoor posts; they were inside the train station checking tickets and fighting Chechen terrorism where it was warm.

Part of Arkady was back in the Kuznetsovs' bloody apartment, where he and Isakov seemed to have exercised a gentlemen's agreement not to mention Eva. No, neither of them took things personally.

Arkady searched between shuttered kiosks and flushed out a pair of drunks so unsteady they couldn't stand except against a wall.

"Stay together!" he told people. Present a solid front, even yaks knew that much, he thought.

But it was each for his own. People closest to the Metro doors clung to their position; those behind pressed harder to the fore, while the crowd further back began to scatter. It was like watching wolves cull a herd as boys flowed out of the dark in packs of five or six, wearing black garbage bags and balaclavas that made them virtually invisible. Old people they plucked where they stood. Bigger game they swarmed; a monk was pulled down on the ice by his cassock and stripped of his gilded cross. One moment he had two boys in his grasp, and then nothing but trash bags.

Arkady was circled by boys. The leader wasn't more than fifteen, not afraid to show his moon face and wispy mustache. He pulled up his bag to produce a slim revolver he aimed at Arkady. Arkady was not amazed that a kid could get a firearm. Railroad police, the lowest level of law enforcement, were still issued hundred-year-old revolvers. Had Georgy come upon a drunken guard sleeping in a boxcar and stripped him of his gun? At Three Stations stranger things had happened.

"Bang," the boy said.

Melting snow coursed down Arkady's back.

"Hello, Georgy," Arkady said.

"How would you like a hole in the head?" Georgy asked.

"Not especially. Where did you find that?"

"It's mine."

"It's a real antique. It outlasted the Soviet Union."

"It still works."

"Where's Zhenya?"

"I could blow your brains out."

"He could," said the smallest boy in the circle. "He practices on rats."

"Isn't that what you are?" Georgy asked Arkady. "Aren't you a rat?"

After two days without sleep anything was possible. The pistol was a Nagant, a double-action, and the hammer was cocked. On the other hand, the trigger demanded a serious squeeze; Georgy wouldn't fire accidentally. Arkady couldn't see how many rounds were in the cylinder, but you can't have everything.

He rolled back the cap of the smaller boy. "Fedya, you're up early today."

Georgy prodded Arkady with the gun. "Never mind him."

"Fedya, I just want to talk to Zhenya."

"You're not listening," Georgy said.

"He plays chess," Arkady told Fedya. "You should ask him to teach you how to play chess."

"Shut up!" Georgy said.

Fedya stole a glance at the dark of a doorway, where a foot stepped back beyond the reach of the light. He felt Zhenya's gaze and saw the scene from Zhenya's point of view: the snow-covered battlefield, casualties nursing their dignity and winners dragging off packages like Christmas presents.

A chorus of police whistles promised that authority was on its way. The militia had clubs but, in the dark, who could tell whom to beat? They did their best. Meanwhile, the boys disappeared, not so much retreating as dissolving into shadows. Georgy backed off, the gun still pointed at Arkady, who watched the boys gather and slip away.

"Zhenya!"

Georgy's group slipped between trash bins, climbed a chain-link fence, and in a moment were gone in the direction of the railroad yard, a confusing array of sidetracks and trains on any night and now a white maze. Arkady followed their prints through the snow until all the footsteps went in separate directions and left him spinning.

Arkady retreated to the station. He staggered into the still atmosphere of the station's great hall, the suspended breath of the chandeliers, the rows of motionless bodies. As if sleep were the first business of the station, train departures were not announced. Take me to romantic Kazan, Arkady thought, to the land of peacocks and the Golden Horde. He was coughing so hard he dropped his cigarettes. Disgusted, he crumpled the pack and tossed it aside.

As he came out the front of the station he saw—briefly, before snow obscured his view—Georgy and Fedya with a boy that could have been Zhenya crossing the traffic island in the middle of the square. Arkady stumbled down the steps and squeezed between parked cars onto the street. Even blinkered by snow the lights of the square were bright. No trolleys out yet, although overhead cables hummed. By the time Arkady reached the island the three boys were halfway to the opposite sidewalk, but he had caught his breath and was gaining with every step when the blast of a horn brought him up short.

The three turned at the sound.

"Zhenya!"

Arkady retreated out of the way of a snowplow. The machine traveled in a haze of headlights and crystals, snow spewing from the blade. Arkady couldn't run in front because a second plow followed at an angle, and a third, lumbering and grinding, walling off the sidewalk with snow.

4

Arkady and Eva lay in a gray light that spread through rooms mostly bare of furniture. Arkady had inherited the apartment from his father; it was huge in comparison to his old flat, which they had left because there she felt the presence of Irina. "I won't compete with a ghost," she said. A table here, a portable television there were more like claims of residence than actuality. Arkady had disposed of all his father's possessions, any toehold the dead man might retain, except for his books and pictures, which were boxed and sealed in the office closet.

From the outside the building was an architectural collision of Gothic buttresses and Moorish arches, but, inside, the digs were fairly grand, with high prewar ceilings and parquet floors. The apartment house had been built for Party and military elite, who were proud of their address, although during Stalin's time it was also where the most people were taken away in the middle of the night, not to be seen again for years, if ever. Residents had listened with dread for a knock on the door or even the ascent of an elevator. Rumor claimed that special passages had been built into the walls to accommodate the agents of the state. What Arkady found interesting was that, even knowing the building was a chopping block, no one had dared decline the honor of moving in.

The truck with all their earthly possessions was a week late and they had been living in a makeshift way, their base a mattress they laid directly on the parquet floor. A quilted coverlet spilled off the bed, but Arkady and Eva were warm because the building was a prodigy of heat. They had slept the day away next to a tray crammed with bread, strawberry jam and tea. The wind had died and snow fell in thick, feathery clumps that drifted as shadows down the curtains.

Her body could have been a girl's, her breasts small and her skin so pale and unlined that he half expected it to carry an imprint of him. With her black hair, she was the perfect creature of dusk. At night when she couldn't sleep, which was often, she walked around the apartment in a robe and bare feet. Some rooms, like the office, they didn't use at all, except for storing boxes of photographs of his father and Irina he had brought by car. At night the parquet floor would groan; she preferred sleeping in the daytime, when fewer ghosts were about.

Eva didn't need his ghosts, she had her own. She had been a schoolgirl in Kiev, marching in the May Day parade four days after the meltdown at the Chernobyl nuclear reactor station because the authorities assured the public that the situation was under control. A hundred thousand children marched into an invisible rain of radioactive plutonium, potassium, strontium, cesium-137. No one in the parade curled up and died on the spot, but she was labeled a survivor, it being generally understood that survivors, especially women, were both barren and contagious.

In Moscow she had found a position at a medical clinic. Eva was good with the younger patients, especially those who couldn't sleep. She recorded them and sent the tapes to their families. Her portrait, Arkady often thought, could be painted in just black and white, although lately more and more in black alone and with sharper angles.

The further apart they grew, the more the bed was their mutual safe haven. Words were their enemy, the expression of failed hopes. Sex was performed in silence and it was difficult to say how much of their lovemaking was passion and how much the desperate scraping of a dead match.

The phone rang. Neither Arkady nor Eva wanted to connect with reality, so the caller talked to the answering machine.

"Where are you, Renko? We have a situation that has to be dealt with. If just anyone dead popped up on a Metro platform, it could be a hoax. Stalin is different. To use a likeness of Stalin is a clear provocation. Somebody is behind it. Why did you turn off your cell phone? Where the devil are you? Call in!"

"That was Prosecutor Zurin. What was he going on about?" Eva asked.

"Stalin has been seen a couple of times late at night at a Metro station."

"Stalin in the Metro? Really? Just what does this Metro Stalin do?"

"Not much. He stands on the platform and gives passengers a wave."

"Doesn't execute anyone?"

"No, not a single one."

"What will Zurin do?" Zurin generally bored Eva, but now she hiked herself up on her elbows.

Arkady was encouraged. This was more conversation than they'd had in a week.

"Well, as the prosecutor says, Stalin is different. Stalin is a minefield and there are no good moves. Call anything about Stalin a hoax and Zurin will have superpatriots to deal with. Do nothing and let rumors spread and he'll have a shrine on his hands. When the tsar's bones were found, pilgrims showed up the following day. The Metro will be a mob scene and Zurin will go down as the man who brought the Moscow subway system to a stop. Or—Zurin's third choice—embrace the situation, announce that the sightings are genuine visions and be left high and dry as a raving lunatic if no more sightings occur."

"And Zurin called you. So he wants to send you into the minefield first."

"Something like that."

"But you're staying here? I didn't know you were going to be here all day."

"I am. Did you have other plans?"

"Except you're always thinking about work, so you're not really here when you are here."

"Not all the time."

"Yes, all the time. Which is good, I suppose, in an

investigator. I know when a ghost joins us. I feel the company." This was a loaded statement, because there were ghosts and there were ghosts. "I suppose you can't help becoming involved."

"Actually, it's better not to get involved."

"You can do that?"

"I have to. I can't spend my life brooding on the dead."

He closed his eyes and saw the man with the cleaver in his neck. The odds were astronomical against a drunken woman's dispatching her husband with a single, perfect swing of a cleaver between the vertebrae and through the spinal cord, as Isakov and Urman maintained. A woman so drunk she most likely wouldn't remember anything she said, let alone a confession. However, the blood spatter pattern on the kitchen walls did seem to match the stains on her housedress. The cleaver handle pointed to the victim's left shoulder, indicating a right-handed attack; she was right-handed. The fact that no neighbors called the militia about the noise of the fight suggested that the husband and wife had gone toe to toe before. Had they argued over who had the dragon? Enough snow, enough vodka, a ready blade? With that combination you didn't need professional killers.

Either way, Arkady was annoyed at himself for drawing the attention of Isakov and Urman. Asking questions was the last thing he should have done, although it was instructive watching the captain and his eager lieutenant.

"You're doing it now," she said.

"Sorry."

"I know your secret," she said.

"What's my secret?"

"In spite of everything, at heart you're an optimist." She amended that. "In spite of *me*, you're an optimist."

"We have our moments."

"I have proof. It's all on tape." When Eva and Arkady were first together she would take a pocket-size tape recorder and cassettes to record what they were doing, whether it was a day of skiing or a simple walk, to play back later and laugh at. When was the last time he heard her laugh?

He held her heartbeat in her breast. With her he was always half aroused. If that wasn't cause for optimism, what was?

Outside the day faded, the sun a bonfire in the snow.

Down on the street, a road crew was attempting the repair of a pothole. Four sturdy women dug while a man supervised and occasionally held a lamp. Each day for a week they had poured steaming asphalt that settled into a widening hole, a daily demonstration of futility.

The phone rang. A sugary Zurin talked to the answering machine this time, apologizing for disturbing Arkady on his day off and hoping that Arkady wasn't using his machine to avoid calls. "You wouldn't be as low as that."

No problem, thought Arkady. He pulled the phone line from the jack, then remembered Zhenya and reconnected.

Eva watched. "You still expect Zhenya to call?"

"He might."

"He will be fine. He's a fish in water."

"It's cold out."

"Then he'll find someplace warm. Are you sure you saw him?"

"No, but I'm sure he was there. Did he say anything to you?"

"Two words: *He's here.* Then he raced out the door."

Nobody knew how many homeless kids there were in Moscow. Estimates ranged from ten to fifty thousand, in age from four to sixteen. Few were orphans; most were running from alcoholic, abusive families. The kids ate and wore what they could steal or beg. They slept on heating pipes or in unwatched trains. They sniffed glue, bummed cigarettes, sold themselves for sex outside the Bolshoi, and the closest thing to a steady roost was Three Stations. The week before, the militia had collared Zhenya, along with his friends Georgy and Fedya. Zhenya was released to Arkady, but Georgy and Fedya had simply been released for lack of shelter space. The president himself called homeless kids a threat to national security. Now that Georgy had a gun, maybe the president was right.

"Arkasha, open your eyes. Your little Zhenya wins more money playing chess than you earn risking your life. You think he's like you, a sweet, agreeable soul. He's not."

"He's twelve years old."

"He's somewhere between twelve and a hundred years old. Have you seen him play chess?"

"Hundreds of times."

"He squeezes his opponent like a python, eats him and digests him alive."

"He's good."

"And you are not responsible for him."

Arkady had looked into adopting Zhenya. However, with no information about his parents, even whether they were dead or alive, legal adoption was out of the question and an arrangement had evolved. Officially, Zhenya was on the rolls of the shelter where Arkady had first met him. In fact, Zhenya slept on the apartment sofa, as if he had happened by and nodded off. Zhenya was Pluto, a dark object detectable more by its effect on the planets than by direct observation.

"Consider me a python." Arkady slipped into bed.

They ate in bed. Brown bread, mushrooms, pickles, sausage and vodka.

Eva filled his glass. "Last night at the clinic, one of the other doctors, a woman, asked me, 'Do you know the curse of Russian men? Vodka! Do you know the curse of Russian women? Russian men!'"

"Cheers."

They touched glasses and downed the vodka in one go.

"Perhaps I am your curse," Eva said.

"Probably."

"Zhenya and I complicate your life."

"I hope so. What kind of life do you think I had?"

"No, you're a saint. I don't deny it."

Arkady sensed a slide in Eva's mood and changed the subject. "Zhenya said, 'He's here.' That's all?"

"He said it as he went out the door."

"He didn't say where he'd been or where he was headed?"

"No."

"He could have seen anyone. A famous chess player, his favorite soccer star. Maybe Stalin. Can we talk about us?" Eva leaned forward and laid her head on Arkady's shoulder. "Arkasha, I can't compete with a wife who died young and beautiful and totally normal. Who could compete with that?"

"She's not here."

"But you wish she were, is what I mean. You know, you never showed me a picture of Irina; I had to find one on my own. Irina was lovely. If you could, wouldn't you want her back?"

"It's not a competition."

"Oh, it is."

He set the tray aside and pulled her close. Her breasts were tender from making love but they stiffened again. Her mouth sought out his even though their lips were sore and slightly bruised. This time the rhythm was slow. With each stroke a soft expulsion of air escaped her lips, so much easier than words. They could go on forever, Arkady thought, as long as they never left the bed.

But they were going someplace. The bed was a magical carpet that took an unfortunate plunge into an abyss when he said, "Don't act as if this is about Irina. It's a lie to pretend it's just Irina. A highly skilled investigator notices such things as strange phone calls and mysterious absences." Well, this is exciting, he thought. They had touched down in the abyss, where the air was thin and the heart bounced around the rib cage.

"It's not what you think," Eva said.

"I'm fascinated. What is it?"

"It's unfinished business."

"You can't finish it?"

"It's not that simple."

"What does that mean?"

"When I was in Chechnya Nikolai Isakov saved me."

"Tell me again why you were there. You're not Chechen or in the Russian Army."

"Someone had to be there. Doctors had to be there. There were international medical organizations."

"But you were on your own."

"I don't like organizations. Besides, on my trusty motorcycle I was a moving target."

"Were you trying to be killed?"

"You forget that I'm a survivor. Besides, Nikolai let it be known that he would slit the throat of anyone who touched me."

"I'm grateful."

She watched him for a flinch. "And I expressed my gratitude in the traditional manner."

"Well earned, I'm sure. So Isakov is a hero in bed and out."

"Everyone had a scheme. Tank commanders sold fuel,

quartermasters sold food, soldiers traded the ammunition for vodka and they went home in coffins stuffed with drugs. Nikolai was different."

"Then why are you wasting your time with me?"

"I wanted to be with you."

"It's getting a bit crowded, don't you think? Two is company and all that. But I appreciate the farewell salute." It was the meanest thing he could think of to say and he had the satisfaction of seeing her eyes sting.

The phone rang again and a voice—not Zurin's—said to the answering machine, "Eva, pick up, it's Nikolai."

It was Arkady's turn to burn.

"Eva," the man said, "can you talk? Did you tell him?"

"Is it Isakov?" Arkady asked.

"I have to take this," Eva said.

She wrapped a sheet around herself before picking up the phone. The cord only stretched so far and she turned away to whisper. Suddenly nakedness seemed ridiculous to Arkady and the scent of sex cloyed.

What was the etiquette of cuckoldry? Should he leave them to their privacy, allow himself to be chased from his own bivouac? It wasn't as if he and Eva were married. It was clear that she could still physically act as if they were lovers and, from time to time, banter cheerfully enough to raise his hopes, at least until tonight, but the performances took more effort all the time. It was rare that their work shifts coincided because she scheduled her hours more to avoid Arkady than to see him. Betrayal was exhausting, weighting every word with double meaning.

Even when they made love he would spend the rest of the night examining everything Eva had said or done, watching her as if she were going to slip away and watching every word he said so as not to jar the mutually constructed house of cards. It had collapsed now, of course.

The funny thing was that Arkady had brought them back together by bringing Eva to Moscow, strolling with her around Patriarch's Pond on an autumn day and not understanding her shock when Isakov called her name.

"Keep walking," Eva had said.

Arkady said, "If it's a friend, I can wait."

"Not yet," Eva whispered to the phone, while her eyes stayed on Arkady. "I will, I will, I promise . . . I do, too," she said and set the receiver down.

Everything but a kiss, Arkady thought.

It wasn't by chance that Isakov called when Arkady was likely to be home. Isakov was rubbing his face in it.

The phone rang again, jarring him. Arkady felt his breathing build. Eva backed away.

"I know you're there, Renko. Turn on your television. Congratulations, you're on the news," Zurin said and hung up.

Arkady turned on the set. There were only six channels. The first showed the president laying a wreath, his eyes twisted one way, mouth another. Soccer. Patriotic films. Chechen atrocities. Finally, Prosecutor Leonid Zurin himself on a snowy street corner with a female reporter. Zurin's white hair whipped back and forth and his cheeks were apple red. He smiled indulgently, a natural actor. After his desperate phone calls to Arkady, Zurin seemed to have regained himself.

". . . a long winter, and sometimes winter is like the doldrums of summer, when all sorts of strange stories seem to be news, only to be forgotten a week later."

"So the rumors of Moscow citizens encountering Stalin in the Metro are fabrications?"

Zurin spent a moment in consideration. "I wouldn't say 'fabrications.' There was a report of a disturbance at a station last night. I sent a senior investigator who was particularly familiar with Stalin issues to the scene and he determined, after interviewing all the so-called witnesses, that no such event had, in fact, taken place. What had happened, according to Investigator Renko, was that some of the older riders got off the train earlier than they had intended and, as a result, found themselves stranded with a blizzard above and no more trains below."

The reporter would not be shaken off.

"Which Metro station?"

"That's irrelevant."

"Are you investigating further, Prosecutor Zurin?"

"Not to chase phantoms. Not while there are real criminals on the street."

"One last question, how did this rumor about Stalin get started? Do you or your investigator think it's a hoax? A political statement?"

Zurin composed himself. "We think no conclusions need be drawn. Stalin is a figure of undeniable historical significance, who continues to draw positive and negative reactions, but there is no reason to make him responsible for every mistake we make."

"Even getting off the train at the wrong stop?"

"Just so."

Arkady sat, stunned, dimly aware that the next news item was on the trial of a war veteran who had shot and killed a pizza deliveryman who resembled a Chechen. Other vets were lending moral support to their brother in arms.

Eva turned off the set. "You are 'familiar with Stalin'? What did Zurin mean by that?"

"You've got me."

The phone rang and this time Arkady picked up.

"Ah," Zurin said. "No more games. Now you answer. Did you see the news? Wasn't it interesting?"

"There should have been no publicity."

"I agree with you but, apparently, someone spoke to the press. I had to deal with reporters because the investigator assigned to the case was incommunicado. Renko, the next time I call you, whether it's your weekend or your deathbed, you will jump to the phone."

"'Familiar with Stalin'?" Eva repeated. "Ask him what he means."

Zurin said, "Explain to your lady friend that she is in a vulnerable position. Today I decided to review her papers. Doctor Eva Kazka is a divorced Ukrainian national with a Moscow residency permit based on her employment at a city polyclinic. Previous employment, a medical clinic in the Chernobyl Zone of Exclusion. A negative word, even a phone call from my office, and she would lose her present employment and her permit and go back to playing doctor for two-headed babies in Ukraine. Do you understand? Just say yes."

"Completely." Arkady watched Eva pull the sheet tight around herself.

"And that's why you will answer every time I call and why you will handle this investigation exactly as I say. Do you agree?"

Eva said, "Whatever it is, say no."

Arkady said, "What investigation? You told the reporter there wouldn't be one."

"What else could I say? That we were going to conduct a ghost hunt in the middle of Moscow? There will be an investigation but it will be confidential."

"Don't you think people will wonder why I'm asking questions if I'm not on a case?"

"You will have a case. You will investigate the claims of a citizen who says he has received threats against his life."

"Then he wants a bodyguard, not me."

Zurin said, "We don't take it seriously. He's reported death threats for twenty years. He's paranoid. He also happens to be an expert on Stalin. You'll be doing an investigation within an investigation. In fact, I've arranged it so you start tonight. The expert has agreed to meet you at the Park Kultury Metro and take the last train of the night for Chistye Prudy station. You will ride in the last car, since that seems to be where the sighting was."

"Who is this expert?" Arkady asked, but Zurin had hung up.

"You weren't going to do this," Eva said.

Arkady filled her glass and then his.

"Well, you changed your mind and now I've changed my mind. Cheers."

Eva left her glass where it was. "I have to go to work. The last thing I need is to tend sick children with vodka on my breath. You are 'familiar with Stalin issues'? What did Zurin mean by that?"

"My father knew Stalin."

"They were friends?"

"That's hard to say. Stalin had most of his friends shot. Let me drive you to the clinic."

"No. I'll walk. I can use the fresh air." Eva was on a different tack. "Did Stalin ever visit this apartment?"

"Yes."

"I'm standing where Stalin stood?" She looked down at her bare feet.

"Not here in the bedroom, but in the rest of the apartment, I suppose so."

"Because I always like to absorb the atmosphere and now I feel that I have really come to Moscow."

"That's the historian in you."

"It's certainly not the romantic."

Ah, that was it, Arkady thought, Stalin was to blame.

For the workers who burned with ambition, for soldiers slack-jawed from hash, for those too old and too poor to wave down a car, for revelers going home with a split lip and broken glass in their hair, for lovers who held hands even wearing gloves, and for the souls who had simply lost track of time, the illuminated red *M* of the Park Kultury Metro was a beacon in the night. They stumbled in like survivors, stamping off snow and loosening scarves while Arkady watched. Fifteen minutes to the last Red Line train and he had seen no one resembling a Stalin expert.

Eva knew he had been less than forthcoming about part of his conversation with Zurin. Now they had both lied. What should he have said? If he had told her that the prosecutor was using her as leverage, she would have packed and been gone in a day. Even if she had promised not to, he would have come home to find the apartment empty.

Something was moving along the banked snow of the sidewalk. It made progress and then stopped and rested against the bank. A faint snowfall sparkled. The approaching something developed an overcoat and the sort of tufted knit cap a Laplander might wear for herding reindeer, and closer, a prow of a nose, woolly brows, and blood-raddled eyes. Grandmaster Platonov.

"Investigator Renko! Look at these fucking boots." He pointed to the felt *valenki* he wore.

"They're on the wrong feet."

"I know they're on the wrong feet. I'm not a cretin. There was no place to sit down and switch them."

"Are you my Stalin expert?"

"Are you my protection?" Platonov's glare folded into resignation. "I guess we're both fucked."

5

"The Moscow Metro is the underground palace of the people." Platonov limped, one boot on and one off, as he pointed at the walls. "Milk white limestone from the Crimea. Now that the riffraff is gone, you can see it properly."

With its arches and tunnels, the hall of the Park Kultury station looked more like a monastery than a palace. A cleaning woman shuffled on towels across a wet section of the floor at about the same speed Platonov was moving.

Arkady asked, "Are you sure you're up to this?"

"To meeting a phony Stalin? This is an idiotic prank. Did you find Zhenya?"

"No."

"You won't, not until he's ready." Platonov stepped onto the down escalator, sat to finish switching boots, stood to put his cap in one pocket, and from another pocket pulled a white silk scarf he flung around his neck. Fumes of liberally applied cologne finished the effect of a bon vivant, a man about town.

Ahead, a man with a violin case hurried down the steps.

Behind, an old man in what had once been an elegant astrakhan cap gallantly carried a handbag for his wife while she pursed her lips and rouged her cheeks.

"Nervous?" Arkady asked.

"No," Platonov said too quickly, and repeated, "no." With his heroic beak, he could have been a Roman senator or King Lear cast out by ungrateful daughters so they could play chess. "Why should I be nervous? I take this subway line every day. It was dug by volunteers during the most difficult times of the thirties and the war. You can't imagine it now, but we were idealists then. Everyone, male and female, the young cadre of the Party, vied to dig the Metro."

"Not to mention brigades of forced labor."

"Some convicts redeemed themselves through labor, that's true."

"Which reminds me, has anybody notified the Communists that Stalin is back? I think the Pope would be informed if Saint Peter were seen in the streets of Rome."

"As a courtesy, Prosecutor Zurin, knowing the Party's interest and concern, did inform us. I've been delegated to make a report."

"So, besides teaching and playing chess, you are also a Party bureaucrat?"

"I told you at the chess club that I was well-connected."

"Yes, I'm sure." Any sane man would have run from the assignment, Arkady thought. "And you chose me?"

"I thought I detected a glimmer of intelligence." Platonov sighed. "I may have been wrong."

The train had collected the dregs of the evening: an inebriated officer of the Frontier Guard who leered at four prostitutes shivering in skimpy jackets and high-heeled boots. Arkady and Platonov took one end of the bench, the pensioners Antipenko and Mendeleyev took the other end. The violinist dropped into a corner seat, set his violin case across his knees, and opened a book. He had a round face and a wispy beard à la Che. Arkady didn't expect many passengers in the last carriage; the Metro was famous for its safety, but the later the hour the more people gravitated toward the front of the train.

As the doors closed, Zelensky, the filmmaker, rushed in and took a seat near the far end, where he emanated nervous energy in a spooky black leather coat that emphasized how thin he was. His frizzled hair looked especially electrified and iPod cords hung from his ears. As the train pulled out he pushed a duffel bag under the bench. If he noticed Arkady he didn't show it.

Park Kultury station fell behind; Kropotkin, Lenin Library, Okhotny Row, Lubyanka and Chistye Prudy stations lay ahead. Lightly loaded, the train flew through the tunnel with added whip. Windows turned to mirrors. A pale man with deep set eyes sat across from Arkady. No one should ever have to confront himself, he thought, not on the last train of the night.

Platonov rambled on about the Metro's glories, the white marble hauled from the Urals, black marble from Georgia, pink marble from Siberia. At Kropotkin station he pointed out the enormous chandeliers. The station was named for Prince Kropotkin, an anarchist, and Arkady suspected that the chandeliers would have made the prince's hand itch for a grenade. There were now six elderly riders including those two from the night before, Antipenko and Mendeleyev. Arkady wondered what the odds were of three passengers riding the same carriage as the night before. Why not, if they had regular schedules?

Zelensky listened to his music with his eyes closed, an occasional nod betraying the beat. Arkady had to give him credit; iPods were the most frequently stolen item on the Metro, but the filmmaker seemed blithely unconcerned. Mendeleyev and Antipenko snatched glances at Arkady, their eyes bitter and bright. Their youth had coincided with the peak of Soviet power and prestige. Little wonder they were wistful and furious at the downward course their lives had taken.

At the Lenin Library station the officer of the Frontier Guard got off and vomited in his cap. The station conductor, a stout woman in a Metro uniform, made sure he didn't spill a drop on her platform. Eight passengers boarded, intellectuals by the thinness of their coats. One attended to his comb-over and vaguely acknowledged Platonov.

Platonov spoke over the rush of the train. "A so-called chess master, but really just a wood pusher. Oslo, 1978, he resigned against me in eleven moves. Eleven! As if he had sudden indigestion instead of a bishop shoved down his throat and a rook shoved up his ass."

"Do you make many enemies?"

"Chess is war. Zhenya understands that." Platonov puffed up a little. "I'm playing the winner of a local tournament match on Friday. That fraud across the aisle pretends he'll show up. He won't."

At the Okhotny Row station two babushkas from the night before joined the car, bringing with them the scent of boiled cabbage to vie with Platonov's cologne. The prostitutes briefly flirted with Arkady before deciding that he was a cold engine. Three were in the death grip of tight Italian skirts. The apparent leader, a redhead in snakeskin pants, seemed to listen to private music without the aid of an iPod. The others gasped when the lights of the car flickered and sparks shot up between the tunnel and the train. This was the oldest section of the entire system. Rails were worn. Insulation frayed. Blue imps danced around the switches.

Platonov asked, "Do you know the sad thing?"

"What is the sad thing?"

"That Stalin was able to enjoy the Metro as a passenger once only. On that occasion he was so loved by the public he was mobbed and the security forces never let him do it again. To think, we're riding where he rode."

The train approached the stop for Lubyanka, the legendary factory of woe, where men were beaten like metal into more useful shapes: collaborators, confessors, victims eager to accuse themselves. They were delivered by car or, in Stalin's day, what seemed an innocent baker's van, but never via the Metro.

Next station, Chistye Prudy. In spite of his skepticism, Platonov removed his cap and made other small adjustments to appear presentable, and Arkady noticed a general stir among the riders: coughs, straightened backs, attention to shoes. Medals suddenly appeared. Antipenko wore the gold star of a Hero of Labor. The babushkas were Heroine Mothers. Zelensky let his earbuds drop around his neck. The violinist dog-eared a page and slipped the book into his violin case. At a depth of seventy meters the train descended further and its breath grew cooler.

The door to the next carriage opened and a man in a warm-up suit entered with a boy and girl in parkas. The man had broad shoulders and a heavy brow, but his physical menace was undercut by his stumbling from pole to pole as he followed the children. They were about ten years old, with blue eyes and golden hair that could have come right out of an artist's tube of paint. The girl held roses wrapped in cellophane. Zelensky took charge of her and the boy and marched them through the carriage to Arkady.

"What a coincidence. I said to myself that looks like Investigator Renko over there, and it is. Two nights in a row, is that coincidence or fate? Which is it?"

"So far, just a ride on the Metro."

"We're going to be on television," said the girl. She raised the flowers for Arkady. "Smell."

"Very nice. Who is the posy for?"

"You'll see," Zelensky said. "Okay, kiddies, go back to Bora. Uncle Vlad has to talk."

Zelensky rocked like a sailor to the motion of the train while the boy and girl returned.

"Is Bora a filmmaker, too?" Arkady asked.

"Bora is protection."

"You must need protection pretty badly."

"Don't underestimate Bora. Bora is a pit bull. But what are you doing here?" Zelensky grinned with bewilderment. "According to the television, you said there was no investigation, that no one saw Stalin. You changed your mind?"

"I thought it over and decided that maybe there was a chance that Stalin had been in hibernation for fifty years."

Zelensky noticed Platonov's interest in the conversation. "Getting nosy?"

"No." Platonov shook his head vigorously.

Arkady asked, "Is this the first time on the Metro for Bora? He looks a little lost."

"He's new to Moscow, but he'll catch on. He's a handy man to have around."

"For crossword puzzles?"

"Things are changing. I've had a bad patch, but I'm coming out of it. I admit I did some adult films. To you that might make me a pornographer."

"That would do it."

"That's because you're concentrating on me. What's important, the messenger or the message?"

"What's the message?"

"You've no idea what you're getting into."

"Will there be special effects?"

"We don't need special effects. We have the secret."

"Share it with me."

"You'll see what you'll see."

Zelensky let his smile hang in the air and returned to his seat. As the train slowed, passengers seated on the left side of the aisle migrated to the right. Instead of displaying the usual subway torpor they were increasingly excited, as if they were in a theater and the curtain about to rise.

Platonov cleared his throat. "Renko, I apologize for not backing you up a minute ago."

"Don't worry about it. You're a chess player, not a policeman."

The train went black and from black to yellow.

"Stalin!"

"It's him."

"Stalin!"

Full lights returned as the doors opened. All Arkady saw was an empty platform and marble columns. Platonov rose from his seat, drawn to the open door. The violinist had exchanged his book for a mini video camera and was taping the scene. Arkady recognized the camera because the prosecutor's office had one similar.

Arkady followed Platonov onto the platform. "Did you see anything?"

"I . . . don't know," Platonov said.

Everyone filed out of the carriage and their numbers grew as curiosity attracted passengers disembarking from forward cars, some with vodka-sloppy steps, bottles tucked inside their coats. Where there had been fifteen people, fifty milled about. The doors closed and the train pulled away. Shorter people on the platform were tiptoe with excitement. Arkady saw no one carrying anything big enough to manufacture special effects, like a strobe light and battery. He also did not see any platform conductors, although they generally allowed no lingering from the last train. Every Metro station had a militia post at street level, but Arkady didn't feel he had time to go up the escalator, wake the officer on duty and tell him . . . what?

"What do you mean, you don't know?" Arkady asked Platonov.

"I . . . don't know."

Arkady turned to a babushka who looked as sweet as the Virgin's mother and asked if she saw anything.

"I saw Stalin as plain as day. He asked me to get him a bowl of hot soup."

Two men in fur hats and parkas hung back on the platform. They hadn't been on the train or boarded it. They weren't Russian. In winter Russians in general just added another layer of clothing, Arkady thought. It was Americans who wore parkas as round and bright as hot-air balloons.

"Friends, fellow Russians, brothers and sisters," Zelensky said. "Please give us room." He indicated how much platform space he needed and where his cameraman should stand, acting the role of a director very much in charge, moving slowly to intensify the moment. From his duffel bag he took a framed photograph of Stalin that he set against the base of a platform pillar. Bora relieved the children of parkas to show off their embroidered peasant shirts. Zelensky dug into his bag again and came out with a spindly votive candle and a candleholder he placed in the boy's hands. While Bora lit the candle, Zelensky looked toward the men in parkas. The shorter one pantomimed holding something. Zelensky arranged the flowers in the girl's hands. The cameraman went on taping. From the flesh trade to Stalin's ghost, it was all the same to Zelensky, Arkady thought, but Zelensky was not even directing, he was taking his cues from the American. The children made a short procession and placed the candle and flowers before the photo. Stalin wore a white uniform in the picture. His vigorous mustache and hair were unmistakable, and the shifting flames of the candles brought his eyes to life.

In singsong, the children chirped, "Dear Comrade Stalin, thank you for making the Soviet Union a mighty nation respected by the world. Thank you for defeating the Fascist invaders and imperialist aggression. Thank you for making the world safe for its children. We will never forget."

The American pointed and Zelensky beckoned Mrs. Astrakhan Cap closer to the photo. She daubed her tears with her shawl.

"What did you see, Grandmother?" he asked.

"A miracle. When my husband and I came into the

station we saw our beloved Stalin surrounded by radiant light."

Other voices answered that they, too, had seen Stalin. It was contagious, despite their different versions.

"He was writing at a desk!"

"He was studying war plans!"

"He was reading Tolstoy!"

"Pushkin!" claimed another.

"Marx!"

The American drew circles with his finger. Speed it up.

Zelensky addressed the camera. "We Patriots declare this Metro station sacred ground. We demand a memorial to the military genius who, from this very site, victoriously defended the motherland. How can any Russian government deny us that? Where is Russian pride?"

The American lifted both hands.

Zelensky held up a red-on-white T-shirt that said, "I am a Russian Patriot." Bora began to circulate through the crowd to distribute similar shirts. An interesting group, Arkady thought: the elderly joined by the mildly curious, the seriously drunk, four cold prostitutes and American puppet masters.

"'I am a Russian Patriot,'" Zelensky read the shirt aloud. "If you are not a Russian Patriot, what are you?"

The pensioners Mendeleyev and Antipenko each took a shirt. The American waved, and the camera found the photogenic Marfa Bourdenova. Until now the schoolgirl had hidden in the crowd like a dove on a bough. She looked likely, by the way she hung on Zelensky's every word, to miss her curfew once again. Arkady felt a rush of anger at the filmmaker, at the willing believers and the make-believe shrine, because in Moscow this was enough to summon the past. The videotape might be even more effective for being clumsily staged and poorly lit, the sort of documentary that was the stuff of rumors. And all of it stage-managed by Americans. Arkady asked himself, what would Stalin do?

Zelensky caught Arkady's approach and began to rush his delivery.

"Russian Patriots honor the past. We will return to the visionary and humanitarian—"

Arkady walked behind Zelensky and kicked the candle and holder across the track. He took a step back and did the same with the flowers.

"Are you crazy?" Zelensky said.

Arkady held up his ID for all to see and announced, "Filming in the Metro is prohibited. Also this gathering is delaying the scheduled cleaning and maintenance of the Metro, putting the public safety at risk. It's now over. Go home."

Zelensky said, "I don't see any cleaning women or maintenance men."

"A schedule is a schedule." Arkady picked up the Stalin photograph.

"No!" A dozen voices protested.

"Then we'll trade." Arkady shoved the photo into the cameraman's free hand and relieved his other of the camera. Arkady popped out a mini cassette and slipped it into his coat.

"That's my property," Zelensky said.

"It's evidence now," Arkady announced and gave back the camera. He went into the crowd to grab Marfa Bourdenova by the wrist and started for the escalator. She screamed. Platonov padded alongside. Uncertainty froze everyone else except the two Americans. They had disappeared.

Ahead, Bora set down the duffel bag. No longer on the rolling deck of a subway car, he seemed more sure-footed. Arkady headed straight at him.

Zelensky shouted after, "We'll just shoot a new tape tomorrow. We don't even need to do it in Chistye Prudy Station. We'll just say it's Chistye Prudy."

"Each station is individual," Platonov shouted back. "People will know."

"Please, don't help," Arkady said.

Bora waited for a signal from Zelensky.

"Let me go, you bastard!" Marfa Bourdenova tried hitting Arkady but he dragged her too fast for her to connect solidly.

Bora reluctantly gave way. Once on the escalator, Arkady kept moving.

Marfa shrieked for help.

Arkady said, "I'll let you go at the top. I know you'll run back to him, only notice, he's not going to wait for you at the bottom. He only wants the tape."

At the top of the escalator Arkady released her wrist

and, as predicted, the girl bolted for the down escalator. Bora and the cameraman were already on their way up, two steps at a time.

The night sparkled. Platonov wanted to search for a taxi, but Arkady struck out for the park behind the station.

"Renko, we won't find a taxi this way, that's obvious."

"Then it's also obvious to Zelensky. He'll look here last."

"Shouldn't we discuss this?" Platonov said.

"No."

"I thought you were supposed to protect my life, not endanger it."

"If no one sees us, we'll be fine."

The park was open space the length of a football field, slightly dished, a white sheet of snow edged by a blur of plane trees and wrought iron fences. The snow reflected the light of boulevards on either side, but there were no paths or lamps within the park and even side by side the two men looked to each other like shadows.

"Do you mind if I smoke?" Platonov asked.

"Yes."

"Consider yourself fired, dismissed."

The footing was uneven, a surface of fine snow over icy sled tracks. As a kid, Arkady had sledded and skated in the park a hundred times.

"Be careful."

"Don't worry about my health. This is the man who asked me if *I* made enemies."

"If you have to talk, whisper."

"I'm not talking to you. Consider this conversation finished." Platonov trudged in silence for a step or two. "Do you even know who the Russian Patriots are?"

"They sound a lot like Communists."

"They *sound* like us, that's the idea. The Kremlin brought in Americans. The Americans polled people and asked which political figure they most admired. The answer was Stalin. They asked why, and the answer was that Stalin was a Russian patriot. Then they asked people if they would vote for a party called Russian Patriot, which didn't even exist. Fifty percent said they would. So the Kremlin put Russian Patriot on the ballot. Just on their name they'll get votes. It's a subversion of the democratic process."

"What if Stalin comes back from the dead and campaigns for them?"

"That's the outrageous part. Stalin belongs to us. Stalin belongs to the Party."

"Maybe you can copyright him, like Coca-Cola."

Platonov stopped to catch his breath. Arkady heard shouts and saw two figures on the snow fifty meters behind. The beam of a flashlight swung from side to side.

"It's Bora and the cameraman," Arkady said.

"I knew we should look for a car. Why did I listen to you?"

Platonov started moving again, but at a slower, shambling pace.

"How is your heart?" Arkady asked.

"It's a little late to be concerned about my health. Don't you have a gun?"

"No."

"You know the trouble with you, Renko? You're a pantywaist. You're too soft for your job. An investigator should have a gun."

What they needed was wings, Arkady thought. Bora seemed to fly over the snow, correcting the false first impression of clumsiness.

"Where are we going?" Platonov demanded. They had been headed down the middle of the park. Now Arkady turned toward the street.

"Just stay with me."

"This makes no sense at all."

Bora had already halved the difference and far outstripped the cameraman and the reach of the flashlight. By the way he pumped his knees he might have been a professional athlete, Arkady thought. Arkady admired men in that sort of physical condition; he never seemed to find the time.

Platonov took air in gasps. Arkady pulled him by the sleeve back in the direction they had originally been headed; it was like helping a camel through the snow. The two turns had cost time and distance. Finally, Platonov could go no further and hung onto an oil barrel in which shovels were deposited.

Bora approached through hanging flakes. Something bright hung from his hand. Left far behind, the cameraman shouted at him to stop. Bora took quicker, more purposeful strides.

"You laughed," he told Arkady.

"When?"

"In the Metro. For that I will carve out your eyes and fuck you in the face."

Bora drew his arm back. He was in midstride when he plunged through the snow and vanished. Snowflakes seesawed in his place. Arkady brushed snow aside and saw a hand pressed against the underside of ice.

The cameraman caught up, his beard frosted from his breath. He was just a boy, soft and heavy with red flannel cheeks.

"I tried to warn him," the cameraman said.

"The name should have been a hint," Arkady said.

The wartime Kirov Station had been renamed Chistye Prudy for the "clear pond" that cooled the park in the summertime and provided skating in the winter. Soft spots were posted with Danger—Thin Ice! signs that were perfectly visible in the daytime. The pool was shallow and the hole Bora had plunged through was just out of reach, but by a freakish chance he was on his back under more solid ice and faced the wrong direction. He couldn't get his feet under him and, with such poor leverage, could only use his fists, knees and head. Arkady had only expected Bora to get soaked in icy water. This was a bonus.

"Your name?" Arkady asked the cameraman.

"Petrov. Don't you think we should—"

"Your flashlight and papers, please?"

"But—"

"Flashlight and papers."

Arkady matched the cameraman to the ID photo of a clean-shaven Pyetr Semyonovich Petrov; age: twenty-two; residence: Olympic Village, Moscow; ethnicity: Russian through and through. Petrov was a pack rat. Arkady delved deeper into the holder and came up with a business card for Cinema Zelensky, membership in Mensa, video club cards, a second mini cassette, a matchbook from a "gentlemen's club" called Tahiti and a condom. A telephone number was scribbled inside the matchbook. Arkady pocketed the matchbook and tape and gave the ID back.

Bora squeezed his face against the ice. He was moving less.

Arkady put his arm around the cameraman. "Pyetr, may I call you Petya?"

"Yes."

"Petya, I am going to ask you a question and I want you to answer as if your life depended on it. Do you understand?"

"I understand."

"Be honest. When passengers on the Metro think they see Stalin, what are they really seeing? What is the trick?"

"There's no trick."

"No special effects?"

"No."

"Then how do people see him?"

"They just do."

"You're sure?"

"Yes."

"Okay." Arkady took a snow shovel from the oil barrel, raised it high, walked onto the ice and chopped at the ice over Bora's head. The blade skipped and sang. No other effect. Petya aimed the flashlight at Bora's eyes. They had the flat stare of a fish on ice. A second chop. A third. Bora didn't flinch. Arkady wondered whether he might have waited a little too long. Platonov gaped from the edge of the pond. Arkady swung the shovel and the first cracks showed as prisms in the flashlight's beam. Swung again and as the ice split Arkady sank halfway to his knees in water, no worse than stepping into a tube of ice cubes. He worked from the head down until he got a hold under Bora's arms and hauled him out onto land. Bora was white and rubbery. Arkady turned him face down, straddled him and pushed on his back. With all of his weight, he pushed and relaxed while his own teeth chattered. Pushed and relaxed and chattered. When Arkady had come to Chistye Prudy as a kid, he was always watched by Sergeant Belov, who taught Arkady to catch snow on his tongue. The sergeant would tell Arkady, this delicious one has your name on it. Here's another. And another. When Arkady skated, he chased snowflakes like a greedy swallow.

Bora gagged. He doubled up as pool water spewed from his mouth. Caught a deep breath draped with saliva. Retched again, wringing himself out. Sodden and freezing, he shivered not in any ordinary way but violently, as if he were in the grip of an invisible hand. He twisted his eyes up toward Arkady.

"It's a miracle," Petya said.

"Back from the dead," said Platonov. He hovered, blocking half the light.

Bora turned onto his back and laid a knife against Arkady's throat. He had returned from the dead with a trump card. The blade scraped a hair Arkady had missed when shaving.

"Thank you . . . and now . . . I fuck you," Bora said.

But the cold overwhelmed him. His shivering grew uncontrollable and hard enough to break bones. His teeth chattered like a runaway machine and his arms wrapped straitjacket-style tight around his body.

"Find the knife," Arkady told the boy with the flashlight.

"What knife?"

Arkady got to his feet and took the flashlight. "Bora's."

"I didn't see one," Platonov said.

"He had a knife." Arkady nudged Bora over not with a kick, but firmly. No knife. Arkady played the beam in and around the water where Bora had fallen through, where he had freed Bora from the ice and finally, trying to reverse time, on Bora's tracks across the snow.

"A magnificent night," Platonov declared. "A night like this you can only find in Moscow. This is the most fun I've had for years. And that you had your car parked here by the pond? Brilliant! Thinking two moves ahead!" He slapped the Zhiguli's dashboard with satisfaction. The lamps of the Boulevard Ring rolled by; Platonov still hadn't said where he wanted to go.

Arkady said, "Make up your mind. My feet are wet and numb."

"Want me to drive?"

"No, thanks." He had seen Platonov walk.

"You know who I saw tonight? I saw your father the General. I saw him in you. The apple does not fall far from the tree. Although I'm sorry you let that hooligan go."

"You didn't see his knife."

"Neither did the boy with the flashlight. I take your word for it."

"That's what I mean. All you could testify to is that Bora fell through the ice."

"Anyway, you taught him a lesson. He'll be frozen solid for a day or two."

"He'll be back."

"Then you'll finish him off, I'm confident. It is a shame about the knife. You think it will turn up in the pond?"

"Tomorrow, next week."

"Maybe when the ice melts. Can you hold a man in prison until the snow melts? I like the sound of it."

"I'm sure you do."

Platonov said, "You know, I met your father during the war on the Kalinin Front."

"Did you play chess?"

Platonov smiled. "As a matter of fact, I was playing

simultaneous games to entertain the troops when he sat down and took a board. He was very young for a general and so covered in mud I couldn't see his rank. It was extraordinary. Most amateurs trip over their knights. Your father had an instinctive understanding of the special mayhem caused by that piece."

"Who won?"

"Well, I won. The point is he played a serious game."

"I don't think my father was ever on the Kalinin Front."

"That's where I saw him. He was cheated."

"Out of what?"

"You know what."

Snow had stifled the usual twenty-four-hour assault of construction crews across the city. The drive along the Boulevard Ring's white-trimmed trees felt like passage through a more intimate town.

"There were atrocities on either side," Platonov went on. "The main thing is that your father was a successful commander. Especially in the beginning of the war, when all seemed lost, he was superhuman. If anyone deserved a field marshal's baton it was him. In my opinion he was smeared by hypocrites."

"So, who is trying to kill you?" Arkady changed the subject. He was, after all, supposedly trying to find out.

"New Russians, mafia, reactionaries in the Kremlin. Most of all, real estate developers."

"Half of Moscow. Have there been threatening phone calls, ominous notes, stones through the windows?"

"I told you before."

"Remind me."

"They threaten on the phone, I hang up. They send a poison pen letter, I throw it away. No stones yet."

"The next note, don't open it. Handle it by the corners and call me. Can you give me any names?"

"Not yet, but all you have to do is find out who is trying to have the chess club shut down. They'll probably turn it into a spa or worse. What we need are the names of the developers. Not the public names, but the silent partners in City Hall and the Kremlin. I don't have the means to do that. You do. I was afraid that the prosecutor was fobbing off some incompetent, but I'm pleased to say that after tonight I have great faith in you. Boundless faith. Not that I don't have my own ruses. We'll have a little exhibition soon and get some publicity."

"At the chess club?"

"At that dump? No. At the Writers' Union. In fact, we're off to see the sponsor right now."

"At this hour?"

"A friend of the game."

Arkady's cell phone rang. It was Victor.

"What the devil were you doing picking a fight with Urman? He and Isakov cover a domestic homicide and you run their pricks through a wringer."

"Are you all right?"

"Well, I'm at the morgue. I got here on my own, if that's a good sign."

"Just don't fall asleep." Around a morgue, Victor might look deposited. "Why are you there?"

"Remember Zoya, the wife who wants her husband dead? Who dialed Urman's phone? She keeps calling me demanding progress, so I'm using my imagination."

"Wait for me. Don't do anything until I get there." Arkady hung up. He desperately wanted to get into dry shoes and socks but Victor's imagination was a frightening thing.

"Stalin loved the snow," Platonov said. Both men pondered that information while wipers swept the flakes on the windshield. "In the Kremlin they had snowball fights. Like boys. Beria, Molotov and Mikoyan on one side, Khrushchev, Bulganin, Malenkov on the other and Stalin as referee. Grown men in hats throwing snowballs. Stalin egging them on."

"I'm trying to picture that."

"I know that some innocents died because of Stalin, but he made the Soviet Union respected by the world. Russian history is Ivan the Terrible, Peter the Great, Stalin and since then, pipsqueaks. I know you feel the same because I saw you rescue Stalin from those so-called Russian Patriots. This corner will do."

Platonov heaved himself out under a streetlamp. Arkady leaned across to say that Stalin killed not "some," which sounded incidental, but in cold blood sent millions of Russians to their death. However, Platonov was enveloped by a redheaded woman in a fur coat and high heels. She was a well-maintained sixty or seventy years old, a whirlwind of lipstick and rouge. A foaming bottle of champagne swung from her hand.

"Magda, you'll catch your death."

"Ilya, Ilyusha, my Ilyushka. I've been waiting."

"I had business."

"My genius, dance with me."

"Upstairs, we'll dance." To Arkady, Platonov said, "Pick me up at noon."

"This is the sponsor?" Arkady asked.

"Better make it two o'clock," Platonov said.

She peered at the car. "You came with a friend?"

"A comrade," Platonov said. "One of the best."

Arkady had intended to set the record straight. Instead, he drove off as fast as possible.

6

When Arkady arrived, Victor had the morgue's body drawers open to a biker with long matted hair, an old man as green as verdigris and a young man fresh from a gymnastics accident.

"I've been here too long. They're starting to look like family."

Arkady lit a cigarette but the reek of death was overwhelming. Cigarette butts littered the red concrete floor under a sign that said No Smoking. Walls were white tiles, although the hall to the autopsy room was uphill and dark, awaiting new light fixtures. From the far end came the sound of a door being punched open by a gurney and feet stamping off snow.

Victor considered the three bodies. "It makes you think."

"About mortality?"

"It makes me think I should open a flower shop. People are always dead or dying. They need flowers." Victor pushed in the gymnast, green man and biker and rolled out a crisply burned body in a fetal position. Pushed it in and rolled out a woman on a bed of gray hair. Rolled her in and pulled out a male punching bag of cuts and contusions. Rolled him in and rolled out a goose-necked suicide, pushed him in and balked at the next shelf's pong of decay. "Anyway, it occurred to me that maybe we're taking the wrong approach. Our problem isn't necessarily the tattoo—we can always find an artist who can copy that—but the skin." Victor pulled out a body with a morose face and a deep wound across the back of the neck. Kuznetsov.

Arkady looked at his watch: four in the morning. He was cold and wet and a little dizzy. Maybe he was dreaming. He hadn't noticed in the dead man's apartment that Kuznetsov's right knee looked as if it had been shattered and badly reconstructed.

"What are you saying?"

"I'm saying we need a more proactive approach."

"You mean, you want to take the skin from one of these bodies?"

"I talked to a tattoo artist. He says all he needs is the canvas, so to speak, if we just keep the skin hydrated."

"Wet?"

"Moist."

"You would do this?"

Was it possible to enter negative hours? Arkady wondered. Extra time that was entirely off the clock? Because skinning the dead wasn't done in any normal twenty-four hours.

Before Victor answered Arkady said, "What do we know about Zoya's business? Wasn't the husband a partner? Why don't we find out more about that before we start on poor souls at the morgue? Autopsies are enough. Do you know how this would sound in court?"

"Skin is skin."

"Whose skin?" Marat Urman approached from the dark of the hallway, emerging from silhouette to solid reality, armored in his red leather jacket but amiable, ready to join the conversation once he knew the subject. "Whose skin are we talking about?"

Arkady said, "Anyone's. It's wise to keep it."

"Good idea. The chief of the morgue doesn't like detectives tampering with the evidence, dead or not." Urman stopped at the open drawer and gazed down at its occupant. "Why it's our friend, Kuznetsov. He's not wearing a cleaver anymore, but I recognize him." He looked up at Arkady. "Why are you so interested in this case? His wife tried to chop off his head. We have her confession and the weapon she used. We make a good case and you try to screw us."

Arkady said, "I'm not trying to do anything."

"Then why is the drawer open? Why are you here in the middle of the night looking at the body? Is there a chance you're just trying to fuck Detective Isakov? This looks, how to say, personal. This is about Doctor Kazka, right?"

"We were looking at all the bodies."

"For head lice? I understand. What's worse than losing a woman is finding out how little you know about her."

"I know Eva."

"No, you don't, because you don't know Chechnya. The three of us saw shit you can't imagine. It's natural that

Eva and Nikolai gravitate to each other. It's only human. You should step back and let them work it out. Don't go sneaking around. If she chooses you, so be it. Be civilized. I'm sure you'll see her again." Urman let a smile develop. "In fact, I can see her right now. Isakov is fucking her and fucking her and she's saying, 'Oh Nikolai, you are so much bigger and better than that loser Renko.'"

"Do you want me to shoot him?" Victor asked Arkady.

"No."

"No," Urman said, "the investigator doesn't want a brawl. He's not the brawling type. I wish he was."

"Piss off," Victor said.

Urman looked down at the corpse that was Kuznetsov. "You want to see bodies? These are nothing. They look like a swim team. Now in Chechnya the rebels left Russian bodies by the road for us to find. They were rigged, so that when you picked up a dead mate a bomb or a grenade would go off. The only way to retrieve a body was to tie it to a long rope and drag it. What was left after the bomb detonated you scraped up with a shovel and sent home in a box." Urman rolled the drawer shut. "You think you know Eva or Isakov? You know nothing."

While Urman made his exit Arkady was stock-still. He tried to erase the image of Isakov and Eva together, but it returned because the suggestion was poison and the taste lingered.

"Are you okay?" Victor asked.

"Yes." Arkady tried to rouse himself.

"The hell with this place. Let's go."

"Why was he here?"

"To shake you up."

Arkady tried to think straight. "No, this was an opportunity Urman seized; it wasn't planned."

"Maybe he followed you."

Arkady thought back. "No, I heard a delivery."

He headed up the ramp toward the sound of water. Water ran from spigots all the time on the autopsy room's six granite tables. Half were occupied by a blue-tinged threesome, all male, who had shared a fatal liter of ethyl alcohol. They held their organs in their open bellies. The new arrival was a woman still in a gray prison gown. She was joyless gray from head to toe and her head arched back so strangely that Arkady recognized Kuznetsov's wife only because he had met her just the night before. Her eyes bulged in their sockets.

Victor was impressed. "Fuck!"

Arkady pulled aside a pathologist working the last of the drunks and asked about the woman's cause of death.

"Asphyxiation."

"I don't see any bruises around the neck."

"She swallowed her tongue. It's rare. In fact, it's been long debated whether it's even possible, but it happens now and then. She was arrested last night and did it in her cell. We have her husband in a drawer. She killed him and then she killed herself."

"Who brought her here?"

"Detective Urman followed the van from the prison. Apparently he'd just finished questioning her when she did it." The pathologist spread his arms in awe. "Some women, you never know."

Signs of the prosecutor's disfavor: A red carpet that did not quite reach Arkady's door. A small office so crammed by a desk, two chairs, locker and file cabinet that it was difficult to turn around. A mere two phones, white for the outside line, red for Zurin. No electric teapot. No plaque on the door. No partner. Other investigators were aware of Arkady's pariah status; he was the golden example of how not to run a career. No matter, Arkady liked working at night when the staff was gone and the light of his lamp seemed to cover the known world.

He tried calling Eva on her cell phone. It was off, which didn't necessarily mean she was with Isakov. More likely, he told himself, she was dealing with a patient in the emergency room and didn't want to be interrupted. He checked the apartment phone for messages. Nothing from her or Zhenya, and Arkady fought off the dark allure of masochism. To clear his head he wrote a report on the events at the Chistye Prudy Metro station, making it as objective as possible; let Zurin sweat over the fact that an investigator of his had rudely disrupted a séance with Stalin. It was one thing to close down a simple hoax, it was another to interfere with superpatriots, and the entire affair illustrated how out of the loop Zurin was. Arkady suspected that when Zurin was put into the loop the prosecutor's bowels would experience a sudden loosening.

Arkady was more circumspect about what transpired at the skating pond. He had looked through Bora's pockets and found sodden papers for Boris Antonovich Bogolovo, age thirty-four, ethnic Russian, resident of Tver, electrician, former honored sportsman. A newspaper clipping of a boxing match and a condom seemed to sum up Bora's past triumphs and hopes for the future. Arkady noted in the report that Bora had followed him and fallen through the ice, but there was nothing to be gained by mentioning a knife when there was no knife to offer in evidence. Arkady had been unable to find it, Platonov and the cameraman Petrov never saw it, and without the knife the report might sound as if Arkady had, for no good reason, lured Bora onto thin ice and almost let him drown. Arkady had to admit to himself that he couldn't describe the knife. He had seen something shine in Bora's hand and felt something sharp against his throat. "The investigation is not concluded," Arkady wrote. Finding a weapon would make a big difference.

Arkady's eyes rested on his closet. Bolted inside was a combination safe that held his video camera, notebooks, snitch money, a war-era Tokarev pistol and a box of bullets. He kept the gun in the office ever since he found Zhenya stripping it at home. Where Zhenya learned how to take apart and assemble a Tokarev, Arkady didn't know, although the boy claimed he had learned from watching Arkady, and it was true that Arkady took good care of a gun he never used. If he had had the gun would he have shot Bora? Was the difference between him and a killer simply a matter of remembering to carry a gun?

Arkady turned to the file from Victor. A skilled suborner of clerks, Victor had assembled enough information to cover the desk, starting with a photocopy of the internal passport for Nikolai Sergeevich Isakov, an ethnic Russian born in Tver. Again, Tver. A Ministry physical found Isakov to be a thirty-six-year-old male; hair, brown; eyes, blue; height, 200 cm; weight, 90 k. Education: two years at the Kalinin Engineering Institute. A five-star student who dropped out of school for no reason. No degree. Military service: army, infantry, trained as a marksman with VSS sniper rifle. Two tours, no disciplinary problems, reaching the grade of warrant officer before segueing smoothly into OMON, a select police force also known as the Black Berets. The Black Berets were hostage rescuers, not negotiators. Their training included rappelling, marksmanship and the subtleties of silent hand-to-hand combat. Only one in five candidates made it through. The instructor notes on Isakov called him "at the top of his class." A special note mentioned that Isakov's father had been NKVD, the forerunner of the KGB.

Starting on a far-off but converging track was Marat Urman, half Tatar with a first name from the French Revolution. The product was a combustible 35-year-old male; hair, black; eyes, black; height, 190 cm; weight, 102 k. Arrest records as a juvenile for assault and public disturbance. One year of university. Six years in the army, with repeated disciplinary issues, rising no higher than corporal. In his last year he and Isakov were at the same base and somehow the cool Nikolai Isakov and wild Marat Urman became fast friends.

Black Beret candidate school appreciated Urman's proclivity for aggression. Much of the training was done as duels; a candidate might fight five opponents one after the other. When Urman broke an opponent's jaw, the instructor had noted with approval that Urman "continued to beat his foe unconscious." He might not be officer material, but he was "an excellent battering ram." Besides, his friend Nikolai Isakov was there to rein in Marat, in case he got out of control. In their black-and-blue fatigues, black boots and berets, the two made a formidable unit.

They went to Chechnya together. In the first Chechen war, in the early nineties, the rebels had bloodied a Russian Army of young, poorly trained conscripts. In the second Chechen war, started in the late nineties, the Kremlin sent a spearhead of mercenaries and elite troops, which meant the Black Berets.

Victor had copied an article from *Izvestia*, datelined Grozny, about a raid by Chechen rebels on a Russian field hospital. The reporter described the horror of wounded men having their throats slit in their beds and the rebels' dash from the scene. "An estimated fifty terrorists in two stolen trucks and an armored personnel carrier headed east to a small stone bridge that crosses the Sunzha River. There their luck apparently ran out.

"A squad of Black Berets from Tver, a mere six men led

by Captain Nikolai Isakov, a decorated officer on his second tour of duty, had heard news of the attack over a cell phone and were waiting among the willows on the river's eastern bank. The narrowness of the bridge forced the vehicles to cross single file, directly into the sights of Black Beret rifles. Isakov himself took out the driver of the APC with a single shot, effectively blocking the bridge. A fusillade greeted the other terrorists as they poured out of the trucks, expecting to overrun the small number of Black Beret troops in their way.

"A firefight raged up and down the banks of the picturesque mountain stream as Captain Isakov consistently exposed himself to enemy fire to rally his men. The terrorists first mounted a frontal attack and, when that failed, attempted to outflank the Russian marksmen, who would fire and change position. Eventually the Black Berets were down to their last rounds. Isakov had no ammunition left in his rifle and only two bullets in his handgun when the Chechens suddenly retreated in one truck, leaving behind the other truck, the APC and fourteen dead insurgents. Remarkably, when the smoke lifted, only one Black Beret was hit, shot in the knee. Captain Isakov said, 'We hope we avenged the cowardly attack on our wounded men. We thought of them and did our best.'"

The name of the reporter was Aharon Ginsberg.

"The army is everything!" Arkady's father used to say, until he was denied a field marshal's baton, then it was "The army is shit." Arkady wished he had such clarity of vision. For a semblance of order, Arkady reassembled the dossier as neatly as he could and slipped it in a drawer.

Before he forgot, he called the phone number he had found on Petrov's matchbook. It was five a.m., a good time to wake and ponder the fact that there were four more hours of dark.

A voice furred with sleep answered, "Metropol Hotel. Reception."

"Sorry, wrong number."

Very wrong. The grand Metropol Hotel and the shaggy cameraman Pyetr Petrov didn't add up at all.

Arkady had two mini cassettes, one he had taken from Petrov's video camera at the Metro platform and a second from Petrov's pocket. He slipped the first mini cassette into the video camera, connected the camera to the television, and sat back to watch.

The tape began earlier than Arkady had anticipated with the filmmaker Zelensky in Red Square. Snow had just started to fall and clouds dirty as cement bags gathered over Saint Basil's. The format was documentary and the news, according to Zelensky, was dire. Russia had been "stabbed in the back by a conspiracy of ancient enemies, a moneyed oligarchy and foreign terrorists to undermine and humiliate the motherland." Zelensky had cue phrases. "Idealism was gone." The Soviet Union had collapsed, "removing the barrier between Russia and the decadent West on one side and Islamic fanaticism on the other." Russian culture was "globalized and debased." The camera panned from an old woman begging for coins to a banner for Bulgari. "No wonder patriots so yearn for the firm guidance of another era." What the videotape would explore, Zelensky gravely told the camera, might be a miracle, a sighting of Stalin on the last train of the night.

Arkady watched the entire event again from a different point of view. Petrov had started recording with an establishing shot of the subway car and its passengers, mainly pensioners like the cronies Mendeleyev and Antipenko, the babushkas, literati from the Lenin Library, but also prostitutes, Zelensky and his golden niece and nephew, the delinquent schoolgirl, Platonov and Arkady, not exactly a cross section of society, but what might be realistically expected at that hour. Arkady was impressed by how little illumination a video camera needed and how the microphone picked up the rush of the train and how those factors combined made a package that seemed more authentic than the actual experience.

"Coming into Chistye Prudy station, what Stalin called Kirov Station," Petrov whispered to the camera.

Up and down the carriage, riders shifted in anticipation. Mendeleyev and Antipenko were already half to their feet. The babushkas twisted to see sparks, blackness, the approaching light of the platform, and in an extra moment of total dark, a woman's cry, "Stalin!"

As the doors opened everyone streamed out but Arkady, who watched Platonov, and Zelensky, who watched Arkady.

The tape cut to the platform and a crowd that had grown with the addition of passengers who had disembarked from forward cars. Stalin's photograph rested against a platform pillar. Young Misha and Tanya lit a candle at the photo and expressed their gratitude to Stalin for saving mankind and being the beacon of his age. Veterans solemnly nodded; women dabbed their eyes. Zelensky smoothly interviewed some sweet old ladies and handed out Russian Patriot T-shirts and the party was rolling along when, from nowhere, a madman in a pea jacket kicked the candle onto the tracks, stopped the meeting by diktat, and seized the camera. Arkady didn't look good.

At no point did the tape show the two Americans or Bora. Also, in slow motion it was the prostitute with red hair who first shouted Stalin's name, then Mendeleyev and Antipenko.

Arkady decided that he should eat something, which remained a theory because there was no food in the desk except a rind of cheese wrapped in greasy paper. He had a cigarette instead. And tried Eva's cell phone again. Still off. Arkady would have expected a slower night at the clinic. A snowstorm usually kept people—even the criminal set—at home.

The second videotape had obviously been shot earlier for purposes of rehearsing the boy and girl. They walked across a room, the girl carrying a feather duster in place of flowers, the boy holding a pen for a votive candle. The children couldn't walk for giggling at the graffiti on the apartment walls: oversized sexual organs, phone numbers, "Olga Loves Petya."

Zelensky directed from off screen. "This is not a joke. Do it over, slower, like in church. Have you ever been in church? Okay, back to your mark and go! Like that. Even slower, kids, this isn't a race. Pay no attention to the camera. Look straight ahead and concentrate on the picture, the man's friendly face. He's a saint and you're bringing him these special gifts. Stay together, stay together, stay together. That's more like it. Petya, how did that look to you?"

The cameraman said, "They missed the mark."

"Hear that, kids? The camera doesn't lie. The blue tape on the floor marks where you start and where you stop. Tonight there's going to be a lot of people. You have to block them out and the only way to do that is to practice."

The children walked across the room again.

"Dear Comrade Stalin," Zelensky cued.

"Dear Comrade Stalin, the children of Russia thank you . . ."

And again.

The boy said, "You rallied the Russian people and threw back Fascist invaders."

The girl said, "As a beloved humanitarian you led a Russia that the peace-loving nations of the world admired and respected . . ."

Again and again until Zelensky clapped and said, "I love you, kids."

It was clearly the end of the rehearsal and Arkady expected the television screen to go dark. Instead, it switched to a bedroom scene of three men and a woman.

The men were Bora, Zelensky and an individual whose face was hidden by lank, long hair. It took Arkady a moment to recognize Marfa, the schoolgirl from the Metro, because her face bulged like a goose with a funnel down its throat. Zelensky had seduced her and used her in the space of a single day. So much for Arkady's advice.

Petrov was conserving cassettes, recording new material over old. Arkady jabbed Fast Forward and the tape speeded to a race of men running around the girl, taking turns, on and off, on and off.

When Arkady found Marfa crying he returned to Play. She sat on the edge of the bed, naked, her face turned away from the camera as she wailed. The way she twisted emphasized the baby fat on her waist.

"She sounds like a bagpipe," Bora said off camera.

A hand came into view and pointed to her tattoo. "A butterfly. How did I miss that before? Cute."

Zelensky said, "Marfa, you were great."

"You were great," Bora said.

"You were great," the third man said. "You were born to fuck."

"This is a private tape," Zelensky assured her. "No one's going to see it. I had to find out how good you were and you were a pro."

Marfa went on sobbing.

Zelensky said, "Remember, you told me you were a big girl and I took you at your word."

The third man said, "Vlad makes porn, that's all he does. What did you expect?"

"That's not all I do," Zelensky said.

"Really? Name something else."

"I have other projects, other movies. You'll see."

"Right. It seems to me that as a film director you have one piece of direction. 'Suck faster.'"

"Sasha, go fuck yourself."

"No. Thanks to your little friend I'm set for the day."

"Get the fuck out."

"I'm getting out in a new Mercedes."

"Heil Hitler!" Zelensky shouted as a door opened and closed. "Bourgeois prick."

The camera remained on Marfa. Run, Arkady thought. Get out while you can.

She stifled a sob. "What other movies?"

By the time Arkady finished viewing the tapes it was seven in the morning. He locked the dossier and tapes in his safe and dragged himself to his car on the off chance Eva or Zhenya had returned to the apartment and ignored his phone calls; although it was rude, some people did that sort of thing.

But no apartment could have been emptier. There were no new notes, no messages on the machine. His footsteps sounded clumsy and intrusive and he couldn't help but think of Eva moving lightly in bare feet. The mattress on the bedroom floor looked more temporary than ever.

An acrid smell drew Arkady to the window. Down on the street the road crew was boiling tar to fill the same pothole as the day before. The women shoveled while the man, the chief, waved cars by. A blue plastic tarp was set up as a shelter, a sign that the crew was settling in.

Eva's clothes hung in the closet, which suggested that she was coming back to pack, at the very least. Her tapes were still in a box, fifty or more audiotapes stacked chronologically beside the recorder. He fed one into the recorder and pushed Play.

The heavy breathing of exercise.

"Arkasha, catch up."

His voice from a distance. "I have a better suggestion. You stop."

"I'm recording you. I am compiling evidence that on cross-country skis the senior investigator couldn't catch a snowman."

He listened to a winter day, a trail that wound through birches and voices ringing in the cold.

"Eva, I am carrying brandy, bread, sausage and cheese, pickles and fish, the full weight of luxury, while you carry nothing but a seductive smile. Perhaps you would like me to carry you, as well."

He heard laughter and an accelerating slap of skis.

Another tape caught the arm-in-arm quality of a stroll. "Between the two of us, Adam was innocent." His voice.

"Seriously?" Hers.

"He had no choice. Between keeping Eve happy and displeasing the Lord, the creator of the universe, any sane man would have made the same decision."

"I should hope so."

Nothing profound, the throwaway lines of life.

A third tape had only the drone and counterdrone of motorboats and the shouts of water-skiers treading water, for some reason a happy memory. Eva was a light sleeper and Arkady would find her in the middle of the night sitting up with a cigarette and vodka, concentrating on the tapes as if they were her proof of a new life.

He put the tapes and recorder back the way he had found them, stretched out on the mattress and closed his eyes. For just ten minutes. Just to keep going.

Snow pecked at the window. When the wind was stiff the window stirred in its sash. The grinding of plows seemed everywhere.

Arkady was on a frozen lake. Between the fringe of trees and gray clouds was a stillness and a pleasant nip in the air, and the length of the lake were dark dots, fishermen at their holes. The gear for ice fishing was simple: an auger, a hook, a line, a box to sit on and vodka to drink.

There was no better fishing companion than Sergeant Belov. He was insulated by layers of clothing, a fur hat and felt boots, but his red hands were bare, the better to jiggle the lure just so and feel any tug on the hook. The temperature could drop to minus ten, minus twenty, Belov never wore gloves. His prize, smelts the size of silver coins, lay frozen on the ice. "*Zakuski* size!" Belov said. "Appetizers!" When his hands and cheeks started to freeze he chased the chill with vodka.

The sergeant was usually full of good stories about tanks and trucks falling through the ice, or an entire company of troops who drifted away on ice floes never to be seen again. This time Belov was so silent that Arkady wandered off on a private dare toward the middle of the lake.

Only one fisherman had drilled his hole so far out. Arkady told himself that a word of conversation with the man would cap his achievement, although when Arkady looked back the sky was darker and all the other fishermen, including Belov, had picked up and gone. A spiderweb of cracks spread across the ice, but since the fisherman ahead seemed so busy and content Arkady pressed on.

The fisherman was wrapped and hooded in tattered coats and blankets, his face lost in shadow, his hands manipulating many strings simultaneously. Arkady couldn't put a name to him, although he had seen the man many times before. Then the sun tunneled beneath the clouds and cast a sudden light. Under the ice Arkady saw Marfa, Eva and Zhenya. He hadn't saved a single one.

7

The harpist onstage in the Metropol dining room played in languid, circular strokes, eyes closed, apparently oblivious of the Americans having breakfast at the nearest table. Wiley had a full face and fine hair like a six-foot baby in a business suit. He filled his bowl with cereal; here was a man, Arkady guessed, who planned to die healthy. Pacheco looked like his protection. In his forties with a bald spot and a bull neck, Pacheco was starting his day with steak and a stack of blini.

Why, Arkady had asked himself, would a scruffy character like Petya Petrov write the Metropol telephone number in a book of matches for a "gentlemen's club" called Tahiti? What members of the Metropol's international set might Petya know? Arkady could only think of the two Americans on the Metro platform at Chistye Prudy, and he recognized them as he entered the dining room. The maitre d' surrendered their names from a buffet sign-in sheet and Arkady waited for the Americans to begin eating before he wended his way between pink tablecloths and red banquettes.

"Do you mind if I join you?" Arkady showed his ID as

he sat. Socially, it was a little awkward, like pushing into a rowboat already occupied.

The Americans were unfazed. Wiley handed the ID back. "Not a bit. Cup of coffee? Breakfast? Load up."

"Just don't kick everything over like you did last night." Pacheco had a voice deepened by a lifetime of cigarettes.

"Coffee at the very least." Wiley waved to the waiter.

"So you do remember last night? Stalin on the Metro?"

"The way you broke it up? How can I forget?"

"I apologize."

Pacheco had a rough face and small black eyes. "The man speaks English better than me."

"Ernie is from Texas." Wiley said. "He's a cowboy."

"Shh." Pacheco put up a finger as the harpist drifted from "Für Elise" to "Lara's Theme." "Ever see *Doctor Zhivago*?"

Wiley said, "There's a chance that Investigator Renko has even read the book."

"Two Americans show up at a Metro platform in the middle of the night. They don't get off or board the train. Instead, they participate in the illegal videotaping of a ceremony in honor of Stalin. Do you both speak Russian?"

Wiley said, "I minored in Russian."

"I was a marine sergeant at the embassy." Pacheco sawed his meat and corralled it. "Back in the Cold War."

"All I can tell you is that we were doing our job."

"In Moscow? What would that job be?"

"I'm in marketing. I help people sell things. They can

be soda pop, faster automobiles, fresher detergents, whatever and anywhere, Moscow, New York, Mexico City."

"You want to sell Stalin in America?"

"No. In the States, Stalin is dead. Now, Hitler's different. In America, Hitler continues to be hot. History Channel, street fashion, video games. But here in Russia, Stalin is the king. Long story short, we're using nostalgia for Stalin to publicize the Russian Patriot political party. It's a start-up party with only three weeks left before the election; it needs an instant identity and an attractive candidate. A good-looking war hero, if possible."

"Brandy?" Pacheco asked Arkady.

"For breakfast?"

"It's not over yet."

Arkady tried to get back on track. "But Russian elections are Russian business. You are Americans."

Wiley said, "Remember Boris Yeltsin's return from the dead? He had an approval rating of two percent—he was a drunk, he was a clown, you name it—but American political consultants like me came on board, ran an American-style campaign and Yeltsin won, thirty-six percent to thirty-four percent for the Communists. Nikolai Isakov's favorable rating is at least that. He will make an impact."

"You do this for anyone? For either side?"

"Yes."

"You're a mercenary."

"A professional. The main thing is—and I want to stress this—what I do is perfectly legitimate."

"How is the campaign for Isakov going?"

Wiley paused. "Better than expected."

"My questions aren't offensive, I hope."

"No, we've been expecting them. To be honest, Arkady, we've been expecting you."

"Me?"

"You see, with any candidate we do a kind of questionnaire. Pluses and minuses. Mainly minuses because we need to anticipate any potential line of attack the opposition may take: drugs, assault, corruption, sexual orientation. We need to see the client naked, so to speak, because you never know when personal issues are going to go public. So far it looks like the only thing we have to worry about is you."

"Me?"

Pacheco had twisted in his chair to watch the harpist. "Isn't she an angel? Golden hair, white skin, white gown. All she needs is a pair of wings. Imagine what it's like for her, getting up at five in the morning, dressing, riding the subway from God knows where to waste beautiful music on a crowd with their faces in their shredded wheat."

Wiley hunched closer to Arkady. "Your wife ran off with Isakov. Are you going to make a stink about that?"

"She's not my wife."

Wiley's face lit up. "Oh, I misunderstood. That's a huge relief."

The brandy came and Arkady drank half a snifter in one hot swallow.

"See, you did want it," Pacheco said.

"What was the trick?" Arkady asked.

"Pardon?"

"Getting people to say they saw Stalin. What was the trick?"

Wiley smiled. "That's simple. Create the right conditions and people will do the rest."

"What do you mean?"

"People create their own reality. If four people see Stalin and you don't, who are you, Arkady, to dispute the majority opinion?"

"I was there."

"So were they. Millions of devout pilgrims believe in visions of the Virgin Mary," Pacheco said.

"Stalin was not the Virgin Mary."

"It doesn't matter," Wiley said. "If four out of five people say they saw Stalin in the Metro, then Stalin was there as much as you. From what I'm told, your father did pretty well by the old butcher, so maybe you should have given him a salute instead of breaking up the party."

As soon as Arkady left the Metropol he used his cell phone to call Eva's. There was no answer. He called the apartment phone. Again, no answer. He called the number of the clinic desk and the receptionist said Eva wasn't there either.

"Do you know when she left this morning?"

"Doctor Kazka wasn't on duty this morning."

"Last night, then."

"She wasn't on last night. Who is this?"

Arkady turned the phone off.

The sun was up, backlighting the snow. From the parking lot of the Metropol he looked directly at Theatre Square. The Bolshoi was being renovated and a chariot drawn by four horses was trapped high in the scaffolding. A man and woman walked arm in arm along the theater steps. They had a melancholy air, the classic scene of lovers hiding from a jealous mate.

"How would you describe yourself? A cheerful, sunny personality? Or serious, perhaps melancholy?" Tatiana Levina asked.

"Cheerful. Definitely sunny," Arkady said.

"Do you like the outdoors? Sports? Or do you prefer indoor, intellectual activities?"

"The great outdoors. Skiing, soccer, long walks in the mud."

"Do you have books?"

"Television."

"Would you prefer a concert of Beethoven or gambling at a casino?"

"Of who?"

"Smoke?"

"Cutting back."

"Drink?"

"Perhaps a glass of wine with dinner."

Arkady had told Tatiana that he was a Russian American hoping to find a Russian bride. The matchmaker eyed him dubiously from his thin Russian shoes to his winter pallor, but her salesmanship responded to the challenge.

"Our women expect to meet American Americans, not Russian Americans. Also, I have this feeling you are a little more intense than you may be aware of. We try to match men and women who are alike in their interests and personalities. Opposites attract . . . and then they divorce. Tea?"

Tatiana had bright hennaed hair, an optimistic smile and a scent of sachet. She filled two cups from an electric kettle and wondered aloud how Arkady had found Cupid's basement office with so much snow on the Arbat. The Arbat was a pedestrian thoroughfare designed to funnel strolling tourists into shops selling amber, vodka, nesting dolls, imperial knickknacks and T-shirts with Lenin's face. Or, in Cupid's case, introductions to Russian women. Today the snow had blown away the sketch artists, jugglers, Gypsies and all but the hardiest tourist. Arkady had seen Zoya leave, sleek in a full-length fur coat and matching hat, but the office lights had stayed on and he thought that before Victor descended on the morgue again it might be wise to see the business Zoya co-owned with the husband she wanted dead. Victor had stopped by the apartment and jumped to copy Petrov's mini cassettes. Pornography was wasted on Arkady, who had dashed through it, but all evidence demanded study, Victor maintained. Anything less was unprofessional.

Cupid had a waiting area, a conference space where the

matchmaker and Arkady sat, two cubicles separated by frosted glass and a closed inner office he assumed was Zoya's. Framed photographs of happy couples covered the walls. The wives were young and Russian; the husbands were middle-aged Americans, Australians, Canadians.

"What is most important is that you and your mate are alike. Wouldn't you want someone educated, cultured and deep?"

"That sounds exhausting. Did you introduce some of these?" He pointed to a photo of a man in a cowboy hat with his meaty arm wrapped around an embarrassed woman transported from Moscow? Murmansk? Smolensk?

"I'm here only part-time, but I have put some very nice couples together. The problem is we don't usually do Russian and Russian."

"I noticed." His eyes fell on a stack of American visa forms.

"Well, what can I say about Russian-American matches? Nothing in common, true. But Russian women don't want a Russian man who lies on the couch and does nothing but drink and complain about life. American men don't want an American woman who's either spoiled or aggressive. We serve mature, traditional men who want women whose intelligence and education does not get in the way of their femininity."

The cell phone vibrated in Arkady's jacket pocket and he checked the caller ID. Zurin. Arkady turned the phone off. "I'm sorry."

"We're not just a Web site and a telephone. We're not a club or a dating service. We don't just take fifty dollars and send you a list of e-mail addresses of God knows what kind of women, or of women who have moved or married or died. At Cupid we take you by the hand and lead you to your soul mate. May I?" She opened what looked like a wedding album and turned the pages for him. On each was a professional-quality photograph of an attractive woman in a gown or tennis gear; her first name—Elena, Julia, or whatever—and her vital statistics, education, profession, interests, languages, and a personal statement. Julia, for example, yearned for a man with a good heart and his feet on the ground. Once or twice Tatiana stopped at a page to mutter, "She's been on the shelf awhile. Maybe . . ."

Arkady noticed a blonde named Tanya in a ski outfit who looked like she could have a good man's heart for dinner.

"A dancer, I believe."

"Not only a dancer, a harpist. She plays at the Metropol. I just saw her."

"Take my word, she's not your type."

As distant as Tanya had seemed with the harp, her smile in the picture was fully charged. Her ski suit was made of tight silvery material only very good skiing could justify. The signs in the snow behind her were black diamonds.

"Anyway, she's taken," Tatiana said. "Not available."

"Well, if I were interested in someone else, what is Cupid's fee?"

"American men pay for quality," she said. For $500, Cupid promised three serious introductions, preparation of the man's special "fiancé visa" to Russia, and if romance bloomed, all the legal paperwork for her visit to his American hometown. Travel and hotel were his responsibility. "We make sure you find your soul mate."

She opened another album and flipped through photos of satisfied couples at the front door of a house, at a fireplace, around a backyard grill, by a Christmas tree.

"If I don't find my soul mate in three tries?"

"We discount for the next three."

"Maybe because I'm Russian the price could be adjusted even further."

"I'd have to ask the owner."

"Who is?"

"Zoya. You nearly met on the stairs."

"I met a man who said he ran an agency like this. His name was Filotov."

"Hardly. Zoya's in charge."

"Now that you mention it he didn't seem the type. He had a short fuse."

"When he drinks."

"When does he drink?"

"Every day."

"He seemed . . ." Arkady paused as if looking for the right word.

"Disruptive. He advised some girls to get tattooed. An American adult is going to marry a tattooed Russian girl? I think not. Filotov even told them where to hide it, but sooner or later, the American finds it. He'd have to be blind not to."

Arkady was afraid to ask more than "Any particular tattoo?"

"I wouldn't know. I tell the girls, if you have a tattoo join a motorcycle gang, don't waste our time."

"What about the American? How do you know he isn't a serial killer and has two or three dead Russian girls in his freezer?"

"My God!" The matchmaker looked around as if someone else might hear. "We don't joke about such things. What an awful imagination."

"It's a curse." He thought of Petya's matchbook and decided to go for broke. "Have you ever heard of a gentlemen's club called Tahiti?"

Ice formed on Tatiana's gaze.

"Perhaps you should try another agency."

While Arkady returned to his car, he called the *Izvestia* editorial office and was told that Ginsberg, the reporter who wrote the newspaper article about Isakov's heroic OMON troops, was covering "the pizza trial," the case of the ex-Black Beret who killed a pizza deliveryman. The trial was being heard in a new courthouse still under construction.

"How will I recognize Ginsberg?" Arkady asked.

"Unless there's more than one hunchback there shouldn't be any problem."

8

Igor Borodin sat sweating in a cage of bulletproof glass. He had gone to fat since his OMON days, his suit stretched to the breaking point, and he had shaved badly. Winter sunlight sifted from high windows onto the emblem of a double eagle above the judge's bench and filtered down to the jury box, the advocates' tables and, separated by a wooden rail, the public. The colors were the pastels and wood tones of a Swedish kitchen and the smell of sawdust and plaster was a reminder that much of the courthouse was still under construction. Arkady tiptoed to the last available seat, next to an olive-skinned woman in a black dress and shawl. A row back a short man with a grizzled beard was making notes. Half of the public section was taken over by men in the blue and black camouflage suits of Black Berets, a corps of hard individuals whose faces expressed impatience with the judicial process. One man was missing an arm, another's face was seared a slick violet and some simply had the hollowed-out look of war veterans. The room was overheated and most people held their coats on their laps; one of the Black Berets had opened his shirt enough to display the tattoo of an OMON tiger.

Nikolai Isakov and Marat Urman had the place of honor in the front row. Isakov showed no reaction to the sight of Arkady, although Arkady had the impression of intense blue eyes watching through a mask. Urman saw Arkady and shook his head.

It was the second day of argument. The facts were that Makhmud Saidov, twenty-seven, married, with one child, had delivered a pizza to the apartment of Borodin, thirty-three, housepainter, divorced. Saidov expected a tip and was disappointed. While waiting for the elevator Saidov wondered aloud when Russians would learn that pizza deliverymen around the world depended on tips. Borodin reopened his door. Words were exchanged. Borodin left the door a second time, returned with his service pistol and shot Saidov fatally through the head.

The defense was that Saidov had verbally abused Borodin, a war veteran suffering from post-traumatic stress. While insults were not sufficient excuse for murder, they had triggered a reaction in Borodin that he had no control of. In fact, according to a psychiatrist, Borodin fired the gun in what he sincerely considered to be self-defense. He didn't see a pizza deliveryman; he saw a terrorist who had to be stopped.

"But he was not a terrorist," whispered the woman to Arkady. "My Makhmud was not a terrorist."

Borodin took off his jacket. He was rapt, as if hearing a story new to him. From the public seats his old comrades sent him thumbs-up and the citizens in the jury box were thoroughly hooked. Juries were a reform urged by the

West. Defense attorneys had always been supplicants, judges omnipotent and prosecutors ran the show. The show had a new audience now.

Borodin's attorney called Isakov to the witness podium, established the detective's illustrious record as a captain in the Black Berets and asked about Borodin's. Isakov's answer was not necessarily to the point, but it was effective.

"I was Sergeant Borodin's commanding officer for ten months. In that time OMON spearheaded Russian forces in Chechnya, which meant constant engagement with rebels. Sometimes with four hours' sleep out of forty-eight, sometimes so far ahead of logistical support that we went days without food, fighting an enemy that hid in the population and observed none of the rules of war. The enemy could be a hardened soldier, a religious fanatic or a woman transporting a bomb in a child's stroller. We made friends where we could and tried to build lines of trust and communication with village elders; however, we learned from experience to trust no one except the men in our own unit. In ten months in those conditions, Borodin never failed to carry out an order. I can't ask more from a man."

Borodin sat up for the highest accolade in his life and opened his collar. At the base of his neck was a tattoo of the OMON shield. Arkady felt the dry swallowing of the veterans and the way they leaned forward to catch every word.

"He was involved in the famous Battle of Sunzha Bridge?"

"More a skirmish, I'd say, but yes, he was."

"More than a skirmish, I'm sure. Could you recount for the judge and jury the events of that day?"

"Our assignment that day was to control and check traffic at the bridge. An attack in force was not anticipated and when we heard about the terrorist raid on the OMON field hospital it was too late to bring up reinforcements."

"But you stood firm."

"We carried out our orders."

"Sergeant Borodin stood firm."

"Yes."

"Against odds of eight to one."

"Yes."

"In that fight, was there any communication between the terrorists and your men? Not radio communication, but shouts or insults."

"Not from us. We were too few and didn't want to give away our positions. The Chechens shouted a number of insults."

"Such as?"

"'Russians, you came a long way to die!' 'Ivan, who is seeing your wife?' although they didn't say 'seeing.' 'Dogs will eat your bones.' Things of that nature."

"Again, how many terrorists were there?"

"Approximately fifty."

"How many in your squad?"

"Six including me."

"And including Borodin?"

"Certainly, Borodin too."

"Under attack, outnumbered, with bullets flying, Igor Borodin heard, 'Dogs will eat your bones.' Is that correct?"

"Yes."

"I refer to the transcript of the testimony of Borodin's neighbors, who heard a heated argument on the landing and Makhmud Saidov shout, 'May dogs eat your bones!' At which point, Borodin snapped. He was again Sergeant Borodin back at the Sunzha River, protecting his country."

The woman in the shawl turned her dark eyes to Arkady. She whispered, "And then he ate the pizza."

Lunch break.

Ginsberg was a short, angular figure in a black coat and cap who walked with his huge head leading the rest of his body. Arkady followed him out of the courthouse and down a raw path between saplings with roots wrapped in burlap to a sidewalk ice cream cart. Up close, the reporter's beard and brows were a disheveled gray, his eyes slightly scrambled and Arkady realized that the man was drunk. At noon. Arkady had a chocolate ice cream cone; Ginsberg had an orange popsicle and a cigarette. They ate as snow swirled around them, like a pair of Eskimos, Arkady thought.

Ginsberg said, "Give me fresh air, nicotine, sugar and artificial color. A cappuccino wouldn't hurt. Although it is important to keep foam and artificial color out of the beard so as not to be too comical. What do you want, Investigator Renko?"

"A little information."

"A little information is a dangerous thing." Ginsberg slipped off the curb and would have fallen if Arkady hadn't grabbed his sleeve.

"You wrote an article for *Izvestia* on the battle that helped make Nikolai Isakov a national hero." Looking into Ginsberg's eyes, Arkady saw intelligence try to surface.

"Yes."

"You interviewed him?"

"I traveled with his unit for a month on his first tour of duty. I was the only journalist along. He said regular-size journalists took up too much room."

"The two of you became friendly?"

"Russians generally have two reliable reactions: beat a Jew and laugh at a hunchback. Which makes me doubly vulnerable. Isakov was free of all that."

"So you were friends."

"Yes."

"You admired him."

"He was a well-read man. Not what you'd expect from a Black Beret in a combat zone. Of course, I admired him and now he's a candidate for the Russian Patriots. He's changed."

"I thought as much, so it struck me as odd that today you weren't sitting with him or even offering each other a few words. You ignored each other. Why is that?"

"That's your question? What is my personal relationship now with Detective Isakov?"

"Him and Marat Urman."

"You want my official opinion? Isakov and Urman are Black Beret veterans and respected Russian Patriots, and the Battle of Sunzha Bridge exemplified the fighting spirit of OMON. How's that?"

"Then why did OMON keep Isakov at the rank of captain?" Arkady asked. "Why wasn't he promoted after a victory like that? What was wrong?"

"Ask Major Agronsky. He was head of the commendation panel."

Ginsberg swayed off the curb and laughed. "Maybe Agronsky could count. Can you? Fifty rebels against six Black Berets. No, I never said it. Salute the red flag. Oorah! Oorah! Oorah!"

The entrance to the new courthouse was plate glass; Arkady saw Black Berets gathered in the lobby. Bottles of beer appeared from nowhere. Alcohol was banned on the courthouse grounds, but the guards had made a sensible retreat. From the lobby Urman returned Arkady's gaze.

Ginsberg saw Urman too. "Marat calls me a dwarf. What I really am is abridged. An abridged version of a reporter, not only in height but in what I write. They say only the grave can correct the hunchback. Not true! My editors correct me all the time. And the editors say that in these troubled times we need heroes to defend us from terrorists. We need riot police even if that means that OMON runs riot and beats every 'black' they find on the street, a 'black' being anyone darker than delicate Russian pink. Chechens, Caucasians, Africans, a Jew or two. I'm not saying that OMON is following orders, no, worse, following the darker impulses of the Kremlin. So some blood flows and the police don't touch OMON because Black Berets are the police. Although, a person might ask how good these supermen are. As for rescuing hostages, remember the school siege in Beslan? OMON botched that operation and hundreds of schoolchildren died. Hundreds!"

"Do you want to go someplace and sit?"

"No. I'm not saying they're all rotten. A lot are good. He was the best." Ginsberg nodded toward the lobby, where Isakov had arrived and seemed to be offering calming words. "All in their black-and-blues here. In Chechnya they looked like pirates with beards, bandannas, tattoos, and Isakov was the pirate captain. They loved Isakov."

"But there's more?"

"There's always more. That's war. It's like being dipped in acid. Sooner or later it gets to you. It eats you." Ginsberg lit one cigarette off the butt end of another, a delicate operation. "What's your interest in Isakov?"

Envy, Arkady thought. He said, "Isakov's name came up in an investigation. It doesn't necessarily incriminate him."

"Is it an internal matter of the militia?"

"I can't say anything more."

"If it is, let me warn you, Isakov has powerful friends."

"Let's just say I want the truth."

Ginsberg stepped back to take in Arkady whole. "A seeker of truth? I was afraid of that. You'll want a unicorn next. There is no truth. No two people agree on anything;

there are only versions. I am a prime example. I can't even agree with myself. For example, the Battle of Sunzha Bridge. One version describes a stand by six Black Berets against fifty Chechen terrorists. In this version the battle ranged up and down the Sunzha, the opposite sides firing across the river until the Chechens beat an ignominious retreat. The end result: fourteen rebels killed by our sharp-shooters and only one of our men more than scratched. The second version says that of the fourteen dead rebels, eight were shot in the chest or the head at point blank range, two in the back, two with food in their mouths. And not a wasted bullet. Unbelievable marksmanship. No nonfatal shots in the arms or legs. In other words, in the second version, what took place at the Sunzha Bridge was not a battle but an execution of any Chechens who happened to be in Isakov's camp that day. It was revenge. It was a slaughter."

"Were the Chechens armed?"

"No doubt, Chechens usually are. And if they weren't, Isakov's squad had been searching houses and confiscating arms for weeks. They had plenty of weapons to add."

"Were there any surviving witnesses?"

"No. I arrived by helicopter minutes after the killing because I was scheduled to ride with Isakov's unit again. I'd been invited by Isakov personally. As we approached I could see Marat Urman directing Borodin and the others running around a truck. Half the Chechens were around a campfire. It wasn't like any firefight I ever saw before. When we came in to land Marat waved us off. They canceled from the ground. No interviews, no joining the squad. It was a complete turnaround. Suddenly even I took up too much room."

"What about the rest of the squad? There were six Black Berets at the bridge. Isakov, Urman and Borodin make three. Who were the other three?"

"I don't know. They were new to me. Men were being rotated in and out."

"Were they here today?"

"No, but I have their names in my notes."

"You kept the notes?"

"A reporter always keeps his notes."

"Did you ever hear about death squads in Chechnya?"

Ginsberg had to laugh. "Chechnya was nothing but death squads. That was how soldiers got by."

"Russian troops hired themselves out?"

"When necessary. But in that bloodbath there'll never be a charge. We're the winners and we don't hang our dirty laundry in public. If you are after Isakov you'd better act fast because if he wins this election for the Senate he'll be immune. You'd have to catch him standing over a body, a knife in his hand and blood pooling at his feet, to arrest him."

Arkady asked in as flat a voice as possible, "Do you remember, when you were in Chechnya, hearing about a doctor named Eva Kazka?"

"No, although there was a doctor on the wrong side."

"What do you mean?"

"On the Chechen side. I never got her name. She didn't

take up arms but she worked in the hospital in Grozny. They say she showed up on a motorcycle; can you believe that? We were shelling the city and there wasn't much hospital left, but supposedly she treated rebels and Russians alike. Then she disappeared. OMON looked for her but never found her. Maybe she was a fantasy."

The number of Black Berets in the lobby was thinning out, moving back to the courtroom. Isakov and Urman were gone. Arkady was late for picking up Platonov, and here he was out in the snow with a small, crooked drunk.

Ginsberg said, "I have pictures from the helicopter. Just two."

"Can I see them?"

"Why not? Mayakovsky Square at eleven. Is that agreeable?" He took Arkady's card, dropped it, clumsily picked it out of the snow. "What do you think? Do you think the pizza deliveryman was a terrorist? I hope so because I got him killed by not turning in Isakov or Marat or Borodin." He stared vacantly at the pile of saplings. Anyone could see that they had just been tossed off the back of a truck. "But if it's my word against Isakov's, who's going to believe me? Marat said if he heard I was telling stories, he was going to come and straighten me. Apparently some people he straightens, some people he bends. I deserve it." He snapped out of his reverie. "Anyway, there you are, two versions of the truth from one man. You choose."

9

Time in a refrigerated drawer had altered Kuznetsov. He looked as if a four-year-old had colored him, crayoned his face, belly and feet a livid maroon and the rest of his body a cool blue sewn up in front with heavy twine. He'd flattened a little, sucked in his eyes and let his jowls hang loose. Because of the sugar in alcohol he smelled of spoiled fruit.

His wife occupied the adjoining table. His and hers. Arkady took off his jacket and pulled on latex gloves while Platonov stood aside, like a man waiting to be properly introduced.

"You're poaching." A junior pathologist came chugging. He was small, with a damp, freshly hatched quality. "It's no bother, but the detectives said these were finished. I'd just hate to get on the wrong side of Isakov and Urman."

"As would we all. Busy night?" Arkady asked. All six granite tables were occupied, spigots running, although he didn't see any autopsies under way.

"Hypothermics. It's a cold night. We pick them up but we don't perform autopsies unless they're violent deaths."

"Which you did for the two Kuznetsovs."

"Yes."

"And now you're done?"

"Unless someone claims them."

"If not?"

"It's the potter's field."

"So you have time to help us."

"Do what?"

"Get the flute."

Platonov's ears pricked up. "A flute in a morgue? See, that's the sort of thing I only encounter with you, Renko."

The grandmaster had arrived at Arkady's apartment in a foul mood, having waited hours to be picked up and full of complaints about old paramours. "At a certain age women don't want the lights on for sex, they want pitch-dark." He had shown Arkady the bruises and scratches suffered from crossing the bedroom. "Whereas a man that age has to visit the bathroom during the night fairly often. Between the champagne bottles, the fucking cat and the coffee table it was an obstacle course."

Platonov seemed invigorated to see the morgue's dead, the day's hypothermia cases, a windfall of frail, bleached bodies that were old but not as old as he. "This is the House of the Dead, the ferry on the River Styx," Platonov announced. "The final checkmate!" In his disheveled coat and shapeless hat he wandered among cadavers, reading charts, pleased with himself and saying, "Younger . . . younger . . . younger . . . younger. It makes a man philosophical, doesn't it, Renko?"

"Some it makes philosophical, some just throw up."

The pathologist returned with a hair dryer and a flute case. From the case he took a velvet cloth and unwrapped a glass cylinder more the dimensions of a pennywhistle than a flute. The cylinder was packed with purple crystals. Each end had a rubber stopper.

"This is the flute." Arkady put the cylinder in Platonov's hands. "Your task is to warm it up."

"What's inside?"

"Iodine crystals. Try not to breathe the fumes."

"Such interesting evenings with you, Renko. Sincerely."

With the pathologist's help Arkady rolled Kuznetsov onto his face. The cleaver wound on the back of the neck gaped to the bone.

"One swing; quite a feat for a woman too drunk to stand," Arkady said.

The pathologist said, "I heard that she confessed twice, once at the murder scene and once in her cell."

"And then swallowed her tongue."

Kuznetsov's back was dotted with moles, and tufts of wiry hair that sprouted on the shoulder blades, where angels had wings.

Between the shoulder blades was a tattoo the size of a hockey puck of a shield with *OMON* written across the top, *TVER* across the bottom and, in the center, the tiger's head emblem of the Black Berets.

Arkady unfolded a copy of the photo Zoya had given him of her husband's tattoo of a tiger facing down wolves. The head of Filotov's tiger and the OMON tiger were identical. Now that he had a reference point, Arkady saw that the rest of Filotov's more elaborate tattoo—the craven wolves, deep woods and mountain stream—was a later addition, including the city name *TVER*, which the tattoo artist had inscribed on a branch.

The pathologist turned on the hair dryer and ran warm air up and down the dead man's arms. "Fingerprints on skin are tricky because skin is always growing, shedding, sweating, stretching, folding, rubbing off. This is just a demonstration, right?"

"Right," Arkady said.

The pathologist inserted a plastic tube into the rubber stopper at one end of the cylinder, removed the stopper from the other, slipped the loose end of the tube between his lips and blew. He blew smoothly while he moved the open end of the flute up and down the dead man's arms, forcing out warm iodine fumes that would combine with skin oils to make a latent print visible, a simple task that demanded care because iodine fumes could corrode metal, let alone the soft tissues of the mouth.

Like a developing photo, the prints of the palm, heel and fingers of large hands appeared in sepia tones around Kuznetsov's wrists.

Platonov was excited. "You found what you were looking for!"

"Smudged," the pathologist said. "Too much twisting and torquing, not a single usable print."

In a way it was the worst possible outcome, Arkady thought, more a matter of fears confirmed than knowledge gained. A call came in on his cell phone, a text message: "Urgent meet, U know where. ;)" That had to be from Victor. Arkady acknowledged the call and turned to Kuznetsov's wife. She was the indeterminate color of an old rug and possibly that was what she had been in life, Arkady thought, with her scabs and bruises, something Kuznetsov had wiped his boots on. Her head arched rigidly back, mouth and eyes agape.

"Can someone swallow their tongue?" Platonov asked.

The pathologist said, "The tongue is a muscle firmly attached to the base of the mouth. You can't swallow it."

"There's dried blood in the nostrils," Arkady said.

"She didn't die of a nosebleed."

"Then what happened to her? She doesn't look happy."

"Between congestive heart failure, pneumonia, diabetes, cirrhosis of the liver and her level of alcohol, who knows? Her heart stopped. Should I fume her the same as him?"

"Please."

The pathologist played the flute around her arms and found no prints, smudged or otherwise. But her eyes said something, Arkady thought.

"Her face," he said. "Try her face."

The pathologist bent over her with the flute and when he stood back the print of a hand appeared across her nose and mouth. Individual prints were blurred; still there was that shadow hand sealing her face shut.

Arkady said, "If someone kept her mouth closed and pinched her nose, maybe from behind, a big man trained in hand-to-hand, who lifted her off the ground first and squeezed the air from her lungs . . ."

"Then the tongue might fall back and, yes, obstruct the airway to some degree. I don't know how significant."

"How long would it take?"

"If she lost her breath at the start, with her heart and alcohol content, no time at all. But I thought she was in a holding cell in militia custody."

"She was. We want to get some pictures of these prints before they fade."

"What are you going to do with them?" Platonov asked.

"Probably nothing."

All the same, Kuznetsov had been a Black Beret from Tver, as were Isakov and Urman, and all three served in Chechnya. It was hard to believe the detectives had not recognized their old comrade even with a cleaver in his neck.

What was left of the Communist Party fit into a two-story gray stucco building off Tsvetnoy Boulevard opposite the circus. On the ground floor was a security desk with a gray-haired guard and a hall of stockrooms of pamphlets and mailing materials. On the second floor were Party headquarters: offices, secretary pool, conference room and coats everywhere, coats hung and boots piled, in the rush to the conference table where sweet champagne was poured and platters offered red caviar, silvery smoked fish, fatback so fine it was translucent, black bread and slices of seasoned horsemeat. On the wall hung a portrait photograph of Lenin, a red Soviet flag and a campaign banner that demanded, Who Stole Russia?

"Like the old days," Platonov said. "Pigs to the trough." He stacked sausage on a pamphlet of "Marx: Frequently Asked Questions." "Have some?"

"No, thanks."

Arkady hadn't seen such a concentration of *Homo Sovieticus* for years. Supposedly extinct, here they were unchanged, with their bad suits, dull eyes, self-important frowns. These were bellies that had never missed a meal. He saw none of the elderly that picketed Red Square in the bitter cold for their miserable pensions.

Arkady moved back to the hall. "I'm going. You're safe now you're surrounded by friends."

"These freeloaders and cretins? The smart ones, my real friends, left the Party years ago. This is what's left, nothing left but the stupid rats swilling wine on a sinking ship."

"Why didn't you leave?"

"I was a son of the Revolution, which means I was illegitimate. A bastard, if you will. I tagged along with a regiment—that's how I picked up chess—and when Hitler and his gang invaded Russia I volunteered for the army. I was fourteen. My first battle, out of two thousand men, twenty-five survived. I survived the war and then I represented the Soviet Union in chess for forty years. I am too old a leopard to change my spots. Stay and eat and give me someone to talk to."

"I'm meeting a colleague for dinner." If that described having a drink with Victor, Arkady thought. And after, meeting the journalist Ginsberg for a list of Black Berets who had served with Isakov in Chechnya.

Arkady flattened himself to let latecomers through. Among them was Tanya, the harpist from the Metropol, in the same white gown. With her golden hair she looked like a figure from a fairy tale. She whispered apologies as she squeezed by, not at all the reckless skier that the Cupid photo had made her seem.

"You'll come back?" Platonov asked Arkady. "It will be an early night; I have to be sharp tomorrow."

"Our grandmaster Ilya Sergeevich is going to a chess tournament and do the honor of playing the winner." A plump little man bobbed at Platonov's elbow. "It will be televised, won't it?"

"Taped. Taped and burned, hopefully," Platonov said.

"Surkov here, chief of propaganda." The man offered Arkady a damp hand to shake. "I know who you are. You need no introduction here."

Platonov informed Arkady, "This is one of the cretins I was telling you about."

Surkov said, "The grandmaster is one of our most renowned and respected members. A link to the past. He's always joking. The fact is, we're a completely different Party these days. Streamlined, open and willing to adjust."

"Ever since we went in the shit can," Platonov muttered.

"See, that sort of talk doesn't really help. We have to be

upbeat. We're giving people a choice," Surkov called after Arkady, who was headed for the door.

Arkady's only regret was that by the time he returned Tanya would be gone. He wasn't so much attracted as curious. Something about her was familiar, something besides skiing or plucking the strings of a harp.

As Arkady drove away he passed a statue of a clown on a unicycle planted on the boulevard to mark the circus. With the snow spinning around the clown he seemed to Arkady to pedal toward the circus entrance one moment and to the Party offices the next, bowing to slapstick and then to farce.

The Gondolier offered murals of the Grand Canal, but the restaurant was on Petrovka Street, half a block from militia headquarters, and the regular customers were detectives who came to get hammered. The usual order was a hundred milliliters of vodka for a good day, two hundred milliliters for a bad. The regulars at the bar were reinforced by OMON officers in blue and black camos celebrating the acquittal for homicide of their former colleague Igor Borodin. Shouts of "Pizza delivery!" drew great laughs and the clamor had driven Victor to a back booth, where he sat like a brooding spider.

As Arkady joined him Victor indicated the vast distance to the bar and said, "I feel I'm too far from my mother's tit."

"You seem to be set up."

Victor's forearm protected a bottle.

"You have no sympathy at all, Investigator Renko. You're an unsympathetic person. If you're drinking at the bar the bottle is right there within your reach. Sit back here at a table and you could die of thirst waiting to be served. Vultures could pick at your bones, nobody would notice."

"It is a sad picture. This is what you've been doing all day?"

Victor asked someone invisible, "Have you ever noticed how smug sober people can be?"

Arkady looked toward the bar. In the main, detectives tended to be older men who were fairly silent, often overweight, with cigarette ash on the front of their sweaters and a pistol tucked in back. By comparison, the Black Berets in their black-and-blues and holstered guns were young and pumped with muscle. There were also civilians, women as well as men, who liked to rub shoulders with police, buy them a drink and hear a story.

"Quite a crowd tonight."

"It's Friday."

"Right." Always good to keep track, Arkady thought. "International Women's Day, in fact."

"I don't think I know any women."

"What about Luba?"

"My wife? You have me on a technicality."

Arkady checked his watch. He was supposed to meet Ginsberg in five minutes. "You haven't scalped anyone today, I hope."

"No, thank you. I reviewed the Zelensky tapes—"

"The Stalin tape or the porn?"

"—and circulated a still of the four prostitutes who saw Stalin on the Metro platform among my colleagues in Vice. No one recognized them. Prostitutes and pimps are pretty strict about their territory. These girls must have parachuted in."

"Good." Victor could have told him as much over the phone, but Arkady wanted to be encouraging.

"Also I suspected that someone as virtuous as you hadn't looked at the porn as closely as I would."

"I'm sure you didn't miss a thing."

"Remember Skuratov?"

"Yes." Skuratov was a prosecutor general who threatened to investigate corruption in the Kremlin. He was undermined by the release of the videotape of him or someone who looked like him frolicking in a sauna with a pair of naked girls.

"Skuratov denied he was the guy getting the ultimate massage, but a spy chief named Putin analyzed the tape and declared Skuratov was the man. Soon we have a new prosecutor general and the spy is president. Once again, history turns on a woman's ass. The moral is, examine all the evidence. You never know when or how your chance will come."

Arkady checked his watch. "I have to go."

"Wait." Victor untied the office folder and drew out a photograph of a couple tangled in bed. "The man is Boris

Bogolovo, called Bora, from Tver. You had an encounter with him outside the Chistye Prudy Metro."

"He slipped on the ice." Arkady recognized the schoolgirl Marfa, but what caught his eye was the tiger's head tattoo on Bora's chest. "OMON."

"Correct. Here's the kicker, though." Victor produced a still of a man whose long hair hid his face. On his shoulder was a tattoo of the OMON tiger facing down a pack of wolves. The words OMON and TVER were set in an intricate background of a stone bridge, willows and a mountain stream. Next to the photo Victor placed the photo supplied by Zoya Filotova. "It's Alexander Filotov, her husband. And the tattoo, I have to say, is a masterpiece."

"Or a bull's-eye."

As Arkady left he had to push through Black Berets drinking at the bar. They were sizable men, and they drank in unison, rapping their glasses on the counter, letting the bartender pour vodka to the brim and on "Go!" downing the drink in one swallow. Warm work; every man was sweating and red-faced.

"Pizza delivery!" the loser shouted; it never ceased being funny.

10

The first reaction of many Russians when Chechnya declared itself an independent nation was to laugh. The Moscow criminal world was so dominated by the Chechen mafia that the announcement was viewed as nothing more than a gang declaring itself a government. The problem was that Chechens believed the declaration and, more than ten years later, the war went on.

Arkady had never tried to extract Eva's past in Chechnya, not forcefully enough; when the war came up in conversation she always fell silent. All she would say was that she rode a motorcycle from village to village to make her rounds. She made it sound like a Sunday drive. Others called the route Sniper Alley. Certain questions demanded attention. If she entered the conflict on the rebel side, how did she end up with Russian troops? How long had she been with Isakov? How ridiculous a figure had Arkady become? Late for his meeting, would he by running to Mayakovsky Square cause his lungs to explode?

There was no sign of Ginsberg at Mayakovsky's statue. The brawny poet of the Revolution loomed overhead, a bronze arm raised against the snow. Arkady wondered whether the journalist was coming by Metro or by car. The crush in the subway might be unbearable for a hunchback and a taxi would be sitting in the traffic Arkady had escaped by parking his car in the middle of the street and telling traffic police to guard it. Still, he was half an hour late and anxious that Ginsberg might be the first Russian ever to be punctual.

Arkady pulled up the collar of his pea jacket. The heat lamps of outdoor cafés were inviting. He and Ginsberg could sit under one and turn themselves like toast. On Arkady's second tour of the square he noticed two militia cars with their lights off blocking a corner where a snowplow operated. The plow went back and forth over the same spot. As Arkady approached, an officer jumped out of the near car to intercept him.

"An accident?" Arkady showed his ID.

"Yeah." With a hint of fuck off.

"Where are the cars?"

"No cars."

"Then why don't you let traffic through?"

"I'm not supposed to say anything."

Arkady saw no metal parts or sparkling glass on the street.

"A pedestrian?" Arkady asked.

"A drunk. He was lying in the street when the plows came through. With snow falling and snow coming off the blade, the drivers don't see much. They just rolled right over him. Rolled him flat."

The other patrol car hit its headlights. The beams illuminated mounds of rosy snow.

"Did you hear his name?"

"I don't know. A yid, I think."

"That's it?"

"A midget. A midget yid. Who's going to see that on a night like this?"

"Was he carrying anything?"

"I don't know. The detectives say it was an accident. The detectives—"

"Isakov and Urman?"

The officer returned to his car to check. The plow packed and scraped the snow into rosy marble. He shouted back over the roof of the car, "Yeah, Detectives Isakov and Urman. They say it's a shame but it was an accident, nothing to make a fuss about."

"Well, they're busy men."

By the time Arkady returned to Party headquarters the celebration had dwindled down to Platonov, the propagandist Surkov and Tanya. Why she had stayed wasn't clear, although it was obvious that Surkov was desperate to impress—beautiful women who wandered into Party headquarters generally had the wrong address—and the group had squeezed into his office so that he could show off his four phones, three televisions, and all the remote controls that a media-wise professional would need. A laptop open on the desk emitted an azure glow. The walls were covered with photos of past Soviet glory: the Russian flag lifted to the roof of the Reichstag, a cosmonaut in the space station Mir, a mountain climber exulting on Everest. A glass case held a gilded saber from Syria and a silver plate from Palestine, final tributes rendered to the Party.

Arkady wanted to say something about Ginsberg, to register the journalist's death in some manner. It was possible that Ginsberg was drunk and had fallen under a plow; Arkady himself had seen the man stumble off the curb outside the courtroom. And it was possible that Isakov and Urman only happened to get the call. It was possible the moon was made of cheese. It was certain only that the two detectives were always a step ahead of him and that whatever Ginsberg had wanted Arkady to see was gone.

Everyone else's attention was fixed on a white uniform tunic that Surkov lifted out of a wooden crate stamped Classified Archives of the CPSU.

"His uniform." Surkov opened the tunic and hung it over the back of a chair facing the laptop. The cloth was yellow along the fold lines and gave off a faint scent of camphor.

Platonov told Arkady, "I told him about the Stalin sighting in the Metro. That set him off."

"I'm going."

"Just a few more minutes."

"His personal effects." Surkov laid out an antique sewing kit, a snapshot of a freckled girl in an oval frame, a velvet pouch that yielded a briar pipe with a cracked bowl. He tapped the laptop's cursor pad. "His favorite film."

On the screen a man in a leather apron swung on a jungle vine. Tarzan landed high on the limb of a tree and sent out a wild ululating call.

"We know the human Stalin," Surkov said.

The harpist shrugged; she seemed to be more interested in the film. "I don't think vines grow that way, from the top down." A faint sibilance touched her consonants, a hint of speech corrected, which only made her more endearing.

Surkov asked, "Tanya, what is your full name?"

"Tanya."

"Tanya Tanya?"

"Tanya, Tanechka, Tanyushka," said Platonov.

"You're all drunk. Except for you." She pointed at Arkady. "You have to catch up."

"Wait, this makes it perfect." From a cabinet Surkov added a white plaster bust of Stalin to the tableau on his desk. "Here he is."

Arkady remembered his father saying, "Stalin loved films." The General and Arkady were polishing boots on the back step of the dacha. Arkady was eight, in a bathing suit and sandals. His father had removed his shirt and let his suspenders hang. "Stalin liked gangster films and, most of all, *Tarzan of the Apes.* I went to the Kremlin for dinner once with the most powerful men in Russia. He made them all howl like Tarzan and beat their chests."

"Did you beat your chest?" Arkady had asked.

"I was the loudest." The General suddenly stood and bayed while he thumped his chest. Heads popped out of windows, which put him in a rare good mood. "Maybe I will leave you something in my will after all. Don't you want to know what it is?"

"Yes, certainly."

"At staff meetings Stalin draws wolves, over and over. I got one from a wastebasket and someday that drawing can belong to you. You don't seem excited."

"I am. That sounds nice."

His father looked him up and down. "You're too skinny. Put some meat on your bones." He pinched Arkady's ear hard enough to draw tears. "Be a man."

"Spencer Tracy and Clark Gable," Surkov was saying, "those were Stalin's favorites. And Charlie Chaplin. Stalin had a wonderful sense of humor. Critics say that Stalin was an enemy of creative artists. Nothing could be further from the truth. Writers, composers and filmmakers deluged him with requests for his opinion. 'Please read my manuscript, Comrade Stalin' and 'Look at my painting, Beloved Comrade.' His analysis was always on the mark."

"But no kissing," said Tanya.

Surkov said, "Soviet films like *The Jolly Guys* and *Volga! Volga! Volga!* didn't need sex." He made a stab at holding her hand and missed. He turned to Arkady. "That was your father's heyday, right? Grandmaster Platonov has told us all about you. Men like you pretend to be neutral or undecided, but as the grandmaster can testify you are not afraid to act. Certain quarters rail against Stalin because they want Russia to fall apart. He's the symbol they attack because he built the Soviet Union, defeated Fascist Germany and made a poor country into a superpower. Granted, some innocent people suffered, but Russia saved the world. Now we have to save Russia."

Platonov said, "You see how outrageous it is for the Russian Patriots to claim Stalin. Stalin is and always will be ours. Don't you think that if he was going to be resurrected on the Moscow Metro, he'd let us know?"

Things were getting a bit rich for Arkady. "We have to go."

Tanya said, "Take off your jacket and stay awhile. Don't leave me with these stiffs."

"After all the trouble I had getting you through security," Surkov said. He told Arkady, "She attempted to smuggle in a roll of steel wire under her coat."

"Wire for my harp."

Arkady said, "Tanya plays the harp at the Metropol. I've seen her. I just never know when she's going to pop up next."

"Steel?" Platonov asked her.

"It lasts longer than sheep gut and it's cheaper than silver or gold."

Surkov said, "Before you go I wanted to tell you that I was a great admirer of General Renko's campaigns and never put any stock in those rumors. War is terrible, but no Soviet general collected enemy ears."

Arkady said, "They were dried and strung like apricots. He had pilots drop the ears with flares over German lines.

If you're a boy from Berlin and it's your first night in the trenches and ears start falling from the sky, you may not be there in the morning."

"You saw them?"

"He brought souvenirs home."

"Well, the main thing is that he came home and God knows what he saw out there on the front. Being who you are, I have something here that you might appreciate. Something very special."

On his desk the propaganda chief set a gramophone with black enameling, a felt turntable, and an arm and horn decorated in silver arabesques. From a record album with no title, notes or credits he slipped out a stiff and heavy 78 rpm disk. He handled the record on its edge with his fingertips and let it settle on the spindle.

"The label is blank," Arkady said.

"A pressing of one, not for release to the general public." Surkov set the needle in a groove.

"Will I know the performer?" Tanya asked.

"Before your time," Platonov said.

The acoustics of the office seemed to expand and tap into another room's nervous coughs, shuffling feet and stage fright. Finally a piano picked out a tune.

"Beria on piano," Surkov said.

Beria, who had signed death orders for perhaps millions of his countrymen as head of state security, was tentative at first, but gained confidence as he played.

"Faster!" someone ordered and Beria immediately picked up the tempo.

Tanya was surprised. "I know this. It's 'Tea for Two.' I play this."

"Beria was also quite the dancer," Surkov said.

Tanya whispered to Arkady, "I remember you, too. You were sitting with Americans at breakfast at the Metropol."

"I thought your eyes were closed."

"It makes people nervous if you watch while they eat. Why were you with Americans?"

"We had a mutual friend." Using the term loosely for Petya.

"Dance?" Surkov offered her his hand.

She shrugged and let him drag her into a seesaw sort of polka around the desk. Platonov watched wistfully, missing a playmate his own age.

"How well do you know her?" Arkady asked.

"Not a bit, but a pretty woman always dresses up a place."

"Any more threats?"

"Not since I placed myself in your hands. You're doing an excellent job."

The needle hissed. A hymn followed and Tanya released herself with an audible sigh.

Orthodox hymns were a slow blending of voices, repetitive and hypnotic. Arkady wondered who was in such a butchers' choir. Brezhnev? Molotov? Khrushchev? A strong baritone carried them all through the crackling of scratches.

"That's Marshal Budyoni, the Cossack," Surkov said.

As Arkady recalled, his father had considered Budyoni

the stupidest man in the Red Army, an old cavalryman who never made the transition from horses to tanks, and worth at least a battalion to the Germans.

Tanya said, "Communists singing hymns?"

Platonov said, "In wartime you pray, whether you're an atheist or not."

None of the songs had introductions, but as if by command the hymn gave way to a single voice singing, "I searched for the grave of my beloved while grief tore at my heart. The heart aches when love has gone. Where are you, Suliko?"

Surkov mouthed, "It's him."

Stalin's everyday voice was as dry and ironic as a hangman's. Singing brought out a pleasant tenor and a sentimental feel for melody. It was a solo, just Stalin and the piano, with Beria, presumably, back at the keyboard. The Great Leader had a Georgian accent, but then the song had originally been Georgian, and the tale was classic. A forlorn lover discovers that the girl he seeks has been transformed by death. When he calls, "Are you there, my Suliko?" a nightingale answers, "Yes."

Surkov said, "He could be standing here with us, he sounds that close."

"Then it's definitely time to go," Arkady said.

Tanya begged a ride. "The people I came with are gone and my coat is right downstairs."

"Stay with me, Tanyushka." Surkov reached out.

She took Arkady's arm. "Save me from this crazed Bolshevik. It's International Women's Day. Protect me."

"Coming?" Arkady asked Platonov.

"I'll be right there."

The stockroom was outlined in white by the light of a streetlamp. Inside the stockroom coat hangers, a copying machine, scanner, and shredder sat in the dark. Platonov had yet to come downstairs; instead, "Suliko" was playing again and the sentimental tenor sang, "I saw a rose drip dew that fell like tears. Are you crying too, my Suliko?"

"Dance with me," Tanya said.

"Haven't you danced already?"

"Surkov doesn't count." She eased Arkady's pea jacket off his shoulders and took his hands in hers. "You know how to dance."

Arkady was capable of a waltz. It was an appropriate interlude on such a night: Stalin singing, the windows shivering, Tanya resting her head on Arkady's chest. What a ridiculous couple they made, he thought; she was the belle of the ball and he looked like he should be shoveling snow. There were calluses on her fingertips, but they were from stroking a harp.

"I'm sorry I'm in the same dress you saw me in this morning. I played for receptions all day long. I must look like a pressed cabbage."

"A bit."

"You're supposed to say I look like a white rose. You don't say much, do you?"

He considered opening gambits. "Do you really want to marry an American?"

Her head lifted briefly.

"How did you know?"

"The Cupid agency. They described you as a dancer. What sort of dance?"

After a moment, "Modern. What else did they say about me?"

"That you weren't my type."

"You see, their problem is they don't like spontaneity. I believe when an opportunity comes you have to seize it. How do you feel about adventure?"

"It's almost always uncomfortable. Tell me, what sort of friends would bring you here and then leave without you?"

"Well, now I can tell them I heard Stalin." The name provoked a sibilant *s*.

"It's amazing. I know some people who just saw Stalin."

"Are they crazy?"

"I don't know." They brushed against the sleeves of a coat rack. "You deserve a better partner."

"You're exactly who I wanted. Are you lucky with women?"

"Not lately."

"Maybe your losing streak is at an end."

When the song ended Tanya let go reluctantly. "Suliko" was replaced by a speech, one of Stalin's harangues, which could go on forever because the Great Instructor was always interrupted by applause described in the newspapers as "steady and thunderous." Anyway, nothing to dance to, Arkady thought and although he sensed that Tanya was disappointed, he pulled on his jacket.

"We must smash and overthrow the theory that proclaims that the Trotskyite wreckers do not have the use of large resources." Here was the other Stalin, a voice like a hammer and words like a carpenter's nails. "This is untrue, comrades. The more we move forward, the more successes we enjoy, then the more hateful become the remnants of the exploiter classes. We must smash and overthrow them!"

Applause broke out as Surkov turned up the volume and let the high tide of adulation pour from the gramophone. Arkady said nothing because Tanya had slipped a garrote around his neck and pulled it tight. Arm strength was where playing the harp paid off. The garrote was steel harp wire attached at each end to a wooden handle. Tanya stood behind Arkady, but he wasn't going anywhere and all she had to do was lean back to stop him in his tracks. The wire dug into his neck and crossed in back to her strong hands. If he hadn't turned up the collar of his jacket, the wire would have been a circular knife.

All the same, the wire dug too deep for Arkady to pull it off or loosen. When he tried to reach back or turn she applied more pressure the other way. He couldn't draw air or call out because his windpipe was closed.

Mounting applause and shouts of "Root them out!" and "Throw them to the dogs!"

Arkady felt his face balloon. She kept him moving backwards and off balance, letting him flail and spill pamphlets off a copier. "Marx: Frequently Asked Questions." Arkady had a question or two. She missed a kick toward the back of his knee. If he did fall she could drag him by his neck and he'd be dead all the faster.

Sustained applause and calls of "Bullets are too good!"

Strangulation came in stages. First, disbelief and a wild thrashing of resistance. Second, dawning recognition of dwindling resources. Third, spasms, limpness, and acceptance. He was well into stage two. He kicked the copier and propelled himself backwards. In the momentary slackness, he snapped his head into hers and heard the crack of bone.

Swelling applause and shouts of "Beat them and beat them and beat them again!"

They began skidding on blood. He got one hand on hers, eased the wire enough to find a straw's worth of breath, plunged backwards and sandwiched her into the shelves and a cascade of lightbulbs, poster board, markers and scissors. She abandoned the wire and snatched a scissors as it flew by.

Thunderous applause and demands to "Stamp on them like vermin!"

She stabbed him in the neck but the raised collar befuddled penetration. When she swung for his eyes he blocked her arm and threw her over the worktable. She came up scissors first over the photo cropper, where he caught her by the wrist and, with one hand, held her hand secure over the cropping deck while he raised the blade.

Hysterical applause, everyone on their feet, shouting

themselves hoarse, waving their fists and again applauding with burning hands.

He could cut her at the wrist. Across the palm. The middle knuckles. Perhaps, for a harpist, fingertips would do.

Arkady found himself stepping into the picture, taking in the blood coursing from Tanya's broken nose, her outstretched hand and the way she stared at the cropping blade.

"Behave," he said in not much more than a croak.

She dropped the scissors and sank to the floor, shook as if she had the chills and let him tie her hands together behind her back with an extension cord.

"My God!" Surkov stood at the door. He turned on the lights and a blood red picture jumped to life. "My God! My God!"

Platonov followed Surkov in, each step slower than the one before. "What happened here? Did you slaughter a pig?"

Shelves, paper, overturned copier lay in a pudding of blood and broken glass. Tanya sat against a printer, legs splayed from gown smeared red. She held her head back to stanch the flow of blood.

"My pamphlets." Surkov tried to peel one blood-soaked "Frequently Asked Questions" from another. "Are you crazy, Renko? What have you done to Tanya?"

Arkady's throat hurt too much to waste words on Surkov. Hoping for an address book, he laid the contents of Tanya's handbag on the worktable: cigarettes, lighter, house keys, change purse, Metro card, memberships in fitness and foreign film clubs and an Internet café, a pass for the Conservatory, a calendar of saints from the Church of the Redeemer and identification papers for Tatyana Stepanovna Schedrina, an innocent who wouldn't harm a fly. He was looking at the only snapshot she carried when headlights swept across the courtyard. Arkady ran outside but only caught a glimpse of a blue or black sportscar. Of course there would be transportation for her to leave in; he would have thought of that if he hadn't poured all his attention into the photograph. It was the same picture of Tanya he had seen enlarged in the Cupid album. Same snow princess on the same black diamond slope. However, the agency photo had been only half the picture. Tanya's photo included her skiing partner, a barrel-chested man in daredevil red and, although Arkady suffered the surprise people experience from seeing familiar faces in unfamiliar settings, he had no trouble recognizing Detective Marat Urman.

He looked up at flakes crossing the light of a streetlamp. He opened his jacket to let the cold in. Later every turn of the head would be agony.

Right now, numb was good.

11

At five in the morning a table and chairs were brought into a basement room at Petrovka. The room was maroon, no windows, only a toilet, a mop sink and an oversized drain in the floor. Arkady sat facing Prosecutor Zurin and a major of the militia. The major's cap was the size of a saddle, gray with red trim. He removed it to take notes because taking notes was a serious business; more careers were built by going to meetings and taking notes than by triumphs on the battlefield. They all stood as a deputy minister arrived with a pair of Kremlin guards and took the last chair. He did not introduce himself and didn't need to. He relieved the major of his pad and pencil and when Zurin started to tape-record the session the man shook his head and, poof, the recorder disappeared.

"It didn't happen," he said.

"What didn't?" the major asked.

"Any of it. The Communists do not want their headquarters to be known for drunken debacles. There will be no militia report. The accounts of what happened last night are so contradictory it would take a trial to sort them out, and a trial is the last thing we will allow. There will be no medical report. The girl and Renko will receive medical attention but the official cause of injuries is their choice. She ran into a door and you, Renko, I suppose, accidentally scratched yourself shaving. It won't go on your record, but in a few weeks you will be quietly cashiered and an appropriate occupation will be found for you. Tending a lighthouse, something like that. In the meantime, there will be no mention of Stalin. No mention of Stalin sightings or Stalin singing or anything having to do with Stalin at all. This is considered a matter of state security. If and when Stalin is reintroduced to the public we will do it on our own terms, not as part of a brawl or an attempted rape." He stood to go. "This meeting did not happen."

Arkady said, "I won't go." He had to push each word through his throat.

"You won't go?"

"I won't leave Moscow."

"We will ship you in a railway car for pigs."

"I can't go."

"You should have thought about that before you attacked the girl."

"I didn't."

Zurin and the major shifted their chairs, putting some distance between themselves and Arkady. In the Vatican, did priests defy a message from the pope? The deputy minister slapped a dossier.

"You killed a prosecutor."

"Long ago. Self-defense."

"So who am I to believe, a man with a history of violence or a girl? You're getting off very lightly. You broke her nose."

"In self-defense."

"So you did attack her? That's what the witness Surkov said."

"He didn't see."

"Didn't see what? That she led you on and then stopped? Naturally, you got angry. It got a little rough, a little out of control. Did you threaten to cut off her hands? The hands of a harpist?"

Arkady meant to say he never would have done it but his throat seized up.

"And you say you didn't attack her. A girl has a broken nose and you hardly have a scratch. Let's see this famous neck of yours."

Arkady stood still while the bodyguards braced him and the deputy minister undid the top button of Arkady's jacket, spread the collar wide and involuntarily sucked air. Even the guards flinched, because despite the fact that Arkady's collar had been turned up during the attack, his neck bore the deep blue bruising and red rope burn of a hanged man.

"Oh." The deputy minister covered his confusion with the last of his outrage. "At any rate, you should be ashamed to drag your father's name through the mud. Renko was a respected name."

*

Snow had stopped falling and had left a bell-like resonance in the air. Traffic lights blinked awake and the noise of plows subsided, but halfway home the pain of driving—turning his head to look right and left—was more than Arkady could bear and he left his car by the river and walked the rest of the way, head down, following his feet, letting the few flakes of snow lifted by the breeze settle in his hair, melt and cool his neck.

At least the search for Stalin was over. Which meant, presumably, that Arkady no longer had to listen to the imaginary threats that Grandmaster Platonov concocted to stall real estate developers. An American-style apartment house with a spa and sushi bar could soon rise from the ashes of the chess club. To Platonov's credit the old Bolshie had stoutly defended Arkady in his police statement. Anyway, Arkady was free to rest up for his next assignment, which sounded as if it might be east of the Urals and north of the Arctic Circle.

Arkady headed for the yard behind his building. The parking area consisted of three rows of metal sheds smacked up side by side and so narrow that a driver had to squirm to emerge. Cutoff plastic bottles shielded padlocks from snow and ashes had been thrown on the ground for walking but the lamp that usually lit the yard was dark. Arkady hesitated beside a playground set of monkey bars sheathed in ice. He stayed still; the stiffness of his neck worked for him and the burns on his neck kept him warm. No blinding headlights rose. Merely, a dot like a moth's eye swirled in a car: a cigarette brought to the mouth, inhaled and released. The driver had parked at the far end of the row opposite Arkady's shed. Had Arkady driven in as usual he never would have spotted it.

Arkady backtracked from the yard and went to the front of the building, pausing at the corner. He did not feel up to a physical confrontation or even conversation. All he saw under the streetlamps was an early-morning road crew morosely assembled around a heavy roller sunk in the same pothole they had been working on for a week.

Arkady took the elevator two stories above his own floor and waited for any movement below before descending the stairs. Finally his neck hurt enough for him not to care whether vipers were waiting on the other side of the door and he went in.

He left the lights off. The first thing he did was go to the kitchen and make an ice bag with ice cubes and a dish towel and chew a handful of painkillers for the throat. Still in the dark he checked the closet by feel whether Eva's suitcase and tapes were still there. They weren't and he wondered whether she had heard about him and Tanya. News that bad traveled fast.

His last hope was the tiny blinking light of the answering machine. There was a message. Three messages.

"This is Ginsberg. I'm at Mayakovsky Square, in the sidewalk café, a little early because I finished the pizza trial story faster than I thought. And now I need a drink. In fact, what I really need to do is take a pee. I could step between cars and no one would be the wiser. (A nervous cough.) I'm sorry to use your home phone, but the card you gave me got messed up and I don't have the number of your cell. Look, Renko, I don't think it's such a great idea, the two of us getting together. This is all about a woman, isn't it? That's what people say. It doesn't sound as if it has much to do with Chechnya. It sounds personal. So I'm going to pass on this."

The second call, received five minutes later, was a hang-up from the same number.

The third was from the same number ten minutes later but it was not a hang-up.

Ginsberg said, "It's me again. Did you know that when Mayakovsky shot himself he left a cautionary note about suicide. He wrote, 'I do not recommend it to others.' So, Renko, you should be happy. I apologize for my spell of cowardice and, although I would not recommend it to anyone, I will help you. Not face to face. Phone only." Ginsberg went silent for a moment and Arkady was afraid the message machine would disconnect but it kept turning. "I don't have to find any old notebooks. Of course, I know who was with Isakov and Urman the day of the so-called Battle at Sunzha Bridge. I saw them all from the helicopter and I checked the roster again when we returned to the base. I'll take those names to the grave." Arkady heard Ginsberg light another cigarette. "The roster of heroes: Captain Nikolai Isakov, Lieutenant Marat Urman, Sergeant Igor Borodin, Corporal Ilya Kuznetsov, Lieutenant Alexander Filotov, Corporal Boris Bogolovo. All OMON officers from Tver and all on their second or third tour in Chechnya. Six Black Berets either beat off an assault by forty or fifty heavily armed terrorists or slaughtered a dozen rebels in the camp. As I said before, you choose. Either is possible. I've seen Isakov in action. With bullets flying he's the calmest man I've ever seen and his men would follow him anywhere. Especially Urman. They make an unusual team. Isakov's philosophy is, 'Immobilize your enemy and he is yours.' Marat's is, 'Cut off his balls, fry his balls, make him watch.' We were friends then. Now I'm jumping at shadows." It was a long message, as if the journalist was calling in a story while he could. "Isakov said I was his mirror. He said I was made the way I was so that I wouldn't be wasted in the army, that I could watch and report the truth. When he waved off the helicopter I put my camera down because I thought, 'He doesn't want a mirror anymore. He doesn't want to see himself.' I still don't understand. Given the worst possibility, that at Isakov's order his men murdered rebels he had allowed to stay in the camp, I ask myself why the Chechens were there to begin with. Anyway, Fate has a way of settling scores, right? *Insh'Allah*—," Ginsberg was saying as the tape ran out.

Kuznetsov and his wife were dead and Ginsberg hadn't jumped at shadows high enough. Arkady gingerly touched his neck. People didn't have to go to Chechnya to be killed; they could do it right here in Moscow.

Arkady's cell phone rang. He answered and Victor said, "Are you in a drunk tank with inebriates and addicts puking on your shoes?"

"No."

"Well, I am. They picked me up outside the Gondolier. Police arresting police, what is the world coming to? I'm the one who suffers the hangovers, isn't that enough? Children ask me, 'Why do you drink?'"

"I can imagine."

"You sound awful."

"Yeah."

"Anyway, I tell the children I drink because when I'm sober I see that life is not a primrose path, no, life is shit. Well, a road with bumps."

"Potholes." Arkady edged closer to the window. The women of the road crew had harnessed themselves to the roller handle and were slowly pulling the roller free of the pothole while the foreman urged them on. He looked like he wouldn't refuse the loan of a whip.

"So I was at the Gondolier when who comes in but Detectives Isakov and Urman, along with some politicians handing out free T-shirts that say 'I am a Russian Patriot.' I got one."

"Eva?" Despite the ice against his neck Arkady's voice was a croak.

"She wasn't there. But can you picture it, politicians in our bar? You know what this means? Isakov's picture will be everywhere and our little plot with Zoya Filotova is over, after all we did."

"We didn't do much."

"Some did more than others."

Arkady let that enigmatic statement die; he was good for maybe four more words.

"You think Eva will come home?" Victor asked.

"Yes."

"And Zhenya?"

"Yes."

"Hope springs eternal?"

"It's pathetic."

As Arkady turned off the phone an ice cube squirted out of the dish towel and pinged the windowpane. The foreman on the street looked up. One of the women stumbled. Coins and keys spilled from her jacket and the roller began rolling back into the hole, dragging the women behind, but the foreman only stood and watched the window.

Arkady's intention had been to stumble to the mattress and collapse, but it occurred to him that Eva had not left her key to the apartment. Eva tended to approach life in an all-or-nothing way. She may have taken the suitcase, but if she had been actually leaving for good she would have locked the door from the outside and slid the key under the door. He found himself on his knees searching the parquet with a penlight. What could have happened, he told himself, was that Isakov came for the suitcase and kept the key so he could get back in when he wanted, a possibility that Arkady was willing to call good news.

The little beam swept the floor like hope at the bottom of a well.

12

Amid the car lots and body shops that stretched along Leningrad Prospect the Casino of the Golden Khan was a fantasy of Oriental domes and minarets. Outside crouched the Russian winter. Inside spread a hush of luxury, of columns carved from malachite around a pool for golden koi and murals of a dreamlike Xanadu. A gilded statue of a Mongol archer presided over a gaming hall with tables for blackjack, poker and American roulette. Only members and their guests made it through the security check at the door and membership cost fifty thousand dollars. That way the club didn't have to run a credit check.

Because the Golden Khan was more than a casino. It was a social club for millionaires. More business was done informally in the intimate lobbies and bars of the Golden Khan than in any office, and nothing impressed a client as much as dinner at the Khan; the casino's restaurant featured steak tartare, naturally, and the most expensive wine list in Moscow, keeping in mind the mafia chief who sent back a bottle because it wasn't expensive enough. A walk-in humidor stored cigars in mahogany drawers with the millionaire's name etched in brass. A Russian *banya* and a Siamese spa refreshed the exhausted millionaire and sent him back to the tables. Escorts, Russian and Chinese, were available for a millionaire's company or solace or good luck. Waitresses wafted by in harem pants carrying drinks. In the Xanadu tradition, the club had originally boasted an indoor menagerie of falcons, peacocks and a rare Tasmanian devil. The devil proved to look like a large rat that shrieked hideously and continually in competition with the peacocks until it dropped dead of exhaustion, while the peacocks were succeeded by parrots that said in a variety of voices, "Hit me!"

On occasion, as a civic gesture, the Golden Khan televised a beauty contest for the victims of a terrorist attack, a lingerie show for wounded soldiers or a chess tournament to benefit homeless kids. Admittedly, chess was a castaway. No one had time to play chess anymore, although every Russian knew how to play chess, agreed it was a measure of the intellect and assumed it was a special Russian talent. So, on what the management expected to be a slow winter morning—the millionaires tucked in their Swedish bedsheets or SUVs—the general public was allowed into an area of the hall where mahogany blackjack tables with blue felt and padded armrests were temporarily replaced by folding tables, chessboards and game clocks. Parrots sidestepped on their perches. Security men in black suits set up a barrier of brass stands and golden ropes as players and supporters filtered in: veterans full of craftiness, a team of university students who were serenely confident, teenage girls with evasive eyes and a prodigy toting his booster seat. Each was a local legend, the winner of wars fought in dormitories and city parks. They had until ten to check in under a banner that declared "Blitz for Moscow Youth!" The event would have been a perfect challenge for Zhenya, but Platonov had checked the list of entrants and failed to find any sign that the boy had risen to the bait. Even so, it might lure him out as a spectator.

Arkady and Platonov stayed out of sight with the show's producer in a van parked outside and watched on monitors as the presenter rehearsed her marks. She was petite as a gymnast and so excited she looked like a sparkler waiting to be lit.

The producer had the short ponytail of a part-time artist. He said, "A month ago she was runner-up for Miss Moscow; now she's a presenter. We're breaking her in by taping a somewhat inconsequential event. Chess? Give me a break." Madonna sang from his pants and he pulled out a cell phone. "Excuse me."

The van's interior was cold and close, dimly lit by the glow of the screens and full of the sharp edges of audio, video and transmission gear. For the occasion Platonov had found a bow tie. Arkady wore, under his pea jacket and turtleneck, gauze swathed in salve; he was learning how many times a day a man had to turn his head. Walking to the car had been difficult. Driving was torture. Speaking was nearly impossible. Arkady had said hello when he boarded the van; otherwise he was mute.

After an animated conversation on the phone the producer began madly throwing switches at a console and said, "There's been a change. The soccer game is canceled due to weather and we have to fill in. We're going live in two minutes. You may have noticed there's not enough room here to swing your dick. So you don't touch anything—and maintain silence except to pass along any information about chess if I need it. If I need it I will hold up my right hand. Otherwise, act like your friend here, the one with nothing to say." He pulled on a headset and tipped back for a better view of the presenter. "Lydia, Yura, Grisha, I have some news for you. We have to start early. We're going live."

On the screen Arkady saw the presenter's personal candlepower rise as she got the word. The two cameramen with her finished mounting an overhead camera over the number one table before they picked up their handhelds. In the van the producer launched three conversations at the same time, choreographing the cameras and cueing her. At five, four, three, two, one, Lydia appeared next to a roulette table to welcome viewers to "a special benefit live at the exclusive Casino of the Golden Khan, the world-famous home of high-stakes gaming."

A plastic shade on the van's rear window was open a crack. Arkady squinted through it at a parking lot that was a maze of ruts in old snow. It was weird, the geometry of reality, he thought. How it changed depending on where you stood.

Platonov muttered in Arkady's ear, "Chess is not gaming. Cretins! Besides, this tournament is not even chess.

We used to play in real chess halls with real rules. It's blitz. It's not even blitz, it's television."

On screen the presenter asked herself, "For those who don't follow chess closely, you may ask yourself what exactly is blitz?"

"In a regular . . .," the producer said.

She said, "In a regular game of chess a player has two hours to make forty moves. In blitz he has five minutes. For this tournament, for motivation, in case of a tie the winner will be determined by the flip of a coin. The pace, as you can imagine, is rapid and exciting."

"Like a mugging," Platonov said.

The producer said, "Knockout. . ."

She said, "The competition will be a knockout system. Who plays white will be determined, again, by a flip of a coin, actually a casino chip. White or black, if you lose, you're out. We have sixteen competitors, players of all ages who have survived preliminary rounds."

Platonov stared at the monitor. "I recognize some. Whack-offs, dilettantes, anarchists."

The producer shot Platonov a warning scowl.

The presenter said, "Our tournament champion will win a thousand dollars and the Casino of the Golden Khan will donate to children's shelters across the city a thousand dollars."

A thousand? That much was swept up in loose chips every night, Arkady thought.

"And there is a special bonus. The tournament champion will play a game with legendary Grandmaster"—she stopped to hear the producer's feed—"Ilya Platonov. Are we ready?"

Platonov spied a different question in Arkady's eyes and said, "They're giving me five hundred. An honorarium. They say I can talk about the chess club."

Arkady doubted it. They'd trot Platonov in and out like a dancing bear.

She unhooked a golden rope. "Find your tables, please."

In the van the producer punched in music to scurry by as the players milled around and found their assigned tables. One camera scanned a player with shaky hands that had shaved him badly, a girl chewing on her hair, a fresh-cheeked university student Buddhalike at his board. The other camera focused on supporters: an anxious mother who pressed a handkerchief to her mouth, a girlfriend with chess books stacked on her knees and on the back row, fresh from the drunk tank, Victor. Fifteen players were in their seats. One was missing.

"We seem to be short one player." The presenter found a place card at an empty seat. "E. Lysenko. Is there an E. Lysenko here?"

Arkady was jolted. E. Lysenko was Zhenya. Was he there?

The opponent was a stickler for the rules. He folded his arms and informed her, "You'll have to give me a bye."

"We'll have to give him a bye," the producer said into his microphone. "Start the games. Come on, Lydia! We need action."

"It looks as if we will have to give you a bye," she said

at her end. "So, you go through the first round and you didn't have to lift a finger."

In the van Arkady said, "It's not ten o'clock yet. There are five minutes to go. You're starting early."

The producer waved him off.

"It's not ten," Arkady said.

The producer told Platonov, "I liked your friend more as a dummy. Get him out of here."

Arkady pulled the microphone off the producer's head and spoke to the presenter directly. "Wait! Give him a chance."

"He's here," she said.

In an anorak with the hood halfway up, Evgeny Lysenko, called Zhenya, looked like a sentry posted at a miserable border. At twelve years old he was short and slight and his natural gait was a reluctant shuffle. His hair was drab, his features ordinary. He habitually looked down to avoid attention and Arkady realized that Zhenya must have been among the spectators the entire time, waiting in the shadow of his hood until the last second before claiming his seat.

"How did his name get on the list?" Platonov asked.

"Sorry." Arkady gave the headset back. His throat burned.

"Get fucked," said the producer.

The opponent won the flip and chose white. He observed to Zhenya, "No time to clean your fingernails?"

Zhenya's nails had black moons from his living in railroad cars around Three Stations. He stared at them as his opponent opened with his king pawn. Zhenya went on studying the dirt that lined his hands. The opponent waited. Every second was precious in blitz. Other boards jumped with moves and the slap of time buttons.

The producer told Arkady, "After all that, your boy froze."

A minute passed. Players at the nearer tables stole glances at Zhenya, who left the white pawn alone and unchallenged in the center of the board. Early moves were the easiest, but Zhenya looked transfixed. Two minutes passed. The time clock was digital, with two LCD faces set in tough plastic for the occasional toss by an unhappy loser. The camera zoomed in. It was difficult to tell in all the motion on other boards who was winning or losing, but Zhenya's board and clock made it immediately plain who was falling further and further behind. His opponent didn't know how to set his expression. At first he was pleased to see Zhenya, by all appearances, at a loss. As the seconds passed he felt more and more uneasy, as if forced to dance alone. Someone was being humiliated; he could no longer say who. He said nothing to Zhenya; speaking over the board after play began was against the rules. Zhenya stood and the opponent half stood, expecting the boy to quit. Instead, Zhenya took off his anorak and hung it over the back of the chair to settle in for longer analysis.

With two minutes to go, Zhenya went into action. It wasn't so much the development of black pieces that was extraordinary as the rapidity with which he met white's every move. White would advance a piece and hardly hit the time button when black did the same, so that the clicks of the buttons came in pairs and the enormous time advantage white had for his moves came to seem pointless, even ridiculous. He began to play at Zhenya's pace, conceding doubled pawns for a promising queenside push. He traded pieces at a slight disadvantage, saw the queenside attack fade, was stampeded into a high-speed exchange that cleared the board and, stripped, watched as a black pawn strolled to promotion. Cameras, guests and finished players watched as the white king dropped. The loser sank into his chair, still confused. It was the sort of loss that could kill a game for a man, Arkady thought. Zhenya looked for the next opponent.

Platonov's verdict in the van was, "Nothing but tricks. If you let Zhenya set the rhythm, of course he'll overwhelm you. In blitz you don't play with your head. There's no time to think. You play with your hands and the little shit has very fast hands. But now everyone knows how strong he is. Vanity will be his downfall."

Zhenya's second opponent was the prodigy. Perched on his booster seat the boy leveled an unblinking gaze at Zhenya, who had picked his fingernails during intermission. The producer ate it up.

"Two boys from different planets and neither of them Earth. Get tighter."

When the prodigy won the coin toss, the camera closed in on a smile trying to hide in a corner of his lips. He had the voice of a choir soprano. "White, please."

Playing black again, Zhenya answered from the start,

simply countering and developing his pieces, castling, leaving no obvious weaknesses and mounting no clear attack. Trench warfare. He was even in material until the prodigy did to Zhenya what Zhenya had done to his first opponent and lumbered him with doubled pawns, the first chink in black's defense. It had promise. Trying to protect his men Zhenya lost offense, and no offense made for an overburdened defense. Targets started to appear. It was so hard to choose, the prodigy squirmed in his seat. It wasn't until he was down to fifteen seconds on his clock that he realized Zhenya had almost a full minute left on his. At which point, black unveiled a long diagonal across the board and a pin on white's queen. Not a serious pin, not one that couldn't be refuted with no more than two or three minutes of analysis. The prodigy's hand hovered. It was still in the air when his clock said 0:00.

Platonov sneered. "Some victory. He fooled a baby. He managed time better than an opponent who could barely see over the chessboard."

"It's down to four players," Arkady said.

"I never said he wasn't talented. I said he was wasting his talent. He only plays for money and this, this, this is the proof. In a casino. Look at him." Platonov pointed to the television screen. Zhenya had pulled up his hood, as good as hiding his face. "He thinks he's Bobby Fischer."

During the intermission, a girl Zhenya's age dared to break into Zhenya's solitude to offer him a stick of gum the careful way someone feeds a half-wild animal. When the intermission was over she stayed in the player's seat opposite him and he chewed more thoughtfully.

Playing black, she immediately challenged Zhenya for control of the center of the board. Her style was as cold-blooded as his, sacrificing a pawn to gain tempo and reach level ground with white. Blitz was a sprint and it was hard to distinguish the beginning from the middle game and the middle game from the end. Forty moves in five minutes. No draws. On the other board still in action—the university champion versus a grizzled veteran—the need for speed encouraged exchanges for simplification's sake. In contrast, Zhenya and the girl developed an intricate structure of poison pawns, veiled threats and phantom attacks. The slightest push could bring it all down. She studied the board with a penetrating gaze. Zhenya closed his eyes. He liked to play blindfolded; Arkady had seen him do it many times. In his mind, Zhenya once told him, he saw all the variations in three dimensions. Not analyzed. Saw.

Zhenya opened his eyes. He pushed. Starting equal in material, he and the girl machine-gunned the board for the next five moves, ending in positions that were identical with one exception: she attacking his king with a bishop while he attacked hers with a knight. A bishop had more sweep than a knight, but a knight jumped enemy lines and in crowded quarters that was the edge.

She saw it. "Mate in five," she said and set her king on its side.

"The girl has possibilities," Platonov said.

"We have our finalists!" the presenter announced. "Moscow University undergraduate champion Tomashevsky and our tournament surprise."

"What did you think of Zhenya's game?" Arkady asked.

"What did you think?" Platonov threw the question back. "You've wondered for days what he's been doing. He's been preparing."

Lydia pulled Tomashevsky and Zhenya in front of the camera and asked what they would do with a thousand dollars if they won.

"Buy a new road bike," Tomashevsky said. He looked athletic. "And beer."

"And you?" Lydia asked Zhenya.

"A tricycle," suggested Tomashevsky.

Zhenya said nothing. He looked at a cage of gaudy parrots that huddled together and blinked their leathery eyelids.

"It must be a secret," the presenter let him off the hook.

"This is the truth about chess," Platonov said. "People don't win a match, they lose. They find a way to lose. Chess is one choice after another and people get tired of choosing. The body gets tired and the brain gives in. The brain says, what are you doing here pulling your wad when you could be out in the midst of life, with women and song and good champagne?"

"How do you think the university champion will do?" Arkady asked.

"Against Zhenya? He doesn't stand a chance."

Platonov was right. The game was an anticlimax.

Although they played under the overhead camera, the finalists revealed no original or interesting strategy. Television viewers watched the systematic demolition of a university scholar by a boy who did nothing but rapidly offer him choices, one after another. With each wrong choice the scholar's position deteriorated a little bit. After twenty moves he was only down a pawn but he had nowhere to go. Every move involved some small loss. He was bound by invisible knots that tightened with resistance because he saw that with every succeeding move his situation would be more obvious. Before his friends and admirers. Professors. On television. He did the only rational thing and moved the same piece twice.

"A double move, disqualified!" said the producer, Platonov, all the players and half the people in the gaming hall.

"What a shame," said the presenter. "The match is decided by a disqualification, a mistake on the part of Tomashevsky, accidentally handing the match to his opponent, Evgeny Lysenko. What a terrible way to lose the tournament when he was doing so well."

The student Tomashevsky rose from his chair in disbelief, like a man betrayed by nothing more than eagerness and stunned by the magnitude of his error. He'd gotten ahead of himself was all. It happened to the best players and there was nothing to do but be a good sport, although when he offered his hand to Zhenya the boy regarded him with contempt.

"Anyway, we have a champion." The presenter tried to

be bright. "And, fortunately, we also have a bonus match between young Evgeny Lysenko and Grandmaster Ilya Platonov."

"Are you all right?" Arkady asked.

"A little lightheadedness," Platonov said. "Have you got a smoke?"

Arkady accompanied him out of the van into the cold bite of a wind that drove flakes across curlicues of ice. Both men sucked fiercely on their cigarettes.

"It's not a tournament that Zhenya prepared for," Platonov said. "There was never any doubt about the tournament."

At the club door, the security squad waved and called Platonov's name.

"They're waiting for you."

"It's hard to explain to someone who is not a player," Platonov said. "There is a time in your life when you imagine chess so perfectly that your intuition is as solid as any game from any book. Like music, if you can hear the entire suite in one moment. You may seem to move your pieces in a hurry but you're simply following a score. And then one day this magical ear disappears and you find yourself hawking chess sets to schoolboys for a living. Or worse." The door of the television van popped open, and the producer yelled for Platonov to move inside the club. Platonov hunched his shoulders. "One day it's just gone."

*

Platonov played white. Between the parking lot and the chessboard he seemed to have found his usual arrogance and wrapped it around himself like a cape. In rapid moves he sacrificed three pawns, opened up the center and developed his pieces while black was still digesting its easy prizes. For the first time since the opening round, Zhenya seemed surprised. Arkady stood in the shadow of a column, out of the boy's line of sight, and followed the game on a screen from the overhead camera. If Arkady had expected the old man to play it safe and eke out a win he was wrong. Platonov had given Zhenya a huge material advantage. On the other hand, Zhenya's power pieces hadn't moved, while the grandmaster's bishops and knights were already on the battlefield. It was an assault that was too reckless for chess. It was pure blitz.

Zhenya rested his chin in his hand and, with the calm of a young gargoyle at a height, looked down on the pieces on the board. Arkady tried to imagine what it would be like to see the game as Zhenya must. The bishop slyly insinuating himself on the diagonal, the knight leaping barricades, the queen a diva, the king anxious and nearly useless. Or was that too romantic? Did Zhenya see the game merely in bytes, like a computer?

Zhenya pushed his forward pawn closer to the fray, a provocation, and the assault began. As fast as they could hit the clock, Platonov attacked and Zhenya defended. They shuttled pieces in, snatched prizes out, castled under pressure, offered and declined gambits. The thought process could not have been involved, Arkady thought;

reason wasn't enough. This was tempo, pressure, intuition. The shape of the board changed and changed again. Even on the club's large game screen it was hard to follow the game's ebb and flow, and just when Arkady expected the entire match would be over in less than a minute Platonov paused to assess the damage. Half the pieces were off the board and somehow, as if Zhenya had reshuffled a deck of cards, the situation was reversed. Platonov had an extra pawn and Zhenya, on the strength of doubled rooks, controlled the center.

Seconds went by. Platonov looked like a man trying to hold a gate closed against a greater force. Arkady wondered whether the grandmaster was trying to find, in the hundred thousand games stored in his mind, a similar position. His precious pawn was an isolated pawn but it was his only winning chance and he assigned a rook to protect it, which opened a hole that Zhenya's knight immediately filled. Platonov covered up like a hedgehog, which was effective in chess. Blitz, however, was not meant for hedgehogs because moves had to be made at once, at once, at once. He fended off one threat after another and, at the same time, nursed his pawn toward the eighth rank and possible transformation into a second queen. The black king took up the hunt, angling across open squares toward the pawn. The white king was smothered by its own defenses.

While Platonov paused again someone sneezed and Zhenya glanced at the rows of seated spectators. He drew his head in between his shoulders and looked again. The grandmaster was still studying the board when Zhenya laid down the black king.

Platonov was astonished. "What are you doing? You have the advantage."

"I counted moves. You'd win."

The teacher in Platonov was outraged. "You counted wrong. How could you do that?"

"You win."

"Hit me," said a parrot.

The television van was gone. The tournament participants and their supporters had left. The girl who played Zhenya had waited for half an hour in the cold but, shivering, had given up. Arkady waited by his car at the street end of the casino parking lot and Victor and Platonov stayed with him. They'd tried sitting in the car but the windows fogged up.

"The little shit gave me the game," Platonov said. "It's insulting. Then he goes to the restroom and disappears."

Victor wiped his nose and regarded the minarets of the Golden Khan. "Does it snow in Samarkand? Sounds like the title of a song, doesn't it? 'When It Snows Again in Samarkand.'"

In spite of his throat, Arkady had to ask Victor, "Did you sneeze? When Zhenya looked up, was it at you?"

"I have allergies."

"To what?"

"Things. Certain colognes."

Which begged the question, wearing or drinking, Arkady thought.

"Anyway, Zhenya did not see me," Victor said.

"I don't need charity," Platonov said. "And they never did let me talk about the chess club."

"That would have made gripping television." Victor stamped his feet to stay warm. "Oh, look. Someone actually has to do some work. Front door security has been issued snow shovels. Work beneath their station. So sad."

The throat was closing Arkady down to a whisper. He asked Platonov, "How good is Zhenya?"

"You saw."

"Really?"

"Complicated."

"Speak of the devil," Victor said.

Zhenya came out of the Golden Khan in the grip of a man who hustled him past security, who bent over their shovels and gave him no more than a glance. At fifty yards Arkady could see that one side of Zhenya's face was deep red. The man wore a mismatched canvas work coat over suit pants and pointed shoes.

The scene was wrong. Zhenya's face was starting to swell and turn one eye into a slit. Arkady had never seen him cry before. It was hard to believe no one at the door asked why. Halfway to Arkady, the man reached into a trash can, took out a dirty hand towel, and unwrapped a gun. Security cameras topped poles all around the lot; someone was bound to notice. Victor and Platonov stayed by Arkady's side.

The man had a thin face, long nose and stringy blond hair. Exactly what Zhenya would grow up to look like, Arkady realized. This was the missing father, Lysenko père. The man's eyes were different, charred, as if he'd looked too long at the sun and at close range his canvas jacket gave off the acrid smell of tar. He was the Tar Man, the foreman of the road crew that had labored so futilely all week on the street that ran before Arkady's building. Zhenya tried to squirm free and the man shook him like a goose held by the neck.

The Tar Man shouted as he marched up to Arkady, "He tore up the check. He saw me and quit the game and when they gave him the check he tore it up. Part of that thousand dollars is mine. I'm the one who taught him."

"Then the money is yours. Fifty-fifty?" Arkady was agreeable. He wanted to negotiate before too much help showed up.

"Five hundred dollars, right now."

"Give me the gun." It was another antique Nagant, like Georgy's.

"First the money."

"First the gun," Arkady insisted. "We have to go to the bank for the money."

"I need it now."

Then he needs it now, Arkady thought. He heard shouts from the casino. The last thing he wanted was Zhenya in the middle of a standoff between a madman and heavily armed guards.

"We'll leave the boy here and you and I will go directly to the bank. I'll vouch for you."

"I know who you are. You're the one that hid him."

Hid him? Arkady had thought Zhenya was trying to find his father. Anyway, this was not a direction Arkady wanted to take.

"You and I will get the money and then we'll have some vodka." Arkady moved closer.

"I looked for a year."

"First give me the gun because the guards are coming, and if they see you waving it, you know how they'll react." Arkady reached out. "You don't want to be shot down in front of your son."

"A son who runs away?"

"It's not working," Victor said.

Zhenya's father pressed the gun against Arkady's head. The muzzle tickled his hair.

Platonov tried to make himself as small as possible, perhaps the size of an atom. This was the difference, Arkady thought, between reality and chess. No next game. Traffic tore blindly by. His car, a couple of meters away, was too far for cover. Victor's hand snaked forever to his holster.

"Give me the gun."

"This is bullshit," Zhenya's father said after consideration, and fired.

Arkady had the sensation of a ripple on a lake, but one expanding at incredible speed, on and on and on.

13

The brain is intact, but it's bleeding. Massively. We can drain it, but we can't stop it. As simply as I can possibly put it, the brain is a gelatinous mass and the skull is bone. The brain expands, the skull does not. Right now, our patient's tender brain is trapped and compressed against the sharp ridges of the interior of his cranium. Which is the least of his problems, because pressure alone brings more bleeding, which only increases the pressure and brings yet more bleeding until his brain physically shifts to one side or herniates, in which case the game is pretty much over. We can keep his head up, pump in oxygen, drain and mop, but we won't know more until he reaches the peak of the bleeding in, we estimate, twelve hours. If he survives that, then we can start worrying about his faculties. He may be the man he was or he may not be able to count to ten. While I probe, Natasha, take the drill, please, and give me the fiber optic."

"Can he hear?"

"Yes, but it will mean nothing to him. He is in a void. No doubt he is losing brain cells. As the brain deconstructs, who knows what is uncovered? Greatest joys, worst fears? He was not conscious when he came in, and that is not a good sign. The vitals?"

"Heart rate seventy-five. ECG normal. Blood pressure one sixty over eighty."

"When will the neurosurgeons arrive?"

"They are all occupied. Children, you are the team. With brain trauma we do not wait for anyone or anything. Seek and you shall find. Here inside the entry wound, between the occipital bone and the dura, a bullet, bone fragments and a good-sized clot. Gauze, please. This is not a hopeless case. Maria, now that you have the tube in, please keep this man asleep."

"I have no halothane. I'm using ether."

"Ether? Wonderful, the choice of the nineteenth century."

"Elena Ilyichnina, this is not what I trained for."

"You are all doing an excellent job. We want to be sure everything is nice and clean. We will have to remove the clot before we secure the bleeding point. I stand corrected, bleeding points. Valentina, step in or step out."

"I'll stay."

"You do it, then. Delicately. You're not drilling for oil."

"I don't understand. When he was prepped there was gunpowder in his hair. He was shot at point-blank range, but the bullet only penetrated the skull?"

"Evidently he is a hard nut to crack."

"Did you see the ligature marks on his neck? I understand that strangulation can sometimes be a sexual game."

"How do you know these things, Tina?"

"Only saying, he's been hung by the neck and shot in the head and he's still alive. He's a lucky man."

A silence.

"We will see. It depends on what you call lucky."

Snipping and the ping of monitors.

"Good. Drill, please. Remember, the brain has no nerve endings; it feels no pain. Suction, please, and for the forehead a smaller bit on the drill."

"The forehead?"

"To monitor pressure on the brain. Not pretty, but accessible."

"Are you sure he doesn't understand?"

"Let's hope not. He would be very discouraged."

Arkady started by wandering among picnic blankets looking for Zhenya. Instead he saw his parents, who were sitting with an open hamper on a quilt weighted with bottles of champagne.

"Reporting in?" the General asked.

Arkady saluted. "Reporting in, sir."

"Is the camp secure?"

"The camp is secure."

"You hear that, Belov? Arkasha is going to be my new aide de camp. You're out of a job."

"Yes, sir," the sergeant said.

"But we'd better check, hadn't we?" He easily swung Arkady up onto his shoulders and ran across the lawn. They called it a lawn even though it was mostly an untended meadow of wildflowers bounded on one side by the dacha—a four-room cabin and porch—and, at the lower end, birches and willows and the bright glints of a river.

His father whipped through high grass and the white heads of daisies and Arkady, even in short pants, felt like a Cossack with a saber.

"You're getting too big." His father let Arkady down and they were at the quilt with Arkady's mother and Belov enjoying tea sandwiches. They had champagne, he had lemonade. The lawn was covered with the blankets and hubbub of officers and their families. None were as handsome as Arkady's father in a tailored uniform with stars on his shoulder boards or as beautiful as his young wife, Arkady's mother. In white lace, her black hair falling to her waist, she was wrapped in a dreamy aura.

"You know what you remind me of?" his father said to his mother. "During the war I spent a few days in a nondescript place with a beautiful legend of a lake where all the swans go. A lake that only the truly innocent can find, hence no one has seen it for hundreds of years. But you are my swan, my redeeming swan." He leaned across the blanket to collect a kiss and then turned to Arkady.

"How old are you now, Arkasha?"

"Seven, next month."

"Since you're almost seven I have an early birthday gift for you." The General gave Arkady a leather box.

His mother said, "Kyril, you'll spoil him."

"Well, if he's going to be my bodyguard . . ."

From the smell of gun oil Arkady knew what the present was before he opened the box, but it was better than he imagined, a revolver his own size.

"You two are a pair," said his mother.

His father said, "A lady's gun to start with. Don't worry; you'll grow into bigger ones. Try it."

Arkady aimed at a small, brown bird that trilled on a wooden post.

"A finch is God's choir," said his mother.

It exploded into feathers.

"Is it dead?" Arkady was shocked.

"We'll know more in twelve hours," his father said.

"I'm going for a walk." His mother got to her feet. "I'll hunt for butterflies."

His father said, "I have to play the host, I can't go with you."

"Arkasha will take care of me. Without the gun."

Arkady and his mother walked along hydrangeas bearing globes of pink blossoms. With a butterfly net for a gun, he shot American agents as they sprang from the bushes. She moved in an absentminded way, eyes down, smiling at something only she heard.

When they reached the river she said, "Let's gather stones."

1822. ICP: 18 mm Hg. BP: 160/80. HR: 75.

*

"What does that mean?"

"May I have the patient's chart back? BP is blood pressure, HR is heart rate, and ICP is pressure inside the skull. Normal ICP is up to fifteen millimeters of mercury. Damage starts at twenty and fatal starts at twenty-five. Are you a family member?"

"A colleague. I was there when he was shot. I thought he was dead."

"The bullet penetrated the skull but not the covering of the brain. I don't know why."

"Ballistics says the gun was old enough to be from the war and so were the bullets in it. Gunpowder degrades. A round that old might barely clear the barrel. When I heard this I thought Renko would be walking out in a day or two. Then I get here and—"

"You can't smoke here."

"Sorry. I get here and he's on a ventilator, a drip in his arm and tubes running out every side of his head."

"His brain is bleeding and swelling."

"Is he going to live?"

"We'll know more in twelve hours."

"You're not going to look at him for twelve hours?"

"He is constantly monitored and observed. He's lucky to be alive. We're at half staff because of the weather. When he came in I had to organize a group of interns."

"Interns?"

"Getting a tube down such a contused windpipe was no simple feat. You can't drink here either. Put the bottle away. Detective, first let us deliver him to you alive, then you can blow smoke in his face or put him on a vodka drip, whatever you want. Am I clear? Do we understand each other?"

"Okay."

"Has the family been notified?"

"There's a woman who's not his wife and a boy who's not his son. The boy was at the scene. Is my friend hearing all this?"

"Yes and no. He's in an induced coma to preserve brain function. Words are mere sounds."

"Can I talk to him?"

"Keep it positive."

"Arkady, about Zhenya. The little prick took off after you were shot. Nobody's seen him since. Here's the kicker: the shooter's last name was Lysenko. Same as Zhenya."

"Can you think of something more positive? I assume this assailant Lysenko has been detained."

"He took three in the chest and two in the head. That sounds positive to me."

Arkady moved upstream as he hunted so that when he nudged stones with his toes the sediment he raised flowed away. Although the surface of the water was slick with light his shadow unveiled a multitude of guppies dashing back and forth over a bed of rounded stones striped red or blue, green or black.

"Do you prefer hunting butterflies or stones?" his mother asked.

"Rabbits."

"You used to hate hunting rabbits."

"I changed my mind."

"Well, today it's stones. See, I already have a net full."

She waded barefoot like Arkady, gathering her frilly dress in one hand and carrying the butterfly net with the other. From time to time she stopped to receive messages. Not from Arkady, but from people only she heard. The tumbling of water covered her conversation.

"What do they say?" he asked.

"Who?"

"The people you talk to."

She gave him a confidential smile. "They say that the human brain floats in a sea of cerebral fluids."

"What else do they say?"

"Not to be afraid."

2322. ICP: 19 mm Hg. BP: 176/81. HR: 70.

"I see, I see. He's going to die and if he does live he'll be a vegetable."

"Not necessarily."

"But surely, not up to the rigors of criminal investigation."

"He might get medical permission to return to work. That would also be up to you. You're the prosecutor."

"Exactly. My office is not a rehabilitation center."

"Don't you think we're getting a little ahead of ourselves? The crisis will come tonight. If he gets through that, then we can assess the damage. Frankly, I'm surprised we didn't see you here before. Your investigator is shot, perhaps fatally, rescuing a boy from an armed lunatic and no one from your office comes to see how he's doing?"

"All we know for sure is that he was shot outside a casino. The circumstances of the incident are murky. Can he hear?"

"No."

"Then what's the point in coming? Call me in the morning if he's still alive."

Arkady and his mother watched from a distance as officers decorated the porch.

She sighed. "Paper lanterns. I hope it doesn't rain. We don't want anything to ruin your father's party."

"What do we do with the stones?" Arkady asked. His pockets were so full it was hard to walk.

"We'll think of something."

"There is no visiting. How did you get in?"

"I am a physician, but not his."

"Then what is your relationship?"

"Personal. You've drilled?"

"And drained."

"ICP?"

"Five millimeters above normal and we're nowhere near floodtide. Another five and we're looking at a fatal outcome or, at the least, permanent damage. Read the chart. Everything that can be done has been done."

"The other vitals aren't that bad."

"Or that good. You said 'personal,' but you don't seem upset. Please do not tell me that you have recently broken off this relationship. Depression would be a very bad element at this point." Silence. "I see. Are you willing to lie for at least a while?"

"Lying is my specialty."

"I thought you were a physician."

"Exactly. I lie all day to dying children. I tell them they have a chance to run and play when I know they won't live out a week. And I tape-record their voices as a game when really the tape is for their families as a memory. A souvenir. So I have small regard for the truth if a lie serves better. The problem is that an investigator has an excellent ear for lies."

"You're Ukrainian?"

"Yes."

"How did you and the investigator meet?"

"At Chernobyl."

"Romantic."

His father's pride was a pond, sixty by forty meters and deep enough for swimming. Sluices from the river brought water fresh enough for communities of sunfish and perch, frogs and dragonflies, cattails and reeds. A rowboat was tied to a dock. A yellow raft and a white buoy floated in the center of the pond. Every morning the General walked in a bathrobe through a stand of firs down to his pond and swam for half an hour. In the afternoon everyone was welcome. It was a golden time as Arkady's father waited for his long overdue elevation to marshal of the army, which people said was finally coming. They were days of badminton on the lawn and long tables full of guests and endless toasts.

When they were alone his parents rowed picnics out to the raft. One evening they rowed out with a gramophone and danced on the raft.

0120. ICP: 20 mm Hg. BP: 190/91. HR: 65.

"One hour to go."

"Maria, all I've been doing is staring at that idiotic monitor, trying to will the pressure down and not doing a very good job. Anyway, you children did well; I'm proud of you. Where is Valentina? Weren't you going home together?"

"She's out front."

"Alone?"

"She couldn't be safer. She's talking to a detective."

*

His mother smiled as she rowed as if she and Arkady were launched into a secret adventure. Wet stones and butterfly netting lay between her feet. The stones in Arkady's pockets made them bulge uncomfortably and he tossed one in the water.

"Oh, no, Arkasha," his mother said. "We'll need every one."

0403. ICP: 23 mm Hg. BP: 144/220. HR: 100.

"You're back and you're drunk."

"I don't need a doctor to tell me that. The point is, Elena Ilyichnina, if I may use your patronymic, I'm not drinking on the premises. Not even smoking. Just visiting."

"Why are you here?"

"Ask my friend Arkady. I'm his shadow. I may be his drunken shadow, but I am still his shadow. So I am not leaving."

"I could call security."

"There is no security here. I've looked."

"It's disgraceful. You're too drunk to stand."

"Then prop me up. Give me some pillows."

"Dear God, what is that for?"

"It's for shooting people. And the bullets are fresh."

*

Arkady went up the ladder clumsily, trying not to lose any stones. He emptied his pockets onto the raft and helped with the stones his mother handed up from the boat. They were larger and more purposeful than his.

She sat beside him while the raft slowly rotated, taking in the zigzag of dragonflies, nodding cattails, wormwood and willows that straggled along the riverbank under the peach-colored sky of late afternoon. The dacha was out of view, behind ranks of firs.

"It won't last," she said. "It's not a natural pond. It will just become a mud hole, a stagnant swamp."

"What do we do with the stones?"

"Keep them here."

"Why?"

"We'll see."

"When?"

"You have to be patient."

"It's a surprise?"

"No, I don't think it's a surprise at all. I'm going to row you back to the dock now. When you get back to the house don't bother your father. Wash the dirt off and change into clean clothes by yourself and then you can join the party. Can you do that?"

Although his mother's sleeves and the hem of her dress were just as wet he said nothing. But when he was on the dock and before she started to row back to the raft, he asked, "How do you feel?"

She said, "I feel wonderful."

*

0750. ICP: 24 mm Hg. BP: 210/100. HR: 55.

"Detective, wake up. Detective Orlov, wake up. Somebody is—wake up. The lights just went out. You're in the hospital. What an incredibly useless man. Wake up!"

Arkady wiped off the dirt with a washcloth, found a clean outfit, and joined the crowd on the porch, where the fruit punch was spiked with vodka and a Gypsy trio had been chased by the younger staff officers to make room for the mambo, a popular import from Cuba. Arkady was drawn into a conga line that circled in and out of the house. He didn't see his mother, but it was exactly the sort of affair that she hated.

Sergeant Belov led him aside to ask, "Arkasha, where is your mother? The General is looking for her."

"She's coming."

"She told you that?"

"Yes."

Arkady returned to the festivities. Now that night had fallen, fireworks were in the offing. He looked forward to Saint Catherine wheels and rockets spraying the night with color.

Half an hour later, his father pulled him out of the dance line. "Where is your mother? I've looked everywhere. I thought you said she was coming."

"That's what she told me."

"Arkasha, where did she tell you this?"

"At the pond."

"Show me."

His father organized a party of eight, including Arkady. They moved through the firs with flashlights that swept shadows left and right. Arkady half expected her to dart out from behind a tree, but they reached the dock without a sign of her.

The rowboat was tied to the raft.

"She swam back?" someone suggested.

The General pulled off his boots and dove into the water. Holding the flashlight high, he swam one-handed to the raft, where he treaded water and directed the beam underneath the barrels of the raft. He hauled himself up the ladder and said, "Not here." His voice carried across the water. He played the flashlight around the pond and its fringe of cattails and reeds. "Not there."

"Where are the stones?" Arkady asked. "I helped her find stones."

"Stones for what?"

"I don't know."

His father looked to the heavens and then brought the flashlight down to the white buoy. As the raft rocked the barrels made a gulping sound. Arkady wished to be somewhere else, anywhere else. His father climbed down to the boat and rowed to the dock.

"Just the boy."

Arkady sat in the stern as his father rowed.

"Take the flashlight."

They coasted the last few meters.

His mother floated upside down beneath the surface, one arm tied by a cotton strip to the buoy anchor of a cinder block and rope. The light on her white dress made her milky and luminous. She was still barefoot. Her eyes and mouth were open, her hair stirred and, with motes moving by, she looked like an angel flying. She had taken no chances. Not only had she tied a hand to the cinder block, but she had weighted the hand with butterfly netting full of stones.

"Are those the stones?"

"Yes."

"You gathered them?"

"I helped."

"And you didn't come tell me?"

"No."

Without another word, his father turned the boat around and rowed to the dock, where his staff officers waited, stripped to their pants. Sergeant Belov helped Arkady out.

His father said, "Get him up to the house, anywhere, before I kill him."

0830. ICP: 17 mm Hg. BP: 120/83. HR: 75.

"Those are good numbers, aren't they?"

"No thanks to you, detective. Someone visited the ICU

last night. Fortunately, they must not have noticed that you were in an alcoholic stupor."

"Totally pissed. So, Renko is through the crisis? He's okay?"

"He's alive. As what, no one can say."

14

Arkady was in a ward with eight beds, each with a curtain for privacy, a night table without a light and a call button that was disconnected. On the other hand, Elena Ilyichnina came every morning to check his incisions. She was a big woman with beautiful eyes and in her lab coat and high white toque she looked like a master baker.

"Don't talk. Your airway is still raw. Nod or shake your head or write on the pad. Are they giving you enough water? Chicken broth? Good." She smiled sweetly, but Arkady had seen her terrorize the nursing staff with threats of what she would do if any patient of hers was left unattended. "You're healing nicely."

He pointed to his forehead.

"So you have a little hole in your head. Don't be a baby. In three months no one will be able to tell. You have much bigger holes in the back of your head, believe me. Also a little titanium. When your hair grows back no one will know. Look at the bright side. Practically no brain death, and because the trauma was a bullet, not a tumor, the recovery should be straightforward."

Arkady wrote, "Headache."

"Two days after brain surgery, what a surprise. It'll go away. In the meantime, don't sit up too fast. There is a risk of seizure; in your case, very small. We'll give you something for the pain. The main thing now is no sneezing. Then you'll know about a headache."

Arkady wrote, "Mirror."

"No, not a good idea."

He underlined "Mirror."

"You're not a princess in a fairy tale. How to put this kindly? You're a man with a hole in his head, a black bruise around his neck, and no hair. You will not like what you see. I know your type. You're the dedicated investigator who goes right back to work. Bullets bounce off you." She held up a box of tissues. "What shape is this? Write it down."

Arkady went blank.

"It's a square," she said.

She put the tissue box down and pulled an orange from her lab coat.

"What shape is this?"

It was familiar to him, but he couldn't put a name to it.

"What color is it?" she asked.

The word was on the tip of his tongue.

"The area of the brain that the bullet impacted processes visual information, that is, shapes and colors. If your brain cells are only damaged they can gradually repair themselves."

Arkady looked at the patient in the next bed, an accident victim with a leg in traction. He had a something-shaped cast and he was sipping something-colored juice through a something. The words were right there, behind a pane of glass.

"What's the last thing you remember?"

He wrote, "Going to casino."

"You have no memory of the man who shot you?"

He shook his head. He recalled arriving at the casino and getting into the television van with . . . Who was it? What kind of brain was this? He started to get out of bed and was stopped by nausea and dizziness. Elena Ilyichnina caught him and helped him fall back against his pillow.

"That was ambitious. There is a problem. The bullet also insulted the cerebellum, which controls balance. I had no idea how difficult a patient you are going to be. You survive a bullet in the head and think you're the same man you were before." She held up the orange. "What shape did I say this was?"

It didn't come to Arkady's mind.

"What color did I say?"

The answer was a fog.

"By the way, when I was sitting with you and your friend Victor in intensive care, the elevator opened and I had the distinct impression someone came to the ICU. I didn't hear footsteps, I simply had the impression that they were at the door and then gone. They must have noticed Victor. Victor was drunk and passed out, but I suppose they couldn't tell."

Often the case with Victor, Arkady thought.

"Back to work," Arkady wrote on the pad.

She balanced the orange on his chest. "Practice."

Victor asked, "Did Elena Ilyichnina tell you about the other night? I was like El Cid, dead, strapped to my saddle, riding out to face the Moors one last time."

Arkady wrote, "Shitfaced?"

"Yeah. But it worked. Whoever it was took off."

"Dead man," Arkady wrote. The man who shot me.

"The assailant at the casino was Osip Igorivich Lysenko. Recently out of incarceration, eighteen months for dealing methamphetamine. His first employment on getting out was road repair. Worked all over the city. I interviewed the women on his crew. They said that they were doing a patch on your block when Lysenko started to act strangely, as if he was in charge. He was weird to begin with, believe me. I went to his digs, a filthy rat hole with plates of garbage and stacks of books on chess by Kasparov, Karpov, Fischer, all the champions. Scribbled in all the books? Better moves. At least, he thought so. He was a meth-head, though, so he might have thought a lot of things."

"Zhenya."

"There was a picture of the two of them playing chess, what else? That was the family scam, the Trans-Siberian scam. Osip Lysenko used to take little Zhenya on the train. You know what a long train trip is like. You get bored of looking out the window. You get bored of reading. Two days down and four more to go and you're bored. Then you notice the door to one compartment is open and inside a father and son are playing chess. It's a cute scene and you stop for a second to watch.

"The kid wins and the father informs you and everyone else around that the kid never loses. You're amused. You're a hydrologist or an engineer or a gold miner from Kamchatka. The father says, 'If you don't believe me, play him yourself.' The kid's eight, nine, looks younger. And he fucking hands you your head. You, a man of science or a rugged outdoorsman, have your ass kicked in public by a boy because by now the corridor is crowded. This is entertainment, the only entertainment for thousands of kilometers. Lysenko must have made an arrangement with the carriage attendant to stay by her samovar and out of the way.

"Now you're serious. The first game doesn't count. How would the kid perform with money on the line? He whips you a second time, which leads to double or nothing. Soon that's what you've got, nothing, and the next sucker steps up. The father warns them that the kid never loses. They're forewarned and that just draws them in.

"The Lysenkos did two round-trips a month for a year. They hardly touched the ground. The scam only ended when they tried it on the same miners two trips running. Unhappy miners. They messed Osip up pretty bad. That's when he started dealing meth."

"Mother?"

"Nothing. I had the feeling she was long gone. Of

course, we're not going to get any information from Zhenya because he's disappeared. Don't ask me why or where. The kid could hole up a hundred places."

"Yesterday. Drunk?"

"Oh, not just drunk, fantastically drunk, drunk on a new level. I have your friend Platonov to thank. We took his five hundred dollars and went straight to the Aragvi. Georgian cuisine, blini, caviar, vintage champagne, hysterical women. It was a beautiful gesture." Victor hiccupped. "We drank to you."

Like being prayed for, Arkady thought.

He fell asleep in the middle of Victor's visit and when he awoke it was four in the afternoon and each bed was an aerodrome of flies. They circled, dove, tied knots in the air while patients moldered. Some men moldered with family members behind discreetly drawn curtains, others moldered flagrantly out in the open in negligent one-size-fits-all hospital gowns. Without vodka and cigarettes, life had lost its purpose. Their last pleasure and solace had been taken away and with a certain grim determination they moldered and considered how to make life for the nurses more difficult. The nurses, in turn, lowered the volume of the overhead television to an unintelligible murmur and raised the volume of the radio at the nurses' station. Walking was allowed only along a central corridor that connected with other wards. Patients stumbled along, pushing their IV stands. He heard the squeal of a gurney as it went by the door. Elena Ilyichnina had warned him that irritability was a side effect of the medication. How could anyone not be irritable after being shot in the head?

There was more to it than that. The brain was outer space; a billion galaxies, poetry, passion, memory, imagination, the world and more dwelt there. Then a surgeon with good intentions comes along and drills the skull like a bucket holding a pulpy pink-gray mass. Arkady felt curiously undressed and at the same time wanted to shout, that's not me!

He took up the pad and pencil to make notes on everything Victor had told him. Spassky . . . Karpov . . . Fischer . . . chess. That was all he remembered.

There was an orange on his nightstand.

What was its color?

When he woke it was evening. A plastic cup and straw of lukewarm broth had joined the orange. He lifted his head a millimeter at a time, reached and delicately felt the bandage in back. Elena Ilyichnina had said that if fluid gathered he would hear it move, so he did remember some things.

He had his blood pressure taken and dressings changed by a young nurse who couldn't keep her eyes off his forehead and he decided that it was probably just as well not to have a mirror. When she left, his eyes strayed to the television, where a cartoon was followed by the news: improved conditions in Chechnya, fraternal solidarity with Byelorussia, sober reassessment in Ukraine. Internationally there was relief that Russia had reassumed its traditional leading role and returned balance to the world order. In Russia itself, polls showed public confidence growing and that the people were united against terrorists. Nikolai Isakov spoke at an outdoor rally of ultranational Russian Patriots.

"Tver again." Elena Ilyichnina returned to Arkady's bedside.

"How do you know?" All he saw on the screen was a crowd.

"I'm from Tver."

The city of Tver was on the route from Moscow to St. Petersburg. Beyond that, Arkady knew nothing about Tver.

"Do you go there often?"

"I take the train every Friday after work."

"That's a slow train in the middle of the night. Why not drive up Saturday morning?"

"If I had a car I would. It sounds luxurious."

"You have a friend there?"

"No. My mother is in the hospital, not quite dying but on her way. I work there on weekends to be sure the staff treats her well. That's enough about me." She redirected his attention to the television, where a corps of boys was dressed in army camouflage. "Tver is very patriotic."

Banners waved, a colorful display, although Arkady couldn't name the colors.

15

The ring-shaped pillow that protected the incision in the back of Arkady's head allowed one position only.

Into that restricted view loomed Elena Ilyichnina.

"I understand from the nurses that you are asking about going home. After all, it's been four whole days since brain surgery, four days since you arrived here half strangled and shot in the head. No wonder you want to get back into the swing of things."

He whispered, "I want a mirror."

"Not yet. When you can walk there is a mirror in the men's room."

"Put me in a chair and roll me over."

"You're all hooked up."

"Do you carry a mirror on you?"

"Not on my rounds, no. Did you sleep well?" she asked.

Arkady mentioned a tapping he had heard half the night, an irregular tap that seemed to emanate from one side of his bed and then the other. The doctor said it was in his head. He had to admit, she should know.

"I need a phone."

"Later. With your throat I don't want you talking overly much or turning this into an office."

"I'd still like a mirror."

"Tomorrow."

"You said that yesterday."

"Tomorrow."

He exercised his memory by reading a page in a magazine, *Men's Health* or *Russian Baby*, whatever was available, waiting five minutes and testing his recall, when he remembered to. Or recollecting telephone numbers and connecting them to names. The oldest numbers came to the fore, reestablishing their precedence: passport, army service, phone numbers for faces he hadn't seen for years. More recent numbers like Eva's cell phone were wisps of fog.

Time nibbled at the afternoon. Motes rose and sank in steady circulation.

The man in the opposite bed died. His neighbor, a tracheotomy, urgently squeezed a call button. In the corner of Arkady's eye, further down the floor, doctors made their rounds, always asking about the liver; care of the liver was paramount in the land of vodka.

He continued to wrestle with his memory. Some telephone numbers emerged whole, some in part: 33-31-33, for example, was most of a phone number or a complete combination to a safe.

Whose phone?

Whose safe?

"We checked your incision and white blood cell count and determined that you have excellent healing and no infection. You want to chance all that for a walk?"

"I need a stroll, Elena Ilyichnina. A little exercise."

"I wouldn't have taken you for an exercise fanatic. Let me tell you about exercise. We are concerned about your balance and, God forbid, a fall. So your first 'stroll,' when you are detached from your IV, will be in a wheelchair. Then a perambulation indoors with someone ready to catch you if you trip. Then short walks in your neighborhood with friends."

"And then?"

"Stay away from the Metro, don't drive, don't drink, don't swim, don't run, don't play football, don't get strangled, don't get hit on the head. Perhaps you should consider a different line of work. For someone in your condition I can hardly think of a worse one. The problem is that you don't know who you are. You will encounter unexpected gaps and changes in different faculties. Mood swings. Changes in your sense of smell or taste. Limits in problem solving. You don't know yet what you don't have. The bullet sent a shock wave through the entire brain. You have to let it mend."

"I'll hardly use it."

Elena Ilyichnina was not impressed.

"Did I ask about depression?"

"No. Aren't things bad enough?"

"Is there any history of depression in the family?"

"The normal."

"Any suicide?"

"The usual."

"Attitude has a great deal to do with your recuperation."

"I will recuperate if no one else shoots me."

At night the ward slipped into a narcotic torpor. Nurses on duty rubbed their eyes and rustled through paperwork. A microwave tone announced that something was warm.

Arkady raised himself as slowly as a deep-sea diver rising to the surface of the water. The bed hardly spun at all and when the nausea was manageable he slid to a standing position on the floor, from which he laid his ring-shaped pillow on the bed and let his head become accustomed to the altitude. He pulled the IV from his arm and, except for a few drops, stemmed the blood with his thumb. For quiet he set out without slippers, although he slid his feet as much as walked. The distance to the toilet was an endless void. His legs shook. Who knew that staying upright was such a feat?

By the time he reached the toilet door the paper envelope that was his hospital gown had adhered to the sweat on his body. First he was afraid a light might come on automatically when he opened the door and then he was afraid of the pitch black when he closed the door behind him. He felt his way with both hands until he found a switch.

The room had a toilet stall, sink and mirror. He urinated and on the way out noticed a creature with a shaved scalp of blue and a violet ring around his neck. Arkady turned enough to show the tip of a black suture and the clown displayed one just the same. Together, Arkady and the clown peeled off the bandages on their foreheads to reveal an eyelash row of sutures.

Arkady staggered away from the mirror and through the door, one hand against the wall of the corridor for balance. He went some distance before he realized he had gone the wrong direction, that he wasn't in the ward but in some totally different area of the floor. He wasn't even clear which way he had come.

What were his choices? Left, right or stay where he was in a paper gown for the rest of the night until there was enough light to find his way back. Wouldn't a nurse notice his empty bed before then? If this was the best his new brain could do he was badly disappointed.

He listened for the sound of an elevator; elevator bays were always lit and gave directions. Or of a floor being mopped; the cleaning person might be a kindly soul who would point the way. Instead, he heard tapping, the sound that had slipped in and out of his consciousness for the better part of a week.

Arkady followed the sound two more doors. The knob turned easily and opened to a room with an examining table, sink and charts of the human digestive system. Zhenya was on the floor in a nest of hospital blankets playing chess on a plastic computerized board by the light of a desk lamp he had carried down with him. He stared up at Arkady. Another boy might have screamed.

"Go ahead." Arkady settled into a wheelchair. "Finish. I have to sit."

Playing black, Zhenya was down to an endgame. White had more pieces but they were scattered, while Zhenya's knight drove white's king into a panic. Zhenya finished with a pinned rook, a swindled pawn, and a series of rapid checks, each move quickly accompanied by the simulated tap of a game clock, *click-click, click-click, click-click.* Mate.

Zhenya's face hovered over the small pool of light cast by the lamp. His eyes were wide and lit from below. He was still in his anorak.

"What are you doing here?" Arkady asked.

"Visiting."

"At night?"

"I'm here at the hospital, I might as well stay. It's easy. I just go from one waiting room to another. They have Coke machines."

That was a speech coming from Zhenya.

"Next time visit me during visiting hours, when I'm awake."

"Are you angry?"

"Because of the . . ." Arkady gestured to the general mess that was his head. "Not at you."

"I ran. My father shot you and I ran."

"I've done worse."

Arkady's eye fell on a telephone. When he picked up the receiver he heard a dial tone.

"Who are you calling?" Zhenya asked. "It's pretty late."

"It's not just late, it's the hour when men with heads like eggplants walk the earth." Arkady punched in 33-31-33, waited, and hung up. He was exhausted.

"Like Baba Yaga."

"The witch who ate small children? Sure."

"Like my father."

Baba Yaga lived in the woods in a house that stood on chicken legs in a yard surrounded by a fence of human bones. Zhenya used to say nothing at all and Arkady would make up adventures about the children who escaped.

"What do you mean? Every weekend we used to go looking for your father."

Zhenya said nothing.

The mute routine. Zhenya could play that like an artist; it might be a week before he said another word.

"Your father tried to kill me and he would have killed you, but you had us search for him every weekend. Why?"

Zhenya shrugged.

"Did you know what he was going to do?"

Zhenya dropped the chess pieces into a chamois sack in order of value starting with black pawns, another of his rituals. Arkady remembered how in Gorky Park the younger Zhenya would walk around the fountain a magical four times.

"You take good care of your pieces."

Zhenya placed the rook in the bag.

"It's like they're alive, isn't it?" Arkady said. "You're not just playing them, you're helping them. And it's not just you thinking, it's them too. They're your friends." Zhenya's eyes shot up, although Arkady was simply using the key that Zhenya had given him. "You said your father was Baba Yaga? Is that who your friends are fighting?"

It was two o'clock in the morning by the digital watch on Zhenya's thin wrist. An hour suspended in the dark.

"They're not alive," Zhenya said. "They're just plastic."

Arkady waited.

"But I take care of them," Zhenya added.

"How do you do that?"

"By not losing."

"What happened if you lost?"

"I didn't get supper."

"Did that happen often?"

"In the beginning."

"He was pretty good?"

"So-so."

"How old were you when you beat him in chess for real?"

"Nine. He said he was proud. I broke a dish and he whipped me with a belt. He said it was on account of the dish, but I knew." Zhenya allowed himself a tiny smile.

"Where was your mother?"

The smile disappeared.

"I don't know."

"I understand your father liked to ride trains. He must have been gone a lot of the time."

"He took us with him."

"Did you play chess on the train?"

No answer.

"Did you play chess with other passengers?"

"My father wanted me to bring them down a peg or two. That's what he always said, bring them down a peg or two."

"Did anyone ever ask why you weren't in school?"

"On a train? No."

"Or why you didn't have a little color in your cheeks?"

"No."

"Did you ever lose?"

"A few times."

"What did your father do?"

No answer.

"Finally some gold miners recognized you."

"They beat my father and threw my chess set under the wheels."

"Of a train?"

"Yeah."

"Your father retrieved the set?"

"He sent me. I would have gone anyway."

"So, you spent a year going back and forth from

Moscow to Vladivostok playing chess in a train compartment? A year of your life?"

Zhenya looked away.

"Did you and your father ever have a holiday, go to the beach, run on the grass?" Arkady asked.

Zhenya said nothing, as if such a childhood was a fantasy. But Arkady felt that there was something else missing.

"When I first asked about your father traveling, you said, 'He took us.' Who besides you?"

Zhenya said nothing and showed no expression at all.

"Was it your mother?"

Zhenya shook his head.

"Who?"

Zhenya maintained his silence but his eyes grew alarmed as Arkady took the white king from the chamois sack. Arkady turned the piece over in his fingers and hid it in his fist, opened his hand and let the boy snatch the piece back.

"Dora."

"Who was Dora?"

"My little sister. She wasn't good at chess. She tried but she lost."

"What happened?"

"She didn't get her supper."

Clarity descended on Arkady and clarity was crushing. For a year he thought he had been helping Zhenya search for a loving father, and all that time Zhenya had been stalking a monster.

"So all those times we were searching for your father, what did you want me along for?"

"To kill him."

Arkady had to rethink everything.

16

Zurin gave a going away party for Arkady, a quiet affair in the prosecutor's office, just espressos and pastries with other investigators. That Senior Investigator Renko was being bundled off was all the staff knew. Not really demoted, but certainly not promoted. Moved sideways. Reassigned.

"The choice of his post," Zurin said. "The choice of his post in some beautiful—"

"Backwater," said a wit.

The prosecutor continued, "Some historical town like Suzdal, a quiet setting far from the stress of Moscow. It has been only a month since Investigator Renko was shot in the line of duty. No one has been more concerned about his recovery than I. I speak for the entire office when I say, Welcome back."

"And good-bye, it seems," Arkady said.

"For the time being. We will reassess the health situation periodically. I understand it takes a year for a full recovery. In the meantime, younger hands will have their turn at the oar and gain some experience. Of course, we all look forward to your return. The main thing for you is to not hang about aimlessly. Not linger."

Arkady looked on the faces of the office staff, the time servers who moved at half speed, the spent and bitter, the up-and-comers who aped Zurin's bonhomie. And what did they see in him but a pale man whose black hair was growing in mixed with gray and a small livid scar on his forehead? Lazarus barely back from the dead and already being shown the door.

"My choice of reassignment?"

"It's been cleared with the prosecutor general."

"You don't think that because of the Stalin sightings anyone would want to keep me away from reporters?"

"Not at all. To a man we envy you. We'll be tripping over corpses while you will be reconnecting with the true, authentic Russia."

Arkady considered Suzdal as he drove. Suzdal, holy beacon of holiday buses. Suzdal, two hundred kilometers from Moscow. Suzdal, the perfect place for a damaged man to rusticate.

He stood on the accelerator, forged a new lane between two legal ones, slowed on Petrovka and then plunged into traffic headed for the river. As in chess, position was everything. A cardboard box carrying leftover evidence, personal effects and a spiral notebook with a cheerful cover of daisies bounced on the back seat of the Zhiguli.

Snow had melted away in weather that was freakishly

warm, swinging from one extreme to the other with no stop in between. Caused by global warming? No matter, the city basked in its false spring, in balmy breezes that teased out daffodils and uncovered Igor Borodin.

Borodin had been found in a culvert in Izmailovo Park, an empty vodka bottle by his side. Forensics found no sign of violence. The contents of his stomach matched what he had consumed after his acquittal for shooting the pizza deliveryman a month before. His doctor confirmed that Borodin suffered from depression and had nearly killed himself binge-drinking twice before. This time, with so much to celebrate, he had succeeded. It seemed only fitting that the investigating detectives, Isakov and Urman, had served with the dead man in OMON.

So far as Arkady knew, no one drew a connection between the fatal domestic quarrel of Kuznetsov and wife and Borodin's overindulgence. All they seemed to have in common was alcohol and the crackerjack team of Isakov and Urman, whose solution rate was a thing of joy.

At an outdoor market Zhenya hopped into the car with a fistful of pirate CDs and DVDs. Arkady hoped the boy hadn't shoplifted; the mafia had rules about that sort of thing. As they drove to the chess club Arkady worked on his visuals. A blue truck. A rectangular poster. A gray traffic officer. A golden onion dome. A green something. A blue bus. A priest like a black cone. A checkerboard pattern of maroon and something bricks. A black and something-striped something. He remembered Elena Ilyichnina had said that injured brain cells could repair themselves but that dead ones never came back. So, one brain, slightly trimmed.

They found Platonov sitting on the club's basement stairs. Although weeks had passed since his five-hundred-dollar celebration, the grandmaster was still a wreck.

"I am proud that I defied the banality of a savings account but debauchery has come at a cost. I have to say that your friend Victor stood by me shoulder to shoulder in my resolve. Most men would have broken and said, 'My dear Ilya Sergeevich, set some aside for a rainy day.' Not Victor. Will you see him soon?"

"This afternoon."

"Dear Lord, make him suffer. My liver is as tender as a balloon and I had hoped to make some small improvements around the club. Not that I'm complaining to somebody who was, you know—bang!—in the head."

Down the stairs the same unwashed basement window allowed the same murky light. A fluorescent tube sizzled over a dozen games so deep in progress the players seemed somnambulists. In scummy glass cases not a single chess set, time clock or layer of dust seemed disturbed. Heads swiveled, however, as Zhenya took over the board tacitly reserved for the strongest player in the room. He opened his backpack and chamois sack and sniffed the air as if for prey.

Platonov said, "If the little shit induces any member to

play for money he will learn that no member of this club has any. They are carefully screened to be pure and poor."

"Like an anticasino."

"Exactly. Renko, they're not going to tax me on the five hundred dollars, are they? It went through my hands so quickly. It's not even as if I won the money fair and square. Zhenya gave me the game."

"How far can he go?"

"Hard to say." Platonov dropped his voice. "He's like a boy born with perfect pitch. He may lose it when his voice changes. He's of ordinary intelligence. His idols are the Black Berets, which is normal for a boy his age. At the chessboard he is a different creature. Where more intelligent players analyze a situation, Zhenya sees. He's a bratty little Mozart who composes music as fast as he can write because it's already complete in his head."

"Any Black Beret in particular?"

"A Captain Isakov seems to be the main hero. Did you know that he led six Black Berets against a hundred Chechen terrorists?"

"Do you believe it?"

"Why not? At Stalingrad we had snipers who killed Germans by the score. Look it up. We had the Volga River at our back. Stalin said, 'Not one step back!' One step back and we would have been in the drink. So how has the recuperation been going? You're looking well, everything considered. Are you yourself?"

"How would I know?"

*

Arkady had mineral water and Victor a beer at a sidewalk café under a leafless tree on the Boulevard Ring. Arabs swept by to their embassies. Babies rolled by in their strollers. Victor read Arkady's spiral notebook and when he was done he waved to the waiter.

"This is not a notebook of beer-sized insanity; this merits vodka. To begin with, Arkady, are you crazy? Maybe this is a result of the shooting?"

"These notes are just to jog my memory of certain cases."

"No. These notes cover cases that were never yours. Kuznetsov chopped by a cleaver, his wife stuffed with her own tongue, the journalist Ginsberg run down and Borodin drunk. These cases were disposed of by Detectives Isakov and Urman as a domestic squabble, a slip on the ice, the dangers of drinking alone and not sharing. But you insinuate murder."

"Just suggesting they were inadequately investigated."

"Did you see Ginsberg run down?"

"No."

"Was there any evidence of foul play with Borodin?"

"No."

"What have they got to do with the Kuznetsovs?"

"Isakov and Urman."

"Do you hear the circularity of your argument?"

"The notes are just for me."

"You had better hope so, because if Isakov and Urman get wind of it your body will be found, but the notebook will not. I feel bad. I got you involved with Zoya Filotova killing and scalping her husband. That blew up in our face."

"The notes aren't well organized."

"Well, you just tossed everyone in."

"I tried to give everyone their own page and a list of facts and near-facts. Isakov and Urman to start with. Then the Russian Patriot video crew—Zelensky, Petya, and Bora—each got a page."

"They're campaigning in Tver today." Victor paused reverently as a short carafe of vodka arrived, then reached across to flip pages. "You gave Tanya a page."

"Urman's girlfriend and handles a garrote well. Bonus points for playing the harp."

"Here's Zhenya's father, Osip Lysenko? What the devil has he got to do with this?"

"Anyone who shoots me automatically earns a page."

"If you keep this up you will get shot again. Who knows? Isakov and Urman may be the ones to find your body. I thought you had a ticket out of town."

"So they say."

Victor turned another page. "The rest of the notes are crazy. Arrows, diagrams, cross-references."

"Connections. Some are sketchy."

"You worry me, Arkady. I think you're coming undone."

"I wanted to be complete."

"Is that so? You know whose name I haven't seen? Eva. Doctor Eva Kazka. I think she deserves a page."

Arkady was startled by the omission. He wrote Eva's

name on a fresh page and wondered what else about her he had missed.

"I think you have it all now," Victor said.

Arkady watched a bus roll by advertising a day trip to Suzdal. "See the Soul of Russia." The trip included lunch.

"There's a number," he said.

"What number?"

"I don't recall the shooting and there are some other blank patches, so I've been working on phone numbers, addresses, names. What does thirty-three, thirty-one, thirty-three mean to you?"

"You're serious? It means nothing."

"What could it mean?"

Victor took a first sip of vodka like a butcher whetting his knife.

"Not a phone number; that would be seven digits. Maybe the combination to a padlock or a safe. Right twice to thirty-three, left to thirty-one, right to thirty-three, turn latch and open, only . . ."

"Only I don't know whose safe or where it is."

"Visualize the number. Typed? Handwritten? Who wrote it, you or somebody else? A man or a woman's hand? What was the number originally written on? A paper napkin or a bar coaster? Is it a license plate number? The winning number of a lottery? How can you remember and not remember?"

"Elena Ilyichnina says that bits of my memory will come back. I have to go."

Arkady paid for Victor's vodka, the price of his expertise.

"Do you think I drink too much? Be honest."

"A touch."

"It could be worse." Victor looked right and left. "Did Elena Ilyichnina say anything about me?"

"No."

"Did she recognize me?"

"Why should she?"

Victor pulled back the hair at his temples and revealed a small puckered scar on each side.

"You always astonish me," Arkady said. "You too?"

"A little different. I had a tiny drug addiction problem about ten years ago, so I had myself drilled."

"Drilled?"

"On local anesthetic. I talked to the doctor while he took some brain tissue from each hemisphere. A dab. The procedure was a wonderful example of Russian ingenuity. It's outlawed now because Elena Ilyichnina turned him in, but it worked. I've been drug-free since."

"Congratulations. And the drinking?"

Victor patted his hair down. "It fills the gap. It completes me. It's my veneer. Everyone has a veneer, even you, Arkady. Everyone sees a peaceful man. There's nothing remotely peaceful about you. We started off, you and I, investigating two detectives. Now you're after the Black Berets."

"Something happened in Chechnya."

"Horrible things, no doubt; it's war. But why would

heroes like Isakov and Urman come back to Moscow and kill their friends and former comrades in arms? Do you know what this notebook adds up to? Wishful thinking. Ask yourself what you're after, Isakov or Eva? I speak as the man who killed the man who shot you. What makes you think Eva is unhappy with him?" When Arkady said nothing Victor dredged up half a smile. "Fuck, forget about all this. I'm rambling. I'm drunk."

"You sound sober to me. Think about thirty-three, thirty-one, thirty-three. I just wonder why my brain chose this number to fix on."

"Maybe at this point your brain hates your guts."

With the thaw a moving truck had finally delivered Arkady's furniture and earthly goods, including a cot, although Zhenya maintained his independence by sleeping on the couch with a backpack ready for instant departure. He still bore the stamp of early malnutrition but he had started lifting weights and developed hard little muscles like knots in a rope.

He did schoolwork quickly so that he could turn on the television and watch a nostalgia channel that ran grainy wartime documentaries on the siege of Leningrad, the defense of Moscow, the carnage and valor of Stalingrad, renamed Volgograd but forever Stalingrad. Also, war films about pilots, tank crews and riflemen who shared snapshots of mothers, wives and children before attacking a machine gun bunker, piloting a burning plane, crawling with a Molotov cocktail toward an enemy tank.

"I'm sorry," Zhenya said.

Arkady was a little startled. He was at the desk writing in the notebook and hadn't heard Zhenya approach.

"Thank you. I'm sorry about your father."

"Did you see it?"

"No, not actually."

"You don't remember it?" Zhenya asked.

"No."

Zhenya nodded, as if that were a good option.

"Do you remember going to Gorky Park?"

"Of course."

"Remember the Ferris wheel?"

"Yes. Your father ran it."

Osip Lysenko had hit on a perfect situation for dealing drugs: young people paying in cash for a five-minute ride in the open-air privacy of a gondola. That no one tried to fly from the top of the wheel was a miracle.

"He was never there," Zhenya said.

Thank God, Arkady thought. Each had gone to the park with a false assumption. Arkady thought that the boy sought a missing father. The boy thought Arkady carried a gun.

One minute was usually the time limit on discourse with Zhenya, but he stood his ground and brightened. "Winter is a bitch."

"It certainly can be."

"In the rail yard you could freeze to death. Sniff glue

during the day and turn blue at night. That's when you go to the shelter."

"Like wintering in the Crimea."

"The problem is, if a parent shows up they hand you over, even to my father. He said the law was on his side; I'd never get away."

"You saw him here?"

"Right across the street. He was with a crew filling in a hole."

"Just bad luck."

"It was snowing. I didn't see him when I went out the building. I walked right by him. The wind pushed my hood back and he said my name. He said, 'Do you still play chess?' And then he saw my book bag and said, 'Do you have your chess set with you?'"

"Did you?" Arkady asked.

Zhenya nodded. "Then he told me to give it to him to keep it safe and that we'd pick up where we left. 'Partners again,' he said. That's when I ran. He was in rubber boots, but he slipped on the ice and went down. He yelled. He said, 'I'll wring your neck like a chicken! The judge will give you to me and I'll wring your neck like a chicken!' I heard him for blocks."

"Where did you go?"

"Where Eva works. She told me to stay away from the apartment."

"That makes sense."

"And not to tell you because it would end badly. She

knew people who could arrange things so that no one got hurt."

"That's a special skill. Who did she have in mind?"

"I don't know."

Arkady let the lie go by. Zhenya had unloaded quite a lot.

"Eva was right," Arkady admitted. "It didn't end well."

And it wasn't getting better. He had no memory of writing 33-31-33. Perhaps it was an imaginary number and his notebook was a fiction concocted to smear a better man. He considered the lengths he'd gone to, casting suspicion on the Kuznetsov investigation and, on no evidence, trying to tie Isakov to Borodin's solitary death in the woods.

Even drunk, Victor had nailed it. Eva had left him. What made him think she wasn't happy?

The Great Patriotic War paused for the evening news. Five minutes in, Arkady realized that a Russian Patriot demonstration in Tver was being covered. Nikolai Isakov was in the front rank helping to carry a banner that read Restore Russian Pride! At Isakov's side Marat Urman continuously scanned the crowd, and in the second row stood Eva, sharp and exotic among round faces.

Through a bullhorn Isakov announced, "I was a lad in Tver, I served in the Tver OMON, and I will faithfully represent Tver in the highest levels of government."

The day was warm enough for many to wear Patriot T-shirts, making the Americans, Wiley and Pacheco, all the more conspicuous in their parkas. As Arkady entered pages for the two political consultants he remembered breakfast in the Hotel Metropol, the harpist's closed eyes and the hotel phone number scribbled in ballpoint pen inside a matchbook.

Arkady went to the closet and tore through the cardboard box he had brought from the office until he found the matchbook he had taken from Petya, Zelensky's all-purpose cameraman. "Tahiti—A Gentlemen's Club" was printed in red letters against a plastic field of pink. The Metropol number was handwritten inside the flap. There was no phone number for the club itself, initially, but as it warmed in his fingers the imprint of an open hand appeared on the front and the back divulged the phone number 33-31-33. Like a mood ring. One digit less than Moscow. He had no conscious memory of seeing the number before; his mind, out of habit, had collected it. The Tver area code was 822.

He called on his cell phone. On the tenth tone a deep voice said, "Tahiti." Arkady heard a background of heavy metal, laughs, arguments, the sociable clatter of glasses.

"In Tver?"

"Is this a joke?"

On the chance, Arkady asked, "Is Tanya there?"

"Which Tanya?"

"The one who plays the harp."

"She's on later."

"Her nose is better?"

"They don't come here to see her nose."

Arkady hung up. He got a short glass of vodka and a cigarette. He was starting to feel like himself. Zhenya watched the war again. The Hitlerites were in full retreat. Their trucks and caissons wallowed in mud. Dead horses and burnt tanks lined the road. Arkady picked up his cell phone and called a Moscow number.

"Yes?"

"Prosecutor Zurin."

"It's you, Renko? Damn it, this is my emergency line. Can't this wait?"

"I made up my mind about my next post and I want to get there as soon as possible. Not linger, as you say."

Zurin reorganized himself. "Oh. Well, that's the right spirit. So, Suzdal it is. I envy you. Very picturesque. Or perhaps you have some other quiet destination in mind. What will it be?"

"Tver."

A long pause. Both men knew that if in their long professional association the prosecutor could have found any excuse to send Arkady to Tver, Zurin would have seized it. Now that Arkady volunteered for the abyss the prosecutor audibly held his breath.

"You're serious?"

"Tver is my choice."

Isakov was from Tver. The Black Berets at the Sunzha Bridge were all from Tver. Tanya was from Tver. How, Arkady asked himself, could he go anywhere else?

"What are you up to, Renko? No one goes to Tver by choice. Are you on a case?"

"How could I be? You haven't given me one."

"That's right. Very well, Tver it is. Don't tell me why. Just say good-bye to Moscow."

On the television screen a victorious Red Army carried Nazi standards upside down and hailed the man on Lenin's Tomb.

Feeling expansive, Arkady added Stalin to his note-book, for good measure.

17

On the way to Tver, Arkady left Moscow and entered Russia.

No Mercedes, no Bolshoi, no sushi, no paved-over world; instead mud, geese, apples rolling off a horse cart. No townhouses in gated communities, but cottages shared with cats and hens. No billionaires, but men who sold vases by the highway because the crystal factory they worked at had no money to pay them, so paid them in kind, making each man an entrepreneur holding a vase with one hand and swatting flies with the other.

For a winter day the weather was freakishly warm, but Arkady drove with the windows up because of the dust pouring off trucks. The Zhiguli had no air conditioning or CD player, but its engine could run on vodka if need be. From time to time the land was so flat the horizon opened like a fan, and meadows and bogs stretched in all directions. A dirt road would branch off to a handful of cottages and a tilted Easter cake of a church framed by birches.

From the passenger seat Elena Ilyichnina looked sadly at the passing countryside. To Arkady's astonishment she had accepted the offer of a ride to her hometown to visit her mother. Villages on the way were dying, hollowed out by the mass evacuation of the young, who went to Tver, to Moscow or St. Petersburg rather than suffer what Marx called "the idiocy of rural life." A village shop sold gum boots and canvas jackets. Moscow offered supermodels and video arcades. An entire generation went to the city to make a fortune, gain computer skills, to hang, to temp, to wear a paper cap and fry chicken, to—one way or another—take part in the future. The death of a village could be tracked by the number of houses that, unpainted, turned to gray and disappeared among the trees; in most villages gray was epidemic.

During the war Tver had been called Kalinin, in honor of Russia's president. Kalinin had a distinguished goatee and, more important, was an organ grinder of secretary praise. In Kalinin's estimation, Stalin was "our best friend, our best teacher, the pathfinder of the ages, the genius of science, brighter than the sun, the greatest military strategist of all time." Stalin tried to get Kalinin to please stop, no more, but he wouldn't. As soon as the Soviet Union fell apart Tver reclaimed its ancient name.

Although the day was warm Elena Ilyichnina's ears were a vivid pink and it struck Arkady that she was many men's ideal: a big woman, Victor often said, was a rock in stormy seas. She had organized a lunch of sausage and bread to eat on the way.

Conversation never really got started. They were like two dancers so out of synch that they finally abandoned the floor. Also, Elena Ilyichnina had worked one shift in Moscow and was about to start a shift in Tver and she took the opportunity to nap, which was fine with Arkady. She made a companionable presence as long as she didn't talk.

As they neared Tver he became aware that she was awake and watching him. She said, "I hear that you are an investigator who doesn't carry a gun. What is the philosophy behind that?"

"No philosophy. In some situations the gun becomes an issue. You start worrying about when to show it, when to use it. It's like a locomotive; it takes you where it wants to go."

"And then someone has to pick a bullet out of your head."

"It's not an air-tight system. Are you telling me I'll need a gun in Tver?"

"No."

"What is Tver like, then?"

"Patriotic. In Moscow, people pay doctors to concoct reasons why their precious sons can't serve their military duty. Of course, the army is brutal and stupid, but in Tver, where boys are just as precious, everyone goes."

"Moscow sounds unpopular."

"I would get a new plate for the car."

That sounded unnecessary to him—after all, he didn't know how long he would even be in Tver—and he changed the subject by asking about her mother's health.

"Day to day." She looked suddenly exhausted. "I'll be back in Moscow tomorrow. Here's the hospital now."

They drove up to the admissions door of a dismal six-story building, a structure of plate glass and pre-cast concrete that once looked modern. Grit covered the glass and the concrete was stained from the rust of low-grade rebars.

"It's better on the inside." Elena Ilyichnina scribbled on a card and gave it to Arkady. "I've added my cell phone number. In case . . ."

"Just in case," he agreed.

As Arkady got back on the road a group of motorcycles overtook him, maybe twenty bikers in scruffy combinations of dark glasses, facial hair and leather jackets. Their bikes shone like gems set in chrome. With his long red hair and bandanna the lead rider could have passed for a buccaneer. His machine was low set, elongated, the color of rubies and as it cruised by, he signaled Arkady to lower his window.

"Fuck Moscow!" the biker shouted.

The pack rolled by.

Arkady decided to change his license plate.

"Welcome to Tver." City Prosecutor Sarkisian made a sentence sound like one sibilant word. He maneuvered Arkady around the office, so that he could enjoy professional certificates, oil paintings of Mount Ararat and, in a place of honor, photographs of the prosecutor in judo gear with the President himself. Otherwise the office was the same as Zurin's, the Soviet red carpet, dark paneling, drapes in deep maroon. A window looked down on a square with a statue of Lenin overdressed for the weather. "Too bad you missed lunch. You're going to find this is a very friendly city. Having our ups and downs, as who isn't. Once you're settled in, though, friendliest place on earth. There are no secrets in Tver." Sarkisian squeezed Arkady's shoulder. "You did volunteer for Tver?"

"Yes."

"I had a conversation with Zurin, prosecutor to prosecutor. You have a reputation as a, let's say, unusually active investigator. You like to get to the crime scene."

"I suppose so."

"I have a different approach. I think of my investigators as editors rather than writers. Let the detectives do the detecting. Your role is to take their findings and edit them into a case I can take to court. It's like geese flying south. They don't fly each in a different direction. They fly in formation. Correct?"

"Yes."

"Less wear and tear too. The doctors have given you the go-ahead?"

"Completely healed."

"Excellent, but before you come to work, take a few days to learn the lay of the land. I insist. You'll meet the men later. If I had been given more notice of your arrival we could have prepared a proper ceremony. As it is, we were lucky to organize a room for you to sleep in."

"Tver is that full?"

"Oh, Tver is a busy town. We've put you up at the

Boatman. I'll give you directions." The prosecutor had already printed them out. "So, as I said, take the next few days to settle in. That will give you a chance to really make up your mind whether or not to transfer here. Then we'll talk about work."

Sarkisian steered Arkady into the hall. By the elevator bay a glass cabinet displayed judo medals, trophies, belts.

"We work together, we play together. Is that how it is in Moscow?"

"We drink together." The elevator, a prewar Otis with an armed operator, finally arrived. Arkady stepped in but held the door. "Moscow does not seem to be well-loved here."

Sarkisian shrugged at the obvious. "Moscow wants to be the only pig at the trough. The rest of us can starve as far as Moscow is concerned. So, here in Tver, we take care of ourselves."

Tver had been an elegant city with an imperial palace and, in the Volga, a river that was an inspiration to poets. Then came the revolution, the war, Soviet implosion and economic pillaging, and, it seemed to Arkady, Tver became a couple of boulevards of classical architecture—the drama theater was a Greek temple trimmed in pink—surrounded by desultory shops, idle factories and gray postwar housing. Arkady drove around to see the city while daylight was left, because Russian maps were one thing and reality often something else. There were detours, road work, one-way streets, guarded streets, streets that did not exist, all sorts of surprises.

Short-term memory was an issue for Arkady. Three times he found himself unexpectedly at Lenin's statue. Arkady consumed a *pirog* he bought at a kiosk while he contemplated Lenin, who studied a pigeon. Finally, Arkady walked down to the river.

Here the empress Catherine had built a palace for her amours. Here the poet Pushkin had wandered along the river and weaved together "emotion, thought, and magic sound." Any ordinary winter the Volga would have frozen and Arkady could have walked across the river's back, but the Volga that he found was swollen with snowmelt and flying through the chute.

As a boy Arkady had taken piano lessons from his mother, and one of the first pieces he learned was "The Volga Boatmen." The boatmen hired themselves out as dray animals with straps across their chests to haul barges and ships, pitting their strength against the implacable current of the river. "Heave ho! Yo, heave ho!" Arkady's left hand would pound dramatically while he picked out the tune with his right, expressing the fatalism of men whose only relief was vodka and whose beds were the rags on their backs.

At the Boatman Hotel long-haul truckers maintained the tradition, sleeping on greasy sheets, showering in cold water, dressing in front of a broken mirror. The wallpaper was a mural of stains. A spray can of insecticide stood on the bureau like a bouquet of flowers.

Arkady set down a duffel and athletic bags and asked the night manager, "Prosecutor Sarkisian arranged this?"

"Personally."

Arkady gave the man a second look. The night manager's head was shaved and slightly flattened. He carried a plastic sheet. "You're the elevator operator from his office. You have two jobs."

"What the prosecutor wants, I do."

Arkady ran his fingers along cigarette burns on the television cabinet. "Don't take it the wrong way, but I think I'll look for other accommodations."

The night manager had a smile. "Doesn't matter. You cross the threshold, you have to pay."

"How much?"

"A thousand rubles for a night."

"A night of what?"

"Doesn't matter." The night manager spread the plastic on the floor, although Arkady thought it was a little late to be fastidious. "This room was reserved for you."

"Not by me."

"You crossed the threshold."

It was hard to argue with a man of such few words. Arkady wasn't feeling too bright himself, but a cosmic ray passing through his brain tickled his memory. "I've seen you before. You boxed."

"So?"

"The semifinals, International Boxing Tournament,

1998. You and a Cuban. After two rounds you were ahead, but in the third you got cut and the match was stopped. It was a great fight. What was the Cuban's name? What was his name?"

The night manager was pleased. "Martinez. His name was Martinez."

"He butted you, didn't he?"

"Yeah, no one remembers that, only that I lost."

There was a general contemplation of the unfairness of life. Arkady thought about his gun, safely locked away in Moscow.

The night manager had to shake his head. "You have some kind of memory."

"Off and on. So this is what you do now, break bones?"

"Sometimes." The night manager was embarrassed, like a master carpenter ordered to build a birdhouse. He slipped brass knuckles over his hand. "Arthritis."

"Is it painful?"

"A little."

"Well, this may sting." Arkady picked up the can of insecticide and sprayed the night manager's face.

"Shit!"

Arkady hit him on the head with the can. Blood spread over the manager's face. He did cut easily.

"Bastard!"

The night manager took tentative half steps and got tangled in the plastic sheet.

"Son of a bitch!"

*

From the Boatman Hotel Arkady drove to the railway station, one place where a man waiting in a car would not draw attention. The insecticide's cloying scent followed him and he rolled the windows down. He didn't know what the night manager had intended—a mere scare, some rib work, a split lip. Arkady did feel that a threshold had indeed been crossed. In one day he had gone from being a senior investigator in Moscow to homeless in Tver. He had wanted to provoke a reaction and he got his wish.

The cell phone rang. It was Eva.

"I don't believe this," she said. "You gave the man a towel?"

"I suppose I did."

"You spray a man who is attacking you and then throw him a towel to wipe his eyes? Did it make you feel better?"

"A little." He wrote the caller ID in his notebook while he remembered it. The number and "Hotel Obermeier." "How did you hear about it?"

There was silence on the other end before Eva said, "The main thing is for you to leave Tver."

"Not yet."

"Nikolai has promised hands off. It won't happen again."

"Hands off me or hands off you?"

"You. Until the election, at least."

"Do you think he'll win?"

"He has to win."

"For the glory or the immunity from prosecution?"

Again a pause.

"Please, Arkady, go home." She hung up.

Immunity would be the icing on Isakov's cake. Senator Isakov would be bulletproof. The law protected lawmakers from arrest for any crime unless they were caught in the actual commission of, let's say, a murder or rape. As for old cases like the Kuznetsovs, Ginsberg and Borodin, there would be no sifting through the ashes. Their cases were already closed and would soon be forgotten.

The cell phone rang. He hoped it was Eva, but the ID panel said Zhenya, the last person Arkady wanted to talk to. He was not in the mood to talk about chess and with Zhenya everything related to chess, chess books or chess tournaments. So he let the phone ring. He did not want to be Zhenya's chess coach or father or uncle. Being a friend would do. The phone rang. Why was Zhenya so persistent? It was midnight. And rang until Arkady surrendered and picked up.

Zhenya whispered, "Are you near Lake Brosno?"

"I have no idea."

"Find out if you're near Lake Brosno," Zhenya said.

"Okay."

"There was a program on television last night that said Lake Brosno was near Tver."

"Then it is, I suppose," Arkady said. "What about it?"

"Lake Brosno has a monster like the Loch Ness monster but better. They have pictures and all the old people have seen it."

"What makes it better?"

"The Lake Brosno monster comes out on land."

"Well, there you are."

"During the war it came out and snatched a Fascist plane out of the air."

"A patriotic monster." Not only had Stalin enlisted the Orthodox Church and all its saints, Arkady thought, but the nation's monsters as well. "How big is it?"

"Big as a house," Zhenya said.

"Does it have legs?"

"No one knows. Some scientists are going to take some electronic gear out in a boat and test for anomalies."

"Anomalies?" A good word.

"Wouldn't it be amazing if the monster came out?"

"And laid waste to the countryside and spread panic and fear?"

"We'd have to bomb it. That would be so cool."

"Zhenya, we can only hope."

After the call Arkady was too on edge to sleep. The trams had shut down. He left the car at the train station and walked toward nowhere in particular. There was little point in checking into another hotel; there weren't that many in Tver, and Sarkisian could alert them in minutes. Or Arkady could drive back to Moscow.

The street led, as all streets in Tver seemed to lead, to the river. The Volga gathered two smaller rivers in the center of the city and, fed by them, rushed against the embankment in a hurry to a faraway Caspian Sea. It was no wonder why he was drawn. Palace, parks, statues, two illuminated bridges, almost everything in Tver looked toward the river, homely faces gazing at a silver mirror.

There were two approaches: attack Isakov or pursue Eva. Both were shameless but in different ways. Since he didn't have the evidence or the authority to go after the detective in any official manner, he would have to provoke Isakov into a misstep. Or he could forget Isakov and justice and concentrate on Eva. She had slept with another man? At his age that meant less and less. People had histories.

He could keep either his dignity or her.

His choice.

18

Sofia Andreyeva said, "I don't show nice apartments to just anyone. I always look at their shoes. If they don't take care of their own shoes, how will they take care of an apartment?"

"Absolutely," Arkady said, although he could take no credit for it; any son of an army general automatically kept his shoes polished.

She winked at Arkady as she drove and hummed to herself. Her car was the tidiest Lada that Arkady had ever been in. No cigarette wrappers, beer cans, wilted newspapers or rust in the floor. A bit like Sofia Andreyeva herself. What once was a distinguished nose had, with age, become a beak, but she had a fresh bloom of rouge on her cheeks and, wrapped in a black shawl, she looked cheerfully bereaved. She was a real estate agent, meaning she met each train as it arrived at Tver Station and studied the disembarking passengers before offering, "Apartments to let. Best choice guaranteed." Other real estate agents wore sandwich boards, which she considered déclassé. She liked Arkady at first sight. Clean shaven, no apparent hangover even early in the day. And she was pleased that, although he had his own car, he had gone to the train station instead of some stuffy, overpriced office.

Sofia Andreyeva showed him a studio apartment with Danish details and wireless connection and took him to a spacious flat on Sovietskaya Street, the city's central boulevard. For Arkady's purposes neither would do. As they walked down Sovietskaya, Sofia Andreyeva surprised Arkady by casually, deliberately, spitting at a gate. Before he could ask why, she said, "There's one more apartment, a dear friend's. He is taking a leave of absence from the university. He phoned me yesterday to say that with the euro being what it is, he could use some extra income. Anyway, the apartment is not ready to be shown, and his personal effects are everywhere, but with new sheets you could move in today. Do you speak French?"

"No. Is that a requirement?"

"Not at all, not at all." She sighed. "It's just, well, a shame."

The apartment was on the second story of a housing block that flew laundry on the balconies. The lobby was filthy and mailboxes were ripped open. The apartment, however, harbored a fantasy. Posters of Piaf and Alain Delon hung on the walls. Michelin guides filled the shelves. A pack of Gitanes lay on the desk, and the smell of forgotten cheese overpowered all. She had Arkady change into slippers at the front door.

"The carpets."

"I understand." It was hardly unusual to change footwear if slippers were provided.

"The professor's pride and joy." She pointed to the most threadbare carpet on the floor. "A minor carpet to be sure, but it was on a professor's salary." She sniffed. "Such ambience. Perhaps an open window would be a good idea."

Arkady looked at a photo of a middle-aged man striking a pose with a beret squashed on his head and a cigarette dangling from his lower lip.

"Does he have a family?"

"The professor's son is an anarchist. He travels the world protesting international conferences by setting cars on fire. Notice the television and videotape player. Two bedrooms, one bath. The carpets, of course. The shower and kitchen have been redone. Gas and electricity are connected. I'm sorry to say that the telephone has been turned off, but you no doubt have a cell phone. Everyone does."

Moving into such a completely furnished apartment was like wearing someone else's clothes, but on the plus side the building directly opposite was commercial, not the roost of curious babushkas. The ground floor offered two exits, a front door to the street and carport and a back door to a courtyard with a playground and bicycle stand. Across the courtyard was a row of small enterprises—an Internet café, a weight-lifting club and a beauty salon. A couple of men loitered in sweat suits outside the club's back door. Sofia Andreyeva was willing to rent month to month at a fraction of what a hotel would cost.

Arkady said, "I like it. Is the son likely to pop in?"

"I doubt it. He's in jail in Geneva. In case there is a problem . . ." She tore off a corner of the newspaper and wrote a phone number. "My business cards are still at the printer's. Just call in the afternoons and ask for Doctor Andreyeva."

"A medical doctor? Two occupations?"

"For the sake of eating."

"I'll see you if I catch a cold."

"Let's hope not, for your sake. Are you married?"

"No."

"You may not know, but men from America, Australia, from all over the world come here to meet Russian brides. I don't think we really need a written contract. Keys count more than paper. Will you be getting any mail here?"

"No, that will go to the office."

"Much better."

Sofia Andreyeva buttoned her coat, ready to fly.

Arkady said, "Before you go, I didn't get the professor's name."

"Professor Golovanov. He likes to say that his liver is Russian and his stomach is French. I am, in a sense, midway between Russian and French myself."

"Polish?"

"Yes."

"I thought I saw something. A certain flair."

"Yes, yes." She was delighted but froze at the sound of footsteps in the hall. A piece of paper slid under the door and the steps moved on. "What is it?"

"A flyer for a political rally."

One side of the flyer promised music and clowns, while the other bore a photograph of Isakov in combat gear riding the fender of an armored personnel carrier.

"Politics." Sofia Andreyeva treated the word like dirt. "Of course, we must register your new address with the militia. You being a prosecutor's investigator, I'll leave that to you."

"Of course."

Arkady understood perfectly. Sometimes it was better not to ask too many questions. Granted, there was a chance that a resuscitated Professor Golovanov might return from a holiday in the south of France, swilling wine and singing the Marseillaise. All the same, Arkady had rarely seen the law broken with such elan.

The day was comfortably crisp, more Easter weather than winter, the pastel walls of Lenin Square glowing in the sun. A balalaika ensemble entertained on a stage decorated with the white, blue and red of the Russian flag. Clowns swayed on stilts. Teenagers on in-line skates distributed "I am a Russian Patriot" T-shirts. Volunteers spun cotton candy, pink and blue. Technicians laid cable and every minute or so the sound system erupted with a shriek. A truck-mounted outdoor video screen rose on hydraulic lifts behind the stage while a camera crew worked on a platform facing the stage, Zelensky on the camera, Bora extending a microphone boom. Zelensky was as emaciated as ever. Bora appeared at the limit of his technical abilities. Arkady spotted Petya handling a mobile camera on the ground. Arkady took one of the Patriot shirts being handed out. The photo of Isakov printed on the back was similar to one on a T-shirt he had seen before, except that the hero carried a shovel instead of a rifle and the tiger's head patch of OMON was replaced by the emblem of a red star, a rose and a third element Arkady could not identify.

More people than Arkady expected had come. Besides the usual steel-teeth pensioners, the rally had attracted coal miners and veterans of the wars in Afghanistan and Chechnya. Miners and veterans were serious men. Some of the veterans were in wheelchairs, driving home the point that Isakov was one candidate who had not weaseled or bribed his way out of serving his country. Speeches had been scheduled to begin at one in the afternoon and last for an hour. At two, the minor candidates began even though the stage crew was still fighting feedback and the screen crew was still adjusting its angle. But a festive atmosphere prevailed. This was a taped event, not live. No one paid particular attention to the time except Arkady. He wanted to buy a car with Tver license plates before the day was out. A white Zhiguli with Moscow plates was too easy to track.

As the crowd grew, Arkady moved to the side so that he could see backstage as well. Two trailers, the kind afforded actors on a movie set, stood on either side of the video truck. One was for the lesser candidates; the Russian Patriots had a score of them to present to the public, decoys chosen to fill a slate. The party's only genuine candidate was Isakov, who stood outside the opposite trailer with Urman and two figures that Arkady hadn't seen since the Metropol Hotel, the American political wizards, Wiley and Pacheco. Isakov was entirely in black. Black was New Russia's favorite color for German cars and Italian suits, but he also possessed the stillness of a movie actor resting with his entourage. Wiley's fine comb-over lifted in the breeze.

Arkady wondered why the men were outside. Why didn't they take advantage of the trailer?

He called Eva's cell phone and watched the group.

At the first ring, Urman and Isakov looked at the trailer.

On the second they looked at each other.

"Hello."

"It's me," Arkady said.

"Are you in Moscow?" Eva asked. "Tell me that you are back in Moscow."

"Not quite. Are you all right?" That seemed to Arkady a question apropos for a woman living with a murderer.

"Why wouldn't I be? I just need time to sort this out."

"You said we would talk."

"After the election."

At that moment the stage sound system emitted a squawk. Eva appeared at the trailer window. She had heard what he heard.

"You're here?"

"This is better than the circus."

"Go home. You're safe if you go home."

"Who told you that?"

As Isakov climbed in the trailer, Eva moved out of sight. Words were murmured. Arkady heard Isakov's "please" and felt the surrender of the cell phone from Eva's hand.

"Renko?"

"Yes."

"Stay where you are," Isakov said.

Arkady watched Isakov open the door to speak to Urman, who opened his cell phone and punched in a number. Arkady knew whose when Zelensky's telephoto lens sorted through the crowd and locked on him like the scope of a rifle.

Arkady's image leapt onto the video screen, only for a second because Isakov came onstage.

"You know me. I am Nikolai Sergeevich Isakov from Tver, and I stand for Russia."

Fervent applause, as they used to say, Arkady thought.

Isakov described a nation under siege by religious fanatics and shadowy alliances. Out in the world were nuclear warheads, human bombs, and fair-weather friends. Closer to home was a circle of vampires that had stripped Russia of its treasure and, worse, subverted its values and traditions. It was an ordinary rant, but what did people actually take away from such an event? Arkady wondered. That Nikolai Isakov withstood magnification on a large screen. That he was handsome in a hard-used way. That he was accustomed to command. That he was one of their own, a son of Tver. That they had reached up and touched a hero.

Urman stood next to Arkady. "I think that bullet must have really addled your brain. You should be as far from here as you can get."

"That occurred to me, but I wanted to hear Isakov in person."

"So, what do you think?" Urman asked.

"He's going from murder to politics. Is that a step up or down? What do the Americans think?"

"They're happy. I told them you were harmless. Are you harmless?"

"As a babe."

"Were you a babe at the Boatman last night? Are you fucking with me?"

"Oh, I wouldn't dare fuck with you. I don't want to swallow my tongue."

"Because I could take care of you now."

"I doubt that. No, not at a rally days before the election. Wiley is an expert. He can explain to you the negative effect murder has on a rally. In fact, I think I have a little breathing room here." Arkady had tuned out Isakov's speech, but he contributed a polite clap. "What a perfect day for an event like this. You are a lucky man. But what exactly are you? In Chechnya you were second in command to Isakov. You're partners with him in the detective squad. Now you're his campaign manager? What's next? Footstool? Bootlick?"

Urman half laughed, half sighed. "You're trying to provoke me?"

"Well, Mongols do have a history of violence, Genghis Khan, Tamerlane and all."

"You've gone mental."

"Maybe. A funny thing about being shot in the head is—"

"You should be dead."

"That's it, I should be."

"Did you get a glimpse of the other side? Did you see a tunnel and a light?"

"I saw a grave."

"You know, that's what I always figured."

People swarmed by. Eighty-year-old farmers in forty-year-old suits were followed at a quick march by men and boys in military camos and by babushkas at full hobble. A teenage boy rushed by with his father and grandfather. They made a heartwarming picture, three generations in camos with identical shoulder patches of a red star, a helmet and a rose.

"An outdoor club?"

"Diggers."

"Why are they called that?"

Urman shrugged. "They dig. They dig and they love Nikolai; they're what Wiley calls Nikolai's base. They need someone like him."

"A serial killer?"

"That is an unsubstantiated accusation by a brain-damaged man. Prosecutor Zurin will say so, Prosecutor Sarkisian will say so and so will we."

On stage Isakov built to a climax. "Russia's blood sacrifice of twenty million lives stemmed the Fascist invaders. Reminders of that struggle can be found around Tver even today."

Overwhelming applause.

"Why are the Americans here?" Arkady asked.

"Nikolai has momentum. The Americans say momentum is very important in politics. They thought they were setting up a paper candidate to fuck up the opposition. They're taking a second look at Nikolai now."

The real and the projected Isakovs said together, "It is our moral duty to protect Russia's security, rationalize her economic gains, uproot corruption, identify the thieves and connivers who stole the assets of the people, ruthlessly stamp out terrorism, rebuild her defenses with apologies to no one, reject the meddling by foreign hypocrites in our internal affairs, promote traditional Russian customs and values, protect our environment and leave a better world for our children. And I will always remember that I am one of you." He wasn't done. A girl came out on stage bearing the obligatory bouquet and something that Isakov pinned to his jacket lapel. On the video screen the camera closed in on an emblem of the star, helmet and rose. Isakov was a Digger too.

Rapturous, passionate applause. A standing ovation. Shouts of "Isakov! Isakov!"

"What the devil was that about?" Arkady asked.

"It's a good windup to the campaign," Urman said. "It's got everything."

"Like a fruit salad. You really think Isakov has a chance?"

"He's been a winner ever since I've known him. Since we joined the Black Berets. There are twelve candidates. He only needs a plurality."

Isakov had not left the stage. He carried the girl from one side to the other while roses landed at his feet. Urman joined in the rhythmic applause.

"Why did he drop out?" Arkady asked.

"What are you talking about?"

"When you and Isakov met in OMON, he had just left the university."

"He was bored. He was sick of books. They taught us something useful in OMON. Hit first, keep hitting."

"Good advice. But he was a five-point student, at the top of his class, and in his last week, he threw away all that hard work. That doesn't strike me as boredom. Something happened."

"You never let up," Urman said.

"It's an innocent question. Anyway, you're going to kill me as soon as you get the nod."

Urman leaned close to speak confidentially. "Do you know how I kill an enemy? First I cut off his testicles—"

"You fry them and eat them and on and on. I heard all about it. But at the Sunzha Bridge, you simply shot people in the back."

"I was in a hurry. With you I'll take my time." Urman reassured Arkady with a pat on the back and slipped away.

The crowd wasn't leaving. A rhythmic clap continued and so many boys rode their fathers' shoulders they were a second tier of enthusiasm. The sound system poured out the Soviet national anthem, the wartime version that included, "Stalin has raised us with faith in the people, inspiring them to labor and glorious deeds!" The applause doubled when Isakov returned to the stage to say informally, like a personal reminder, "The dig will tell the tale!"

Maybe, Arkady thought. Maybe Urman could make him beg for mercy, although Arkady had trained with a master.

"Skin is sensitive."

Arkady was twelve years old. In Afghanistan. He had returned to camp covered with ant bites, each bite hot and throbbing and his face swollen.

His father sat on the cot and continued. "There have been experiments. Subjects have been hypnotized and told they were burned and blisters appeared on their skin. Other patients who were in pain were hypnotized and their pain went away. Not far away, perhaps, but enough."

The General loosened his necktie and undid the top two buttons of his shirt. Took a sharp breath through his nose and sipped his scotch.

"The skin blushes with embarrassment, goes pale with

fear, shivers in the cold. The question is, why were you riding around on a motorcycle outside the base? Outside the base is dangerous and off-limits, you know that."

"I didn't see any signs."

"There have to be signs posted for you? What were you doing on the bike when you fell?"

"Just riding."

"A little too fast, maybe? Doing some stunts?"

"Maybe."

The General finished the glass and poured another. He lit a cigarette. Bulgarian tobacco. For Arkady, the match flame focused the pain of the bites.

"So far as the natives are concerned we are guest engineers building an airstrip under a treaty of friendship and cooperation. That's why we're in civilian clothes. That's why we buy their pomegranates and grapes, because we want to cement our friendship and be even more welcome. But this is still a Soviet military base and I am still its commander. Understood?

"Yes."

The cigarette smoke was aromatic and blue as a thunderhead.

"Were there any natives there? Did any of them see the accident?"

"Yes."

"Who?"

"Two men. I was lucky they were there."

"I'm sure." His father blew the flame out as it reached his fingertips. "It must hurt."

"Yes, sir."

"You're thirteen years old?"

"Twelve."

"Twenty bites is a lot at any age. Did you cry?"

"Yes, sir."

The General picked a flake of tobacco from his lip. "The people who live here and surround this base are tough. These people fought Alexander the Great. They're warriors and their children are trained to be warriors and, no matter what, not to cry. Understand? Not to cry." His father's face turned red. Arkady didn't think it was from embarrassment. Veins spread on the General's forehead and neck. "I am the commander of this base. The son of the commander does not fall off his bike in front of the natives and if he does fall off and is bitten by a hundred ants he does not cry."

Two natives had stretched languidly in the shade of a saxaul tree to smoke cigarettes and watch Arkady on his motorbike chase ground squirrels across the desert floor. The boys were brothers with similar short, swirly black beards. They wore turbans, baggy trousers, oversized shirts, sunglasses.

"They're watching," the General said. "The minute we look weak, we will be under siege. That's why we surround the camp with mines and discourage the natives from coming near and why we have never let them inside to see our electronic gear, until today, when they carried in my son because of his ant stings."

"I'm sorry," Arkady said.

"Do you know the consequences? I could lose my command. You could have set off a mine and lost your life."

A gecko had darted in Arkady's way. He had twisted the handlebars without thinking, and as the back end of the bike caught up with the front he flew over the machine and plowed face first into the gritty mound of an ant colony.

"Do you know what made Stalin great?" his father asked. "Stalin was great because, during the war, when the Germans took his son Yakov prisoner and proposed an exchange, Stalin refused, even though he knew that saying no was a death sentence for his son." The General drew on his cigarette to make it flare. In spite of the ant bites Arkady felt a chill. "Tobacco burns at nine hundred degrees centigrade. The skin knows it. So I will give you a choice, your skin or theirs."

"Whose?"

"The men who brought you, your native friends. They're still here."

"My skin."

"Wrong answer." From his shirt pocket his father gave Arkady two snapshots, one of each brother, bareheaded and stripped to the waist, lying in a bloody heap. "They wouldn't have felt a thing."

19

The sun was setting and the village was a picture of civilization going to sleep: a handful of cottages, half of them abandoned, a power line and the dome of a church. A woman shuffled under a yoke of water buckets. A smoke-colored cat followed. When the old woman shooed it, the cat nipped across the road and slipped between piles of metal and rubber belts, through stacks of fenders and tires. Arkady kept pace in the Zhiguli until the cat squeezed under the closed doors of a garage.

Arkady's day had been spent searching for the right car, something with a Tver license plate and so drab it deflected attention. He had looked at Volgas, Ladas, Nivas of every color and variety of dents and for one reason or another each car was wrong.

Knocking on the door to no effect, Arkady let himself into the garage and immediately blinked from the light of an acetylene torch. A figure in a leather vest and welding mask was welding what could have been a fuel tank amid the pulleys and chains, vises and clamps of a workshop. Anonymous items under different tarps shifted in the glare. The cat jumped up to a shelf of motorcycle helmets and batted at sparks.

"Rudenko?" Arkady had to shout. "Rudi Rudenko?"

The welder turned down the flame and flipped up his mask. "Yeah, what?"

"This is the Rudenko repair shop?"

"So?"

"Do you have any used cars?"

"No. This is a motorcycle shop. Shut the door on your way out. Thank you. Have a shitty day."

Arkady started for the door. He paused. On the way from Tver he had watched the rearview mirror in case he was followed and he could give a brief description of each car that had drawn close. Until his encounter with the motorcycle pack he had ignored bikes, virtually wiped them from his vision. Small motorbikes especially were as incidental as mosquitoes.

"You're still here?" Rudenko said.

"Do you have any motorcycles to sell?"

"You want a car, then you want a bike. How about a fucking cat? I have one of those."

"Do you have any bikes?"

"I don't see you on one of my bikes. That would be like seeing an old man climbing on a beautiful woman. I'm busy."

"I can wait."

"There's no waiting room."

"I'll wait in the car."

"That car?" The welder looked through the door.

He turned off the torch and removed his mask, freeing a ponytail of red hair. Arkady's spirits sank. Rudi was tall and angular with a beefsteak face and a sickly mustache. He was the biker who had welcomed Arkady to Tver with a hearty "Fuck Moscow."

Arkady said, "Sometimes people bring in bikes for repair and never return. Do you have a bike like that?"

Rudi picked up a shovel and held it like an ax. "Let me fix your car first."

"I simply want a bike." The last thing Arkady wanted was a brawl with someone bigger and uglier.

"It's okay!" Rudi suddenly shouted past Arkady, who found an old man coming at him from behind with a pitchfork. The old man must have shrunk because his clothes looked strapped on. "It's okay, Granddad! Thanks!"

"Is it Fritz?" the old man asked.

"No, it's not Fritz."

"Watch for tanks."

"Got my eyes peeled, Granddad."

"Well, they'll be back." The old man shook the pitchfork as he retreated.

"We'll be ready this time."

"For what?" Arkady asked.

"Germans," Rudi said. "If the Germans come again, he's prepared. Where were we?"

"I came for a bike," Arkady reminded him.

Rudi glanced in the direction his grandfather had gone. "Just stand still." Rudi put the shovel aside and patted

Arkady down and found his ID. "A senior investigator from Moscow. Are you investigating me?"

"No."

"How did you even know my name?"

"You're in the telephone book."

"Oh, okay, no harm done."

Arkady appreciated that. Rudi had the arms of a man who lifted heavy bikes. On his right shoulder was a round BMW tattoo and on his left shoulder a Maserati trident. No tattoos of girls or guns, and no OMON tiger heads.

The grandfather returned to the door in a jacket with war medals. He gave Arkady a salute and said, "Rudenko reporting in."

When Arkady returned the salute Rudi said, "Don't encourage him. He thinks he knows you."

"From where?"

"I don't know. Sometime in his past. Ignore him. You really want a bike?"

"Yes."

"I have three." Rudi pulled tarps off a flame red Kawasaki, a tiger-striped Yamaha, and a sidecar Ural the color of mud.

"Beauties. The Japanese bikes, I mean. Two hundred on a straightaway, screaming like a jet."

"And the Ural?"

"You want to go fast in a Ural? Drive it off a cliff."

It was a fact that the Ural was not a racehorse. It was the mule of motor travel, its sidecar used to haul trussed chickens or a farmer's wife. People called it a Cossack for its lack of charm.

"It has a Tver license?"

"Yes, see for yourself," Rudi said. "Two thousand euros for either customized Japanese bike, two hundred for the fucking Ural."

"It needs a new front tire."

"I have a retread somewhere." Rudi waved vaguely toward the pile of tires outside. "You're a real risk taker, I can see that."

"Would you throw in a helmet with a face shield?"

"No problem." Rudi rooted around a trash can and fished out a helmet with a crack down the center. "Slightly used."

"Can you deliver it tonight? Say, ten?"

"To get rid of it? Anywhere. I suggest Pushkin's statue on the embankment. At night the gays move in and the militia moves out." Rudi was suddenly alarmed. "Watch out, Granddad. No, no. Don't come in."

Carrying a paper bag, the old man stumbled against a corner stack of shovels and rods that fell with a clamor on the floor.

"Granddad, why do you always do that?"

"You look familiar," the old man told Arkady. "Were you here in 'forty-one?"

"I wasn't born yet in 'forty-one."

"Would you know if this is Fritz?" The old man opened the bag and took out a skull with a hole in the back.

"All Germans are Fritz to my grandfather," Rudi said.

Arkady said, "I have no idea."

Rudi said, "Call him Big Rudi. He used to be bigger."

"There's no need for formalities between old comrades." Rudi's grandfather found a loose tooth, a brown molar, and plucked it from the jaw. "I never understood that. The Germans were such big strapping fellows and they had such bad teeth."

"Where did you get it?" Arkady asked.

"Everywhere. Believe me, there's nothing worse than fighting with a toothache. I pulled my own tooth out." He dropped the tooth in a pocket. "Don't fret, Rudi, I'll pick up the shovels. Have you got my eyeglasses?"

"You lost them ten years ago."

"They're here somewhere."

"Gaga," Rudi told Arkady. "He lives in the past."

Arkady helped the old man pick up the shovels. Among them was a homemade metal detector, with an inductor coil and a gauge. While Rudi slammed through drawers in a search of sale documents his vest rode up from a gun tucked into the back of his jeans.

The cat leapt up to a shelf of Nazi helmets, some whole and some punctured. On a work counter, a metal canister with instructions in German was the explosive end of a "potato masher" hand grenade. The foggy eyes of an ancient gas mask peeked from a cabinet. A camouflage tunic on a hook had the same shoulder emblem—star, helmet and rose—that Arkady had seen at the rally in Tver.

"Did you go to the rally today?" Arkady asked Rudi.

"For Isakov? He's a fucking Fascist."

"He seems popular."

"He's still a fucking Fascist."

"I met Stalin," Rudi's grandfather said.

Arkady took a second to adjust to such a broad change of subject. It was possible, Arkady thought. Big Rudi was old enough.

"When?" Arkady asked.

"Today."

"Where?"

"On the hill in back. Look out the window, he's there now."

Enough light was cast by the window for Arkady to see there was no Stalin and no hill, only the stubble of winter grass.

"I was too slow. He's gone. Did he say anything?" Arkady asked.

"To go to the dig." The old boy became excited. "Come with us tomorrow. Stalin will be there."

"Will Isakov?"

"Maybe. It doesn't matter," Rudi said. "You're not a Digger. It's members only."

"Why?" Arkady asked.

"One, you'd be in the way. Two, since you don't know what you're doing you might get hurt or hurt someone else. Three, it's strictly against the rules. Four, no fucking way. Why do you even ask? What did you expect to see there?"

That Arkady did not know. Signs? Maybe revelations?

*

"The monster not only knocked down an invading Fascist plane," Zhenya said, "it came out of Lake Brosno and chased away the invading Mongols hundreds of years ago. Now scientists have to find out if it's the same monster or a descendant. That's what the expedition is all about. They have a picture of it, a photograph, not a drawing. I saw it on the television."

Arkady switched his cell phone to the other ear; when Zhenya was excited his voice tended to be shrill. Nothing had excited him more than the Lake Brosno monster.

"What did it look like?" Arkady asked.

"It was kind of blurred. It could have been a form of apatosaurus. Definitely. The scientists went out in a boat with special equipment and detected something really strange underneath the surface."

"What did they do?"

"They dropped a grenade on it."

"Any man of science would." Arkady looked out the apartment window at the roofs of Tver. He saw church spires but no onion domes to lend the city grace or fantasy. On the other hand, Arkady appreciated the local monster for turning Zhenya from a virtual mute into a chatterbox. "What did the monster do then?"

"Nothing. It escaped. It would have been great if it swallowed the boat."

"And it would have been proof."

Zhenya said, "I'd like to see a video of that."

"Wouldn't we all?"

*

Pushkin's statue had a top hat, iron poise, perhaps a smirk. Arkady had no such style. Every few minutes, different men would come out of the dark, pass him and the statue in a speculative fashion and continue on their way. Fifteen minutes late Rudi rode the Ural up the embankment to Pushkin's statue, followed by another biker on Rudi's red bike.

Rudi climbed off, removed his helmet and shook his ponytail free. For the cool of the evening he wore camos, army green, not OMON blue. "Sorry, I'm late. I had to take back roads and alleys so no one would see me on a tricycle."

"I understand. You have a reputation to protect."

Rudi's fellow rider was a heavyset man upholstered in leather and chains. His name was Misha. Misha rattled impatiently while Arkady counted out money.

"The helmet?" Arkady asked.

"In the sidecar. I filled the fuel tank."

That was more than Arkady had expected. He unsnapped the sidecar cover and found a scuffed but uncracked motorcycle helmet with a visor.

"Thanks."

"You know my granddad."

"Big Rudi with the pitchfork?"

"Right. He is really sure he saw Stalin. He heard there was a man in Moscow who was shot in the head. Stalin appeared and the guy got up and walked away."

"That's quite a story."

Misha said, "Rudi, are we going or what?"

Rudi waved him off and told Arkady, "I gave you a new tire. A knobby, for off-the-road action."

"That's generous of you." Arkady did not plan to go off the road.

"You realize you're coming out ahead on this deal, Renko."

"What do you want?"

"You're so fucking suspicious."

"That's right."

"Okay, my granddad wants to see you again. It would mean a lot to him and I'd personally consider us even. He's positive he saw you here during the war."

"I wasn't even born."

"Humor him. He lives in the past and he remembers old stuff better than new. Sometimes he gets mixed up. He sees you and now he's all wound up. Big deal, you drop by the shop for a visit. A fucking hour of your precious time."

"At the dig."

"I can't do that. Like I said before, you're not a Digger."

"I'll talk to Big Rudi at the dig. Nowhere else."

"I explained, it's not allowed. You have to be a Digger."

"Too bad," said Arkady.

"What a son of a bitch."

"The dig."

Rudi and Misha got on the red bike, which came to life with a vibrato that warned the world to move aside while Rudi went in circles around Arkady.

"You know, Pushkin's not the only one here with brass balls."

Rudi made another turn.

"We leave for the dig at six."

As soon as Rudi had gone Arkady checked out his new acquisition. New to him. The Ural had to be thirty years old, at least. A spare tire was secured on the back of the sidecar, which looked like a large sandal and had the major amenities: a shovel and a windshield. The machine-gun mount had been cut off. Arkady had noticed when he first saw the bike that it was stamped in various places with a star, meaning it had come off a military assembly line.

Stalin's engineers got their hands on some German BMWs, took them apart, strengthened this, simplified that and when they put the bikes back together they were Russian. Cossacks might be a lowly transporter of potatoes now, but they had once carried heroes to Berlin.

Arkady rolled through Tver. The Ural's engine wasn't symphonic but it was steady, its power dedicated not to speed but to traction, and since the sidecar was connected to the bike it drove like a car. No leaning. He rode by one dark restaurant after another, from one empty square to the next, like a chess piece alone on a board. If half the city was on the crawl, he was looking under the wrong rocks. He swung back toward the embankment, gathered speed along the river and had yet to see an open enterprise apart from an all-night casino that, compared to Moscow's, had the allure of a pachinko parlor.

He was stopped at a traffic light when a Porsche

convertible rolled alongside. Urman was at the wheel, looking more like a detective from Miami than one from Moscow. He was too occupied with smoothing his wind-whipped hair to give Arkady more than a glance; he might not have seen the bike at all. When the light turned green the Porsche took off like a rocket. Six blocks further on, Urman was entering a hotel as Arkady rode by.

Arkady U-turned and coasted back to a playground of seesaws, gnomes and kiosks opposite the hotel. The Porsche was in the driveway. The Hotel Obermeier was a fortress of brick. The ground floor, however, was plate glass and fountains, and Arkady had a sweeping view of the reception desk, concierge's podium, elevator bank, bar and restaurant. All was dark except for a table by the restaurant window, where Urman joined Isakov, Eva and Prosecutor Sarkisian. Two waiters slumped over a corner table.

The party had reached the brandy and cigar stage, had possibly reached it hours ago but Sarkisian was holding forth. Urman laughed and filled a snifter. Was the subject humorous homicides or the election odds of the home-town hero? Isakov listened stoically, while Eva made no effort to hide her distaste. Sarkisian put his finger by his nose, signifying Armenian powers of insight. When he raised a glass, Isakov and Urman followed suit, while Eva rose from her chair and stood by the window to smoke a cigarette. Arkady trusted that on her side the plate glass had to be a mirror. Isakov waved to her to return to the table. She ignored him and rested her forehead against the pane. It wasn't a happy scene.

Isakov motioned Eva again to rejoin the group at the table and she continued to ignore him. Urman covered the moment by humoring Sarkisian until, finally and without a word, Eva went to the elevator bank, pushed a button and disappeared behind metal doors. The men sat stupefied by her desertion. A room lit in the middle of the second floor. The waiters went on sleeping, heads deep in their arms.

Sarkisian pointed in the general direction of Eva and apparently said something less than complimentary, because Isakov picked up a fork and pressed it against the prosecutor's neck. Arkady remembered what Ginsberg had said about Isakov's calm; the detective's move was unhurried and he didn't appear to raise his voice, but he conveyed conviction. He seemed to tell Sarkisian what he probably should not do or say ever again and the prosecutor nodded in emphatic agreement. The waiters slept on.

Urman went to the window where Eva had stood and cupped his eyes against the glass. He saw something because he moved through the restaurant and lobby and out to the front steps of the hotel to scan the playground. Gnomes were bigger at night and more menacing, as if they were on the march. What seemed smaller was the kiosk. Was the Ural's front tire showing? The rear? Arkady realized that Urman was waiting for a car to pass by. He was waiting for headlights.

Urman had to break off when Isakov came out of the hotel, half jollying, half carrying Sarkisian to the Porsche. They were all pals again, although the prosecutor's eyes were white with terror. Together, the two detectives loaded Sarkisian into the convertible and belted him in.

Arkady heard the prosecutor say, ". . . every effort."

Isakov said, "He can't be far."

Sarkisian sputtered something Arkady didn't catch.

"I'd rather find him first," Urman said.

Urman got behind the wheel and started the Porsche, which drowned further conversation. The car took off, gear changes whining the length of the street.

Isakov turned wearily to the hotel. He paused in the restaurant to wake the waiters and pay them, generously by their expressions, and took the elevator. The room on the second floor was still lit. It brightened briefly as a door opened and closed, and Arkady got a sense of bodies in motion.

More he didn't want to know.

20

A drab world came out of the dark: an abandoned field of winter wheat bordered by scrub and brambles on three sides and, along the bottom, a dirt road that led to willows and fog.

The Rudenkos left their truck at a broken-down gate. Arkady had followed on the Ural and the three marched with flashlights and a wheelbarrow full of hemp sacks and tools to a mound of loose earth. Big Rudi seemed rejuvenated by the morning air: perhaps crazy, Arkady thought, but not the befuddled grandfather of the night before. The old man aimed the flashlight on the mound while Rudi selected a shovel and set to work, moving the loose dirt aside. The Ural had nothing as fancy as an odometer, but Arkady guessed that they were about fourteen kilometers south of Tver.

As the sun broke from the horizon the field developed contour and dimensions, about two soccer fields' worth of flattened grass and sodden earth, a reminder that winter had started heavy with snow. The men's shadows seemed to stand on stilts and a massive shadow spread from a stand of pine trees in the middle of the field. The trees must have been an impediment to farm machinery; Arkady wondered why they hadn't been pulled as saplings.

Military camos were the dress code of the day and Arkady had borrowed a uniform from Rudi, who said, "Renko, you look like a POW."

"No, a general," Big Rudi insisted.

The sun up an hour, Rudi was using a pick to pry the earth around a skeleton lying on its side.

"Ours or theirs?" Big Rudi asked.

"Can't tell yet," said Rudi. He added for Arkady's benefit, "This weather is fantastic. This time of year the ground is usually frozen solid. This is like cutting cake."

"Check the teeth."

"Present and accounted for."

"But you think it's December 'forty-one?" Big Rudi asked.

Every schoolboy knew that in December '41 Stalin performed his greatest miracle. The Red Army had lost four million men dead and wounded. The Germans were on the outskirts of Moscow. Leningrad was under siege, its population starving to death. Tver, which was the center of the entire front, had already fallen. And then, incredibly, the Russians counterattacked. Stalin had secretly moved hundreds of tanks and thousands of troops from Siberia to the low hills outside Tver. This new army, seemingly created out of thin air and launched in the middle of a snowstorm, was a total surprise to German intelligence. The Red Army crossed the frozen Volga and chased the Wehrmacht for two hundred kilometers. Not only was Tver liberated and thousands of Germans killed and captured, they no longer resembled a superrace. The shape of the front changed. The nature of the war changed. The enemy stalled outside Moscow, never to threaten it again.

Two women, bent over and, blinkered by their shawls, moved along the far side of the field gleaning stunted potatoes that had been left to rot. Crows strolled behind. When the women saw Rudi they crossed themselves and left. Arkady wondered whether Big Rudi had stood in the same scene with tanks belching black smoke and Siberian riflemen moving across the river.

"There are Red Diggers and Black Diggers," Rudi said. "Red Diggers find the bodies of Russian soldiers so they can send the remains home to be reunited with their families. Black Diggers find bodies, German or Russian, and strip them of medals, belt buckles, SS gear, any shit they can sell on the Internet."

As the shape of a skeleton became evident at his feet, Rudi probed the bottom of the hole with a metal rod attached to a wooden pole.

"Remember that you're not only digging up bones, you're digging up unexploded shells, mines, hand grenades, booby traps, Molotov cocktails. Before you dig anywhere, take the rod and feel around. You do it enough, you can tell what you hit, wood, metal or glass. Every year somebody gets a big surprise. Well, we're provoking it, aren't we? Provoking the past."

Satisfied, Rudi exchanged the pole for a spade and shaved the walls of the hole for elbow room. The man was a human power shovel, Arkady thought. Rudi's friend Misha arrived with a metal detector and began sweeping the field, but not before he pointed to cars and vans arriving on the dirt road. "Diggers."

Rudi said, "That's okay. They had to load up with shish kabobs and beer. We got here early and the early bird got the worm, right?"

"So to speak," Arkady murmured.

"There's enough to go around, all skeletonized and picked clean." Rudi scooped dirt with a short spade. "Bodies in trenches, bunkers, outhouses, you never know where. The first one I ever saw was up in a tree. I was out skiing on my own. I guess the body got tangled in the branches and the birch grew and lifted it until the body could grin down from the sky. I was eight years old."

Men and boys streamed through the gate onto the field like an army with portable tables and hampers of food, bed rolls and tents, metal detectors and guitars. Not everyone was in camos, but it was the best way to blend in.

Arkady said, "If they don't find anything they're going to be very disappointed. How do they know where to dig?"

"They follow Rudi," his grandfather said.

"And how do you know?" Arkady asked Rudi.

Rudi freed a clavicle and chose an ice pick to work

around a tea-colored rib cage. "I study old war plans, maps and combat reports. I ride around on my bike and I know what to look for. A lilac bush where a house once stood. Depressions where the earth settled. Anything out of place, such as pine trees in the middle of a wheat field. Trees were a favorite way to hide a mass grave. Besides, I can feel it."

"How big is this grave?"

"Big. Before they ran, the fucking Germans killed a lot of prisoners. Anyway, the Diggers will scratch around, work up an appetite, build some campfires, get drunk and sing songs. Tomorrow is the big day, when they dig in the trees."

"Why wait until tomorrow?"

"Television. It had to fit their schedule."

"Is it Fritz?" Big Rudi stared down at the hole.

"Well, Granddad, there's no ID, medals or shoulder bars." Rudi knelt. The uniform was brown gauze that disintegrated in his hands. "He's not from a tank crew. Too big. They're short and broad-shouldered because they have to be small enough to fit in the tank and strong enough to open the hatch. Also, they tend to be fried to a crisp. So, who are you?" Rudi asked the bones directly. "Are you Fritz or Ivan? Do you have a picture of Helga or Ninochka?"

"Check him for foot wraps," Big Rudi suggested.

Russian soldiers had wrapped cloth around their feet instead of wearing socks.

"No feet," Rudi reported. "No legs. Cut off at the

knees. Not a very neat job, either. Probably blown off and then trimmed. Poor bastard, to go through that in the middle of a battle. That's what happened."

"What you think?" Big Rudi asked Arkady.

"I wouldn't know."

"Go ahead," Rudi said. "You're the investigator from Moscow."

"I'm not a pathologist."

"Don't be scared. It won't bite you."

Arkady squatted by the edge of the hole.

"Well, a fairly young, fit man, a little less than two meters tall. Good nutrition. The ring finger of the left hand is missing, so I'm supposing that he was married and had a gold ring. As for the legs, I suspect they were taken for their boots."

Rudi said, "You don't have to take the legs off to get boots."

"You do if they're frozen. You have to warm up the boots at a campfire. Since you don't want to drag a body around the camp, you saw off the lower legs and carry them. Especially if they're leather boots made to order. So, I'd say he was a young, newly wed German officer who thought he would be home for Christmas. That's just a guess."

Rudi said, "What a shovelful of bullshit that is. From Moscow, too."

"It probably is," Arkady agreed. "Tip him over. Misha detected something."

Rudi pulled on the rib cage. The earth gave reluctantly,

but the skeleton rolled away from a metal spoon on a chain attached to the cervical vertebrae. On the chain was a black spoon with a swastika stamped on the handle. Rudi rubbed the spoon with a chamois cloth. Silver shone through. He snapped the neck with his hands, freed the chain and spoon and wrapped both in the cloth. He looked up at Arkady and said, "It's still bullshit."

Arkady took a break. He left the hole and walked into the field to try Major Agronsky on the cell phone, only to discover the obvious, that the countryside around Tver was on the fringe of cell coverage and he had to fight waves of static. He shouted his number into the phone a few times and gave up. The major had headed the army commendations panel and Arkady wanted to ask him one question, why were Captain Isakov and his Black Beret squad denied a single medal or promotion for their heroism at the Sunzha Bridge?

Clutching his hat, Big Rudi caught up. "I want to apologize for Rudi. He's a good boy at heart."

"There's no reason to apologize. It is absolute bullshit, I'm sure. Professional bullshit, the best."

"He was taken advantage of by some bike distributors in Moscow."

"There you are."

"He and the Diggers do good work. It's still important who is who."

Arkady understood. On Stalin's orders any Russian soldier missing in action was presumed guilty of going over to the enemy. It didn't matter whether he was last seen bleeding to death or charging a German tank, he was guilty of treason and his family was punished for associating with a traitor. Widows lost their rations, their jobs and sometimes their children. The family lived under a cloud for generations. Rehabilitation, even sixty years late, was better than nothing. Over the years, said Big Rudi, the Red Diggers had identified and sent home over a thousand Russian dead from the fields around Tver.

He asked Arkady, "How did you know about frozen boots?"

"I don't know. It seemed a possibility."

"This wasn't the only case like that." Big Rudi pulled his face in for a shrewd study of Arkady. "Rudi says you weren't here in 'forty-one."

"That's right."

"So it must have been your father. He told you about the boots."

"He was never here."

"He never said his name but I remembered him as soon as I saw you. He made a strong impression on me."

Arkady did not want to get into an argument with an elderly veteran. Some people worshiped the General. Stalin praised his initiative and willingness to pour blood like a river.

"You wanted to talk about something," Arkady said. This was his part of the bargain.

"The counterattack was so confusing. First we were on our knees and the next we were beating Fritz to his. It was a madhouse."

"Fortunes were reversed."

"That's right. That's straight to the point."

Not exactly, Arkady thought. The old man seemed to be unburdening himself, but of what Arkady couldn't tell. Big Rudi kept turning as he walked, as if getting his bearings, gazing at the sky one moment and the ground the next. In a distracted way, he said, "When Fritz stalled he froze. He was in his summer uniform; he wasn't prepared for a Russian winter. His horses dropped dead. The engines of Fritz's planes froze solid." The old man halted. "Here! There was a farmhouse right here. Here we are."

"Where?" All Arkady saw was matted wheat and a few green shoots of grass.

"Five days after the counterattack your father and I sat at the kitchen table right here facing each other. I was wounded from fighting on the front line, but I was detained and brought back because accusations had been made. Someone said I had gone over to the Germans the day before the counterattack began, when things were so grim."

"Had you?"

"That's what your father asked."

"And?"

"In war, everything is upside down. One moment you're pinned down, your comrades are dead and you shit your pants, and the next you're running after Fritz, spraying him with a tommy gun, then another and another. You're behind his lines, he's behind yours. It's all confusion."

More cars and vans pulled off the dirt road to let out an army carrying not weapons but portable grills. Boys marched with the somber faces of inductees to a secret rite, their camos freshly stitched with the Diggers' emblem of the red star, rose and helmet.

"Were there any witnesses?"

"No. Finally, your father said he calculated there was one chance in seven that I was telling the truth and he emptied his revolver, all but the seventh bullet, spun the barrel and gave me the gun. What could I do? They were, like the General said, better odds than a firing squad. I put the pistol to my head and pulled the trigger. I missed because the action of the trigger was so stiff and the barrel kicked and all I did was burst an eardrum and burn the side of my head. I thought your father was going to fall off his chair from laughing. How he laughed. He gave me a cigarette and we had a smoke. Then he picked up the gun and spun the barrel and said to try again and keep the barrel level. So I put the pistol to my head again and pulled the trigger, determined to do as he said, but the hammer came down on the empty chamber."

"And then?"

"The General was a man of his word. He had me released."

"That's what you wanted to tell me?"

"Yes, how he saved my life. With a burst eardrum I was unfit for frontline service. When you see him next, tell him I was the only one in my group to survive the war."

The old man was wrong on so many counts, Arkady thought. First, so far as he knew, the General had never been at the Tver front. Second, he owned a Nagant revolver, but he usually carried a Tokarev pistol, so there had been no dramatic spinning of the barrel. Third, when soldiers were executed they were often told to strip, so that their uniforms could be passed without bullet holes to the next man. That was a touch his father never would have missed. But there was no good reason to set Big Rudi straight. What would it gain him?

True, the General did enjoy the occasional game of Russian roulette, especially toward the end. People said he must have been insane. Father and son were so estranged that Arkady claimed what the General was really suffering from was a late onset of sanity, that he finally saw the monster he was.

A sense of organization was taking hold by the time Arkady and Big Rudi returned to the dig. A poster on a stake assigned squads of Diggers by color to sections of the field marked by pegs tied with matching tape; none of the sections were near the trees. A curious thing about the trees: as the day got brighter, they grew darker and more solid.

The Red Diggers seemed to be both a paramilitary organization and a social club. As Arkady understood it, they pitched their tents, hiked, sang and exhumed the dead. Who could argue with an agenda like that? Separate tables were set up for sorting bones, others for food, vodka and beer. There was the good cheer of a reunion, a fair turnout for an unexpected wintertime dig. Arkady recognized one of the lesser candidates from the Russian Patriot rally. He was digging furiously.

"Wait until tomorrow, that will be a show," the candidate told Arkady and jumped aside as Rudi came through to dump a wheelbarrow load of bones at a poster that said, "Germans Here."

Arkady's cell phone rang. He got an earful of static when he answered but he didn't move for fear of losing reception entirely.

"I apologize. I can barely make you out. Could you speak loudly, please?"

"This is Sarkisian. Where the devil are you?"

Arkady said, "I'm sorry, this connection is terrible."

"What have you been up to?"

"Would you repeat that?"

"Where are you staying?"

"We're breaking up."

"Damn it, Zurin told me you'd play tricks like this."

"Sorry." Arkady pressed END.

He hardly took a step before the cell phone rang again. Now the reception was loud and clear.

A deliberate voice said, "This is Agronsky. Whatever you're selling, I don't want it, whoever you are, I don't care," and hung up.

Arkady put down the shovel.

Bones would wait.

*

The retired Major Gennady Agronsky, a round man in a raveled sweater, surveyed the daffodils that bordered his vegetable garden.

"Fool's gold. Beautiful but brief. This kind of deceitful weather draws them out and a frost lays them low. But good for the Diggers, I suppose."

"Yes, it is. Major, you're a hard man to reach."

"I don't answer the phone or the door. Most people get the message. Then I saw that you came on an old Cossack. What a beast! It went right to my heart."

A white picket fence was the boundary of his domain, a trim cottage in front and in back a patio of terra-cotta pavers with rows of vegetables to come, several raw stumps, sawdust and a small cherry tree with a satiny bark. His neighbor's yard was a junkyard.

"They plant nothing, not even cucumbers. In the summer I have pickles, tomatoes, coriander, dill, you name it. These young people, these good-for-nothings, complain there's no work. Just pick up a hoe and put your back into it. At least you'll eat, I say."

Arkady noticed a pit bull pretending to be asleep on the other side of the fence. "What do they say?"

"They say, 'Stuff it, you old fart!' or 'Pull your head out of your ass!' The same with the dealer on the other side. You're sure you wouldn't like vodka, just a touch?"

"No, thanks."

"That's just as well. The doctor says if I drink I might as well shoot myself. My attitude? Everything in moderation, including vice." Agronsky led Arkady to the patio table. "Sit."

"Did you go to the rally for the Russian Patriots?"

"Too far to go. This is almost outside town. We have bears in the garbage."

"I noticed a hunting rifle at your front door. Do bears call at your front door?"

"Not yet."

The rifle was a Baikal Express with over and under barrels. Arkady thought that would discourage even a bear.

"They offered free rides to the rally."

"I saw enough on television."

"The candidate is someone you must know, Captain Nikolai Isakov. He is a militia detective in Moscow now, but he was a Black Beret from Tver. A man rising in the world is Nikolai Isakov."

"You're investigating him?"

"Just asking a few questions. For example, was Captain Isakov a competent officer?"

"What a question. More than competent; a model officer. We held him up as an example."

"He was the hero of Sunzha Bridge, after all. As, I suppose, were all the men under his command that day at the river. All heroes and all from Tver."

"The people of Tver are patriotic," Agronsky said.

"Six Black Berets against fifty heavily armed rebels with an armored personnel carrier and two trucks. The outcome was what, thirteen, fourteen terrorists dead—"

"Fourteen."

"Fourteen terrorists dead, the APC and trucks in retreat and, in return, one Black Beret wounded. Amazing. It was the sort of battle that can make an officer's reputation and win a promotion in rank, especially at a time when there was so little good news coming out of Chechnya. Yet there wasn't a single decoration."

"These things happen in war. Sometimes it's just a matter of missing paperwork or witnesses."

"Which is why there is a citation committee to review commendations. You were the head of the committee that denied the Black Berets of Sunzha Bridge any medals or promotion. Why?"

"You expect me to remember? The committee processes hundreds of recommendations, and on a generous basis. The regular army consists of boys, conscripts, the poorest and dumbest, the ten percent who didn't dodge the draft and the one percent true patriots. They deserve commendations. If they get shot in the ass they get a commendation. If they steal a chicken for their commanding officer they get a commendation. If they get killed their body parts go home in a sealed coffin with a commendation."

"So why wouldn't a real battle merit a medal or two?"

"Who knows? That was months ago." Agronsky looked away. "It isn't as if I were allowed to bring my files with me."

"It was your last case. You retired a week after you submitted your verdict. After thirty years you suddenly retired."

"Thirty years ago, things were different. We were an army then."

"Tell me about Isakov."

Agronsky's eyes stopped dodging.

"The report smelled."

"In what way?"

"Captain Isakov reported a firefight between rebels on one side of the bridge and his men on the other. The medical examination revealed that all the rebels were shot at close range, some in the back, one or two while eating. Where the rebels were supposed to have been shot there was no blood on the vegetation. The leaves weren't shredded, they weren't even disturbed. No doubt Isakov wanted to arrange the bodies in a more convincing manner but a helicopter was coming to the landing zone. A journalist who was on the helicopter described the scene to me."

"That was Ginsberg?"

"Yes."

"Were there any actual witnesses?"

"Only one, a civilian, and she was no help at all."

"What did she say?"

"We'll never know. She was Ukrainian. She went back to Kiev."

"What was her name?"

"Kafka, like the crazy writer."

Close enough, Arkady thought. He held his breath before the next question.

"Are there any photographs of the firefight scene?"

"Only Ginsberg's."

"From the helicopter?"

"His colleagues said he always carried a camera, in case. The pictures completely contradict the statements of Isakov and Urman."

"Do people in Tver know about this?"

"They won't hear it from me. Did I mention that two weeks before the incident at the bridge, rebels captured eight Black Berets and took videos of them, first alive and then dead? Their mothers couldn't recognize those boys. They were all from Tver. Don't ask for any sympathy for rebels in this city."

"Then why not promote Isakov?"

"Because he was no longer a soldier; he was a killer. To me there is a difference."

Arkady was impressed. Agronsky looked more like a retired bureaucrat than someone who would stand up to Isakov. The major's sweater had holes and loose strands, exactly what a man of leisure would wear for gardening, although glints of chrome at the belt line betrayed the gun underneath.

"Was there a follow-up investigation?"

"I suggested one and for that I've been cashiered and all the evidence has been destroyed."

"What about Ginsberg's photographs?"

"Burned."

"Gone?"

"Smoke."

"No copies?" Investigations were usually awash in copies.

"My ruling on honors and commendations was regarded as a slur on the army. My files were thoroughly cleaned out and I was shown the door."

"Did you copy them, scan them, e-mail them to anyone?"

"Renko, when I joined the army they stripped me clean, and when I left the army they stripped me clean."

"What about Ginsberg's office or home?"

"His office was searched and his colleagues questioned. There were no other photos and he wasn't married."

"You wrecked your career over this."

"To tell the truth, at my age if you're not at least a colonel, you're wasting your time. Besides, the citation committee was exhausting work, lifting some to heaven and kicking some into hell. You know, I've told no one about all this. My mouth is dry." The major's smile regrouped. "When I joined up, the army gave each man a daily allotment of one hundred grams of vodka. There must be some good in it."

"One glass."

Agronsky clapped his hands together. "We'll confound the doctors. Before we die we'll shoot ourselves, like Sergeant Kuznetsov."

The major made a beeline for the house and returned with a tray bearing a bottle of vodka, two glasses and a plate of brown bread and cheese because, as he declared, "A man who drinks without something to eat is a drunk."

He unscrewed the bottle's cap and threw it away. An ominous beginning, Arkady thought.

The first glassful slid down, fastidiously followed by bread. Arkady tried to recall whether he had eaten anytime during the day. He asked, "Kuznetsov shot himself?"

"Not exactly. Kuznetsov was ranting and raving as he was being airlifted, yelling that Lieutenant Urman told him that for the good of the team they needed at least one casualty from OMON, not to take it personally. He shot poor Kuznetsov in the leg."

"Urman is impulsive."

"Of course, it has to be said that during the airlift Kuznetsov was under the influence of painkillers. In the hospital he correctly pointed to the photo of a dead rebel as the man who shot him."

"How do you know it was correct?"

"Captain Isakov said so. A little more?"

"Just a little. What did you tell the captain?"

Vodka quivered on the brim. Agronsky begged a cigarette and a match.

"I said I could support neither a promotion for him nor medals to a death squad, because at the end of this war that is all we would be. No armies, just death squads."

His eye on the Tahiti matchbook, Arkady asked, with too little forethought, "Did you happen to know any of the eight boys from Tver who were killed?"

"Rifleman Vladimir Agronsky. Vlad. Nineteen years old."

The major's face fell in on itself.

"I'm sorry," Arkady said. "I'm very sorry."

"Do you have a son?"

"No."

"Then you don't know what it's like to lose one." The words caught in his throat he washed down with vodka. No bread. Deep breaths. He had outpaced Arkady with the vodka and was starting to look sandblasted. "Forgive me, that was inexcusable. What were you talking about? What else?"

"The candidate is protecting his official history, cleaning up loose ends, eliminating anyone who knows what happened at the bridge, including his own men. Kuznetsov and his wife are dead. Borodin and Ginsberg are dead."

"I've taken precautions."

Arkady had noticed the gun under Agronsky's sweater, the double-barreled rifle at the door, trees recently felled for a clear field of fire and the comfort of meth lab security on either side. The situation was strangely snug and highly delusional. The major could build a bunker and not keep out Isakov and Urman.

"Ginsberg's photographs of Sunzha Bridge would be a great help," Arkady said.

Agronsky said, "I wish they still existed."

"Maybe if you looked again you'd find them."

"Sorry, they're gone."

Arkady let it drop. After a last round, Arkady made his good-bye and went out and sat on the Ural. Agronsky's neighbors, a young couple in sheepskin coats, walked by with the soft steps of the truly stoned. To the north a scrim of clouds promised a light dusting of snow. Contradict. Contradicted. Such a small difference, but Arkady had done a thousand interrogations or more. Sometimes he just knew. He killed the engine and returned to Agronsky's door.

"My friend Renko, another . . . ?" The major lifted an imaginary glass.

"I'm trying to stop two murderers. Ginsberg's photographs will help."

"So?"

"You said that Ginsberg's pictures of the firefight zone 'contradict' Isakov. You should have said 'contradicted.' Past tense, the photographs are gone. Present tense, they still exist and you have them."

Agronsky blinked.

"What are you, a schoolteacher? 'Contradict.' 'Contradicted.' So what? Does that give you the right to come to my house, eat my food, drink my vodka and call me a liar?"

Arkady gave Agronsky a card. "This is my address and cell phone number. Call before you come."

"I'll go to hell first." Agronsky threw the card back and slammed the door.

Returning to the bike, Arkady did not feel completely sober. He had handled the major badly. He should have been tougher or more sympathetic or, if necessary, enlisted the dead son in the argument. Whatever, a golden opportunity had presented itself and he had let it slip through his fingers.

Zhenya was excited. "They're launching a new expedition at Lake Brosno to find the monster. A casino is the sponsor."

"Well, that sounds perfectly logical." Didn't the children's shelter have any rules about late calls? Arkady wondered.

"If they find the monster they'll capture it alive and put it in a giant tank in the casino. Is that fantastic?"

"That qualifies."

"If we could be on the team that would be so neat. Have you been to the lake yet?"

"No."

"Why not?"

"I have one or two things to do here first." He was at the apartment changing out of Rudi's camos and into a jacket.

"What are you doing now?"

"I'm going to Tahiti."

"Where's that?"

"It turns out it's in Tver."

"Okay." Zhenya's interest returned to minimal.

Arkady asked, "Have they decided how to catch the monster?"

"I think they want to stun it."

"With what, a torpedo?"

"Something, and then the monster will float to the surface."

"What if he sinks?"

"I don't know. How can anyone tell?"

"It's a matter of buoyancy. The more fat the more buoyancy and mammals are fat and gassy animals. We float."

"On the water."

"Or under."

"What do you mean?"

"Well, there is a theory that in really deep lakes a body will sink only to a certain zone, at which point water pressure, temperature, weight and buoyancy balance out and the body hangs in the water."

"There could be dozens of them down there just hanging around. The police could go there in a submarine and solve all sorts of crimes. That is so amazing. What do you call that zone?"

"I don't know. It's just a theory," Arkady said, although he did have a name for it: Memory.

21

The mural in the bar of the Tahiti Club covered Gauguin's Polynesian period, faithfully copying the artist's paintings of phallic idols and natives in sarongs. Everyone wore knockoff Armani and shouted into cell phones, while on a wide television screen two heavyweights pounded each other like bell ringers.

Arkady followed a disco beat up the stairs, past the scrutiny of body builders in black tie and entered a cabaret where the speakers were so loud that the hovering layers of cigarette smoke seemed to shudder with the beat. He caught a glimpse of two pole dancers on stage before a waitress sized him up.

"You want a stool? A ringside stool down where the action is. The action, you know."

"I'm not sure I'm ready for much action."

"A table?"

"A booth. I'm expecting friends."

He ordered a beer and asked whether Zelensky or Petya were around. Isakov and Urman were probably at a Russian Patriot event, but word would get back to them that he hadn't left Tver. He couldn't provoke Isakov and Urman if all he did was hide.

The waitress asked, "You know Vlad Zelensky? Are you a film producer?"

"A critic," Arkady said.

Spotlights made the dancers bright and blurry. They strutted up and down the stage in platform shoes and thongs, keeping in constant motion like fish in a tank while an audience of men hung in suspended animation. When a dancer paused and sprawled on the runway, ring-side aficionados tucked money in the thong. Otherwise, as a sign said, No Touching.

Arkady settled into a leather booth the color of arterial blood. The table had two menus. A food menu featured tropical cocktails, egg rolls, and sushi. A "Crazy" menu offered a lap dance in the Sportsman's Lounge, a personal chat with a naked woman, "an intimate hour with a lovely companion in the VIP Jacuzzi or an entire evening with an anything-goes beauty (or beauties!!!) in the luxurious Peter the Great Bedroom." The price of a royal romp was a thousand euros, cut-rate compared to Moscow clubs.

The waitress brought his Baltika. "It really ought to be the Catherine the Great Bedroom. She built the palace here and she did a lot more fucking than Peter ever did. Food?"

"Just some black bread and cheese."

"But you'll be drinking?"

"Naturally."

The "Crazy" text informed Arkady that "the women of Tver are legendary for their beauty. Today, some of Russia's top models are daughters of Tver. Their fame has grown worldwide and bachelors from the United States, Germany, Britain, and Australia, to name but a few, travel to Tver seeking the aid of Cupid."

Tanya and a peppy little dancer were up next. The first time he had seen Tanya she was in a white evening gown strumming the harp at the Metropol. In little more than the flesh she was even more in control, with a cool smile and long strides that prompted rhythmic clapping at ringside.

Across the room Arkady saw his waitress lead Wiley and Pacheco to an opposite booth. Pacheco adjusted his tie while Wiley tried hard not to look at Tanya. They couldn't have found the Tahiti on their own, Arkady thought and, soon enough, Marat Urman joined them. His canary yellow jacket brought style to the scene; a Tatar could wear colors that made a Russian quail. Urman blew Tanya a kiss, but her eyes tracked Arkady as he changed booths.

"Look what the cat drug in." Pacheco made room for Arkady.

Urman said, "You can't be serious."

"Tanya looks good," Arkady said.

"She looks magnificent," Pacheco corrected him. "Milky skin, a dancer's body, fabulous tits."

"Her nose looks good," Arkady said.

The music started, a throbbing bass that made the room reverberate, and the dancers climbed the poles.

"*R-E-S-P-E-C-T.* I love this song," Pacheco said.

Arkady said, "Somehow I think they missed the point."

"It's the beat that matters," Pacheco said. "Got any good Mongolian love songs? Like to your favorite horse?"

Urman said, "You should take off your wedding ring."

"Why?"

"It promotes impotence. It's a Slavic tradition to wear a wedding ring no more than four hours a day for reasons of health. Ask Renko."

"Is that true?" Wiley asked.

"Some men believe it. Some believe they shouldn't wear a ring at all."

"It's scientific fact," Urman said. "The ring is like a closed circuit and the finger is an electric conductor."

Pacheco said, "Well, the Slavic dick is a more delicate instrument than I would have thought."

"Where is Isakov?" Arkady asked.

Wiley said, "A visit to an erotic club is not an appropriate image for a candidate of reform."

"Does he have momentum?" Arkady asked. "I understand that's important."

Wiley was happy to avert his gaze from the stage and take refuge in politics. "Momentum is all he's got. He's got no genuine party machine behind him, so one misstep and his campaign is over."

"But he does have momentum," Urman said.

"He was only chosen to steal votes from the opposition," Wiley said. "Nobody expected his candidacy to come alive."

"He has a chance," Urman insisted.

"If he finishes with a bang."

"In the States pole dancing is the new workout," said Pacheco. "Honest."

Tanya was sex wrapped around a pole, with a slow head-down slither that seemed to swallow brass. The other dancer swung around her pole like a dynamo, which seemed quaintly Soviet.

"Tanya had classical training for the ballet, but she grew too big for the men to catch." Urman turned to Arkady. "Well, you've wrestled her, you know."

Pacheco's ears perked up. "Wrestled? That sounds interesting."

"We had a special moment," Arkady said.

"We need a bang." Wiley concentrated on the table top. "A long-shot campaign has to end with a visceral, explosive climax."

"Like what?" Arkady asked.

Wiley looked up. "There's a statue of the Virgin Mary in Tver. The people here swear she cries. They sincerely believe they see it."

"You're going to have the Virgin appear at the dig?"

"Do you have Diet Coke?" Wiley asked the waitress.

Pacheco said, "She plays the harp and she strips. This is a talented young lady."

"If not the Virgin, who?" Arkady asked. "Anyone in mind?"

"People see what they want to see," Wiley said. The smaller dancer peeked at Wiley from between her legs. She had short dark hair and a beauty mark. Her name was Julia; she was twenty-three, spiritually advanced, looking for a man with his feet on the ground. Arkady knew because he had seen her photograph and description in the Cupid album of marriageable women.

"Renko can't do anything," Urman reassured Pacheco. "He's hiding from the prosecutor here and disowned by the prosecutor in Moscow. Besides, he's a dead man."

"You mean, he will soon be a dead man?"

"No, I mean he's dead now. He got shot in the head. If that's not dead, what is?"

"I've noticed that Isakov never actually says Stalin's name," Arkady said.

"Why should he?" Wiley said. "Right now all anyone knows about Nikolai Isakov is that he's a good-looking war hero. Everything stays vague and generally patriotic. Once he actually uses Stalin's name, Stalin is an issue, which has some negatives. Our job is to connect Isakov and Stalin without saying so out loud."

"How do you do that?"

"Visuals."

"At the new dig? As I understand it, a mass grave of Russian soldiers has been discovered. That's a strong visual, isn't it? Any chance that a patriot named Isakov will be there, shovel in hand, when the television cameras arrive?"

Pacheco said, "The son of a bitch doesn't sound that dead to me."

Aretha Franklin sang, *"R-E-S- . . ."*

Tanya slid off the runway, ignored her ringside regulars and climbed onto Arkady's lap, where she breathed heavily and stamped him with sweat and powder. She kissed him as if they were lovers reunited and when he tried to ease her off she clung to his neck.

"Where is this hole I hear about? Is it the size of a bottle cap?"

She pressed herself against his face while she felt his scalp. All that remained of his operation were drain scars, but she found them. If Arkady had humiliated her, she would humiliate him. On stage Julia spun at half speed.

Pacheco reached across the table and gathered Tanya's golden hair in his hand. "Darling, if money is your object, you are humping the wrong man. My friend here is as poor as a church mouse, whereas I am slipping a hundred-dollar bill in your G-string. Am I getting your attention?"

"I told you this was a bad idea," Wiley said.

Tanya held on.

Pacheco said, "I like you and I am a great admirer of the harp, but you have to let go of my friend's head."

Tanya turned enough to say, "Make it two hundred."

"Damn, this is a fine woman. Two hundred it is."

Pacheco gave Tanya a chivalrous boost back onto the runway. Patrons applauded her return.

"Would you like some sushi?" Urman said.

"No." Wiley threw money on the table. "Let's go, let's go, let's go."

Outside, the Americans piled into a black Pathfinder and waited while Urman followed Arkady to the other end of the parking lot. Arkady had come in the Zhiguli because he had intended to be seen.

Pacheco hit the horn.

"I would love to kill that cowboy," Urman said. "Threatening to drag Tanya by the hair? What kind of behavior is that? I appreciate the fact that you restrained yourself."

"No problem."

"Look, do us all a favor. Leave Tver. Go away and we can forget our paths ever crossed. Or did she call already?"

"Who?"

"Eva. She was going to tell you she was coming back."

"But she isn't, really?"

"No, I'm afraid not."

"But she is going to call?"

"You think I'm just trying to fuck up your mind?" Urman had a soft laugh. "Frankly, I wish you would take her with you. I'm sick of the radioactive bitch."

Arkady was taking a long route to the apartment, looking for any car following him, when he saw Isakov on Sovietskaya Street. It was two a.m., the hour between sweet dreams and black despair, a time to pace the floor, not the sidewalk. Arkady went around the block, turned off his headlamps and coasted to the corner.

A light snow melted on the ground. Isakov could have continued down Sovietskaya and taken shelter in the portico of the Drama Theater, instead he walked back and forth along a wrought iron fence. He wore a poncho with the hood back and by the dampness of his hair he had been outside for some time. Arkady thought Isakov might be waiting for someone, but he showed no signs of looking up and down the street.

The buildings behind the fence were obscured by trees, but they seemed to be typical pre-revolutionary mansion turned municipal office. Walls maybe yellow, white trim. The gate had a guard post, but the night guard had been replaced by closed circuit surveillance cameras. Nothing special, except that it was the same gate that Sofia Andreyeva had spit at.

The cell phone rang. Arkady snatched it up. Across the street, in his own world, Isakov didn't appear to hear.

On the phone Eva said, "I want to see you."

He had imagined there would be conversation, explanation, expressions of regret.

Instead, when she came through the door of the apartment, he removed her jacket and pressed her against the wall and found the hook of her skirt, a voluminous Gypsy affair, while she unbuckled his belt. In a moment he was in her, past the cool skin to the heat within. Eva's eyes were huge, as if she were in a car that was rolling over and over in slow motion.

"Take off your blouse."

Just the way she lifted the blouse over her head was graceful, Arkady thought. Her Chernobyl scars melted and every line of her was perfect. He pulled her to the floor. She managed to pull out the lamp plug and in the dark she hung onto the cord as if it were a lifeline. The back of her head hit the floor with every thrust, and when his anger was spent she kept him inside until he was hard again, so that the second time he could be gentle.

22

Arkady said, "I think Napoleon slept here. This bed is about his size."

"It's perfect," said Eva. "I slept like a cat."

He was always struck by her smoothness. In comparison, he was wood, bark and all.

"How is your head?" she asked.

"Improved."

"But you haven't seen Stalin?"

"No."

"Or his ghost?"

"No."

"You don't believe in ghosts."

"Not flying through the air, but waiting."

"Waiting for what?" Eva asked.

"I don't know. Maybe political consultants." He reached to the floor and refilled two glasses of the professor's Bordeaux. "Today is the last day of the campaign. Is Isakov confident?"

"Yes, as a matter of fact, but I don't want to talk about him. This is good wine."

"French. Everything here is French. In fact, even our

situation is extraordinarily French. Until someone dies, then it's Russian. Pushkin had over a hundred lovers and then died in a duel defending his wife's honor. She was a flirt. Is that irony or justice?"

Eva said, "We had a seminar on Pushkin at the hospital."

"Poetry in the workplace. Excellent."

"They said that the bullet that killed him penetrated Pushkin's right pelvic bone and traversed his abdomen."

"I think he would have preferred one through the heart." He set down his glass and pulled her close to draw in the scent of her neck. "Have you ever noticed that when one lover leaves the bed, the other rolls into that space?"

"Is that true?"

"Absolutely true." Something struck him. "Are you aware that Isakov gets up in the middle of the night to pace up and down Sovietskaya Street?"

Eva took a moment to adjust to the change in subject. Her voice flattened a little. "I didn't know he did. Marat mentioned once when we were driving on Sovietskaya that Nikolai's father used to work there."

"Where was 'there'?"

"I didn't notice. You don't like Nikolai."

"All I know for certain about Nikolai Isakov is that he's a poor detective."

"He's a different man here. You don't see the real Nikolai in Moscow or Tver; his natural setting is a battlefield. Do you want to know how we met?"

Arkady didn't want to know.

"Sure."

"The Russians were shelling a Chechen village of absolutely no military value. All the village men were in the mountains and only women and children were left, but I think the Russian artillery had a daily quota of houses to destroy. I was picking hot shrapnel out of a baby when Nikolai and Marat arrived with their squad. It was a situation I always dreaded, caught giving aid to the enemy. I half expected to be shot. Instead, Nikolai shared his medical supplies and when the Russians began shelling the village again Nikolai got on the radio and told them to stop. The colonel in charge of the guns said orders were orders. Nikolai asked his name so he could personally punch his teeth in and the shelling stopped at once. All I can tell you, Arkasha, is that Nikolai and I met under strange circumstances. Perhaps we were both at our best. We were people who couldn't exist in the real world. Anyway, this was all before I met you. It has nothing to do with you. Don't get involved with Nikolai."

Something rustled at the front door. Arkady rose from the bed, pulled on pants and looked through the peephole. No one was in the hall but on the apartment floor was a string-tied envelope. He turned on a lamp.

"What is it?" Eva sat up.

He opened the envelope and drew out two glossy photographs. Major Agronsky had delivered and fled.

"Pictures."

"Of what? Let me see."

He brought them to the daybed. The first photo

was taken from about a hundred meters in the air and included a stream and a stone bridge with a van on one side and an armored personnel carrier on the other. By the APC was a campfire. The picture was grainy and enlarged to the max, but Arkady counted half a dozen bodies slumped around the fire. The Chechens were in sweaters, sheepskin vests, woolen caps, running shoes, boots. Skewers of meat, flatbread and bowls of pilaf were scattered with them. Six more bodies were facedown on the road.

The Black Berets had grown beards and wore a mix of Russian and rebel gear, but their characters shone through. Urman held a Kalashnikov and a skewer of kabobs, Borodin and Filotov waved off the helicopter, Kuznetsov lay wounded and Bora kicked bodies, his pistol ready for a coup de grâce. Treetops bowed in the wash of the rotors. In a corner the camera conveniently tagged the time at 13:43. The second photo, tagged 13:47, was virtually identical. The bodies around the campfire were arranged a little differently. There was food enough for a welcome, but not for a feast. The van was gone. Urman had dropped the skewer and aimed his rifle at the helicopter.

"The Sunzha Bridge."

Eva said, "I thought we were past this."

"I had some questions."

"You have an obsession about Nikolai."

"I want to know what happened."

"Why? This was war. Are you going to investigate

everything that happened in Chechnya? I'm in your bed, but you're in love with questions."

Arkady wanted to drop the subject but was drawn by an irresistible gravitational pull. "So I won't have any more questions, tell me from your point of view what happened. Forget the official report. What happened at the bridge?"

"You know, Nikolai wasn't even at the bridge. My motorcycle broke down and he drove me on my rounds of the villages, mainly because you never knew where the Russian checkpoints were or how nasty and drunk the men would be. If they thought you were with the rebels they would rape you and kill you. There were times that would have happened without Nikolai's protection. That's why neither of us is in the photographs."

"Isakov deserted his post to serve as your personal driver?"

"I suppose you could put it that way."

"Did you recognize any of the rebels?"

"They were in bags when we returned to the bridge."

"You never saw them before?"

"No. I said they were in bags."

"Then the man in charge at the bridge was Marat Urman? He led the fight?"

"I suppose so."

"All this time Nikolai Isakov has been taking the credit for Urman's deeds?"

"Taking responsibility in case there were problems."

"Why should there be problems?"

"I don't know."

"If the Chechens were attacking, why were the bodies in the road shot in the back? Why were the others eating? Where are their weapons?"

"I don't know."

"Didn't Isakov unzip the bags to look at the bodies?"

"I don't know."

"Did Urman resent losing the credit?"

"Marat worships Nikolai."

"Everyone in the squad went along with that story?"

"Everyone worshipped Nikolai."

"What about you?"

"Yes," she said.

Arkady felt his heart race with hers. Well, they were working at something both perverse and difficult, the killing of love. That could raise a sweat.

"But this was all before I met you," Eva said. "If you want to we can get in your car and go. We can do it now, while it's dark. Take the car and go to Moscow."

"I can't," Arkady said. "I can't miss Stalin."

"Are you insane?"

"No, I'm getting closer. I have a feeling this time I might see him."

"Seriously?"

"He knew my father."

"Why are you suddenly so mean?"

"Eva, I have a reliable witness who places Isakov at the bridge with bodies on the ground immediately after the fight. In fact, he's so reliable he's dead."

Eva got out of bed and collected her clothes without looking in Arkady's direction.

"I have to go."

"I'll see you at the dig."

"I won't be there."

"Why not? It's the big event."

"I'm leaving you and Nikolai."

"Why both? Choose one."

"I don't have to choose, since one of you will kill the other. I don't want to be here for that. I don't want to be the prize."

His father said, "I loved her but your mother was a bitch. She came from a stuck-up family. Intelligentsia." He said the word as if it were a species of insect. "Musicians and writers. You and I, we live in the real world, right?"

"Yes sir." Arkady, fourteen, blindfolded with his own Young Pioneers scarf, was assembling a pistol. It was a game his father had invented. As Arkady raced the clock the General would try to distract him, because noise and confusion were an ordinary part of battle. Or move pieces around the table so that Arkady had to relocate them by feel.

"She was very young and wanted to know about women, so I told her in detail. I afforded her a view of sex that was more animal than her fainthearted friends were used to. One evening was devoted to Pushkin. It was a salon. Everyone brought in their favorite verse. Very artsy.

I brought Pushkin's diary. It had all the women he shagged in intimate detail. The man could write. You agree?"

"Yes sir."

"You like that gun?"

"Yes sir."

The gun, a Tokarev, came together in Arkady's hands. He held the slide upside down, inserted the barrel into the recoil spring assembly, one end of the spring hanging loose, cradled the frame into the slide, turned the gun right side up and he was nearly done.

His father said, "I knew a man who swore by the Walther. Now here was an expert. He worked at night in a special room insulated for sound with a felt-lined door. His assistants would bring in a prisoner and he would shoot the prisoner in the back of the head. No conversation or nonsense about last words. All night, every night, one at a time, one hundred executions, two hundred executions, whatever the quota was. The workload was intense and halfway through the night the room was an abattoir. To keep him working, he was given a bottle of vodka. Every night, vodka and blood. The point is, the Walther never misfired, not once." The General kicked the table. The recoil spring and barrel bushing flew off the table and under the couch he was sitting on. Arkady heard the spring roll over the parquet floor and felt his father's boots in the way.

"Excuse me," Arkady said.

His father didn't move. "'Excuse me'? Is that what you

plan to say when you meet the enemy? One minute left. You're running out of time."

The punishment for running out of time varied from a cold stare to standing with arms outstretched, a gun in each hand. The guns were loaded and Arkady occasionally thought his father was trying to goad him into rage.

Arkady dove under the couch, found the spring and felt for the bushing to hold the spring in. It was at his fingertips, but every time he touched the bushing it moved. From the other direction his father was too much in the way.

"I met this expert on guns because I got the dirty work, the assignments no one else would carry out. Stalin himself would take me aside and say there was an error here or there that demanded correction, something that the fewer knew about the better and that he would remember me when batons were handed out. I thought I was the elephant in the parade. It turned out I was the man who followed the elephant with a shovel and a pail full of shit. Ten seconds. Haven't you got that damn gun together yet?"

Arkady extended his reach with the gun to haul in the bushing. He backed out from the sofa, inserted the spring, rotated the bushing into place, slapped the magazine home in the grip and whipped off his blindfold.

"Done!"

"Well, are you? That's the question. Give it."

The General took the gun, put it to his temple and squeezed the trigger. The hammer didn't move.

"It's on half cock." Arkady took the gun and thumbed the hammer back a notch. He returned the gun to his father. "Now it's on full cock."

In his father's eyes was desolation.

"I have homework," Arkady dismissed himself.

It was the last time they played that game.

Victor said, "A New Russian goes into an expensive boutique and asks the clerk what to get his wife for her birthday. Cost is no problem. He's already given her a Mercedes, diamonds from Bulgari, a full-length sable coat."

Arkady asked, "How long is this joke?" It was six a.m. by his watch. A little early for a call.

"Not long. The clerk says, 'There's nothing left to buy. Do something personal, something intimate. Give her a written certificate good for two hours of wild sex, fulfilling any fantasy or desire.' The New Russian says, 'Yeah!' It sounds like a win-win to him. He pays a calligrapher a thousand dollars for an inscribed certificate worth two hours of sex, all fantasies fulfilled, no questions asked."

"God, please strike Victor dead."

"Patience. A certificate for two hours of wild sex. Her birthday comes. He gives her pearls, a new Mercedes, a Fabergé egg as usual and finally an envelope with the certificate inside. She takes it out, reads it, her face turns red. A smile breaks out. She clutches the certificate to her breast and says, 'Thank you, thank you, Boris. This is the most wonderful present I ever got. I love you, I love you!' She grabs her car keys. 'See you in two hours!'"

Black as a pit. Arkady stood in the dim illumination from the street, putting himself in a classic dilemma. Look for cigarettes where they most likely were or search where the light was best. A few snowflakes melted on the asphalt.

Victor said, "So, who is the 'two hours' in Tver?"

"Your ability to reduce everything to sex is astonishing."

"It's the best system I've come across."

A bonanza. Arkady found a pack in his jacket, though no matches.

Victor said, "Zurin called and asked where you were. A prosecutor from Tver, a cretin named Sarkisian, called and asked why you didn't check in at the office. It's given me a chance to hone my antisocial skills."

"Why are you up at this hour?" Arkady remembered seeing matches in the kitchen.

"I'm on a stakeout."

"You called me to stay awake on a stakeout?" Arkady felt for matches on the kitchen counters and table.

"I want to tuck this guy in. He had company before but he's alone now. I just wish he would open the refrigerator door, take a piss, strike a match, anything I can report."

"What's he done?"

"An army deserter. Which is okay with me, but the little prick took his rifle with him."

Arkady looked at the one-car sheds across the street.

A good push and a row of them would collapse. His car was four sheds in.

"Are the lights out?" Arkady asked.

"The whole flat."

"What makes you think he's up?"

"Because he can't sleep."

"Maybe somebody called him in the middle of the night." Arkady found matches on the windowsill. "Have you ever been to Tver?"

"Once or twice. Have you seen any of Isakov's OMON friends in Tver?"

"Once or twice."

Cars outside the sheds were parked haphazardly along the curb and on the sidewalk. They all looked cold except for one: there was a steamed-up windshield on a blue compact, Honda or Hyundai; Arkady couldn't see the license plate. Most likely, the condensation was the heavy respiration of lovers seeking privacy where they could. All the same, he decided he didn't need a cigarette. What he needed was a gun and he had left that in Moscow under lock and key.

Victor said, "An intelligence test is given at OMON."

"Is this another joke?"

"The Black Berets are each given ten wooden blocks of different shapes to put in holes of corresponding shapes. Half the men fail but half the men succeed, from which the researchers conclude that fifty percent of the Black Berets are abysmally stupid and fifty percent are really strong."

"Is that funny?" Arkady asked after a while.

"I suppose it depends on the situation."

Arkady dreamt of a small, hunchbacked man standing in the open door of a helicopter high up. The wind tried to suck him out or shake him free but he rode the bounces with the calm of an athlete.

"Ginsberg! Watch out!" Arkady shouted from a bench.

Ginsberg, meanwhile, was yelling to the pilot to go lower. The sound of the rotors was enormous and everyone resorted to hand signals.

Through the door was a vista of mountains, villages, cultivated land, a flock of goats, a valley stream with a stone bridge and a campfire and bodies on the ground. Ginsberg clung to the fuselage with one hand and held a camera with the other. He began shouting Arkady's name and pointed with his camera hand.

Arkady woke and went to the professor's desk and rummaged through drawers until he found a magnifying glass. What had he missed?

At 13:43, kebabs were cooking on the campfire. In the campfire group three bodies lay on their left side, four on their right. The bodies on the road were facedown because they were shot in the back as they ran for the truck on the other side of the bridge. Altogether they added up to fourteen, meaning none on the far bank of the so-called firefight. No sign of Isakov. The photo was too blurred otherwise by the dust kicked up by the helicopter and its own vibration.

The 13:47 photo was taken from the same position on a pass four minutes later. Urman wore sunglasses as he put the pilot in his rifle sights. The bodies on the road hadn't moved a millimeter, but all the bodies around the campfire had rolled forward as if praying in the Muslim manner and the kebabs were smoking, half on fire. What else had changed from one picture to the next? Something too obvious to see. He apologized to Ginsberg and returned to bed.

So he would keep things simple. Ride out to the dig and wait for a ghost. What could be simpler than that?

His cell phone rang at seven a.m. from a number new to him. He was dressed in camos, ready to get to the dig before dawn. Night was already fading to gray flecked with snow. The blue car was gone and Arkady didn't see any unusual activity around the Zhiguli shed. The phone went on ringing while he paused at the professor's shelves and desk, idly looking for a weapon; all French paperbacks, nothing with heft.

Arkady finally picked up.

"Hello?"

"It's Zhenya. I came on the train. I'm here."

23

The Russian dead sometimes carried plastic cylinders with a scroll of paper bearing a name, rank and blood type, but, otherwise, nature had digested everything but bones and identity was a matter of conjecture. Likely Russian skulls were stacked up in the trenches and German remains piled in a central heap.

Trophies of the first day were as reverently displayed as holy relics. Tables were covered with the flotsam of war: brass cartridges, machine gun belts, aluminum canteens, encrusted bayonets, mess tins, lieutenant's bars, a crushed bugle and half-sized, withered rifles.

Zhenya lugged a backpack heavy with a chessboard, clothes and rubber boots for wading in Lake Brosno. Arkady had brought him only because there was no alternative. Put Zhenya on a train to Moscow and he'd be on the next train back to Tver. So far Zhenya seemed to consider the dig a worthy detour, lingering at each display with fascination, the monster in Lake Brosno temporarily out of mind. He inserted a finger through a bullet hole in a helmet and stole a glance at Arkady.

Crews digging since the day before exposed a network

of bunkers two meters deep and fifty meters long, taking care to keep remains whole and not detach feet or fingers. Two skeletons were found in an embrace, one with a dagger, the other with a bayonet. A tent with the front canvas rolled up was being readied for pathological examination.

All of this was preliminary to opening the ground beneath the pines, marked off-limits by a red tape on stakes 30 meters from the camp. The general mood was one of solemn excitement, and enough snow fell to add an auspicious sparkle to the day.

Big Rudi tugged at Arkady's sleeve. The old man had polished his medals and donned a moth-nibbled army fore-and-aft cap in honor of the occasion.

"My grandson Rudi told them where to look, but they won't put him on television."

"It's all horseshit." Rudi appeared at Arkady's other side. The biker's fashion note was a bulletproof vest. "They're amateurs and they resent a professional."

"I thought you were a Red Digger."

"Do I look like the sort of fuckless wonder who's going to dig up dead bodies for free? If they want to play around mines, let them."

"You don't like mines."

"They're so . . . I can't even find the word for it."

"Perverse," said Arkady.

"Yeah, that's the word. Or mind-fucking. A landmine is just as happy disabling you as killing you. Happier. When you see your pal blow up and come down screaming without a leg, you don't check for tripwires. You rush in to help and trip more mines and disable more men. You can't outrun it either." Rudy hitched up his armor and shirt to show his back, an expanse of mixed colors.

"The German spoon you found?"

"On the Internet, thank you."

"Have you seen Stalin?" Big Rudi asked Zhenya.

"The one that skinheads talk about? I thought he was dead."

Big Rudi patted Zhenya on the head. "He was. Now he's back."

Nikolai Isakov wore camos with the tiger head emblem and the red star shoulder patch of the Red Diggers. He didn't give a speech so much as share stories of battles won and lost. In the war against terror sacrifices had to be made. But sacrifices by whom?

"Has Mother Russia abandoned her children? Or have we been led astray by a superrich elite so devoid of spiritual values that it would steal the coins off the eyes of our dead heroes? The men whose remains lie on the fields around us answered with their lives the order 'Not one step back!' The question is, who will stand fast for Russia now?"

Every word was taped by the television crew that had been at the chess tournament. Arkady remembered the name of the young, upbeat presenter was Lydia something. Bits of that day were filling in, although he still remembered nothing about being shot. With her raincoat and undimmed smile Lydia put Arkady in mind of a doll wrapped in cellophane. Zhenya was transfixed by a charred and twisted chessboard and pieces made of tin. There was no sign of Eva.

A visitors' tent with brandy, cheese cubes and pistachios was set up for the television people. Pacheco waved Arkady and Zhenya in.

"It's a hell of a combination, Stalin's spectral visit and a new Nazi atrocity. You don't get those opportunities every day," Pacheco said. He and Wiley were outfitted in camos but marked by their white, unsullied hands.

"Do you mind?" Arkady speared cheese with a toothpick from a glass.

"Go ahead."

"Thanks." Arkady introduced Zhenya and filled his hand with cheese.

Wiley said, "We have a bit of a coup, an election eve news event that will feature Detective Isakov. We may have a genuine upset here. Isakov may be the real thing."

"Well, he is the only candidate endorsed by both the living and the dead. I doubt you can do better than that," Arkady said. "There are a few loose ends, though, a homicide here and there."

Wiley said, "Those suspicions seem to be limited to you. Anyway, an image of strength is not a problem. Weakness is a problem. A mass grave is a perfect example of what happens when a threat is ignored."

"And good television?"

"He's catching on," Pacheco said.

Arkady looked around. "Where is Urman?"

"Who knows?" Pacheco said. "Urman is like a genie. I think he hides in a magic lamp."

Wiley said, "He's impulsive. He might be a liability down the line."

They were thinking ahead, Arkady thought. Isakov really had a chance.

"Time to cut the cake," Pacheco said.

All work came to a halt as Diggers with metal detectors crossed the field to the pine trees. The men moved at the pace of mushroom hunters and Arkady heard one mutter over and over, "If treasure be hidden here, make the Devil give it back without shaming myself who am a servant of God. If treasure be hidden . . ." Wherever their gauges spiked or earphones squawked, the men planted a red plastic flag on a wire.

Zhenya wormed his way through the Diggers to Arkady and showed him the tin chess set.

Arkady said, "I'm sorry, but you'll have to put that back."

"Nikolai said I could keep it."

Zhenya pointed to Isakov, who was watching them in return.

"Do you know him?" Arkady asked.

"He's Eva's friend from Moscow. Nikolai's famous. He's my friend too."

Isakov acknowledged Zhenya with a wave and the boy swelled. The detective was growing into his role of a media hero. Lydia and a camera moved in for an interview.

"What do you expect to find here?" she asked Isakov.

"We will find Russian prisoners of war who were slaughtered by their German captors at the onset of the great counteroffensive of December 'forty-one."

"Will the spirit of Josef Stalin then walk the land?"

"That's not for me to say. What will walk the land is a spirit of patriotism. The heroes brutally murdered and buried here symbolize the sacrifice of millions of Russians."

By the time the Diggers with minesweepers emerged from the trees they had no red flags left. One man balanced on his shoulder a long-nosed skull that looked like driftwood.

"Moose!" he shouted ahead. "The whole skeleton's in there."

"Our first find. Shot by a hunter?" Lydia was instantly excited.

The man with the moose skull let it slide off his shoulder to the ground. The antlers were grainy, the skull was smooth. "I don't think so. No signs of it being dressed. It could be ten or twenty years old. Nobody goes in those gloomy trees. Why would they?"

"Maybe it died of old age," Lydia said.

"Maybe it stepped on something," said Rudi.

As Diggers with probes moved into the trees Arkady realized how gray the day was getting and what a black palisade the pines made against the sky.

"Why don't you go home and sit at your computer and make more money from death?" a Digger asked Rudi.

Rudi said, "Because I'm the one who found this gold mine, asshole." Arkady pulled him away, although he wondered why Rudenko had told anyone else; this could have been his private gold mine. Rudi shook free. "Amateurs."

One by one the probers replaced red flags with yellow flags. Pacheco asked, "Renko, why does Detective Isakov look as if he'd like to plunge a dagger into your heart? I want my candidate positive and personable. Would you mind taking a walk? Pretty please?"

Arkady intended to search for Eva anyway. As he moved around the perimeter he was joined by Petrov and Zelensky. The filmmaker was furious. "They had us up the ass. As soon as a network showed any interest we were out the door."

Arkady asked, "How did you pull off the Stalin sighting on the Metro?"

"Let me tell you something else about old age: the dick goes first, but when Tanya gets on the train in a wet fuck-me outfit the old boys steam. And when she jumps up and says she sees Stalin, the geezers swear they see him too. Without a law being broken."

"Why the Chistye Prudy Station?"

"It's a wartime station. We couldn't have Stalin show up at a station with a shopping mall."

Petya said, "By the way, watch out for Bora. First you

almost drown him dead and then you spray his older brother and almost blind him."

"The boxer with sore knuckles? Interesting family."

Arkady disengaged and watched for Eva. She had come to him and all he'd had to do was be an agreeable lover and keep his questions to himself and he and Eva would be in Moscow now. People said that good marriages were built on honesty. Arkady suspected that as many solid relationships were based on a lie shouldered by two.

After the top layer of needles and earth was declared safe other Diggers moved in with wheelbarrows and shovels. Arkady completed his circuit and found that Zhenya had moved beside Isakov, who rested his hand lightly on the boy's shoulder. Zhenya was honored, as any lad would be, although Arkady heard Wiley ask Pacheco, "Is this the most photogenic kid we could find?"

A shout from the trees indicated that a body had been found. Lydia and a camera followed as the remains were carried on a litter to the examination tent, which was outdoor theater. Onlookers jockeyed for position to observe a pathologist in a lab coat and surgical mask separate bones, boots and a pot-shaped helmet. She turned the skull and untangled a metal disk—a Wehrmacht ID—on a chain.

"German!" the doctor declared, and expressions of satisfaction went around the crowd.

Marat Urman arrived and Isakov passed him possession of Zhenya, who basked in their attention. The three of them made their way to Arkady.

Isakov said, "Zhenya wants to go to Lake Brosno and

look for sea serpents. I told him that as soon as the election is over Marat and I will take him. We might plug the beast and mount it."

"Arkady doesn't carry a gun," Zhenya said. "I remind him but he always forgets."

Urman said, "That's because he's a member of the hole-in-the-head club. Anything you say goes right through."

Zhenya snickered although his face was red with embarrassment.

The topsoil around the trees yielded a few rusty cartridges, food tins and mess kits. Word came back, however, that when metal detectors were set for a lower level they got more response. Arkady was surprised since execution victims were usually stripped of arms, helmets, watches and rings before they were shot and afterwards of gold fillings. What else would cause a metal detector to spike?

Lydia was a shade paler when she returned with her camera crew from the examination tent, but she was game. "Nikolai Isakov and Marat Urman, as detectives and former OMON officers, people here are talking about the possibility of finding a mass grave at this site. How is this sort of atrocity carried out?"

Isakov said, "Victims are either forced to dig their own grave and then machine-gunned, or killed somewhere else and brought to a grave. If we find Russian prisoners of war, they were probably killed here by German guards afraid of being overwhelmed by the counteroffensive."

Urman added, "You can tell the difference because a

machine gun chews up a body, bones and all. If you're going to transport dead bodies you want as little mess as possible, so you just pop them in the back of the head. Sometimes you have to pop them twice."

It was a reflective moment. A digger raised high a CD player and the wartime anthem rang out across the dig:

Arise, the great country,
Arise for the final struggle,
With the dark Fascist force,
With the accursed horde.

Everyone sang. Zhenya sang with Isakov and Urman. Arkady was sure that when the song was over Big Rudi would point to a shadow or a stirring bough and see Stalin. Before the song ended, however, a voice called from the pines, "A helmet! A Russian helmet!"

"Show time," Pacheco said.

The first helmet was joined by more helmets, bottles, boots, razors, all stained, broken or disintegrating Russian junk. No weapons. Bodies, though, there were. As the day warmed, snow became a soft rain that revealed a cranium here, a kneecap there.

"A two-point bump," Wiley told Pacheco. "If Uncle Joe shows, ten."

The plan was for no retrieval until every red flag was investigated, but the promise of so many Russian heroes waiting to be found was too much. Red Diggers were neither military nor pathologists; when one got a wheelbarrow and started toward the trees he was followed by another and another.

"In an upwelling of patriotism, the people mobilize," Lydia told a camera. "Ignoring red danger flags they are rushing to exhume lost martyrs of the Patriotic War."

Zhenya said, "Let's go with them."

"No one investigated the flags," Arkady said. "They didn't investigate a single one."

Wiley said, "The flags are theater. Decoration. Any ammunition here is sixty years old. It's not going to do anything."

"Can my crew and I get closer?" Lydia asked. "I feel the viewers would want to get closer."

"You'd better have this." Rudi ripped open his vest and handed it to Lydia.

"I can't take it from you."

"Why not?" Rudi said. "I'm not going there."

Pacheco told her, "A little advice. Any time, anywhere you have an excuse to wear body armor on television, you grab it."

"Ready, Captain?" Urman said. "Don't let me down."

Isakov gathered himself together. "Right."

A party of five—Isakov, Urman, Lydia and her two cameramen—trudged toward the trees, following wheelbarrow tracks in the muck. Although Isakov was in the lead, Arkady thought there had been a moment when the bold commander seemed to have cold feet and Urman had to prod him into action.

Something odd was happening ahead. Diggers who had

arrived at the trees in such a hurry spread around the periphery instead of going in.

Zhenya told Arkady, "You're not my father, you can't tell me what to do."

Arkady heard and didn't hear. He was intrigued by Isakov's hesitation.

Wiley said, "The people here must have wondered why there were suddenly pine trees planted in the middle of a productive field."

"They steered their tractors around it until it became invisible," said Pacheco. "You don't see what you don't want to see."

Arkady watched Isakov lead the way to the edge of the trees. All five stopped and crossed themselves.

Zhenya bolted. Backpack and all, he was across the tape and into the field before Arkady had a chance to stop him. Zhenya didn't stay on the wheelbarrow paths but took a mocking, looping route, swinging his backpack as if he'd just been let out of school. All Arkady could do was follow.

As he tramped across the field he reassessed Zhenya and how the boy had shifted his allegiance to Isakov and Urman without batting an eye. Snakes were slower at leaving the nest.

Arkady reached the pines and joined the Diggers staying motionless and mute on the periphery of the stand. A wheelbarrow that trespassed accentuated the unnatural, regularly spaced columns of trees, and rain that escaped the upper canopy fell into silence and a thin blanket of needles. There was no birdsong, no squirrel chatter.

Bodies must have been thrown in sideways, head first, feet first, one on top of the other; Arkady couldn't estimate how many, only that they all appeared part of a violent struggle. A head lifted here, a knee there. Over the years nature's parade of scavengers and microorganisms had stripped the flesh and the remains were not only skeletonized but an interlocking puzzle. Did this skull go on that neck? Did these two hands make a match? When the merest tug pulled the tip from the finger, the finger from the hand, the hand off the arm, where to even begin? The distance between the trees was an unnaturally uniform five meters, but stepping on clear ground meant crushing remains underneath, so Diggers put together composite bodies of whatever they could reach.

"You shouldn't take it so hard," Big Rudi said. He had a way of appearing at Arkady's side when least expected. "War is a meat grinder. Farmers, doctors, teachers? Ground beef. And if Fritz doesn't shoot you, the commissar will. But I miss the camaraderie. I was smoking at your age," he told Zhenya, who was approaching tentatively.

"Did you kill anyone?" Zhenya asked.

Arkady stuck a cigarette in Big Rudi's mouth and lit it. The old man inhaled deeply and coughed up half a lung.

No one stopped the cameraman Grisha from using bones as stepping stones because everyone understood that television ruled. This was the Diggers' moment in the sun. Better than the sun, the camera's eye. Wiley was right, Arkady thought, it was a great visual.

Big Rudi said, "The collective used to have a nice field of wheat here. Nice soil, sandy, well-drained."

"Why didn't the collective take the trees out?"

Big Rudi shrugged. "They had to apply. Someone said no."

"Why would anyone in Moscow care whether a collective farm in Tver cut down trees?"

"Who knows? These were the old days. An order from Moscow took into consideration forces and dangers we knew nothing about."

Arkady watched Grisha's advance through the trees. The cameraman kept each move smooth and slow, a step away a brown line that led to what looked like a pinecone standing up.

"Can I see what—?" Zhenya started toward the cameraman.

"No." Arkady pulled him to the ground and shouted, "Grisha, stop! Land mine!"

Grisha tripped, aimed down, and the ground erupted. When the smoke cleared, the cameraman was soaked in blood, on all fours, blinking, experimentally searching his crotch. Isakov helped Grisha to his feet and out of the trees. Grisha could walk, but Isakov tipped the bones out of a wheelbarrow and put Grisha in. Zhenya disappeared. The Diggers called for a pullback, which became a wholesale retreat to the tents.

Arkady stayed. Now that he knew what to look for, he found more unexploded mines. The POMZ land mine was a Russian creation as successful as the AK-47 and even simpler: seventy-five grams of TNT in a cast iron cylinder crosshatched for fragmentation and mounted on a stake. A trip wire ring looped over the igniter, a cigarette-sized rod that capped the mine. A safety pin hole was provided, although the pin had been pulled long ago. He spread-eagled on the ground studying how to remove the igniter and get to the fuse.

He was tentatively wriggling the stake when he noticed a wire running the other direction. He brushed aside rotten needles and discovered another POMZ. He discovered seven mines altogether on the same trip wire circling a tree, a necklace of ancient POMZs with their safety pins pulled and rigged like a string of holiday lights; if one went off, they all would, spitting shrapnel with a lethal range of four meters.

Probably all duds.

Arkady rolled on his back to dig into his pockets, found his keys, and slid them off the key ring. As occasionally happened under stress, a loud, unwelcome tune began in his head. His brain selected Shostakovich's "Tahiti Trot." *Tea for two and two for tea, me for you . . .*

Although he couldn't straighten the entire ring he did, at the cost of a bloody finger, manage to bend a tip of wire. He rolled onto his front, held the stake steady with one hand, and with the other inserted the wire into the safety pin hole and pulled out the igniter and fuse. Didn't even have to unscrew the fuse. The General always said they came out too easily.

Arkady was wet and covered in needles from head to

toe, unintentionally camouflaged in case Urman came searching. Arkady could tell how much the detective itched to go into action. That was the exciting thing about Urman, his unpredictability. He could be affable company one moment and help you swallow your tongue the next.

Using his makeshift safety pin Arkady disarmed the next two mines in short order. The safety hole of the fourth was rusted shut and demanded exquisite pressure to force open without tripping the wire.

"Nobody near us, to see us or hear us . . ."

What Arkady did not understand was why the mines were set on metal stakes rather than wood. It was as if whoever rigged the POMZs had intended them to stand guard during the war, after the war, forever.

"What are you doing?" Zhenya asked.

Arkady was startled enough to make the trip wire tremble: he had not heard the boy coming.

"Rendering these mines a little less dangerous."

"Huh. You mean, disarming them."

"Yes."

"Then that's what you should say. 'I'm disarming these mines.' That's simple." Zhenya shifted the weight of his backpack. Damp ringlets stuck to his brow. "You're making such a deal out of it. They're all duds according to Nikolai and Marat. Nikolai and Marat would know better than you."

"What about the cameraman Grisha?"

"Scratches. The mine didn't have any real charge left. Marat says Grisha will still be able to scratch his balls."

"Marat said that to you?"

"Yeah. I'm looking for him."

Arkady considered the prospect of Zhenya wandering around land mines and skeletons. Or worse, being near if Arkady tripped a wire.

"I think Marat was looking for you around the pathology tent."

"I was just there," Zhenya said. "That's a long walk."

"Get a lighter backpack."

"I bet Marat could disarm mines like these in his sleep."

"You could be right."

"I'm bored."

"I'm busy," Arkady said with a look that matched.

Zhenya's cheeks went red, the most color Arkady had ever seen in them.

Arkady found a tripwire to follow, but when he crawled forward he felt something scratch his stomach. He rolled away from a mine set as a booby trap deep and on its own. After waiting sixty years, the bomb detonated with the soft pop of a champagne cork.

A dud.

When Arkady looked up, Zhenya was gone, except for his laugh.

24

A steady drizzle could not dampen the spirits of the camp. Although digging was canceled for the rest of the day, no one was leaving because every crew had brought vodka and beer, sausage and bread, fatback and cheese. Besides, twenty remains had successfully been brought in for examination, enough for the pathologist to, once she was done, declare all the victims Russian.

In the visitors tent Arkady listened to Wiley praise Isakov.

"An officer who carries home his wounded men? This is exactly the image people respond to. That tape is being edited in the studio as we speak. It's still only four in the afternoon. If the pathologist gets her act together, you'll make two news cycles as the lead story."

"What if the bodies aren't Russian?" Isakov asked.

"They found Russian helmets."

"What if they aren't?"

Wiley glanced at Lydia, who was occupied signing autographs for admirers at the front of the tent. The cameraman named Yura was on a cell phone to Grisha's wife.

"If they're German?" Wiley dropped his voice. "Admittedly, it won't be nearly as good, but the rescue of Grisha will still sell you."

"Is that what I want to be, sold?"

"With all your heart and soul," Pacheco said. "You crossed that river the day we were hired."

"Nothing like this was mentioned then."

"Nikolai, you're suffering preelection nerves. Relax. This dig is going to put you over the top."

"They're right," Urman said.

"We're just lucky we brought two cameramen." Pacheco raised a glass of brandy. "To Grisha."

"Anyway," Wiley said, "you needed something like this. Your numbers were starting to flatten out."

"Maybe they should," Isakov said. "What do I know about politics?"

"You don't have to. You'll be told what to do."

"I will be informed?"

"That's it." Pacheco said. "It's not a difficult job unless you make it one."

"You'll get plenty of advice," said Wiley.

"And immunity, don't forget," Arkady said. "That has to be a plus."

Yura finished his call. "So, you play chess?" he asked Zhenya.

Zhenya nodded.

"Why don't we have a game while we wait? You can be white."

"D four."

"That's it?"

"D four."

Yura frowned. "Just a second. I thought you had a chessboard in your backpack."

"Do you need one?" Zhenya asked.

Arkady took Zhenya for a stroll.

Despite the rain a good many Diggers tended portable grills. Camping was camping. In their tents crews sang wartime songs overflowing with vodka and nostalgia. A line formed at a laboratory carboy of grain alcohol decorated with slices of lemon. It was a bonding experience for fathers and sons.

"Yura was trying to be friendly," Arkady said. "You could have played on the board."

"It would have been a waste of time."

"He might have surprised you. Grandmaster Platonov was here during the war playing the troops. He played anyone."

"Like who?"

"Soldiers, officers. He said he had some good games."

"With who?"

For Arkady Zhenya's smirk was maddening.

"Anyone," he ended feebly.

They bumped into Big Rudi walking with his ear cocked.

"Can you hear him coming?" he asked Arkady.

A distant cannonade rose and fell.

"I think that's thunder," Arkady said.

"Then where is the lightning?"

"It's too far away to see."

"Aha! In other words, you assume it."

"I'm guessing," Arkady admitted. "Wouldn't you like to get out of the rain?"

"Granddad won't go." Rudi approached with a beer in hand. "He's set in his mind. And he's not the only one."

Arkady looked down along the tents and saw other figures standing like sentries in the rain. He thought that between the patriotism and grain alcohol Stalin was bound to make an appearance.

There was a great bustle at the examination tent, where the presenter Lydia was suddenly illuminated by television lights. She was joined by an older woman with sharp eyes and a sardonic smile. Arkady recognized his real estate agent, Sofia Andreyeva. He remembered how she had admitted to being a doctor and warned him not to be her patient. She changed to a clean lab coat while the Diggers packed together around the tent, boys on father's shoulders, cell phones set on video and held as high as a homecoming salute to heroes finally rescued from the grip of the earth! Let it rain. Every face was bright with zeal. Arkady joined Wiley and Pacheco at the back of the crowd. Zhenya found a chair to stand on. Urman cleared the way to the front for Isakov.

Wiley told Arkady, "At the end of most campaigns I ask myself what opportunity I missed. What could I have done that I didn't do? But this is like breaking the bank at Monte Carlo. You should be happy too. Now that Nikolai has immunity he's certainly going to lay off you."

Arkady decided that Wiley was stupider than he looked.

"Can everyone hear me? Good. I am Doctor Sofia Andreyeva Poninski, pathologist emeritus at Tver Central Hospital. I was requested to attend this mass exhumation and offer an opinion as to the identity of bodies found. Not necessarily individually but as a group. I could carry out an examination in much greater detail in the morgue, but I am informed that you need a conclusion here and now. Very well.

"I examined twenty remains, more or less. I say 'more or less' because it is obvious many of the so-called bodies are a mix of bones from two or three or even four different skeletal remains. This, of course, is one of the hazards of amateurs attempting a task best left to forensic technicians. So, I can offer you only gross observations of mishandled remains.

"First, that all twenty pelvic bones I examined were male.

"Second, by the density of their bones and wear on teeth enamel, that their ages at the time of death ranged from approximately twenty to seventy years of age.

"Third, that by variations in bone density some were active and athletic, some sedentary.

"Fourth, that the skeletons as offered suffered no wounds apart from a single shot to the back of the head. It's possible there were flesh wounds that did not involve trauma to the bones. The absence of trauma also indicates that the victims were not subjected to physical abuse. In twelve instances there are signs of charring of the cranium consistent with execution at contact or very short range, and also consistent with execution one victim at a time, rather than a writhing mass. Which indicates that the deceased were shot at one site and transported here. The location of the fatal shots—twelve degrees below the cranial equator, in other words, below and to the right of the back of the skull—was remarkably similar, suggesting the possibility that a single right-handed individual carried out the execution, although he no doubt had accomplices.

"Fifth, the victims' teeth showed generally good care and no German amalgam fillings.

"Sixth, one skeleton wore a leg brace. I was able to remove rust from the maker's plate, which gave an address in Warsaw. Other objects found in the accompanying soil included a silver locket, perhaps once secreted in a body cavity, that expressed romantic sentiments in Polish; a jeweler's loupe engraved with the name of a stamp dealer in Krakow; a pillbox with a view of the Tatra Mountains, and Polish coins of the prewar era.

"In sum, not enough information is yet available for us to draw firm conclusions, but indications are that the victims were Polish nationals . . ."

Where there was nostalgia there was amnesia. People tended to forget that when Hitler and Stalin carved up Poland, Stalin took the precaution of executing twenty thousand Polish Army officers, police, professors, writers, doctors, anyone who might form a political or military opposition. At least half were killed in Tver. Buried beneath the trees was the cream of Polish society.

The Diggers exhibited deflation and confusion. This was not the outcome the men had expected, not the laurels for a mission accomplished, not the bonding they had planned. This was a definite fuckup. Someone had sent them to the wrong dig and Rudi Rudenko, the Black Digger, the so-called professional, had suddenly disappeared. If Big Rudi said he saw Stalin one more time someone was going to lay him out with a shovel.

Sofia Andreyeva drew herself up and asked, "Did you hear me in the back? Was it clear enough for you? The victims are Poles, killed and buried here on Stalin's orders. Do you understand?"

The Digger crew leaders convened under an umbrella. Understand? They understood that she was a fucking, Polish whore of a doctor. They should have made sure and gotten a Russian. They also knew that it was no fun to camp in the rain. Kids sniffled in camos that had resisted rain all day and were now soaked through on a cold evening that was getting colder when a hot bath and pepper vodka was what the doctor ordered. Not this doctor. A Russian doctor. A thunderclap decided it. They were breaking camp.

In a flurry of flashlight beams the tents came down, crews rolled tarps up from the trenches, boys stuffed Wehrmacht helmets into pillow cases. Unwieldy items like metal detectors, coolers and grills were cursed as they were portered in the dark, and cursed a second time surrounded by milling vehicles attempting to reverse direction over the ruts of a one-lane dirt road. Thunder and the smoke of campfires lent an aspect of retreat under fire.

Yura backed up the television truck to the pathology tent. Lydia dove in and shook her hair. A Mercedes eased its way to Wiley and Pacheco.

"That's it? You're quitting?" Arkady asked.

Wiley said, "The son of a bitch said he was afraid of this. He knew something."

"Who?"

"Detective Nikolai Isakov, our candidate. He said he'd been waiting years for this."

"This what?"

"Something about his father. Believe me, it no longer matters."

Pacheco said, "No one is going to put on the air what we just saw. A Russian atrocity? They'd hang us by our heels first."

"Say good-bye to Nikolai for us," Wiley said.

"We had fun," said Pacheco. "If Stalin shows up, say hello for me."

Zhenya's wet hair was plastered to his forehead because he refused to pull up his hood no matter what Arkady said. Together, they helped Sofia Andreyeva put a skeleton in a body bag. She was laughing and crying at the same time.

"Did you see them run? Poof, the mighty encampment is gone. Stuffed into their cars with someone, I hope, feeling nauseous. What a shame. They came to glorify the past and the past serves up the wrong victim. Some days I curse God for letting me live so long, but today it was worth it. Everybody has a fantasy. Professor Golovanov dreams of a beautiful Frenchman. I dream of a Polish boy, a medical student."

The rain fell heavier. Arkady was on the verge of shouting just to be heard.

"Do you have a ride back to the city?"

"I borrowed a car, thank you. I'm just going to sit here for a while with my compatriots. I have a camp chair. I have cigarettes. I even . . ." She allowed him a glimpse of a silver flask. "In case of a chill."

"The road will be mud soon, don't wait too long."

"It will turn to snow. I much prefer snow; it has panache."

"Where is Isakov?"

"I don't know. His friend headed back to the fir trees for more bodies. He claims that there are Russian remains and that you didn't dig deep enough or in the right place."

Zhenya said, "I bet he's right. Marat's a soldier; he should know. I don't see why we couldn't help."

Arkady said, "Stumbling around explosives in the dark is not a good idea."

"If you're afraid to get into the dig yourself, you could hold a flashlight for someone else. I have a flashlight in my backpack."

"You've come prepared for anything."

"Someone has to."

"No. We're going home. We're going to Moscow tonight."

It felt to Arkady as if it had been night for days. Nothing had worked out as expected. Instead of winning Eva he had lost her. And in Tver there was no way he could escape Marat and Isakov.

Zhenya said, "I'm going to Lake Brosno with Nikolai and then we're going to Swan Lake."

"Swan Lake? Like the ballet?"

Sofia Andreyeva said, "It's a local myth, a haven that does not exist for swans that do not exist."

"Swans, monsters, weeping virgins. And dragons."

"I'm sorry, no dragons," Sofia Andreyeva said.

"You said there were dragons when I took the apartment."

"So you take your shoes off, yes. You walk on an old dragon softly."

It took Arkady a moment. "It's a rug."

A shadow moved across the campground, levitating over paper wrappers and empty bottles left in the Diggers' hasty departure. Closer, the figure became a black and shiny ghost that billowed and snapped in the rain. Arkady watched for Stalin's bristling mustache, greatcoat, yellow eyes. Instead it was Big Rudi in a plastic bag with holes for his head and arms and his cap jammed on his head. Rudi followed with the sort of box flashlight a mechanic might set on a fender. The beam was off.

"Granddad is still looking for Stalin. He's in his own world."

Sofia Andreyeva allowed Big Rudi a sip of brandy using the cap of her flask as a cup. "I don't want to see him in the morning on a slab."

"Any vodka?" Big Rudi inquired.

"I think he's back in our world." She said to Rudi, "I noticed you when I was describing the remains. You stood out."

"Thank you." Rudi was flattered.

"You are a Black Digger, a professional."

"Yes."

"You dig to make money."

"I'm a businessman, yes."

"I wonder how much money would you demand to go into those trees tonight?"

"You couldn't give me enough."

"Why not?" Arkady asked. "Don't you think the mines are harmless?"

"Every year a 'harmless' mine blows off someone's leg."

"But a professional like you would see the mine."

"Maybe."

Arkady looked to see Zhenya's reaction, but the boy was gone. A flap at the back of the tent was untied.

"May I borrow your flashlight for a moment?"

Arkady stepped out into the rain, turned on the beam and did a 360-degree sweep of trenches, smoldering campfires, beer cans, mound of skulls, piles of soil. Zhenya was on the field at the edge of the beam's reach, halfway to the trees. He had his hood up and in his black anorak he would have been invisible except for the reflective trim on his backpack. The reflection got weaker and weaker.

It occurred to Arkady that when he had so abruptly left Moscow for Tver, Zhenya may have felt abandoned. All the conversations on the phone about monsters may have been a boy hanging on for an invitation that was never issued. Arkady hadn't even said when he was coming back. And when Zhenya came to Tver was he appreciated or treated like excess baggage? Valuable insights but a little late.

At night the pines were a solid wall rising from the field, and though the rain eased up, the boughs dripped and with every step Arkady sank ankle-deep in damp needles. He followed winks of yellow light to a lamp set in the center of the stand, a clearing five meters across where Urman dug like a stoker while Zhenya sifted. The detective was stripped to the waist and looked like a muscular Buddha except for his shoulder holster and gun. He had already dug a fair-sized hole.

"Any luck?" Arkady asked.

"Not yet," Urman said. "But things will go a lot faster now that I have a partner."

Zhenya kept his face a blank. Arkady noticed Urman's shirt and leather coat neatly folded on a tree root next to Zhenya's backpack.

Arkady asked, "Zhenya, have you ever noticed how much a pine forest smells like a car freshener?"

Zhenya shrugged, not in a mood for humor.

Arkady asked Urman, "Where is your partner?"

"Nikolai is going to get the Americans back. I'll dig up the right remains and we'll tape for television."

"The Americans are gone. In fact, so is Isakov."

"He'll be back and then he'll get them back."

"What do you think, Zhenya?"

"Like Marat says, if we find the right remains . . ."

Urman said, "Perhaps you haven't noticed, Renko, there are a lot of bodies here. It's a mass grave."

A grave where the dead came up for air, Arkady thought. A skull, half-submerged, stared up from the dirt. In the glow of the lamp leg bones resembled candlesticks.

"It's also a minefield," Arkady said. "I don't see a metal detector or a probe."

"We don't have time for all that. Anyway, there's nothing left to blow here."

"You just didn't find it."

"You're trying to scare the kid."

"Maybe he shouldn't be here. I'll stay. If you want, I'll dig for you."

"I'm going to give you a shovel to swing at my head?"

"Whatever you want, as long as Zhenya goes back."

"He doesn't want to go."

Arkady lost patience. "There's no reason to be afraid of me. Granted, you killed some people, but no one particularly cares about the murders except Ginsberg and me. He's dead and I'm in Tver, which is much the same thing. Why the urgency?"

"The people we killed were terrorists," Urman told Zhenya.

Arkady said, "You shot them in the back and in the head. You executed them. And the ones you killed in Moscow were your fellow Black Berets."

Urman shook his head for Zhenya's benefit. "Poor man, that bullet really did scramble his brains. Look, Renko, now the kid's smiling."

It was a sickly smile.

Arkady said, "Zhenya, don't put on your backpack, just run."

Urman stepped out of the hole. "Why should he run and leave his chess set? And what else? Why is the backpack so heavy?" Urman reached into it and pulled out the stripped frame and barrel of a handgun. "Your gun. He brought it for your protection but there never seemed the right moment. In fact, I think that moment has come and gone." He dropped the pieces back in.

Arkady felt the conversation gain speed. Or maybe it was that they tossed their last few words aside like unplayed cards.

"Watch this." Urman took some casual swings with the shovel, not so much to hit Arkady as to maneuver him to the lip of the hole.

"Run," Arkady told Zhenya.

Urman launched the shovel at Arkady's chest like a spear, but Arkady ducked as soon as Urman set his feet, and as the shovel sailed by Arkady rose with a butt to the chin that snapped back Urman's head. "Hit first, keep hitting." Not bad instructions. Arkady hit Urman in the windpipe and went on pounding him until Zhenya got in between and hung onto Arkady's arm.

"Stop fighting!"

"Zhenya, let go."

"No more fighting," Zhenya said.

"No more fighting." Urman had his gun out. "Not for you, old man. This is for Tanya." Urman hit Arkady in the face with the flat of the shovel; Arkady sucked a tooth back in and felt blood drip from his chin.

"Now you're even," Zhenya said.

"Not yet." Urman motioned with his gun for Arkady to get down on his knees. "Hands in back." He handcuffed Arkady and kicked him facedown into the hole. "This is for me." The shovel blade came down wide of its mark, however, and Arkady heard the sound of wrestling above. Urman said, "Now you want to attack me? You want to go with him, you little creep?"

A body fell on top of Arkady. Dirt followed and the scent of pines and the warmth of blood.

Urman said, "I'll dig you up in a couple of hours, remove the cuffs and we'll go find a nice bog for you and your friend. That's the plan. Otherwise, you know what I hate? Long explanations. Blah, blah, blah, blah, blah."

Zhenya moaned but he didn't sound conscious. He might not be until they were covered with dirt, Arkady thought. He twisted his head to breathe and gathered his knees under himself as best he could.

"Go ahead," Urman said. "Squirm like a worm, but you're still buried alive."

Urman shoveled vigorously. He believed in a full spade; dirt fell in clumps.

"Not Zhenya, please," said Arkady.

"Who's going to miss him? I'm doing him a favor."

Dirt showered Arkady's head. When there was no more loose dirt Urman turned and dug new soil. Despite the dirt in his ear, Arkady heard thunder, a motorcycle winding toward the river road, and a mechanical click.

Urman stopped. He stared at three rusty pressure prongs that had been undisturbed in a bed of old needles until the last shovelful. He took a deep breath as the prongs and a canister the size of a coffee can popped out of the ground waist high, almost near enough to touch. It was packed with TNT, ball bearings, and scrap metal, and all he could say to sum up his life was "Fuck!"

25

They returned to Tver, Arkady on the motorcycle, Sofia Andreyeva and Zhenya in her car. The boy had suffered a concussion when Urman hit him and he was alert but silent. Zhenya had been forced to gather the handcuff key from what was left of Urman. A jumping mine had a lateral blast; at close range it could cut a man in half. As the temperature dropped, rain turned to snow. Zhenya clutched his backpack and stared out the window at passing streetlamps, at flakes dancing by glass, at anything rather than the images in his mind.

Arkady and Sofia Andreyeva agreed to keep the story simple: Detective Marat Urman ill-advisedly went to a hot site alone in the dark, stuck a spade into the ground, and hit a land mine. Evidence that anyone else was there had been shredded into a million pieces.

Arkady's plan was simple too. It was time for him and Zhenya to cut their losses and treat the Tver experience as a high fever or a nightmare. Arkady could pack in a minute and Zhenya carried everything in his backpack. Taking stock, Arkady had lost Eva, traumatized Zhenya and ended his less than illustrious career. How much more damage could a man do?

Arkady turned onto Sovietskaya Street, the main thoroughfare. The snow melted as it landed and the street had a photographic stillness, a contrast of silvery tram rails, the sheen of wet asphalt and a couple walking beside a wrought iron fence.

A block farther on at the Drama Theater, Arkady motioned the Lada to pull over and walked back to Sofia Andreyeva while she rolled down her window.

"Do you usually spit in public?"

"Of course not, what a question."

"There's a building we passed. Whenever you go by it, you spit."

"That's not spitting, that's protection against the devil."

"The devil lives on Sovietskaya Street?"

"Of course."

"I think I just saw him." Arkady gave Sofia Andreyeva the key to the apartment. "He's not alone."

They walked along the wrought iron fence, Eva in a coat and scarf, Isakov's hands plunged in the pockets of an OMON greatcoat. They didn't seem surprised when Arkady fell in step with them, other than to take a long look at a bruise that colored half his face.

Arkady offered a one-word explanation. "Urman."

"And how is Marat?" Isakov asked.

"He was digging a hole when he hit a mine. It was a jumping mine. He's dead."

Eva asked, "Where were you?"

"I was in the hole. So was Zhenya. He's all right."

No one was on duty at the guardhouse at No. 6, although through the bars of the fence Arkady spied a black BMW in the courtyard with a driver dozing at the wheel. Closed-circuit cameras were mounted inside the gate and Arkady thought he made out floodlights on the roofline.

Isakov said, "You killed Marat? I find that hard to believe."

"So do I," said Arkady. "What is this building?"

"This was the headquarters of security during the war."

"It's where Nikolai's father worked," Eva said. "Tver's own Lubyanka."

The Lubyanka in Moscow was the maw of hell, a monolith the color of dried blood. In comparison, the building at No. 6 was a frosted cake.

"He was an agent of the NKVD?" Arkady asked.

"He did his part."

"Tell him," Eva said.

Isakov hesitated. "Eva is a stickler for the truth. So, my father. I always wondered how he could be in the NKVD and be treated with such contempt by his colleagues. He was old when I was born and by then a drunk, but at least he had been a spy in the war, I thought, and he acted as if he had guarded secrets of the state. He had a skin condition from washing his hands and the more he drank the more often he would leap from the table to wash and dry his fingers. On his deathbed my father said there was one more Polish grave. When I asked what he was talking about he told me he was an executioner. He never spied, he just shot people. He not only shot them, he kept track of where they went. That was his farewell gift to me: one more Polish grave. Two gifts," he corrected himself. "He gave me his gun too. I found it this morning in a velvet sack, still loaded."

Arkady asked Isakov, "Why are you telling me this?"

"I think it's safe with you."

"I'm cold," Eva said. "Let's walk."

A civilized stroll in a light snow in the middle of the night. With bonhomie.

Isakov put his arm over Arkady's shoulders. "Marat should have eaten you alive. You don't look that strong and, frankly, you don't look that lucky."

"It wasn't me; he dug up a mine."

"Marat knew better than that. He was a Black Beret."

"The elite?"

"Who else? They sent us down to Chechnya to stiffen the troops. Army officers were too drunk to leave their tents and the soldiers were too scared. They'd call in an air strike if they saw a mouse. If they did go out it was to loot."

"What is there to loot in Chechnya?"

"Not much, but we have a looter's mentality. That's why I was a candidate. I want to revive Russia."

"You had political plans?" Arkady asked. "Beyond

immunity, I mean. You admired Lenin, Gandhi, Mussolini?"

As Eva crossed to the Drama Theater, she sang the old ditty, *"Stalin flies higher than anyone, routs all our foes and outshines the sun."*

Arkady couldn't tell whom she was mocking. Snowflakes on her scarf made him aware more snow was falling, which was a return to normalcy. To hell with warm weather.

Eva returned to her place between the men and put her arms through theirs, the three of them a troika. "Two men willing to die for me. How many women can say that? Will you each claim a half or will you take turns?"

"It's winner take all, I'm afraid," Isakov said. He spotted the motorcycle on the theater portico and placed his hand on the engine. "Still warm. I wondered how you were getting around without being seen. Clever."

The neighborhood was not residential; at this hour of night only a few cars were parked on Sovietskaya and no one else was afoot along the dark offices and shops. A terrific shooting gallery.

Isakov's mind must have been running in the same direction because he looked across Eva and asked Arkady with a note of idle curiosity, "Do you have a gun?"

"No."

Actually, for once a gun seemed not such a bad idea. A Tokarev would do, but it was in pieces in Zhenya's backpack.

"Anyway, no gun could match yours," Arkady said.

"When you think about it, your father's gun may hold the record for a single handgun killing the most people. A hundred? Two hundred? Five hundred? That makes it at least an heirloom."

"Really?"

"I feel for him. Imagine shooting people one after the other, head after head, hour after hour. The gun gets hot as an iron and twice as heavy and there must be some uncooperative victims. It had to get messy; he must have had work clothes. And the sound."

Isakov said, "As a matter of fact, my father had earplugs and he still went deaf. Sometimes he would try to leave the room and they would pour vodka down his throat and push him back in. He was just sober enough to pull the trigger and reload."

"He gave his eardrums for the cause. Did the gun ever misfire?"

"No."

"Let me guess. A Walther?"

"Bravo." Isakov pulled a long-barreled pistol out of a sack. "My father liked German engineering." Even in the light of streetlamps the gun showed its nicks. It also looked eager.

A blue and white militia van cruised up Sovietskaya and slowed alongside Arkady, who expected an ID check at the very least. Isakov tucked the Walther into his belt, showed OMON printed on his jacket and bent his elbow in a drinker's salute. The van flashed its head beams and rolled away, purring.

Eva said, "He recognized you. You made his day. You are a hero in their eyes."

Not to mention a killer, Arkady thought. People were complicated. Who could say, for example, which way Eva would lean? It was like playing chess and not knowing which side his queen was on.

Arkady said, "The fight at the Sunzha Bridge sounds like quite a victory."

"I suppose so. The enemy left fourteen bodies and we lost none. There was a raid on an army field hospital earlier that same day. Thank God, we got the message in time."

"You were at the bridge when the attack began?"

"Of course."

"You got a message that in a few minutes half the Russian soldiers in Chechnya would cross your bridge to chase the rebels. Did you worry what they would think if they saw your squad of Black Berets eating grapes and lounging with the enemy?"

"There were some Chechens at the bridge. They turned on us, but we were ready."

A reply steeped in humility. Wrong choice, Arkady thought. Outrage and a punch to the mouth was always a safer answer. Of course, Isakov was painting himself a rational man for Eva's sake. So was Arkady. They were actors and she was their audience. It was all for her.

By the time they arrived back at the wrought iron fence snow was starting to stick and narrow the bars.

"I talked to Ginsberg," Arkady said.

"Ginsberg?" Isakov slowed for the effort of recollection.

"The journalist."

"I've talked to a lot of journalists."

"The hunchback."

"How can you forget a hunchback?" Eva asked.

Isakov said, "I remember now. Ginsberg was unhappy because I wouldn't let him land in the middle of a military operation. He didn't seem to understand that a helicopter on the ground is nothing but a target."

"The military operation was the fight at the bridge."

"This conversation is boring for poor Eva. She's heard the story a hundred times. Let's talk about rebuilding Russia."

"The operation was the fight at the bridge?"

"Let's talk about Russia's place in the world."

"Ginsberg took photographs."

"Did he?"

Arkady stopped directly under a streetlamp and opened his pea jacket. Inside was a folder, from which he took two photographs, one behind the other.

"Both from the air, of the bridge, bodies sprawled around a campfire and Black Berets walking around with handguns."

"Nothing unusual about that," Isakov said.

Arkady held up the other for comparison.

"The second photograph is of the same scene, four minutes later by the camera clock. There are two significant changes. Urman is aiming his gun at the helicopter, and all the bodies around the campfire have been rolled forward or been moved to one side. In those four minutes the most important goal for you and your men was to ward off the helicopter and get something out from under the bodies."

"Get what?" asked Eva.

"Dragons."

"The man has lost it," Isakov said.

"When Kuznetsov's wife said you took her dragons I didn't understand what she was talking about."

"She was a drunk who killed her husband with a cleaver. Is that your source of information?"

"I wasn't thinking about Chechnya."

"Chechnya is over. We won."

"It's not over," Eva said.

"Well, I've heard enough," Isakov said.

Eva asked, "Why, is there more?"

Arkady said, "The rest of the world puts its money in banks. This part of the world puts its money into carpets and the most prized carpets have red dragons woven into the design. A classic dragon carpet is worth a small fortune in the West. You don't want to spill blood on that and, as you said, there's not much else worth stealing in Chechnya."

"The dead men were thieves?"

"Partners. Isakov and Urman were in the rug business. They rolled out the carpet for their partners and then they rolled it up."

Snowflakes swam across the glossy surface of the photographs, over the coals of the campfire, across Marat

Urman's purposeful stride, around bodies sprawled on bloody sand.

"*Now* I see," Eva said.

Isakov had an ear for nuance. "You've seen these photographs before?"

"Last night."

"You told me you were going to the hospital. I watched you pick up the cassettes."

"I lied."

"Renko was with you?"

"Yes."

"And?"

Eva gave Isakov a drawn-out, emphatic "Yes."

Isakov laughed. "Marat warned me. Look at Renko, look at him, the man looks disinterred."

Arkady said, "I feel surprisingly good, considering."

"You don't care if you're dead or alive?" Isakov asked.

"In a way, I feel I've been both."

The Walther reappeared in Isakov's hand.

"Okay, let's be grown-ups. Marat and I did trade in carpets. So what? In Chechnya, everybody did something on the side, mainly drugs and arms. I doubt that saving a precious work of art from a burning house is against the law. Dealers and collectors certainly don't ask questions and the Chechens, if you treated them with respect, were trustworthy partners. But that day, when I got the message from a Russian Army convoy that they were a minute away from the bridge, there just wasn't time to end the lunch, fold the carpets and make nice good-byes. Sometimes you have to make the best of a bad situation."

Eva laughed. When she wanted to deliver contempt she did it well. "You're a rug merchant? Fourteen men dead for rugs?"

"And in Moscow, murdering members of your own squad," Arkady said.

"Loose ends." Isakov motioned for Arkady to be still and patted him down. "You really don't have a gun. No gun, no case, no evidence."

"He has the photographs," Eva said.

"Prosecutor Sarkisian would tear them up. Zurin would do the same." Isakov aimed the Walther directly at Arkady, a certain threshold crossed. "They'll probably let me lead the investigation. You don't have a gun? Maybe this will do. Maybe you found this old gun at the dig. Mainly, you didn't have a plan. You saw Eva and jumped off your bike. Was it worth it just to win her back?"

"Yes." He realized that she was what he had come back for out of the black lake he had sunk into when he was shot.

But part of him was thinking in a professional mode. Isakov would shoot him first, then Eva, and then wrap the gun in Arkady's dead hand to mimic a murder-suicide, all to be carried out on the street at close range and with dispatch. The Walther was a heavy double-action pistol with a long trigger draw and a huge kick. It filled Isakov's hand. No rush but no hesitation either. Arkady remembered Ginsberg's admiration of Isakov's calm under fire.

Was anyone awake at the security monitors, Arkady wondered? In the BMW? He heard far-off machinery, but where was the white van of the militia? Weren't bakers abroad at this hour, on their way to their ovens? Sovietskaya Street was as still as a tomb.

"No gun, no prosecutor, no case, no evidence." Isakov did not stand back to shoot Arkady; he tucked the barrel up under Arkady's jaw at can't-miss range. "And then your lover left. No wonder you're depressed."

"No wonder you're depressed," Isakov's voice repeated from Eva's coat pocket.

She took the tape recorder from her coat, popped the machine open and held up a cassette. Isakov watched in disbelief as she threw it over the fence. The cassette happened to be white and disappeared on the snowy lawn. The bright lights of a motion detector flashed on and off.

Isakov kept the gun tight on Arkady. "Go get it."

"There's a camera at the gate."

"I don't care if you go over, under or through." Isakov let Arkady go and gave him a push. "Get it."

"Or what? I don't think that tape is going to be easy to find. You'll never have time to find it once you fire that old cannon, and you have to find it because it's a full confession. In chess that's called a pin."

A grinding sound announced the approach of snowplows scraping the street. The trucks traveled slowly but majestically in a blaze of light that Arkady and Eva walked next to. From the motorcycle they saw Isakov still in front of the gate, immobilized.

26

Riding to the apartment, Arkady was exhilarated and exhausted, as if he and Eva had crossed a wasteland of betrayal and misunderstanding, and survived. He knew that later they would talk about it and words would diminish the experience, but for the moment they rode the motorcycle in a happy stupor.

Only once she spoke over the noise of the bike, "I have a gift for you." She took a cassette from inside her coat. "The real tape."

"You are a wonderful woman."

"No, I am a terrible woman, but that's what you're stuck with." Waiting for the elevator doors to close they spoke of trivialities, preserving the bubble of the moment.

"Are you still an investigator?"

"I doubt it."

"Good. We can take a trip to someplace with a sunny beach and palm trees."

As the elevator doors began to close a cat with spiky fur came on board, arched its back in surprise, and ran off.

"And Zhenya?" Arkady said.

"We should take Zhenya with us," Eva said.

Why not, Arkady thought? To golden sand, blue water and a regular drubbing on a chessboard. If that wasn't a holiday, he didn't know what was. Eva removed her scarf and snapped off the snow as they stumbled out of the elevator on Arkady's floor. Being happy was like being drunk. He didn't have the usual ballast.

At the apartment door he asked, "Would you like to see a dragon?"

"Let's just get Zhenya and go," she whispered.

Eva entered first. As she turned on the light Bora stepped out of the bathroom. Arkady recognized the same dagger that he had failed to find on the ice at Chistye Prudy. It was double edged and sharp as a razor and Arkady grabbed it only to have his palm sliced open. Bora turned and drove the knife into Eva's side and carried her backwards over the body of Sofia Andreyeva. Sofia Andreyeva's throat had been slit, her face white under garish mascara and rouge. The walls and posters were speckled with signs of struggle. Zhenya was barricaded behind a coffee table in a corner of the room, a long knife in one hand. On the table lay a partially assembled Tokarev awaiting its recoil spring and bushing.

Bora wore rubber gloves and an easy-to-wash training suit. He asked Arkady, "Are you laughing now?"

As he drew the knife out of her, Eva sank to the floor trying to catch her breath.

In the corner Zhenya fumbled the spring and it rolled off the table. It was unfair, Arkady thought. They had been so clever, Eva most of all.

Bora had the confident approach of a butcher, ready to open the belly but willing to start carving an arm or a leg. In films this was where the hero wrapped a cloak around one arm as a shield, Arkady thought. No cloaks seemed to be available. Instead, Arkady tripped on the carpet and went down. At once Bora was on top of him, pressing the bruised side of Arkady's head against the floor.

Bora's breath was hot and damp. "There's a weight room in your courtyard. I was coming out and who do I see pulling off a motorcycle helmet but the man from Chistye Prudy? Remember the fun you had on the ice there? You laughed at the wrong man."

Bora was all muscle, while Arkady got winded climbing stadium steps. Also, he had only one good hand to fend off Bora. Everything was wrong. The red ring around Sofia Andreyeva's neck. Zhenya's despair as the pistol's recoil spring sprang and rolled out of reach. Eva's hoarse efforts to breathe.

Bora leveraged more weight onto the knife.

"Are you laughing?" Bora introduced the knife to Arkady's ear, tickling the fine hairs of the whorl.

Slowly, reluctantly, Arkady's arm gave way. He remembered a dream in which he had failed everybody. He didn't recall the details but the sense was the same.

A chessboard bounced off Bora's head. He looked up and Zhenya fired.

There wouldn't be a second shot, because the boy pulled the trigger without the recoil spring.

There didn't need to be a second shot. Bora was spread

out on the floor, a black hole the size of a cigarette burn in his head.

With wind and snow constantly shifting, it was hard to tell whether the ambulance was making forward progress.

Arkady and Zhenya rode with Eva and a paramedic, a girl with a check list. Eva was strapped into a litter, blankets up to her chin, an oxygen mask cupping her face and wires connecting her to a rack of monitors. On a jump seat, Zhenya hugged his knees.

"She's taking shallow breaths," Arkady said.

The paramedic assured Arkady that while stab victims could die from shock and loss of blood in a matter of seconds, at twenty minutes after being attacked Eva was still conscious, her eyes focused on Arkady and she had hardly bled at all. Arkady tried to seem confident, but the experience was like being in a plunging elevator. He saw the floors go by, but couldn't get off.

Eva lifted the oxygen mask. "I'm cold."

He pulled Eva's blanket back and tore her dress for a better look at the wound, a slit edged in purple between the ribs. There was no external bleeding from the cut unless he applied pressure, then wine-dark blood seeped out.

Waiting.

Arkady and Zhenya sat on a bench outside the scrub room, trying to catch a glimpse of Eva whenever the door opened to the OR she had been rolled into. Arkady measured the hall in footsteps again and again. He stared at the Do Not Smoke and No Cell Phones signs on a wall. At one end of the hall an Emergency Only door accessed the roof; outside, snow was covering the deck and pushing along cigarette butts and empty packs. He flipped through commercial brochures on a table without really reading, "What to do in Tver," "Sovietskaya's Luxury Row" or "How to Win at Roulette." Felt himself petrify. Zhenya hid in Eva's coat, two legs sticking out, until Arkady put his arm around him and thanked him for saving everybody. They would all be dead if it hadn't been for Zhenya.

"I think you're the bravest boy I ever met. The best one ever."

Zhenya's crying under the coat sounded like the tearing of wood.

Elena Ilyichnina came out in purple scrubs dark with sweat and spoke to Arkady in a soft, special tone that offered no false hope at all. "We drained a considerable amount of blood. Doctor Kazka presented little external bleeding, but internally she was drowning. There are so many organs for a knife to hit—the lungs, liver, spleen, diaphragm and, of course, the heart—depending on the reach of the blade. A complete laparoscopy and repair could go on for hours. I suggest you go to the emergency room and have your hand properly looked at."

Arkady could picture the emergency room and its

nocturnal population of drunks and meth-heads vying for attention. Everything but vampires.

"We'll stay."

"Of course. How silly of me to suggest medical attention."

Arkady didn't see why she was so brusque. "Could you please tell me where I can use a cell phone?"

"Not on this floor. Our instruments don't like them."

"Where, then?"

"Outside." She caught him eyeing the Emergency Only door. "Don't even imagine it."

Sick of gazing at the floor, Arkady returned to the brochures on the table. They were glossy foldouts that offered apartments, manicures, intimate restaurants, the chance to meet foreign men. One said, "Sarkisian Carpets. A fine Persian, Turkish, Oriental carpet is a beautiful investment! Dragon carpets, especially, only gain in value. In the auction houses of Paris and London dragon carpets are valued at $100,000 and more!" In the accompanying photo a well dressed man with white hair pointed to a red dragon skulking in the intricate design of a carpet. Arkady inked in the man's hair with a pen and the family resemblance to Prosecutor Sarkisian was complete.

Victor and Platonov arrived from Moscow with cardboard cups of tea.

"Your doctor called me. I called Platonov."

Platonov said, "You and Zhenya didn't think your friends were going to desert you, did you?"

"Do you have a relationship with Elena Ilyichnina?" Arkady asked Victor.

"Sort of. We sat up together when you were in the hospital. We shared the vigil."

"You were drunk."

"A detail. Drink your tea."

The tea looked weak and felt cold. Arkady took a sip and almost spat up.

"A touch of ethanol." Victor shrugged. "There's tea and there's tea."

"It's vile."

"You're welcome." He offered Arkady a pistol and an extra clip.

Arkady declined. "I don't think Elena Ilyichnina called you so we could have a gunfight in her hospital."

"We would be famous. We would be terrorists on the evening news."

Zhenya and Platonov played blindfold chess, exactly what the boy needed to keep his mind occupied. A catalogue for women's lingerie had Victor totally absorbed.

Arkady nodded off and in a dream went for cigarettes. He found a machine in the basement next to the cafeteria, which was closed, and an exhibit of schoolchildren's art.

There were a good many princesses and figure skaters, ice hockey players and Black Berets.

He got confused on the way back, missed a turn and took the wrong elevator to a different part of the hospital. Now he was hotter, sweatier and it was the middle of the day. He heard the drone of outboard engines, dipping oars, the plop of fish, the lassitude of an aluminum boat adrift. Midges hatched from the water, dragonflies feasted on the midges, swallows snatched dragonflies on the wing and horseflies fed on Platonov. He wore an Afrika Korps-style cap to protect his neck and every five minutes went into a spasm of swatting that rocked the boat.

"Bloodsuckers! This is probably why the creature stays in its murky depths."

Platonov dropped the oars back in the water and managed a stroke. He did the rowing because placing his bulk at the bow or stern made the boat unsteady. Zhenya sat up front in a T-shirt and shorts searching through a box of fireworks. He had attained a light tan and even filled out a little. A camera hung on a strap around his neck.

"We only have one more bomb," Zhenya said.

"How are we with sandwiches?" Platonov asked.

Arkady looked in the hamper. "We have plenty. Some of them are a little wet."

"There's no such thing," Platonov said, "as a sandwich that is only a little wet."

Zhenya scanned the water through the camera. "Did you know that some dead bodies don't sink or float, they just hang in the water?"

"Sounds delightful." Platonov dipped his cap in the water and set it back on his head, luxuriating in the cool runoff.

"Tell me the plan again," Arkady said.

Zhenya said, "We set off a bomb, really a big firecracker. The monster is curious, comes over and I take its picture."

"Good plan."

"It will be on the cover of every scientific review," Platonov said.

A dragonfly began to flash around the boat, make figure eights and loops so close to Platonov that he lost his balance. As the boat jerked, he and Zhenya stayed in. Arkady plunged into the water and sank. He was comfortable under the surface, drifting in the shadow of the boat when a larger shadow crossed his line of vision. A sturgeon hundreds of year old, with barnacles and armored ribs, swam by trailing a white veil from its jaws. The giant fish was a metallic gray and each eye was as large as a platter. Arkady followed the veil down to the dark bottom of the lake, where he found Eva trapped by a massive rock he could not budge. Arkady looked up at the boat and saw Zhenya throw something in the water. The bomb! A huge bubble erupted, creating a shock wave that littered the surface of the lake with fish and, below, dislodged the boulder. Arkady took Eva's hand and they rose effortlessly until Victor shook him awake.

"She's coming out."

*

Eva emerged from the OR a deflated version of herself, drenched with sweat, anaesthetized and deaf to the rattle of the drip stand rolling at her side. Then the doors of the Recovery Unit closed behind her.

"Doctor Kazka had a difficult time," Elena Ilyichnina said. She herself looked all in, with shadows under her eyes and the indentation of a surgical mask running like a seam across her face. "The blade moved in an arc after penetration, so we had a number of sites to attend to. One lung was scraped and the diaphragm was perforated. However, there was no damage to the heart. Usually, I would insist on admitting her here for observation, but I understand your special need to return to Moscow and have organized an ambulance. You can make a financial arrangement with the driver."

"But she's out of danger," Arkady said.

"Not as long as she's with you," Elena Ilyichnina observed, regarding the purple side of his face. "You're taking good care of my delicate handiwork? Being careful when you cross the street?"

"I try."

"You know, we are supposed to report any violent crimes to the militia. I'd like to report a man who had a miracle and threw it away," Elena Ilyichnina said and marched through the door to Recovery, leaving Arkady with the sense that his head was on a pole.

Victor said "Our 'special need?' Our need is to get out of this piss pot of a town. Towns like this, you could be anywhere. Russia has towns like Tver all over, like a thousand ugly daughters. It doesn't matter how big they are, they're the same. Same dreary buildings, same empty squares, even the same statues, because we no longer notice how ugly they are. What do you think, gentlemen?"

"I think you've had enough tea," Arkady said.

"We have to get Zhenya somewhere safe." Platonov was suddenly a mother hen.

Arkady said, "Go to the ambulance bay. Work out something with the driver."

"You're not coming?" Victor said.

Arkady watched the last of the nurses leave the scrub room. "Give me five minutes."

Arkady went out the emergency door to the fifth floor deck and climbed a metal stairway to the roof.

He found himself on a shadowy island surrounded by a faint wash of floodlights and populated by ventilation ducts hooded with snow. The spiral bonnets of a vent spun like a dervish. Fans hummed. A duct with a vane shifted nervously with the wind. High ground, perfect for cell phones.

He called Moscow.

The eleventh ring was answered with "Who the devil is this?"

"Prosecutor Zurin, this is Renko."

"Christ."

"I'm coming back. There are two dead bodies in my apartment in Tver. One older female with her throat slit, a very nice woman named Sofia Andreyeva Poninski, and her assailant, Bora Bogolovo, whom I shot and killed." He gave Zurin the address.

"Wait, wait. Why are you calling me? You work in Tver in Prosecutor Sarkisian's office."

"Sarkisian was involved with Bogolovo. Also with Moscow detectives Isakov and Urman in murder, war crimes and receiving stolen goods. I have Isakov's confession on tape."

"Christ."

"It's shocking. Who knows where this may lead?"

"What are you insinuating?"

"Only that this investigation can't be left to Tver. It must be led by an outside prosecutor whose reputation is above reproach. I left you a key above the apartment door."

"You son of a bitch, are you taping this conversation? Where are you?"

Arkady clicked off. That was enough for a start.

He felt refreshed by the call. He rested his arms against the parapet, took a deep breath and let a shudder of relief roll through him.

From the hospital roof he took in the black course of the Volga and the sinuous light of traffic along the river road. Lenin Square was a pool of light, but away from the center streetlamps were softly overwhelmed. As snow fell the city sank and rose. There was a rhythm to the snow as surely as there were waves at sea, and the illusion, as snow fell, that Tver was rising.

"Not so bad," said Arkady.

Snow settled. Snow settled on a hero at a gate on Sovietskaya Street, immobilized, still thinking of his next move. Snow settled on bones that had come out of hiding. It settled on Tanya and Russian brides. It settled on Sofia Andreyeva's panache.

He thought the doctor had it wrong about a miracle. The real miracle was that the people of Tver would wake to find their city transformed into someplace pure and white.

As for ghosts, they filled the streets.